FALCON'S GHOST

Books by Mike Waller

* * * * *

The 'ECHO'S WAY Series

Solitude's End - Book 1 of Echo's Way (Novella)

Dark World - Book 2 of Echo's Way (Novella)

Enemy Ally – Book 3 of Echo's Way

* * * * *

The FALCON Books

Falcon's Call

Falcon's Ghost

* * * * *

Other

HAWK: Hellfire

FALCON'S GHOST

By

Mike Waller

Published by Rampart Publishing

ISBN 9780648900931

Licence Notes

This is a work of fiction. All characters are fictional, and bare no relation to any person or persons living or dead.

This book is written in American English.

Cover design by Margaret Rainey – Ad Astra Book Covers

TABLE OF CONTENTS

Acknowledgements

Moholes:

The term 'Mohole' first appeared in relation to a failed attempt by the United States of America to drill a hole through the Earth's crust in the early 1960s, to obtain samples of the Mohorovicic Discontinuity (the boundary between the crust and the upper mantle).

The concept of Moholes as giant shafts bored in the Martian Crust as part of terraforming activities was first used in the Mars Trilogy, by Kim Stanley Robinson.

The Soletta:

A soletta is a giant shield built in space to protect a planetary surface from the Solar Wind. This concept was also used by Kim Stanley Robinson in the Mars Trilogy.

We stand on the shoulders of giants......

Prologue

(Falcon's Call)

IN THE DAWNING years of the twenty-fourth century, humanity's perception of the universe changed forever.

An unidentified, alien vessel entered the outer reaches of the Solar System on a direct course for the Sun.

Convinced by scientists the ship could not be manned and was certain to be a derelict or robot, the governments of Earth and Mars each sent fleets to intercept, both worlds seeking to gain any technological benefit the hulk might deliver. Martian authorities, realizing the Terran fleet would arrive first and claim ownership, decided to send an additional ambassador.

The *Butterball*, a small, ancient freighter converted for asteroid surveying, was the only ship in a position to reach the intruder before the opposition. Its owner and captain, Joe Falcon, intercepted the star-ship, a giant vessel over one hundred kilometres in length, and found it apparently deserted. As he began to explore, the derelict ship's systems started to come alive.

When the fleets arrived, they found themselves locked out of the amazing craft, with Joe and his crew prisoners inside.

The visitor continued its journey to the Sun, unconcerned by the warships following in its wake.

Upon reaching the star, the vessel—named the *Minaret* after its general shape—performed a solar breaking manoeuvre and set course for a rendezvous with Earth. Only then did the inhabitants of the ship, dubbed the Visitors, make themselves known. Joe was summoned to a meeting with an individual named Io, a synthetic android created in female, human form to interact with the arrivals. Her purpose: to reveal the reason for the ship's presence in the Solar System.

Close behind the first, a second star-voyager called the *Blackship* approached Sol. According to Io, that vessel had attacked and destroyed her civilization, and now intended to attack Earth in the same manner. The Visitors had rushed to reach Sol first, intent on revenge for their murdered race.

Unable to defeat their enemy alone, Io asked for the fleets of humanity to join her own fighters in the battle. In return she offered to protect Earth with a shield that could not be penetrated, and asked for the use of the moon Titan for one year, to construct a giant factory for the manufacture of fuel for their vessel before they departed to find a new home.

With Joe's help, the bargain was struck. As predicted, the new arrival attacked Earth without warning, but the planet was well protected and suffered minimal loss. The combined fleets dealt with the massive force of *Blackship* fighters while the mother-ship was lured away by the *Minaret* and led on a merry chase to Mars.

Once there, Io's people tricked the *Blackship*, surrounding it with a mirrored shield of pure energy, blinding it and rendering it incapable of manoeuvring. With the blast from its own engines, the *Minaret* nudged the trapped enemy into a lower orbit around the red planet.

The shield turned off seconds before Phobos, the last remaining moon of Mars, hit the vessel. With a mass of over ten and a half quadrillion tonnes, and twenty-two kilometres across, the massive rock slammed into the stationary ship at seven thousand, seven hundred kilometres per hour.

Its engines damaged beyond repair, the enemy vessel was unable to prevent itself from dropping from orbit and crashing into the surface of Mars.

Two murders occurred on the *Butterball* during the voyage. One murdered crewman returned alive and well through the magical technology of the Visitors on the *Minaret*.

Joe's investigations into the perpetrator of those deaths led to another member of his own crew, and in a confrontation with the killer Joe was fatally shot. His body failed him and his memories were downloaded into the vast memory banks of the star-ship, where he awaited the day he would receive a new, cloned body.

The war won, the Earth and Mars saved, the colossal *Minaret* moved to an orbit around Saturn and a gigantic factory complex rose on frigid Titan. Nobody knew precisely what the aliens were doing there, but many feared their presence and rumours abounded.

For one hundred years no human was permitted to land on Titan.

Chapter 01

SIXTY-ONE YEARS LATER:

JOE FALCON BRACED himself against the unsettling shiver that wormed its way up his spine. The sound of his own breathing echoed back from the confines of his space suit as he smelt the canned tang of the air from his life support system. It was not something he enjoyed. The last time he wore a spacesuit was decades in the past.

This moon had an eerie, surreal feel, and something about it set his nerves on a razor's edge. To his knowledge he was the only human to land here since the first exploration ship almost a century ago.

Joe's insulated suit protected him from the hellish environment beyond his faceplate, but a chill still filled his soul. He glanced down, scuffed a booted foot in the grainy sand and contemplated the mark it left, proof of his presence in this forbidding place. With a shake of the head to force himself back to reality, he began the trek around the ship towards the cargo hatch. He had seen all this before, but long ago and from a distance.

Giant, black dunes marched skyward beyond the dark plain at the edge of which he stood, but those high ridges were not normal mineral sands. Composed of fine, hydrocarbon grains that drifted down from the frigid clouds, they extended many kilometres to where higher mountain ranges of rock-hard, super-chilled ice stretched into the ever-present haze of a frozen sky.

On Joe's other side the calm waters of a broad lake spread mirror-like, reflecting the orange murk that filled the nitrogen-methane air. Dominating all, a colossal, multi-coloured orb forced its presence through the overcast, the glow sufficient to bathe the alien landscape with an eerie half-light. The giant gas world of Saturn, unchallenged queen of the Solar System, brooded over its hellish, elder child Titan, its glowering visage counterpointed by multiple lightning flashes that crackled uninterrupted across the moon's sky.

Joe thanked Thoth and Hephaestus, the gods of technology, for his suit and prayed it would not fail him. Outside the hard, protective shell the surface temperature registered at ninety-six degrees Kelvin, or minus one hundred and eighty Centigrade, far too cold for a body to survive unprotected.

Not that he had any right to be standing here; by doing so he broke a convention that had dominated humanity's exploration of the outer planets. No one was permitted here. As Joe was instrumental in the formulation of that decree, he of all people should not be breaking the rules, but for him this was personal.

Six decades ago a colossal alien star-ship known to all as the *Minaret* arrived to warn the people of Earth and Mars they were under threat of attack from a second vessel, dubbed the *Blackship*, which entered the system soon after.

The first arrivals, named by Joe's crew the 'Visitors', offered protection for the worlds of humanity in return for the exclusive use of the moon Titan for one hundred years. Joe helped to finalize the agreement and the decree went out that no human ship was to land there for one century.

Joe had arrived a little early.

In the distance he saw his destination, the near wall of a vast structure that stretched for many kilometres from the edge of the lake to the distant dunes, and soared several hundred metres into the frigid air.

Joe worked his way around the ship, the New Worlds Institute research vessel *Marco Polo*, until he reached the cargo hatch. The short journey was disconcerting, the only sounds those of his breath, the pounding of his pulse in his ears and the multitude of small, whirring noises from the servos operating the limbs of the mini-tank that was his environment suit.

A breath of warm air flowed over his face but did little to ease the chill in his soul. No decent human should ever be in a place like this.

It all began with an innocent observation.

The *Minaret* was missing.

Six decades ago the alien visitors set their giant, silver ship in orbit around Saturn and commenced construction of the massive building ahead. Joe, a guest on the star-ship at the time, observed the structure rise.

The exact nature of its purpose remained unknown but the accepted belief was it was a giant cyclotron used to manufacture antimatter, the supposed power source of the vessel. The Visitors never quite clarified the matter, and most knowledge was based on speculation rather than fact.

They stated the *Blackship* came with the intentions of destroying humanity and occupying the Solar System. Joe believed them at the time, and formed an alliance on behalf of Mars and Earth. The enemy marauder was defeated and destroyed by a joint task force of the Visitors' small but efficient fighters, called *bayonets,* and the war fleets of Earth and Mars. The Visitors had, they claimed, used all their fuel to reach Earth ahead of the *Blackship,* and after the battle, needed to make more before they continued their quest to find a new home elsewhere among the stars.

Or so the people of both worlds believed.

Joe knew otherwise. The giant structure ahead was an illusion, a ghost, but of all humans only he was aware of that.

Io, the ambassador of the aliens, once made a secret admission her ship lacked the capacity for another star voyage. They were here to stay. The Titan complex was intended as a blind to make humanity think the *Minaret* was being refuelled. After one hundred years the ship would leave as promised, but go no further than the Oort cloud where it would wait hidden until a future time when it might be rediscovered by humans. By then they would have developed sufficiently to cope with the sophisticated engineering the star-ship offered.

The Visitors possessed the technology to create or clone any organic body they desired, and it had been Joe who advanced the idea they take on human form and merge with humans. Subject to the same emotions and hormones, the crew of the alien vessel would in time become integrated into the race and after a few generations of interbreeding would be indistinguishable, a part of the varied patina of humanity.

Joe long ago began to doubt the plan, despite the evidence of his own eyes. For reasons both deep and personal he now mistrusted the aliens, and this landing was the result. He deliberately chose to defy the embargo. The time had come for everyone to know the truth of this place, but he needed to reveal it in such a way that his own duplicity would not be discovered.

Io maintained that prior to travelling to Sol the *Blackship* attacked and destroyed her home world, and the Visitors' presence here was as much for revenge as for altruism towards their neighbouring galactic brothers and sisters. True, they protected Earth, but Joe no longer believed it to be so simple.

From the moment the war ended rumours began to spread. Some maintained the Visitors wanted the Solar System for themselves, and took the chance to destroy not only their interstellar rivals but also human opposition. The fleets of both Earth and Mars were decimated in the conflict, and many considered humanity unprepared to defend itself in the future. Joe had worked hard to correct that deficiency in the last six decades.

Others suspected the Visitors walked amongst them in artificial bodies indistinguishable from natural ones. Joe knew that to be true without a doubt, as he had been party to the deception.

Despite the rumours, nothing had been heard from the *Minaret* since it went into orbit around Titan. Only days before the *Marco Polo* arrived at Saturn, the alien star-ship vanished.

"You alright, Joe?" a static voice crackled over the radio. "Your heart rate's up a heap and a half."

"Yeah, still standing." Joe took a deep breath and tried to calm himself. "Suit's working fine. This place gives me the willies, is all."

The embargo on Titan landings did not preclude exploration of Saturn's other moons, and Joe's original objective was to carry out research and survey exercises on several of them on behalf of the New Worlds Institute. After his having spent years as a surveyor in the past, this trip was an opportunity to return to that simpler life for a short time at least.

His ship was one of the first manned vessels ever to come this far, the voyage costing more than most organizations beyond the Institute would consider worthwhile. As they approached Saturn the first thing the crew sought was the starship, but a survey of the system failed to produce any trace. Joe decided the Visitors had not kept their side of the pact, throwing the whole question of the agreement between them and humanity into doubt. He needed to confirm their absence, and so the largest of the planet's moons became the *Marco Polo's* first destination.

On a broad plain near the equator of the little world, between the sea and the black dunes, the solitary monolith stood in isolated grandeur, and the crew were determined to see inside. If the Visitors *were* gone anything remaining might be of value to humanity, but that was not the motivation for Joe. The aliens' original plan had diverged and that troubled him.

He had always been aware the structure was an illusion, but he went along with the charade for the *Marco Polo* crew's benefit. He had to pretend he did not already know its true nature, and was only now making that discovery.

At the rear of the vessel an exploration buggy rolled from its storage bay and waited, tail ramp lowered. One steady step at a time Joe shuffled aboard and locked into the pilot frame, designed to hold the thermal suit in a standing position. A minute later he was on his way, the vehicle leaving deep tracks in the black sand as it rolled towards the nearby monolith.

"This place is bloody enormous," Joe mumbled as the buggy rumbled on, drawing close to the high, black structure before stopping a short distance from the near wall. He demounted and walked nearer, then leaned back as far as practical in the confines of the suit to peer upwards. "Must be a couple of hundred metres up there."

"Any sign of a way in? A door or something? Anything?" asked the voice again. Chan Berry, the man on the radio, was the captain of *Marco Polo* and a close friend to Joe.

"Nope, not here. I'll run around the base a bit."

He remounted and drove along the perimeter ten metres out from the structure. The ship had flown over the building on the way down, and there was no trace of an entrance on the flat, featureless roof. Any way in would be here at ground level.

The monolith was far too large to circumnavigate in the time available, so an hour later, having given up and turned around, Joe returned to his original position. He stopped beside the wall, dismounted and stepped closer.

As he reached out a hand he did not expect to encounter an actual surface. As anticipated, the carbon-fibre glove of the suit passed through without resistance. He jerked the hand back, the faint, tingling sensation one he was familiar with. Memories flooded back of his first landing on the star-ship when he flew through a force field into the airfield deck; it felt just like this.

"Something's not right here," he said, continuing the pretence. "This wall is—I don't know—not real. I can put my hand through it like the hatches on the *Minaret*, but it's not the same. It seems different."

"Sure you're not imagining it, old buddy?" the intercom replied.

"I'm not. Legit, my hand went straight into the damned thing. I'll try walking through. This might be the way inside."

"Are you serious? What if you go in and can't get out again?"

Joe paused for a moment to consider his response. "What else can I do?" He had taken similar risks before and emerged safely, and he could not stop the charade now.

"Drop it and come back. I think we should get off this moon and get on with the job we came here for. This place gives me the willies too."

"Yeah right, but I'm not giving up so easily." Joe stepped forward again, re-inserted the gloved hand and leaned in until the faceplate of his helmet passed through. He felt no sensation beyond the tingling, and no resistance.

The wall had no thickness. Hundreds of metres above, the ceiling of the vast structure was transparent, the dim light from the exterior filtering through to provide minimal visibility. Inside, the black plane continued unbroken.

Joe took several paces forward and stopped. He was in, but it was like he had not gone anywhere at all. Beneath his feet lay nothing but sand, in every direction only blank walls. The structure appeared to be a vast, hollow space.

"Can you hear me, Chan?"

"Yep, you're still coming in clear. I can't see you. Where are you now?"

"I'm inside."

"Cool. What's in there?"

"Bugger all. Nothing." *Fine, now it's common knowledge.*

"What, they stripped it when they left? Damn!"

"No, I mean there literally *is* nothing here and it doesn't appear there ever was. This place doesn't even have a floor. Wait, I can see something in the distance. The light's not so good but I can just make it out. It's a little block-like thingy on a raised platform. Might be worth checking out."

Joe turned and walked back through the wall to his buggy, boarded and drove into the enigmatic structure, heading for the object sitting on the sand several kilometres ahead.

"Not sure you should be doing that," Berry said. "Something stinks to high heaven about this."

"That'll be your jocks, Chan. You haven't showered for a week."

"No, I'm serious. This whole thing is weird. I mean, why would we be ordered away from this moon if it's deserted?"

"We thought there *was* something here, but I guess we were wrong. I'm still going to check this out though. Almost there."

Minutes later the buggy reached its destination, drawing to a halt beside a platform about five metres square and one high, smooth, featureless and by all appearances made from some kind of plastic material. Joe placed a glove on the black monolith and felt the slightest of vibrations.

In the ultra low gravity of Titan he flexed the knees of his suit and launched himself up to the platform, landing with a soft clunk and the slightest of wobbles. He steadied himself and straightened up.

At the centre of the block a thin pylon constructed from the same material rose to a cube structure, the surface of which was broken by dozens of rectangular irregularities that reflected Joe's helmet lamp like glass. He stepped forward and examined the device, moving around until he had viewed it from all sides. Standing tall, he could see across the top.

"Nothing. No access hatches or anything. Can't see any way to get inside. Smooth as a baby's butt. Nothing else here either."

"So, a waste of time coming here, hey."

Joe laughed to himself. "Yeah, I guess. There's something about it though; I don't know what. A feeling I've seen something like this somewhere else." He had experienced the same déjà-vu sensation before. The Visitors had a penchant for building things not unlike their equivalent on Earth.

"Come back. You can stew over it later. The power in your suit is down to thirty-nine percent and if it fails I can't reach you in time. You'll freeze in a minute or less."

"True. Alright, I'm on my way." Joe knew he shouldn't have come alone, but this little subterfuge was something he needed to do by himself.

The buggy was almost back to the ship when realization flashed into Joe's mind.

"Got it," he said. "It's a projector like you see in planetariums. That explains a lot. This building's a phantom, a projection of some sort—a holographic image. That's why I can go straight through it. It isn't real."

"Don't make no sense. Those aliens have been out here for sixty years. Why would they stay so long and put nothing but a hologram here?"

"Who knows? What puzzles me most is I watched them build the damned thing from orbit, and now I wonder if it's a massive charade. A trick, an illusion for our benefit to make us think they were making fuel out here. They weren't doing anything. They were never here at all." Joe hoped he sounded genuine, and that Chan would not realise he was aware of the illusion all along.

"Where are they, do you think?"

Joe hesitated, unwilling to say anything that might give him away. "I'm sure I don't know, but until we can find out I think we need to keep this quiet."

"Sure, but where are they?"

Chapter 02

A HOT, DRY wind from the Outback blasted across the walkway at the Sidings Springs Mountain Observatory Complex and streamed away on its relentless journey eastward to the sea, leaving a swirl of dust and dry leaves in its wake.

Anand Khatri did not mind the heat. He was a child of the tropics, where at any given time of the year it was either stinking hot or flooding, monsoon rains. Most of the observatories he had worked at in his long career were in isolated locations and high up, so often cold and sometimes snowbound like the last he visited in the French Alps. This one, on a plateau well back from the eastern coast of the continent of Australia, was heaven by comparison.

Anand's current benefactor, the Australian National University, maintained comfortable residences in Coonabarabran, a small rural town not far from where the observatory sprawled across a mountain top at the boundary of the Warrambungles National Park. The accommodations suited Anand and his family, and the small town was well endowed with the kind of active social life typical of country communities. He had always considered the people of Australia to be amongst the friendliest in the world, and he felt accepted here.

His current work was with the ANU 5-1, a brand new, five metre telescope located at the westernmost end of the complex. With his mind focused on his latest project he ambled into the administration building and went straight to his desk. The office was cooler than outside, and the coffee machine only metres away.

Perfect!

The first task for the day was, as always, to answer the multitude of emails that awaited him. Some came from colleagues with whom he maintained a regular discourse, others from academic or business associates, members of the media or political organizations. The majority came from private citizens who wanted to ask questions, and he looked forward to those the most.

Anand was a celebrity, and often appeared on the television networks as one of the current 'go-to' scientists in Australia whenever something of astronomical interest pricked the public consciousness. The majority of queries were straight forward, others ridiculous or inane, but he answered every one. For him no question was too simple or stupid. He had acquired a substantial personal following in recent years with over nineteen thousand fans on 'Science Unlimited', and found the notoriety gave him something of a thrill.

One name on the list of unanswered messages stood out, a video call from an old colleague, Garry Denny, now at the Kepler mining station in the Asteroid Belt on a trip of several months duration. Anand opened the file and waited. His friend's face smiled back, a hand waving hello from the bottom corner of the screen. Anand did not return the greeting—the message was over a day old due to the time lag with transmissions from the Belt— and instead, sat back and listened.

"Hey, Anand old pal," his friend began. "Long time no see. I'm out at Kepler at the moment and this'll cost me a mint, so I'll keep it short. One of my associates came up with something interesting last night. Says he overheard something odd in a local bar. All the crews tend to gather in those places and the guy talking was from an NWI research vessel on its way back from Saturn. They went there to check out some of the moons, and discovered the *Minaret* is gone. The Visitors aren't due to leave for another forty years, so that's a cause for concern, don't you think?

"The story is the researchers broke protocol; with no sign of the star-ship, they landed on Titan hoping to investigate the Visitors' factory. Thought they might discover something of value, but guess what they found? Nothing! According to the guy, the whole sight is a hologram. There's bugger all there except a holo-projector. The research team took fright and hi-tailed it; I reckon they figured as soon as the disappearance became public knowledge the place would be swarming, and they had no authority to land.

"I thought you guys should know. Somebody needs to investigate it and you're the only one of my contacts with the resources. I thought you might like to take a look with that big magnifying glass of yours. That's about all, so I better go now before this bankrupts me. Give my love to Karishma."

Anand leaned back in his chair and stared at the screen, a blank expression on his face. If the *Minaret* had departed Saturn this was a massive deal indeed, but what could he do? The orbit of the alien ship was well documented and several observatories still made occasional checks, but ANU 5-1 was not one of them.

For several minutes he mulled over the problem. To use the telescope to check this information would require moving off-line from its current programs, and he would never be given approval. However, the New Worlds Institute was the most respected research and development body on both Earth and Mars, and a major contributor to the university's funding. So if they found anything odd then it meant something.

Anand decided he could not let this go.

"Call Gabriella Ramos at VLT," he spoke to the console and waited until a familiar face appeared. "Hey, Gabby, how are you?"

The striking, Latina woman gazing back at him was one of the directors of the VLT Array, a complex of seven enormous ten-metre telescopes located in the Atacama Desert of northern Chile. Anand knew the facility checked on the alien ship every so often and so possessed the coordinates for an immediate inspection. After the usual pleasantries he explained the situation.

"Well," Gabriella said, "we haven't done a check for several months. *Melipal* has been down for maintenance and we brought her back on line this morning after a complete rebuild and upgrade. We're still making adjustments, but that'll be finished in a day so we can use her to have a quick look as a test run before we move her to other projects. It'll take some time, so I'll call you back."

Anand nodded, made his farewells and ended the communications link.

Melipal, a local term for 'Southern Cross', was the nickname of VLT3, the third of the original quartet of giant telescopes. The observatory began life three centuries ago with four, eight-point-two metre telescopes. Over the years they were upgraded, replaced by larger, more accurate units, and in addition the array had been increased to seven, each capable of working alone or as part of a coordinated whole with sufficient power to detect exo-planets around nearby stars. If anything had the ability to make a proper check, *Melipal* did.

That will have to do, Anand thought. He turned his attention back to the stream of messages yet to be answered.

Several days later, his communicator chimed and Gabriella appeared again.

"Your friend was right. We can't find any trace of the *Minaret*, and it's no longer in Saturn orbit. The committee here decided to refer it upstairs, so we've set up a conference call with the United Earth Council and the Mars Minister for Space. They'll want you to attend, as the person who raised this to everyone's attention."

"But, what can I tell them? I'm just the messenger."

*   *   *

The Honourable Martin Calvin, Minister for Martian Space Operations, drummed his fingers as each of the seats opposite blinked from empty to an actual occupant. Arrayed along the far side of the conference table were six holo-fields, set up for the delegates from Earth to join the meeting. Representatives from various authorities on Mars were there in person, seated to either side.

Calvin sighed. Now in his late sixties, white haired and with a face lined by too many years of fretting over trivial details, he was starting to think the time had arrived to consider those marvellous gerontological treatments so talked about. The

Falcons were his friends, and their treatments cost virtually nothing. In Calvin's occupation image was everything; he was about to book himself in when this business landed in his lap.

To the left sat Professor Stephen Grate, the president of the Mars Institute of Sciences. Steve, also a close, long-term friend and somewhat younger than Martin, was a tall, angular individual with long, gray hair tied back in a stylish ponytail, his hazel eyes glistening with intelligence. Always dressed in cargo pants and a leather jacket, he was the grandson of Alfred Brewer, the faculty head at the time of the *Minaret's* original arrival in the Solar System. After the death of his grandfather, Steve, a physicist of repute, had been the obvious choice to fill the vacant chair. He waited, a patient smile on his face as he toyed with a file of papers.

On Martin's right hand sat Abiko Hirotami, the current Martian home secretary. Abiko, whose parents emigrated to Mars soon after his birth, was also tall, typical of those raised in the lower gravity of the red planet.

The last holo-field flickered and the final attendee appeared. Martin recognized the Honourable Edwardo Mori, chairman of the United Earth Council and the one who called the meeting. Beside him sat Minister Francoise Abreu, the unenviable individual tasked with the job of coercing uncooperative nations into contributing to the re-construction of the Terran Space Force.

The conflict with the alien *Blackship* decimated the original fleet, and while construction of new ships proceeded at a lightening pace the majority of the funding for the Earth contingent came from only ten percent of the planet's nations. The nano-construction techniques used by the New Worlds Institute, which oversaw the project, allowed a criminally small construction cost, so Abreu's task was not as noisome as it might otherwise have been.

Martin's briefing notes told him the other four faces opposite belonged to an uncomfortable looking Anand Khatri, the scientist who first raised the issue of the absence of the *Minaret*, a composed and self-assured Gabriella Ramos, the astronomer who confirmed the discovery, and two other representatives of Terran governmental authorities, David Khan from the North American Federation and Langa Ndaba from South Africa, both senior members of the Council. Martin studied the faces, some of which he knew, others not. Before he could utter a word, Mori spoke.

"Let's not waste time on trivialities," he said. "We all know each other and we've all read the report. The question is, what are we going to do about this?"

"Hello to you too, Minister ... Ed," Martin replied, unwilling to give way to Mori. "What do you suggest?"

Mori cleared his throat. "Yes, well. I think we need to find out where they went. This may be critical for us."

"In what way?"

"Don't be naive, Martin. We're all aware of the power that ship represents. We must confirm if the Visitors are gone or still in the system, and if they *are* still here, what they are up to."

"The rumours say they haven't been doing anything at all. The factory on Titan is nothing more than an elaborate holographic image, according to Joe Falcon."

"Joe Falcon? The nephew or whatever of *the* Joe Falcon? What does he have to do with it?"

"An institute research ship was surveying the other moons when they discovered the absence of the *Minaret,* so they went and had a look."

Mori slapped his hand on something beyond the edge of the holo-field. "That alone is enough for concern. Why would the aliens do this? What purpose is served by their creating an illusion to fool us for so long? We should send a contingent, an official one, to make sure."

"I agree, and we intend to arrange one as soon as possible, but I don't see it as a critical issue. It would be best to focus on locating the ship, don't you think?"

"I also agree," Langa Ndaba said. "Those bastards destroyed our major city." He referred to the destruction of Johannesburg, one of two cities decimated during the *Blackship* attack. "We've never been happy about this Titan arrangement."

"Would it not be more accurate to say," Mori asked, "your government shot down one of the shield devices the Visitors used to protect the Earth, allowing an enemy fighter to enter and destroy Jo-burg? We warned you along with everyone else not to interfere with those generators, but you chose to do so despite the warnings, and suffered the consequences."

"We had every right to..."

"This gets us nowhere," Martin interrupted. He had no wish to get embroiled in Earth rivalries. He turned his attention to Gabriella Ramos, the only female in the group. A clear degree of hostility was present in this meeting and he hoped she at least would be a calming influence. "Any progress locating the ship?"

"No, none."

"May I ask why? You've been looking for two weeks now."

The astronomer gave a long, drawn out sigh, her eyes flicking upward. "I appreciate you're only a politician, Minister, but if you were a scientist you would be aware of the difficulties involved. The *Minaret* is not in orbit around any of the planets and does not appear to be in the Asteroid Belt; we would have found her by now if so.

"We're focusing our attention on the Kuiper belt at the moment and we have four of the VLT array on it, as well as the Franklin B unit in Tasmania and the AAT-3 at Siding Springs in New South Wales. Unfortunately, once you go beyond Neptune this becomes a big-ass solar system, and finding something out there the size of even that star-ship is like searching for the proverbial needle in the haystack."

Martin sat back and glared at the astronomer. He did not like anyone putting him in his place, academics less than most. "Very well, keep looking. So where does this leave us?" He ignored the stricken look of Mori, who realised he had lost primacy in his own meeting.

"The factory on Titan," Abiko Hirotami said. "Perhaps it's nothing, but we do need to check. We must learn what those aliens are doing if they aren't creating fuel for their ship as we thought."

Martin sighed. "Alright, accepted. I'll arrange for our navy to send someone out there. Saturn's a hell of a way, but the new military vessels are well able to make the trip in a few months."

"If those NWI idiots can get there, a naval vessel should be more than capable," Ndaba said. "The ship's landing is in breach of the law, by the way. Has anything been done about that?"

Martin fought to repress a chuckle. "I don't consider it a critical issue. The New Worlds Institute is one of the most respected organizations on either planet, and my understanding is the mission was under the personal command of Joseph Falcon. He's one of the senior directors of the Institute and I would not question his motives. I'm assured a full report of their findings will be sent to us as soon as they arrive home, so the issue of their landing isn't worth our concern. Besides, if they hadn't done so we might not now be aware of this little problem."

For a long, uncomfortable moment the conference fell quiet. Martin expected every member of the group, excepting perhaps the scientists, had a political agenda of their own, and it did not surprise him nothing concrete had so far come from this exercise. Nevertheless both Mars and Earth had, since the *Blackship* attack episode, agreed to a policy of open consultation on any matter concerning alien activities, and in particular the *Minaret* and the Visitors.

What remained of the *Blackship* lay as desiccated remnants scattered around a crater in the Utopia Planitia, a broad plain in the northern hemisphere of Mars. So colossal was the explosion on its crash landing that little of substance survived, but what little information emerged from the wreckage belonged to both worlds.

Of the *Minaret*, naught remained to share. The Visitors left nothing behind when they moved out to Titan, including the remains of the damaged shield generators brought down by South Africa and Kyrgyzstan.

The only avenue remaining was to keep an eye on the ship as it orbited the gas giant, and several telescopes on both planets carried out checks on a semi-regular basis. For that reason it could be confirmed wherever the alien star-ship went it had done so only recently, perhaps only days before the arrival of the NWI vessel.

"So," Martin continued. "The ships we'll send will be ready to leave shortly. It's a long journey and they'll need to prepare. Does anyone else want to add anything—anything constructive?"

Six heads shook on the far side of the table and more with him in the room. All they had to work with was a rumour, a report yet to arrive and the data from the astronomers. There was little they could do at this stage.

"You will keep us advised?" he asked, directing himself once again to Ramos. She nodded. "Excellent. Shall we adjourn for now, Edwardo? Thank you everyone." A second later the holo fields flickered off and Martin turned to his scientific adviser. "Why do I have the feeling there is much more to this than is obvious?"

"I feel the same, but these ridiculous meetings never solve anything, and Mori's not going to appreciate your taking over like that." Steve said. "We've always known little about what the Visitors are up to and speculation is rife, as always. Then there are the stories about their being here, and on Earth."

"Yes, I've heard them too. They live in human bodies and walk amongst us. Tripe, if you ask me."

"Perhaps, perhaps not. We don't know. We gave them Titan for one hundred years on the understanding they would build a factory to create the fuel needed for their next journey, to find the other colonies of their own people. Now we learn it's all a farce, so whatever the truth is, we know one thing for certain."

"Yes, we do. They lied to us!"

Chapter 03

JOE FALCON PLACED one eye to the scanner and waited as the door to his apartment opened. Once inside, he dropped his bags to the floor and took a deep breath. He walked to the windows, sat in his favourite chair and cast his gaze towards the mind-blowing view beyond the thick, pressure-resistant, window glass. He breathed in the familiar, canned smell of the air and let the cool draft from the ventilator wash across his skin. It was good to be home again.

Something was not as it should be. Despite being in perfect health Joe felt old this morning, and getting motivated for the day was proving difficult. He had struggled all the way from the spaceport to home, and accepted it was a hangover from the voyage from which he had just returned, a lethargy that would last for days. He had not been in space for any length of time in decades, and had forgotten the joys of his body attempting to return to normal.

A trip of several months, the journey to Saturn and back took an enormous toll, and Joe expected it would be difficult to pick up his usual planet-side routine where he left off. Experience told him it would take weeks for his muscles to re-adjust to Martian gravity.

Joe also realized it would not be long before his little side trip to Titan came back to bite him, considering the governments of both Earth and Mars now knew of the disapparance of the *Minaret*. He had anticipated that, having long ago discovered one of the crewmen on the expedition was renowned for having a loose tongue after a few drinks. The news was out, as he had intended.

He heard the first rumours soon after leaving Kepler, and contacted his son Jake to issue an official statement of the *Vasco* landing on Titan. While the trip would be accepted as legitimate under the circumstances, he knew some people in government always sought ways to attack the NWI. When and if the issue arose, he would let his son take care of it. The *Marco Polo* was an institute vessel, and Jake was the public face of the family business.

For now Joe wanted to relax. The expedition had been an attempt to kick start his life again, a restorative for his flagging interest in virtually everything. It was over now, leaving him less invigorated than hoped. He was tired, and it was becoming obvious such an adventure was not enough to assuage the demons haunting his soul.

The splendour of Hellas in the morning was an astonishing thing to behold and becoming more so every year. The apartment in which Joe lived was several kilometres above the basin floor, dug into the rim of the eastern wall of the massive, ancient crater.

The sheer rock faces in this district contained many similar dwellings, each with expansive pressure windows looking out to the vastness of the 2,300 kilometre wide impact basin. Some, like Joe's, possessed balconies accessed by airlocks against the future day when it would be possible to stand in the open air without protection. Even though his apartment included one, he did not enjoy being outside.

Joe had always battled with vast, empty voids, and in space it always proved a problem whenever he went extra-vehicular. Here on Mars, looking over a seemingly endless drop, it was even more pronounced, but the view was worth it.

All the dwellings in the area were well separated, connected by a series of tunnels and elevators to local stations on the hyper-loop around the perimeter of the crater. One could easily travel from here to Hellas City, located further along the rim, without once needing a suit.

Joe loved this place. The apartment offered seclusion, enough for him not to be bothered by anyone he did not wish to see, which these days was more or less everyone. A strong security door at the entrance to the tunnel from the shuttle station, and another at the house itself, made sure he kept his privacy. This was a district reserved for the more affluent, and that included Joe, as much as he hated to acknowledge it.

For a little less than sixty years he had been a major shareholder in and a leading contributor to the rapid rise of the New Worlds Institute, the research and industrial conglomerate set up by his son Jake and daughter in law Akira, to develop and disseminate the data received from the Visitors. The organization operated on minimal profit, most of which the Falcons folded back into the business to increase its viability, but the miniscule allowance given its captains was sufficient to amass a respectable fortune, considering the vast scope of the Institute's activities. Joe had invested much of his original worth in the early years and the dividends from that alone exceeded anything he had possessed before.

In the far distance, a glint of light reflected from the ice sheets in Hellas. Drawn from deep, subterranean reserves, water pumped constantly on to the surface, enough to exceed the inevitable sublimation caused by the still thin atmosphere.

Every year the air grew denser and warmer, the sublimation less and the lake of ice larger. One day when the temperature increased sufficiently, the basin floor would be an ocean.

In the glass windowpane a reflection stared back, a face Joe hated.

It looked wrong.

It should have been older.

Much older!

He turned away from the window and reached for the bottle of brandy standing on his side table. Pouring himself a measure, he closed his eyes and tried to relax.

He had occupied this body, his second, for sixty-one years.

He had been fifty-eight when he and his crew flew their spaceship, an old freighter named the *Butterball*, to intercept the first alien visitor to the Solar System. He died on the voyage, murdered by one of his own people. Within minutes of his demise the Visitors, the inhabitants of the star-ship, downloaded his entire memory to one of their computers.

A year later, most of which Joe spent orbiting Saturn on the alien vessel, his mind was uploaded into a new body created from his own DNA with input from his younger crew members to compensate for the genetic deteriorations of age. The clone grew in total isolation from stimulus to prevent it from developing any memories of its own, and at somewhere around a physical age of twenty years Joe took occupancy. It might have been something from science fiction had he not experienced it for himself.

Now, after six decades, his second body should have physically been around eighty years of age.

It was not.

Despite having been force-grown for the first part of its life, the clone aged at less than half the rate of normal human bodies, and Joe now appeared no older than forty five. He still felt ancient, but it was a psychological thing.

Everything about his new incarnation seemed somewhat surreal. Fifty-eight years in his first body, the one he was born in, and sixty-one years in this, the second. That made him one hundred and nineteen years old, and he believed it utterly. In his mind he carried the scars of those long, dry years, every second of each minute of every day, and when he reached his lowest ebb he often expected to feel the cold hand of the Reaper on his shoulder, telling him it was time to move on. It never happened.

Despite its apparent age, Joe's face was a map of a life lived far too long, and the intensity in his eyes mirrored every moment. Technically, he was one of the oldest humans alive, and in his own mind had outlived the right to life. Apart from his relatives all the people who mattered to him were gone, and these days he had few friends, living the life of a virtual recluse unless he chose to emerge for some specific reason like the Saturn trip. He had only his work left, and his family.

In the harsh light of the early morning, his life seemed empty. It was a chore to become motivated and see what the day would offer. Sleep, probably. He needed a rest after the voyage.

For the gift of a forty-five-year-old body he cursed the Visitors every day. It had robbed him of the most perfect love of his life, something he could never forget, or forgive.

At the beginning of his second life Joe entered a relationship with Sarah Cole, his young first-officer from the

Butterball, satisfying both his fondness for the young woman he had come to respect and the deep love she developed for her captain despite their original age difference. His return in the body of a twenty-year-old removed the only real barrier to their friendship, a wall that existed only in Joe's mind and not Sarah's, and they formed a legal partnership.

Joe had expected he and Sarah would spend the rest of their lives growing old together, experiencing the unspoken love for a partner only age and companionship could bring. He had been denied that pleasure when his first wife Helen died young, and now the Visitors' technology had robbed him a second time. While his new body stayed young, Sarah grew old, and passed away four years ago taking much of his soul with her.

His greatest regret was her refusal to take the gerontological treatments now offered by the Institute, unwilling as she was to continue growing older while he remained young. The treatments did slow aging, but not enough for it to matter to her. Joe believed his own lack of aging in some way denied her the longer life she might have otherwise enjoyed.

He opened his eyes again and strained to see along the crater rim to a point several kilometres distant and slightly lower. A small buttress extended out over the basin floor at the place where he placed Sarah's ashes. One day she would have an ocean view, and eventually he would join her, he hoped.

His secret—that he was the original Joe Falcon who died and was re-born long ago on the *Minaret*—was known to only a handful of friends, family and higher officials. Everyone else accepted him as a distant relative with the same name as his famous predecessor.

He continued on as one of the directors of Martian operations for the New Worlds Institute and the official head of the division responsible for research and development for the fleets of diamond ships, the new, advanced warships now being built on both Luna and Mars. Beyond that he kept to himself, a virtual recluse.

There were of course his children Jake, Grace and Raisa, and Jake's wife Akira who Joe considered a daughter rather than daughter in law. Jake was now eighty-nine and the vast industrial and research empire he and his partner had built over the years from data given them by the Visitors was now operated by their own children, a son and daughter both blessed with superior intelligence.

The parents, still active due to gerontological treatments, headed the board of directors and oversaw operations on Earth, but had now decided to move to Mars, the Institute's base having preceded them. They still had the final word in any major undertaking, but from the daily running of the family business they had officially retired. Nobody in government really believed that. The couple were, without doubt, the most powerful individuals on either planet, more so than even the politicians.

Joe's daughter Grace, with whom he long ago became reconciled after years of distancing, lived on the mother world but was also about to emigrate, having now rejoined the Falcon Empire.

Most of all, Joe's youngest, third child Raisa was his pride and joy, the magnificent young woman born halfway through his second incarnation. Sarah had been middle-aged when Raisa arrived, but for her the girl had always been distant, a usurper in the relationship she was already starting to question.

Raisa was a true creature of space. Now thirty-one Earth years of age and Martian born and raised, she had never set foot on Terran soil. She lived the life of a spacer, working for the Institute doing whatever was needed by her father, her step brother or his wife, all of whom loved her deeply.

For a while she captained the old *Butterball*, resurrected from mothballs after its retirement. Now the much-loved, old prospector served as a memorial to humanity's first encounter with visitors from the stars, in a museum not far away in Hellas City. Raisa commanded a new ship, the *Vasco da Gama*, the latest and most sophisticated research vessel belonging to the NWI, and from what Joe heard she was a first-class captain.

He poured a glass of soda to chase the brandy, and resumed his contemplation of the far distance. No, the last sixty years had not gone at all as he hoped.

Not long after the *Minaret's* departure from Mars, terabytes of data were downloaded to a computer terminal in Jake's home as a gift to humankind and an act of goodwill. Or so it appeared at the time.

Some of the information had been useful, but most of it proved to have only academic value. Several of the oldest unsolvable mysteries of science were explained, but only a handful of advances resulted, including a set of guiding principles for the safe application of nanotechnology, high temperature superconductors, and new techniques for the extension of life and control or elimination of disease. Since then, Joe had decided some of those advances were a mixed blessing.

A considerable portion of the data appeared to lead in directions both Jake and Akira agreed should not be pursued. The relevant sections involved the harnessing and use of Dark

Energy and it did not take long to realize following the data blindly could lead to a catastrophe greater than humanity could survive. The discoveries had been made available to nobody, sequestered against the day humankind might grow mature enough to use it.

The Visitors had not passed on any of what Joe most hoped for: the secrets of the amazing shield that protected the *Minaret* and allowed it to fly unharmed through the corona of a star, the generators used to protect the Earth, the principles of the star-ship's space drive, the walkways and gravitational elevators, the bubble-way transport system or the advanced cloning and memory storage techniques that gave Joe his second life. Even the medical technology used to bring Joe's *Butterball* engineer Terry Caldwell back to life after being murdered by the same crew member who killed him, was missing.

The greatest value came not from the download but from the inherent human ability to take a principal and expand on it, making new, serendipitous discoveries above and beyond the original intent.

At this moment, one such endeavour was in progress, preparing to test an invention capable of freeing humanity from its solar-system prison forever. Again, the development came from sheer, human ingenuity. Two researchers studying a completely unrelated block of the alien information found something that drew their attention in a new, unforeseen direction, leading to what was, in Joe's opinion, the most important research ever undertaken.

In the end, Jake and Akira concluded the gift contained little humanity would not have discovered anyway in the next few decades, and did contain many things considered downright dangerous. In light of that realisation Joe now saw the gift as false, possibly a decoy to reduce humanity's suspicions, or even a trap.

Overall, what could be gleaned from the alien data proved more useful on Mars than on Earth. Nanotechnology had never been outlawed on the red planet as in most terrestrial nations, and for an empty world the benefits of safe nanotechnology were beyond estimation. Self regulating nano-bots were building vast domes across the Martian landscape, future sites for a growing population. Square kilometres of covered area waited against the day they would be needed for a growing hydroponics industry. Mars possessed an agricultural and manufacturing capacity far in excess of its current needs.

To increase the density of the atmosphere and release heat and water from the subsurface, giant shafts were being bored by automated machines. They extended several kilometres into the crust and were dubbed 'Moho' shafts by many after an ancient, failed scientific endeavour to drill a hole through the Earth's crust.

From the walls of these shafts, expansive habitation levels were being cut back into the rock for use as anything from future underground cities to industrial or agricultural complexes. The machines kept digging without human assistance or supervision and the spacious chambers grew larger by the day.

Many industries had already converted to the new technology, particularly in the manufacture of spacecraft built from the ground up, molecule by molecule. Mars had suffered greatly from the aftermath as the giant *Blackship* collided with the surface of the red planet. Much of the fledgling atmosphere blew away and the early, successful attempts at vegetation failed, setting the terraforming effort back by decades. Those losses were being restored and next time, Fortress Mars would be ready.

As Joe sat and gazed through his window he could see the real signs of progress. The red world was becoming a living planet again, a new Earth.

Why did this no longer excite him as much as it should?

Chapter 04

DOCTOR LATIKA ADVANI turned on the taps and allowed the warm water to flow over her hands as she began the tedious ritual of the scrub, still considered essential before an operation. Why, she could not imagine.

Once in the operating environment she would not go within metres of the patient, all the surgery being performed by a computerized robo-surgeon she would control from a distance. In fact, she would not be in the same room. The simplest of procedures utilized advanced technologies today, and a critical operation like this would never be done any other way. Still, the routine of the scrub persisted.

That was it, a ritual, as much so as the fact most doctors still carried an old fashioned stethoscope on their person, sometimes even around their neck. Such devices were rarely used in modern medicine, but they held an enduring significance in the mystique of the profession. They were iconic, the symbol of the medical practitioner, though in this day and age a doctor more closely resembled a computer technician than a hands-on healer.

Latika looked up as she scrubbed, peering through the window into the operating room. It didn't much resemble the average person's idea of a theatre. Within was a maze of electronics and robotics at the centre of which lay the patient.

Every action inside the room was carried out by some mechanism or other, the surgeon and assistants restricted to the other side of a glass wall, each seated at the controls of a particular machine. They would perform remotely, viewing the actual procedure through virtual reality.

Truth to tell, many of the simpler, more routine surgical procedures were done entirely automatically, with computers making the decisions and controlling the operating devices. It worked fine for simple ops, but nobody quite trusted the machines enough to allow them total autonomy in a complex undertaking like the one about to be performed.

Following the obligatory but useless ritual, Latika entered the control room and took her seat. This would be a long stint, the subject having been injured in a sky-car crash; a male, middle aged, with extensive physical trauma to the head and thoracic cavity, and massive internal bleeding. The chances of success were close to nil, but this patient was someone of importance so the attempt would be made regardless. Latika wondered if this would be the case for an ordinary citizen. Where *did* the line between a human life and cost lay?

*　　*　　*

Seven hours later Latika sat in the surgical-wing restroom sipping at a piping-hot beverage. The label on the dispensing machine said 'tea', but she was not convinced. Still, it was hot and wet, and anything was acceptable at the moment.

The operation had not gone well, the subject's trauma too great. Latika's patient died despite hours of meticulous and skilled work in rejoining, sealing and repairing damaged tissue. She stopped the bleeding into the brain and repaired the damage to the lungs and heart, but then without warning the patient appeared to give up. No revival attempt succeeded. It was like he had not wanted to live.

Jill Riley, the senior post-op nurse, walked into the room and sat down. For a moment she said nothing, staring at the floor. She started to speak, opened her mouth and then stopped.

"What?" Latika prompted.

"Umm, I'm not sure. I took the patient down to post-mortem, and something's wrong. I don't know, something unnatural, something weird."

"Like what? He was pretty messed up and we were never going to save him."

"No, it's not that. Two things. First, I couldn't find a single blemish on the body. I don't mean the trauma from the accident. I mean normal blemishes and marks from living. This guy is listed as being forty-nine years old, yet his skin is as clean as a new-born baby and he looks about thirty-five. No scars, no moles, or freckles ... nothing. I've never seen a person of that age without some marks.

"Can't say I have either. So, where are you going with this?"

"Well, the lack of blemishes drew my attention, so while he was being prepared for the post-mortem I hung around and took a closer look. The work you did on the cranium..."

"What about my work?" Latika crossed her arms over her chest, a frown on her face.

"No, I didn't mean it that way. After you finished, the assistant closed up while you moved on to the chest injuries. The scalp..."

"Yes?"

"It started to heal immediately—within minutes."

Latika put down her tea cup and stared at her associate. This was getting beyond a joke. "Ridiculous."

"I agree, but it's also true. You can check it yourself if you want. It appears the lesions began healing at an incredible rate, and continued to do so after death."

Unconvinced, Latika stood and made for the door.

"Where are you going?"

"Down to post-mortem. I have to see this for myself. Assuming it isn't all bullshit, we need to take a much closer look at the body. You're *not* bullshitting, are you?"

*   *   *

"This makes little sense, wouldn't you agree?" Using a technique intended to diminish her minions the administrator lifted her eyes from the report and glared at Latika over the top of her spectacles. Three days had passed since the unusual patient's death, and Latika had requested a full autopsy. The results were disturbing in the least. "What do you make of this?" her superior asked.

"I don't know. Never saw anything like it before."

To begin, the autopsy looked at the outer appearance of the unfortunate individual, and the opinion of the nurse had been confirmed. The skin was perfect, with no indication it belonged to a man in his late forties. The operation incisions on the skull showed clear signs of having begun to heal, and that alone gave cause to pursue the matter further. On a whim Latika had ordered a complete internal investigation, and the case became stranger with each discovery.

"The patient's appendix is missing. I don't mean it's been removed: it isn't present and never has been."

The administrator, an elderly, somewhat calcified and aggressive woman named Brixton, with a reputation of avoiding controversy wherever possible and at whatever cost, grunted and dropped the report on the desk.

"A missing appendix? You base your suspicions on that?"

"Not at all; there are other minor differences in the organs. It's all very puzzling and I think we need to check into it a bit further."

Brixton leaned back and crossed her arms, her face taking on the typical intransigence for which she was renowned.

Latika continued. "We found a small implant, a gel capsule about the size of a medication pill, inside the skull above the pituitary gland. It's been implanted artificially, but we don't have any idea of its purpose or what it's made from. It didn't show on x-rays or scans, and we would've missed it if the post-mortem surgeon had not chosen to remove the brain for examination. The capsule dissolved when we removed it."

Administrator Brixton shifted in her chair, her brow furrowed and her mouth slightly twisted. "Doctor Advani, I don't see how this changes what I said. Give the body to the university. I mean, what do you think this is, other than perhaps a mutation?"

"But, the capsule?"

"Probably some kind of cyst."

Seriously? Latika stared down at the floor. She felt a little lost, and the administrator might be right, but if this was indeed a mutation it was a history making one and she expected Brixton to show a little more interest. Mutation did not explain the presence of the implant, but the woman was an administrator, a bureaucrat and a known ass-protector, not a doctor.

"None of the abnormalities would be easy to spot in a normal medical examination. The blemish-free skin is obvious, but not concerning, and the missing bits can only be found by invasive means. This person could have gone his whole life without discovery, barring major accidents."

Brixton said nothing for a moment, her expression blank. "This is all very interesting," she said, "but it strikes me as nothing more. Hand it over to the university wing and let them mess with it. You should be attending to patients I think, and this hospital does not pay you to play around with mutations."

*　　*　　*

"So you got this from where?" Martin Calvin asked, raising his eyebrows.

Steve Grate eased into the vast, overstuffed armchair beside Martin's desk. His constant shuffling betrayed the fact he was uncomfortable, but he maintained his composure.

Calvin's office was located on the summit of Pavonis Mons, on the southern side of the immense volcano's crater at the site of the base-station for the first Martian space elevator, so high it was almost at the top of the atmosphere. The view beyond the window looked out to a virtually airless terrain, and Martin knew Steve found it discomforting.

"A colleague at the Auckland Capital Hospital, on Earth," Grate replied. "He thought it might interest us, considering the current situation with the *Minaret*."

"Well, it *is* unusual; especially the capsule, but I don't see how it concerns us. It's not my area of expertise, or my portfolio."

"It might be. There's more to it than the obvious. After those discoveries they decided to dig a bit deeper. They made up cell slides for a closer examination, and did a DNA map."

"And?"

"The telomeres on the DNA are different, and the map is not exactly human." Grate leaned forward and flicked the reader to a page containing an electron microscope image. "This patient has a different structure to the caps on the ends of his DNA strands. It's like a 'T' shape. I've never seen anything like it; definitely not normal for a human being."

"Interesting."

"Infinitely, but it doesn't end there. The mitochondria in the cells are missing. He has something else, an organelle-like structure that's spiral in form rather than oval. They are still studying it, but it seems to do the same job as the mitochondria, the production of adenosine triphosate."

"Adeno ... what?

"Adenosine triphosate. It's how they provide energy for the cells. They're like little powerhouses."

"Could this be a genetic abnormality? Mitochondria that are deformed in some way?"

"No, the internal structure is different and it's far too neat. There's only one of these—things—in each cell. They tested muscle and liver cells and should have found multiple mitochondria in each, but they didn't, just one of these in every cell except the red blood cells. None there of course."

"Yes, of course." Martin shook his head. He once, as a young graduate, met Steve's grandfather, Doctor Alfred Brewer; grandfather and grandson were alike, and these scientists lived in a world of their own. "So why did they send the report to you? How does this affect us?"

"It's almost like this was a 'better designed' human, with changes that could not easily be discovered by us. Remember those rumours about the Visitors?"

"Sure. The aliens are still here and they walk amongst us in humanoid bodies. Poppycock."

Grate took a deep breath, before forcefully releasing it again. "I'm not so sure any more. The body vanished just after the autopsy. I seriously doubt this particular individual was human, and several Governments on Earth are taking the same view."

Martin swiped through a few more pages and then placed the reader on the desk. He was a politician, not a scientist, and most of the document meant little to him. Not that he was going to admit it. "What are they doing about it?"

"Authorities in China, India, the North American Federation and the Eastern American States all propose plans to check citizens. Other national governments won't be far behind. They are of the opinion this individual is alien, and if he is, there will be more like him."

"Seriously? Do we have any proof?"

"What else could it be? You want my opinion?"

Martin waved his hand for the professor to continue and resigned himself to an afternoon immersed in conspiracy theory. He liked the man, but Steve's penchant for indulging in scientific oddities was sometimes annoying. Still, he was almost always right, so worth indulging. That was the reason Martin kept his friend so close, as a personal advisor.

"Well, it's sixty-odd Earth years, roughly thirty-two Martian years, since the Visitors arrived. They aren't here any longer and we now know they did nothing at all on Titan, right?"

"Yes, so?"

"So, whatever they are up to, they are hiding it from us. They lied to us, Martin. They are somewhere in our system and we don't know where, or why."

"You're looking for them though, aren't you?"

"Yes, of course, but it's a difficult job."

"Accepted, but what's this got to do with Auckland's corpse?"

"I think it's one of the Visitors. Think about it. Assume you are in a strange environment with a warlike species—that's us of course—and you want to conduct your business in secret. You're going to want to keep your eyes on them, right? I think our subject is a spy, a cloned body but improved over the original model, sent here to observe us from within. If there is one of them, there will be more."

Martin, mulled the words over; Brewer had a point, as bizarre as it might seem. "So … what, the Earth governments are planning to check everyone to see if they are missing an appendix?"

"Something along those lines. A simple skin biopsy to examine the cells; if they don't have mitochondria, they are alien. The idea is to start with mandatory testing of all government personnel from the top down, all heads of institutions, big business concerns, military personnel and so on down the pyramid. It'll take forever of course, but if it's true, these individuals are more likely to be positioned high up, I would think."

Martin could see Grate had more on his mind. "And?"

"The Council is considering instigating something similar here on Mars."

"You don't think it's a bit of an overreaction? The Visitors never did us any harm and they did save us from the *Blackship*. Why would they try to deceive us now?"

"They've already done so. They lied about Titan, so what else did they lie about? We took it on good faith the *Blackship* was an enemy, but now I wonder."

"The inhabitants of the *Blackship* tried to deceive us from the beginning, and attacked us without warning."

"Yes, but we don't know the full truth, do we. We took the Visitors' word for it."

Martin stood and turned to gaze out of his window. The logic could not be argued with; the professor was right. All the promise brought by the alien arrival had amounted to little, and after a short period of peace and harmony on Earth the mother world plunged back to its normal state of political bickering and one-upmanship. Perhaps that *was* something the aliens wanted to keep tabs on.

Martin knew about the data download received by Jake and Akira Falcon and the attempts by Jake's company, the New

Worlds Institute, to use the knowledge for change. In fact, he'd been instrumental in deflecting some of the multitude of legal challenges to wrest the rights from the Falcons, terrified of the possibilities if the data became the subject of open slather, uncontrolled research. He also knew most of the information had proven to be of little practical value, and the golden age promised by the Visitors did not eventuate. He turned back to face his adviser.

"I have no authority in this area, but I'll support the council if it recommends we start testing. It's a little thing, and it can't hurt, can it?"

Chapter 05

JAKE FALCON LOGGED out, shut down the computer and leaned back in his chair. Breathing out with a loud sigh, he pushed back from the desk and stood.

The time had come to go.

Finally.

Permanently.

He would never again work from his home high on Mount Maleny, on the outskirts of the mega-city of Brisbane, in Australia. The next time he logged on, it would be from his private yacht, somewhere between Earth and Mars.

The last few decades had not gone as well as hoped following the departure of the *Minaret*. Jake's organization, the New Worlds Institute, had achieved a great deal and made a lot of money from government contracts, but that was not at all what Jake had intended with the information entrusted to him.

The original plan was to use the data from the star-ship for the general betterment of society, and on Mars that outcome had been achieved to an acceptable degree. On Earth his efforts were thwarted constantly by a number of factors. The few true advances discovered would eventually benefit the entire human race, but Jake never allowed for the vagaries of human beings.

When the existence of the data was leaked, many Terran authorities took him to court to gain open access to the information, claiming it was a gift for all. He and Akira fought against this, considering much of the data had as much potential for harm as for good.

Jake was adamant no government would get its hooks into what he considered a Pandora's Box. He always won in court, based on the simple truth the download was given to him alone, without qualification or proclamation, and therefore nobody else had any legal claim. For once, the intricacies of the law on both planets worked in his favour.

To prevent the data's misuse he and Akira, with the help of a handful of trusted associates, created the New Worlds Institute, a network of research establishments that girdled both planets. The NWI intended to release the information piecemeal, as serendipitous scientific breakthroughs, but the first efforts had so far failed to achieve great success on Earth due to the intransigence of government agencies and the unpredictability of the masses.

On the mother world, implementation of the new science collapsed almost entirely. The first major project was the release of the gerontological suite, a number of treatments and techniques for the extension of life, allowing a normal human to live much longer than the average ninety or one hundred years while still retaining health and fitness. That did not go down well.

Clinics opened in the major cities of almost every nation, the cost of treatment kept to the absolute minimum to cover costs. Within months, many local governments shut them down for a variety of reasons not at all to do with the welfare of the people.

In the more enlightened nations—the Western European Union, South Africa, Canada, the North American Federation and the Eastern States of America—the clinics remained under the purview of the NWI and continued to run as intended, but in other countries, such was not the case. In Australia, one of Earth's most over-regulated nations, the treatments received official approval only after strict bureaucratic process, delaying the implementation for years.

In several nations dictatorial or military regimes took over the clinics in order to line their own pockets, forcing the issue until Jake was obliged to choke supply and force them to fail.

In overpopulated nations like India, the governments outlawed the project, unwilling to spend money to provide infrastructure for the inevitable increase in population numbers.

Other countries, including China and several European nations, allowed them, but either placed massive tariffs on their introduction, driving the cost of treatment so high only the wealthy could afford them, or instigated such a restrictive regime of rules for accessing the services only those in favour with the governments could qualify. By doing so, they limited the longevity treatments to the rich and affluent, the exact opposite of Jake's original intentions.

Worst of all, in those countries where the programs were not available but their existence was common knowledge, mobs began rioting in the streets in an attempt to force their governments to remove restrictions. Jake now acknowledged the suite had not been the best choice for beginning his campaign to reshape society.

Another early failure was the plan to introduce nanotechnology-based retail manufacturing hubs in all major cities on Earth. All a citizen needed to do was enter a facility, choose a design, pattern or recipe and in the shortest of times walk out with their item for only marginally more than the cost of the raw materials or ingredients.

Most of the program never eventuated. Jake's original concept was to set up the hubs and all supply lines using nanotechnology, then hand them over to the governments. Profits from the project were to be used to provide services and support to those citizens with jobs at risk, or to find them employment in non-manufacturing industries. No one would end up missing out and everyone would have enough to live a comfortable life.

In theory.

Most governments refused to allow the stations at all, insisting any arrangement be on a contracted basis to permit nanotechnology only in certain areas and under strict government control. Generally that meant the military. For others, nanotech remained illegal.

Jake now knew his original plans to be naïve in the extreme, and considering he was hailed as the Hawking of his age, it galled him. His mistake had been to attempt to integrate the various governments into the process, and he had seriously misread the economic environment. His talents lay in the applied sciences and he was not a politician. Nor was he an economist nor a social scientist, and he wished now he had listened more to those who were. Today, that side of the Institutes concerns were in the hands of others wiser in those areas than he.

A compromise was made by following a more insidious path, accepting certain government contracts and refusing others. Where permissible, a small number of hubs were set up under Institute control to manufacture a limited range of products, the income from those used to further the cause.

In the nations allowing it, factories were constructed to manufacture major items such as spacecraft, aircraft and agricultural machinery, using micro machines rather than nano-technology. It was a beginning, and the network would grow and expand as the populations became more dependent and demand grew, legitimizing the concept right under the noses of the bureaucrats, and despite them. The governments, unlike the general public, paid respectable prices for the technology, money which was funnelled by the Institute into schools, hospitals, universities, research and numerous charities.

In the meantime, many small discoveries and improvements to existing technologies flowed from the NWI. In the end, public pressure always worked best; baby steps, all the way.

On Mars, the situation was very different. The population was smaller by orders of magnitude and the entire planet was controlled by a single government, presided over by scientists, engineers, economists, diplomats and other respected members of the professional community. They held their positions for only three Martian years, although it was acceptable for an individual to serve several non-consecutive terms.

The Congress contained no career politicians who thought only of themselves and the next election, no military personnel who sought only power, and no industrialists eager to gain an economic advantage. There was no party politics and no congress-person sat for more than one term at a time except the elected President, who was permitted two consecutive terms by consensus. Spending time on the Council was an essential community service, not a career.

With unlimited resources and an empty world begging for expansion, Martian authorities had no objections at all to life extension technology, and the number of citizens taking advantage of the treatments was growing daily. Every city and major settlement possessed a subsidized clinic.

The greatest successes so far were the new space fleets under construction on both worlds, in deference to the now certain knowledge humans were not alone in the galaxy and the neighbours might not be friendly.

The Martian fleet, constructed on-planet on the plains of Daedalia, was well advanced, the more efficient and faster warships now numbering over a thousand. The cost was pitifully low at every stage from mining raw materials to completion, and the project allowed the government to employ many thousands of individuals from both worlds to man and maintain the ships. Humanity had long ago learned the fallacy of placing a weapon of war in the suspect hands of machine intelligence.

The Institute also signed contracts with the United Earth Council to build a second fleet on the moon, constructed from pure carbon like those on Mars, using nanotechnology to handle materials at the molecular level. The off-planet location eased the minds of those governments loath to allow nanotech in their territories, and opened the possibility for future expansion in other, more human-oriented fields. It also guaranteed the new warships would remain under the oversight of the UEC, with no Terran nation being able to claim ownership on the basis of the construction site being located on their national territory.

Nanotechnology was being used to construct a wide range of products on both Luna and Mars, and in the Asteroid Belt, for shipment to Earth. Much of the income from these ventures went to setting up or supporting charitable organizations and to apply constant pressure on Terran governments to introduce the health and agricultural innovations made possible by the technology from the *Minaret*.

Another major advance achieved by the NWI was in the field of artificial gravity. The supplied data did not provide the answer, as was so often the case, but did lead some of Jake's brilliant scientists along a line of research resulting in the development of a system which appeared to be the same as the one employed on the star-ship. Those same researchers were also well advanced in technology designed to locate and penetrate the wormholes science had recently proven existed in space.

Walking to the window, Jake looked towards the spacecraft squatting several hundred metres from the back of the house. This was his own private yacht, a streamlined, jet-black ship built using the latest technology and with all the latest advances in engineering, drive system and gravity control. In Jake's eyes it was a joy to behold, and in less than an hour it would carry him and his wife away from the mother world for the final time, to their new base in Hellas City on Mars, without the clearance or approval of local authorities.

The many NWI buildings on Earth, still official Institute premises but empty now, would in the months to come be sold to other concerns. Over the last decade, the Institutes primary facilities had been moved quietly but permanently to the red planet, the move kept from Terran governments to circumvent the inevitable attempts to confiscate or commandeer the local operations. New sites were built in Hellas and elsewhere, and personnel relocated as normal immigrants under the Institute's sponsorship. The process had taken almost a decade, and only after the fact would the local authorities receive official notification.

The official explanation: tax advantages offered by the Martian government as an incentive to move, as if the Institute needed financial help.

The real reason: the need to place the NWI beyond the control of petty, intransigent Terran governments.

Jake's amazing, genius wife of six and a half decades, Akira Hirano, was on board the yacht preparing for the four-week journey. The authorities did not allow Jake to land the ship on his private estate, but this time he accidentally forgot to ask. His pilot brought the sleek craft in at night, flying up the escarpment to avoid detection. So far nobody important had noticed the arrival, or if so, had chosen to remain quiet. In recent years Jake and Akira had become untouchable in the local community in which they lived.

Minutes later Jake stood at the front door preparing to lock down the security system one last time when a large, black, ground car glided down the driveway and drew to a halt outside the entrance. He was expecting someone to take over the house until it could be disposed of, but this vehicle did not appear to be the one he was waiting for. Two individuals dressed in white disembarked and stepped up to the door.

"Mister Falcon?"

"Yes. What can I do for you?" Jake could tell instantly these men were government employees; over the years he had become most proficient at spotting bureaucrats.

"We represent the Australian Federal Security Authority. We're here to take biopsy samples from you and your wife."

"Why would you want to do such a thing?" Jake finished setting the controls and closed the hatch on the security panel, refusing to justify the men by interrupting what he was doing or looking at them.

"Mister Falcon, you must know of the biopsy program. We're testing all personnel in government and the upper echelons of business. You are the CEO of the largest and most powerful organization in Australia, for that matter on the planet, so you must have been expecting us."

"My wife and I are both documented citizens of Earth. We were born here as were our parents, and our entire histories are on public record. Why would anyone want to test us?"

"How old are you, Mister Falcon?"

"Eighty-nine. That's also general knowledge as you well know."

"Yet you look about what, forty-five? Fifty? Would you not agree that is cause for suspicion?"

"My physical appearance is a result of medical rejuvenation techniques pioneered by my institute, which would be more easily available here if your government didn't place so many regulations in the way. I'm sure you're well aware of that as well. Why don't you tell the truth: you want tissue samples because you think we might be aliens. Maybe we got rid of the original Jake and Akira Falcon and replaced them."

"That is not our official line, sir, and if you took those gerontological treatments in this country without the proper documentation, you have committed a breach of the law. Can we get on with this, please? We do have other clients to visit today."

Clients? Really! "No, we cannot. Before you take a biopsy sample from either my wife or me, you'll get a court order. I don't know you, and I won't allow any invasion of my person or my wife's without the proper legal authority in writing. I am well within my rights here and considering who we are, I think you can guess where that authority might come from."

For a moment, the white-coated individual who was doing the talking looked flustered, then rallied. "Really, sir. Nobody does anything on paper any more. We represent the government, and it would be unwise for a man in your position to commit the folly of upsetting officials."

Little tin gods! "Are you threatening me?" Jake faced the man and returned his stare with an even harder one.

Once again the bureaucrat baulked, having not expected resistance. It was unlikely he had ever encountered someone so intransigent before, at least not on this job. "No, of course not, I merely..." He came to an abrupt stop as Jake stepped inside and closed the door.

For a few moments Jake stood motionless in the foyer, until he heard the car pull away and whine its way over the gravel driveway to the gate. Once the vehicle exited, those gates would close and remain so, with the fence around the property electrified until some authority chose to cut off the power supply from the source. Only the individual tasked with looking after the house knew how to get in, and if he did not arrive soon Joe would call him from the ship. When the authorities sent their cronies back they would not be able to gain legal entry, and the house would be secure and empty besides.

Exiting by the rear door and locking it behind, Jake stopped for a moment to take a last look at the place he had called home for over seven decades. He built this place, located on an old Macadamia nut farm perched at the edge of the escarpment with a clear view over the fabled Glasshouse Mountains, a series of ancient volcanic plugs projecting up from the otherwise flat coastal plain between Mount Maleny and the original Brisbane city centre.

The landscape below had once been vast, green swathes of pine plantation, native forest and verdant farm land, and a major agricultural district for the production of pineapples. Now there was nothing but suburbs and industrial sites, the mega-city having spread to encompass almost all of the area. The wonderful view he treasured so much no longer existed.

He and his wife were the last of the extended family to leave. His sister Grace departed for the red planet several weeks ago, and Jake's own clan was long gone. His two children now headed up the new operations on Mars, and his younger step-sister Raisa moved her life to space a decade ago. As captain of her own ship she considered her work brought her closer to understanding the family member she most admired, her father Joe Falcon.

Joe now lived in Hellas. As a young man of about twenty he came to Earth in his brand new, cloned body, complements of the Visitors, and took up residence in this house with his son, and daughter in law. He insisted on retaining his name, his presence explained as a distant relative who returned to the fold to work with his cousin.

In those days Jake had been a master hacker—he could still turn a high card in that respect—and he created a believable fake history for Joe, inserting it seamlessly and undetectably into the public record. Old Joe's assets, including his personal fortune, were willed to Jake and returned, excepting only the old freighter, to his 'cousin' as incentive for joining the Institute and heading up the Mars division. The transaction raised some eyebrows, but not enough to make a difference. The old ship became an NWI vessel, first under the captaincy of Sarah Falcon, then Joe again and lastly Raisa.

The only resistance to the will came from Jake's older sister, who always believed she was entitled to half the fortune, but she withdrew her objections the minute Jake explained to her the curious but real reality of her father's continued existence. Like Joe, she was now a director of the NWI, managing a massive team of legal eagles whose only task was to prevent various governments from trying to take control of Institute property and assets.

Jake looked forward to seeing his father again. Dad looked younger than him now, but it did not interfere with the father-son bond always so strong between them. It was his father's mind he knew so well, not the body.

With a loud sigh, he shoved his hands into his pockets and strolled across the grass to the spacecraft, where Akira stood waiting for him.

Chapter 06

THE *CALYPSO*, ONE of the newest of the New Worlds Institute research vessels, drew to a standstill near Jupiter's L4 Lagrangian point, located along the orbit of and preceding the giant planet.

Scattered through near space, several asteroids hung motionless in the void. A significant number occupied this region, rocks snatched from the Asteroid Belt by the unrelenting power of the largest planetary body in the system. Called Trojans, these lonely sentinels gathered in the L4 and L5 Lagrangian points and wove their merry dance along Jupiter's orbit in close concert with the planet itself.

They were not why the *Calypso* had come. Something else lurked in this lonely place.

Within the cargo hold sat a second, smaller craft, a vessel designed as a high-speed courier but now modified for a very different task. At its physical centre of mass sat a unique creation, a sphere just under two metres across consisting of an external platinum shell inside which spun a core of rare-metal plates, exotic materials and electronics. Outside the structure a maze of cabling and shielding secured and connected it to the vessel of which it was a part.

The exterior of the unique craft was highly modified, the hull covered in a thick layer of foamed titanium and an outer, diamond shell designed to protect it, hopefully, from micro-meteoroids at velocities greater than light speed. The interior of the tiny craft resembled something patched together from a junk yard, belying the true nature of its capability. It was, with recent modifications, the most sophisticated spacecraft yet built, and the end product of decades of dedicated research.

In the claustrophobic cockpit two individuals prepared themselves for the journey to come. No words were spoken, each occupied with their particular role in the test voyage now only minutes away.

Daniel Radelick commanded the mission from the co-pilots' seat, while his research partner, life partner and partner in crime, Jada Saitou, piloted the ship out of deference to the simple truth she was a far better pilot than he.

Dan's forte was physics in its purest form, and in the field of astrophysics few matched him in expertise. He lived in laboratories and spent little of his time in actual space, though his objective had for many years been the conquest of that medium.

In contrast to her partner, Jada had dedicated a considerable part of her life to spacecraft of all types. Her career began with the Mars Fleet and there were few ships in existence she could not fly, or at least figure out how to if given the time. An engineer of high standing, she was responsible for the conversion and preparation of this unique vessel for its groundbreaking task.

She turned to her partner for confirmation, which came in the form of a quick nod of the head, and then tapped the intercom switch on her screen. "Ready to lift off whenever you care to open the doors, Mother."

A concerned voice answered over her headphones. "You sure you want to do this yourself? It's dangerous to say the least, and you two are indispensable. Wouldn't it be better to let a couple of our test pilots do it instead?"

Dan, listening in, shook his head. "No, Jay and I invented this monster and we both decided it would be unfair to risk someone else's life testing it. Our invention, our gamble. Besides, Jay is as experienced in flying as anyone else available, if not more so."

"And if you don't make it?"

"We've allowed for that. All our research and design data is on file for our colleagues to pick up after us if the worst-case scenario eventuates. We're convinced we've got it right though. The odds are acceptable. Fifty-fifty I think."

"How do you figure?"

"Simple. It will either work or it won't. Haha!"

"We can send the ship through on auto. Let the computers take the risk."

Dan contemplated the idea for a moment. This was their baby, and he and Jada were both hands-on individuals. If there was a danger, they were prepared to take it for the thrill of being the first humans ever to do this.

"No, don't think so," he replied.

A loud sigh sounded over the intercom. "As you wish. Doors opening now."

The cargo bay hatches yawned wide, allowing the little ship to lift and slide sideways into deep space. Once clear it moved to a position several kilometres away.

"On point," Jada said. "Switching on locater now." For almost a full minute numbers scrolled across the screens before settling on a single set of coordinates.

"It's still there, right where the survey found it a year ago," Dan muttered, his hands shaking with anticipation as sweat began to pearl on his forehead. "How lucky can you get? We don't have to do a search. Damned right!"

"Distance twenty-point-six-three kilometres. Are we ready for this?"

Her partner nodded and gripped the arms of his acceleration seat. The target in question was invisible, nothing more than a potential, the location of one end of a wormhole anchored at the Lagrangian point. Until now, nobody had managed to prove anything further. Nobody knew what lay beyond.

The existence of wormholes had been mathematically calculated by scientists long ago, and several decades past, the first actual example was located at Jupiter's L5 Lagrangian point. Two more had been found since, one at Jupiter L4 and the third at Neptune L5, the latter discovered by one of the few automatic probes ever to venture that way.

Nobody completely understood the physics of these phenomena but speculation was they stretched between areas of equal physical potential within and between systems, thus forming a highway from one star to another provided a means existed to traverse them without catastrophic effects.

No larger in diameter than a micro-millimetre, they could not be traversed in any normal manner, but in theory any ship able to enter the anomaly without being destroyed by the strange alien reality within would reach the other end in a matter of minutes to hours, instead of the decades or centuries dictated by the speed of light.

That was where the complex device further back in the hull came into the equation. Dan and Jada had dedicated their lives to the study of these strange anomalies from the time the first was detected. They had no clue as to where they led, but believed they had discovered a way to allow a vessel to enter.

At least, they hoped they had.

Once up to speed, the gateway generator formed a sphere of force around the ship, shielding it from any adverse affects of a traverse. As it drove towards the point of potential, the generator would attract the end of the wormhole, forcing it to expand to a size sufficient to permit entry by the magnetic bubble and the spacecraft it contained. As the ship moved forward the wormhole would stretch to pass over and around it, shrinking back to a normal microscopic diameter in its wake.

At least, so went the theory.

Nobody had done it before.

This was the first attempt, and so far the concept was nothing *but* mathematics and a carefully assembled mass of electronics in a carefully junked together ship.

Dan was convinced the science and maths were right. He and Jada were acknowledged as the top of their field and if anyone could get this to work it would be them, but the potential for catastrophic failure gave them nightmares. Each made a will prior to this venture.

"Generator's active," he noted, eyes glued to the readout on the holo-screen. "We have our energy bubble."

"Mother, we are beginning our run ... now," Jada announced.

"Good luck, *Endeavour*," the voice of the research vessel's captain replied, acknowledging the name given the smaller exploration vessel. "Come back safe. We will maintain this position for as long as we are able. God go with you."

"Thank you, *Calypso*. Here we go." Jada tapped the screen and the *Endeavour* began to move forward, encased in its bubble of magnetic force.

When the ship approached to within half a kilometre of the location of the point of potential, the computer announced the anomaly had exploded in size, the gateway floating dead ahead. The generator had successfully accomplished its first task.

A popular misconception of a wormhole was a bell shaped entrance to a tube leading to places unseen, but such was not the case. The anomaly existed in a different dimension to the observable universe and its intrusion into this reality was a three dimensional singularity, a microscopic pinpoint in space. Now forced to expand to a bubble its size was, as expected, sufficient to allow the vessel to enter, and entry was possible from any direction.

"So far so good," Jada said. "We have our gateway."

"Engaging now," Dan said, as the ship nosed up to the bubble, visible only as a mathematical construct on the ship's command screens. He focused on the monitors, his head pounding as the blood rushed through his ears.

His gut gave a sharp wrench.

In a blink, the spacecraft vanished from this reality.

For a brief moment Dan felt numb, his mind shrouded by lethargy the like of which he had never experienced before. The haziness cleared, allowing him to focus on the job at hand. The ship was inside the wormhole on its way to God knew where. Jada increased the speed of the tiny vessel in stages, offering a silent prayer the far end of the anomaly would not carry them into the corona of, or worse, the core of an alien star, or so close to a planetary giant they could not escape its gravity well.

On the monitor the stars behaved in a most disturbing manner. The wormhole stretched through the observable universe and occupied the same space as normal reality, allowing the light from the surrounding stars to reach the ship. At first they flowed outward at high speed like in the holo-vids, but then slowed, stopped and started to converge, congregating into a blinding tube through which the vessel travelled, with nothing but blackness ahead. Rapidly the tunnel closed in, the light becoming brighter as the screens in the cockpit washed to white.

"As predicted," Jada gasped. "Shutting down forward cameras now."

Now accelerating well beyond light speed, the ship drove into the oncoming light so quickly neither the cameras nor the human eye could cope with the hard radiation.

At the speed at which it now travelled, and with the view now inaccessible, it was impossible to determine the exact degree of progress, so Dan and Jada trusted to their calculations and prayed they would arrive somewhere, anywhere, safely.

Dan stared at the now black screen, his hands gripping the arms of the co-pilot's chair until his flesh blanched from lack of blood. Deep inside, he felt a gut-wrenching nausea rising. Without a doubt, this was not something an organic body was intended to do. He was sweating, the smell he detected that of his own fear. He wondered how his partner was coping, glancing across to where she sat with her attention fixed on the readouts. Grasping for breath he summoned up the strength to say something, his voice faint and hollow.

"I don't believe it," he said. "We're in! We're travelling through a wormhole."

"We sure are honey-bunch." Jada's voice was a breathless whisper. "And well beyond light speed. Everything is working according to the mathematical modelling. The generator is operating at, umm ... it's good ... and the bubble is holding. Everything's in balance." The timbre of her voice told Dan his companion was almost in tears. Her hands shook as they rested on the control console.

"It's a shame we can't tell how fast we're moving," Dan said.

"We'll be able to work it out later. Time of passage into the known distance from Sol to wherever we end up."

"Assuming we can figure out where we are when we get there."

"I hope it's soon."

Dan glanced across to his partner. "You can feel it too? The nausea?"

"Yeah, and it's not pleasant. I think I want to heave."

"Same here. I don't think it's wise for us both to leave the controls now, so only one of us can afford to go at a time."

"Me first?"

Dan grimaced, aware of the turmoil in his own gut. "Go ahead."

The ship burst into clear space and glided to a standstill, the nose pointing at a distant, orange orb. Within seconds the A.I. began analysing anything observable in the vicinity. Dan turned the cameras back on and took the first human look at an alien system.

"It's a type K star," he said minutes later, as the astronomical observation data scrolled on the screen. "Orange, point-seven solar masses. And it's a binary. The AI's detected a second type-K nearby."

"Sounds familiar." Jada's eyes were glued to the readout on her own screen. "This one is a—wait a minute—the computer identifies it as 61-Sygni-A, a type K, 'BY Draconis', variable star, ninety-nine-point-nine percent probability. The other one will be 61-Sygni-B, a type K, Flare variable. We sent a probe here decades ago, but it won't have arrived yet."

Dan thumped his fist firmly on the arm of his seat, a broad smile on his lips. "Yes! 61-Sygni. We're still in our own neighbourhood. We've come eleven-point-four light years, just across the block from home, and in ... twenty-nine-point-three-two minutes. Spectacular!" His voice trembled as he spoke. He wasn't sure what drove his emotions the most, the elation, or the shock. "And we're still alive!"

The fifteenth closest star to the Earth, 61-Sygni was first catalogued several hundred years ago, and due to its proximity it had been a favoured subject for many astronomers over the centuries. At first it was believed to be a single star, but later observations identified two, both type K, circling each other in a close but slow dance. They had been named A and B, and at first there had been long and virulent arguments as to whether they possessed any planets.

Long ago it was speculated there were bodies orbiting both, but evidence was hard to come by. Subsequent observations confirmed gas giants and super-Earth type worlds around each. More recently, smaller rocky bodies had been discovered closer in to both stars. Nobody knew if any were inhabitable, or inhabited.

"Get a load of this," Jada said. The A.I. had assumed the gateway at this end would be at a Lagrangian point of a planet, and begun a search of near space. An image of the resulting discovery now filled the screens, a massive, mottled, red-brown, super-Earth world. "That thing is enormous," she gasped, studying the statistics. "Half the size of Jupiter. Too big for us."

Several hours later Dan suggested Jada turn the vessel around. "This is mind blowing, and I would love to stay here and make more observations, but that particular part of the project will have to wait for others. Our purpose is to test the generator, and Captain Henley will be wondering what's happened to us."

"You do realize we are the first humans to travel faster than light, and the first to enter an alien solar system?"

"I sure do, and that will have to be our reward. Let's go home."

"Must we?"

Loath to take his own advice, Dan nodded.

"Fingers crossed," Jada said, her face pale. "Here we go."

Three hours after it disappeared, *Endeavour* reappeared in Jupiter space at the exact point from where it began the voyage, and set a parallel course a few kilometres from the *Calypso*. Soon after, the ship sat once again in the mother-ship's hold.

When the hatch opened and the two occupants stepped out, the smiles on their faces lit up the cavernous chamber. The first test of the Saitou-Radelick gateway generator was a resounding success, and for the first time human beings had travelled faster than light speed to another star with potentially inhabitable planets.

The way to the stars was open.

Chapter 07

WHAT THE HELL are you doing here?

Joe Falcon stared at the image on the holo-screen. Io, the elegant individual standing outside his inner door, should not be there. He had no desire to see her now or ever, and she should have been stopped at the outer entrance. Nevertheless, there she was.

So much for expensive security, dammit.

Io was one of the Visitors, the occupants of the *Minaret,* and few people were privy to her real identity. Only he, his now departed wife Sarah, Jake and Akira, and Ruth Carvalio, Terry Caldwell and Alaine Parish, three of the crew of his old ship the *Butterball,* ever knew the true story, that the aliens did not leave at all and walked amongst humanity in human bodies indistinguishable from the genuine thing.

Joe first met Io in the *Minaret's* habitat drum. She occupied an android body then, an artificial construct based on the features of the female members of the *Butterball's* crew, to allow her to converse with Joe. She was his liaison for the entire duration of the first visit.

Now she was as human as him, her mentality occupying a body cloned from genetic material from again, the females of *Butterball.* That had been Joe's idea. In facial appearance she possessed something of both his ex-wife Sarah, and Ruth, the writer who accompanied them on the first voyage as official historian and media liaison and with whom Joe formed a brief friendship on the voyage.

According to Io, the alien ship left its home world incomplete and unprepared, and its crew pushed it to the limit to reach Earth, as a result of which they had no choice but to stay in the Solar System.

Their initial intention had been to live amongst the human race using synthetic bodies like the one Io once occupied, but Joe convinced them that to remain unnoticed they should use clones, limiting the chance of their being discovered. Joe's unspoken hope was they would eventually merge with and become part of the human population, cease to be a separate species and add to the overall patina that was the human race.

Once occupying human bodies, the only alien thing about them would be their minds, and those would change with time. In Joe's view they were not very different to humans to begin with, their thoughts and attitudes unexpectedly similar. He always assumed the differences would be significant, moulded by the environments in which each evolved, and the similarities struck him as uncanny. Perhaps a bit too much for believability, he thought.

He was no longer convinced his ploy had worked. Recent news articles indicated variations between the alien bodies and natural humans which had only now been discovered after decades. An increasingly aggressive government program was already hunting them down.

Joe glared at the image on the screen. "What do you want?"

Io glanced up to where a hidden camera revealed anyone standing at the door.

How do you know that's there? Joe wondered.

"We need to talk, Joseph. It is important."

"We have nothing to discuss. Go away."

"I cannot. This is critical. Please allow me to enter."

Joe shook his head and shut down the viewer, intending to ignore her. Seconds later a soft click sounded from the foyer of the house.

How the hell can you get past my security?

Io swept into the living area and sat down on the lounge without waiting for an invitation. Dressed in an elegant suit she looked like a successful businesswoman, but beyond that she drew the eye more than most. With long, auburn hair, large eyes, a perfect face and flawless skin she had changed somewhat since their last meeting decades ago. Her appearance was without doubt intended to draw attention, Joe thought, perhaps useful for her life amongst humans in the past but not an advantage in the current environment.

"I have nothing to say to you. Please leave."

"Why do you not wish to talk? Is there a problem?"

Joe gave a slight cough and evaded the question. He shook his head, moved as far from his visitor as possible and scrunched himself into a seat, all the while glaring back at her. "You lied to me."

"I have never done so, Joseph."

"When you gave me this body you told me it was perfectly human, but it's not. It doesn't age at the normal rate. I'm over eighty but I look in my mid-forties. You *did* lie to me."

Io's mouth twisted into a wry smile, her eyes reflecting the light filtering in from beyond the windows. "Is it not the dream of all humans to remain forever young? I thought your new body would please you."

"You thought wrong. You robbed me of my wife, Sarah. She was offered the gerontological treatments being developed by my son's institute, but she refused. Can you guess why?"

Io did not answer, sitting motionless, hands clasped in her lap. Her eyebrows lifted in anticipation.

"She couldn't stand growing old while I stayed young. We were supposed to grow old together but your perfect, bloody clone doesn't age normally. She couldn't accept that."

Io dropped her eyes to the floor, a shadow of realization washing across her face. It was a remarkably human reaction. "I *am* sorry, Joe. We had no intention of taking away your happiness, or Sarah's."

"No, I expect not. You couldn't help it, could you? I suggested you create normal bodies, but you couldn't resist making what you thought were improvements. Now it's turning around to bite you, isn't it? And you did it to me without telling me."

For a moment the silence was palpable, and then Io spoke again. "Yes, I accept that, but we did not intend to cause harm. Sarah could have delayed her aging by taking the treatments. At the time you occupied your original body you were fifty-eight and she loved you then, even though you were old enough to be her father."

"Yes, and my age was a big part of it. She was estranged from her own father and saw a father-figure in me, I think. I don't know if it was love beyond that; I hope so. When you gave me a new, twenty-year-old body she was all for it and I think there was genuine affection there, at least on my part, but over the years *that* changed as well. *Her* issue was being *older* than me."

"This is a problem with humans, is it not?"

"Not always. As a general rule love has no barriers, not age, race, or gender, but for some it does; it did for Sarah. How long is this body going to last me?"

"It ages at about one third the normal rate, so you will live to around two hundred and sixty years. With your son's research you might survive even longer."

Joe shook his head, his eyes wide with shock at Io's last statement. Again, a long silence. His guest looked human, but despite the incredible similarities the mind living within the body still seemed alien, and Joe appreciated it was sometimes hard for the Visitors to understand the way humans thought.

Io gazed directly at him. "I think perhaps you lied to us also. Am I right in assuming you believed if we assumed human bodies we would integrate with humanity and cease to be who we are? Was it your hedge against our being a threat?"

Joe felt his skin flush hot. "Yes, but I never made any secret of it. You knew well enough we're emotionally based creatures, and if you took on our bodies you also took on our hormones. Like I said, love has no bounds."

"Yes, I accept that, but you may be surprised to know we managed to avoid that fate. Most of us maintained our genetic purity and kept to ourselves as much as possible. Those of us who partnered with your politicians and business leaders also remained true to our kind."

"Well, now you've been caught out because you couldn't resist modifying the clones you created. I did warn you of the

danger. Humans are xenophobic, sometimes in the extreme."
And what about the children?

"We did take certain precautions. If a cloned Visitor mates
with a human, the offspring is genetically human. A necessary
divergence."

Dammit, don't do that! Io's apparent ability to read minds
always perturbed Joe. He long ago determined it was not so,
and that she was simply extremely good at reading and
interpreting facial expressions and micro-movements, but it still
annoyed him.

"It is because of the genetics of the clones I am here." Her
face hardened as she took on a more businesslike posture.
"You are in danger."

For the first time since her arrival Joe looked her in the
eyes.

"What do you mean? *Why* am I in danger?"

"The body we created for you is no different to the ones
we made for ourselves. If they decide to test you they will
determine you are one of us and you may be incarcerated."

Joe shook his head again, his face flushed and his hands
trembling. "Bastards! Why would you do that to me?"

"I understand your anger, but we could not know the
current circumstances would eventuate. I am here to warn you
and provide you with an avenue for escape, should you wish
it."

"I haven't been tested. It's not such an issue here on Mars."

"You are still at risk. You have the advantage of the power
of your family, but eventually it will get out of hand. No more
of my people will be discovered on Earth, but many of us lived

here as well and the Martian Council began testing several weeks ago. So far they have not done so beyond members of the government and the heads of Industry, but most of us have already left as a precaution."

"Left to where?"

"We are returning to the *Minaret*. Yes, it is still here, hidden in your outer Solar System."

"Where?" Joe sat bolt upright, his hands gripping the arms of the chair.

"I cannot give you the exact coordinates. Our ship navigation computers have them and the recognition codes needed by us to make rendezvous."

"My son Jake and his wife..."

"Will be tested soon, within the next few days."

"There's no reason for them to worry. Their physical ages are the result of their treatments. They aren't involved with you or your cloning techniques."

"True. The only other person besides yourself who needs to be concerned is your ex-crewman, Terrance Caldwell."

Joe's eyebrows lifted. "He's still alive?"

"Indeed, and like you he still looks to be in his forties. When we brought him back to life we gave him, you might say, an upgrade. That is why it took us so long to return him to you."

Joe felt his blood begin to boil. "What kind of fucking upgrade?" he blurted, his temper rising.

"We could not save him. Like yourself, he was given a new, cloned body."

Joe leaned back in his seat and closed his eyes. He had not seen his ex-engineer for over forty years, but he had always liked the lad. *No, not a boy anymore; he'll look around the same age as me if what Io says is correct.* The idea the Visitors had set him up in the same manner infuriated Joe.

When Terry died, the alien maintenance drones that were everywhere inside the star-ship took the body before Joe could reach it, and Io's people returned him some time later, alive and well but with no memory of what had happened.

The boy was always one of Joe's favourites. His ability to behave in an almost childlike, naïve manner endeared him to the hearts of almost everyone he met. Sarah, who had been in her early twenties at the time, considered him a brother, he being the closest in age to her of all on the *Butterball.*

"Has he been told about this?" Joe asked.

"Not yet. He is here on Mars, and I will contact him after I leave you."

"He's in Hellas?"

"No, he lives and works at one of the shaft sites in the Arsia Mons region. He shares similar concerns to you over his lack of aging, so he moves around a lot and keeps a low profile."

For a moment Joe considered Io's words and wondered how she could have any idea what concerned him, considering they had not met for years. He always assumed the Visitors saved the boy by re-building his old body, but now Io had stated otherwise. Joe knew these aliens could create a new clone and force grow it to adult size in only months. Whatever they did to Terry, it took a matter of weeks.

"We had several human clones in process when Terrance died," Io explained, appearing to read Joe's thoughts again. "When you first docked with the *Minaret* we sent micro-probes into your ship to take tissue samples from each of your crew while you slept. We began growing clones of the younger members, including one of Terrance, so we could more adequately study your biology. His clone was well advanced when his death occurred."

"Alright, why are you here? Not just to warn me, I think."

"No. My few remaining colleagues and I intend to leave soon and return to the *Minaret*. Over one hundred of us have been discovered and incarcerated on Earth, but it will go no further. We maintain a number of ships of our own, and all but one, my own personal vessel, are already on their way home. Those of us still on Mars will soon depart, and I am offering you and Terrance the chance to come with us. I know how you feel about your continued existence here and thought the opportunity might be attractive to you."

Joe glared at Io, his eyes burning with anger. He had for years blamed this woman for his worries, in particular the loss of Sarah, and the idea he might want to go with the Visitors on their travels was never something he contemplated.

She was now offering him the opportunity to join her and her people in their future travels, and it told him a great deal. The star-ship was no longer crippled; if it had been incapable of further star voyages when it first arrived, such was now not the case. For the briefest of seconds he wondered what it would be like to wander amongst the stars.

"Your ship is still out there somewhere? But not at Saturn."

"I am told the commanders considered it safer to move elsewhere. Do you wish to accompany us?"

Joe leaned forward and fixed his eyes on those of his visitor.

"No," he said. "No way will I ever go back to that ship. Not a chance in hell."

Chapter 08

BEAN PELTZ SHUFFLED to ease the pressure on his backside as he drove northwest along the Grand Loop. The road skirted the north-eastern section of Yellowstone Lake, the largest body of water in the national park. It was a magnificent day, the sky blue and cloud free, a gentle breeze blowing.

An overpowering fragrance floated on the air. Most people would have considered it the volcanic presence of Yellowstone or perhaps just a plain stink, but for Bean that particular perfume had been a part of his life for many years. He loved the park, and for him life had never been better.

Apart from the pain in his backside from sitting in the driver's seat all day, that is. He needed a break and not far ahead was a place where he always stopped when travelling this way, which considering his job as a custodian of this magnificent park, was often.

At the much loved spot he pulled over to the side of the road and climbed out to stretch his legs. Most visitors found nothing spectacular about this place—it was a nondescript piece of bitumen on the roads circumnavigating the lake—but for Bean it was special. In this spot ten years earlier he first met his wife, when he stopped to check on a group of lost and confused tourists. From then on it became a place of significance, one he found truly peaceful, where he could stop to contemplate the natural beauty of the park to which he had dedicated his life.

He leaned against the pickup, his gaze drifting past the few scattered trees and across West Thumb, an almost circular body of water pushing out from the western edge of the main lake. In front of him a long, narrow, gravel spit cut across at an angle, separating the lake from a small enclosed pond where Little Thumb Creek flowed out.

Far across the calm, mirror-like surface, a miniscule, black speck appeared, approaching from the direction where Trout Peak reached for the sky in the distance beyond Yellowstone Lake. Still leaning against his vehicle, Bean remained unconcerned but curious as his eyes followed the object.

The ship flew closer and became identifiable as a plane of some kind, or perhaps, considering the stubby wings and the way it moved, a spaceship. It descended low over the water and came to a stop, hovering metres above the surface. Odd, Bean thought, but there was nothing especially unusual about it; private aircraft were frequently spotted over the park. Space craft, on the other hand...

The only possible concern was something dangerous, like toxic waste, might be dropped into the lake, a simple and cost-free expedient to dispose of something that would otherwise cost a fortune to deal with. Since the collapse of the old United States such underhanded tactics were being used with increasing frequency by big industry, which now held a stranglehold over the government and cared less every year about the environment.

Sad, Bean thought. As a ranger he studied environmental practices in depth and he knew the planet had been through all this before. Several hundred years ago the climate reached a critical point for global warming, and only through the efforts of mega-industry and the common people to solve the issue in the face of intransigent governments did Earth win through.

The effects of that fiasco still lingered today, but now those same industrial concerns no longer bothered. They had forgotten the valuable lesson learned by their predecessors, that if one wished to prosper in a densely populated world one first had to ensure the planet survived the ill effects of such prosperity.

Yellowstone sat at the extreme edge of the Eastern American States, in the state of East Montana-Wyoming, the park itself straddling the border with the North American Federation located some kilometres to the west of where Bean now stood. The western portion of the original park lay in that now foreign nation, in what had once been Idaho and western Montana.

This area was once the destination of choice for vast numbers of tourists, but these days comparatively few came. In recent years the district had become hotter and the air less than ideal from fumes, Bean's 'perfume', which increasingly bubbled from certain parts of the lake. He had long ago become accustomed to the smell, but to the uninitiated it was noisome.

Many scientists considered the park to be the most dangerous caldera on the planet. The super-volcano had seen major eruptions before, but not for 640,000 years. Events since then had been minor in comparison, the last around seventy thousand years ago having been little more than lava flows that created the Pitchstone Plateau in the southwest.

For several hundred years the floor of the caldera had been rising infinitesimally, triggering an increased response in monitoring. Nothing had happened yet. The park still survived and attracted visitors in decreasing numbers. The science said the super-volcano would not erupt in the near future, if ever, but tourists were a strange bunch; tell them there was a minor possibility and the World-Wide-Networks could turn it into an existential threat overnight.

Bean watched as doors opened in the belly of the vehicle and dozens of small, black objects dropped and disappeared beneath the water, their passage unmarked in the turbulence created by the downdraft from powerful engines. When the surface calmed no trace of the objects remained and the ship had vanished, having accelerated away as only a spacecraft could.

Damn, Bean thought. *Dumpers! We need to get a retrieval team out here as quick as we can. Bastards!* Returning to the pickup he reached in to grab the radio speaker and then stopped, noticing flocks of birds streaming from the far side of the lake on their way west. Far out in West Thumb water began to boil, as if forewarning an imminent event.

What the fu...

Seconds later the calm waters erupted, tall columns of steam shooting skyward. Bean jumped into his vehicle and slammed the door shut, wound the windows up and turned on the ignition. He paused and glanced back out over the lake. The eruptions were not volcanic, neither lava nor ash. They resembled white, pure pillars of scalding steam erupting hundreds of metres into the atmosphere.

Dozens of plumes towered over the otherwise peaceful lake and then diminished, growing shorter until in less than ten minutes the last vanished, leaving a carpet of bubbling, white water and steam in its wake.

Bean sat dumbfounded. He had never seen anything like it before. His hand shook as he grabbed the radio speaker and pressed the send button.

"Come in, base. You there, Dianne. You ain't gonna believe what I've just seen."

*   *   *

In Salt Lake City, many kilometres to the south-west, Celia Spargo stared at her monitors and shook her head in disbelief. The screen before her displayed data from earth tremors in Yellowstone National Park.

Her office was at the University of Utah Seismographic Stations, or 'UUSS'. Established centuries ago in the original United States and now part of the Eastern American States, the unit monitored the Yellowstone Seismic Network, a sophisticated array of seismometers spread throughout the region of the ancient super-volcano. Since the program's inception millions of quakes had been detected, most of them so minor they registered only on instruments, while tourists remained blissfully unaware.

Something strange was happening. The lines on the monitors indicated an event unlike anything Spargo had seen before. At first it looked like another earthquake swarm, a series of small tremors occurring over a short space of time. Swarms occurred commonly and accounted for at least half the total seismic events in the park.

This time, the network had so far detected fifty-three tremors, each one short, sharp and of the same precise intensity and duration. Each registered at magnitude two-point-one and all occurred within one hour, each sixty-nine seconds after the last. It was almost like someone set off a timed sequence of explosive charges. Such a thing was, of course, impossible, considering the location of the epicentres.

Spargo sat back and shook her head. According to the display the tremors were originating from several different and precise depths. Some were shallow, between one and five kilometres deep. Others were at around nineteen kilometres, but of the most concern was a third cluster even further down near the Mohorovicic Discontinuity, the bottom boundary of the crust. Celia turned her head and shouted over her shoulder to her fellow researchers.

"You guys getting this?"

Murmurs of acknowledgment came back, unheard as she focused on her own readouts.

The Yellowstone Caldera sat on an unstable section of the Earth's crust, located where a magma plume rose close to the surface from deep within the mantle. Between the top of the plume and ground level lay two magma bodies, the uppermost of which was a wide, shallow, rhyolite mass extending from five to seventeen kilometres deep. Beneath this and several times larger, sat a second body of basaltic rock extended from twenty to fifty kilometres into the crust.

Neither of these was entirely molten, only a small percentage of each persisting in a melt state. That was not the principal danger. Beneath the lower body and separated by a thin layer of upper mantle, sat the top of the plume itself.

Spargo's concern was the epicentres were in the barriers separating the three bodies from each other and from the surface. If those became fractured the pressure could increase, weaken the rock and allow more of it to turn to melt, thereby precipitating an eruption.

Celia felt herself turn suddenly cold. She could almost believe the tremors were a deliberate series of explosions placed in precise positions to initiate such an event.

No, impossible. No technology on Earth could get explosive devices down there.

The Mohorovicic Discontinuity or 'Moho', marked the border between the Earth's crust and the upper mantle. Centuries ago the old United States attempted to drill a hole down to the boundary, an undertaking called the Mohole project. It failed. Earth's inner realm was not an easy place to reach.

At Yellowstone the Moho sat at the base of the lower magma body. The plume rose to a point just below the boundary, and between them the melt bodies created a weak spot all the way through the crust.

A new set of data began to scroll up the screen. Spargo's breath caught as the system displayed hundreds of small quakes occurring across the caldera region. As she watched, her mind reluctant to accept what she saw, the number of tremors increased.

"I think," she said to nobody in particular, "it's time to report this to F.E.M.A. We need to start getting people out of there, now!"

*   *   *

From a high vantage point on the Salsabila Hills road, Agung gazed out across Lake Toba, a beautiful, placid body of water at the north-western end of Sumatra. He had been here many times before as part of his research, and its beauty never failed to impress him.

A little to the south, Samosir Island, home to well over one hundred thousand people, filled most of the centre portion of the lake. A mostly agricultural district, it also had a respectable tourism industry, and at this time of the year hordes of pleasure seekers would be in the region, catching the ferry across from Parapat to enjoy the cultural heritage the island offered.

Agung was familiar with the terrible past of this place, something of which the average tourist remained blissfully unaware. Toba was the sight of one of the most devastating volcanic eruptions in history. The super-volcano beneath Agung's feet had erupted four times in one-point-two million years, the last eruption occurring seventy-five thousand years ago.

Now the crater of that cataclysm was a peaceful and beautiful body of water surrounded by forested hills and small-plot agriculture, but the island half-filling the lake contradicted that peace. Volcanologists called Samosir a volcanic resurgence dome, and that was all Agung saw when he studied the scene. As always, his visit this time was to continue his research on the subject of his thesis, the Ring Of Fire and its future consequences for Indonesia, his home.

The floor of the old, water-filled caldera was rising, continuously pushing its way above the waterline to create the ever growing island. One day it would collapse and the monster beneath would be unleashed once again. That would not be for a long time, and meanwhile the ancient volcano provided constant study for academics around the world.

Long shadows began to spread over the water as the sun set behind the western mountains and evening approached. Agung felt the first pangs of hunger in his stomach, prompting him to climb into his vehicle and return to his accommodations in Parapat, where he expected a meal of the finest local cuisine would be waiting for him. It was not far, but the road had a hundred sharp curves and it would be dark before he arrived at his lodgings.

As he climbed back into the car he spotted a small, black spacecraft dropping down over the northern most end of the lake. It descended until only metres from the water and hovered for a moment, the downdraft from its engines sending a series of concentric waves streaming away. From his high and distant vantage point Agung could not see what the ship was doing, but waited until it rose and flew away, accelerating skyward at a phenomenal rate.

The lake returned to its normal, placid state so Agung shook his head and climbed into the car. It was not his concern, but space craft were not supposed to descend over Toba, so he might consider reporting it. The hour was late and he was getting hungry.

*   *   *

The clock struck midnight. A half-moon shone down on the Bay of Naples, drowned by the blaze of light from the nearby mega-metropolis. The city was a major commercial centre and numerous aircraft arrived and departed the international airport day and night.

In the control tower, flight controller Carlo De Amicis observed an unidentified target as it approached the coast. He had spotted the blip at the extreme limit of the radar's range, and now his supervisor stood behind him watching over his shoulder. Every attempt to contact the unidentified vehicle had failed and a minute earlier the intrusion had been reported to the air force. At this moment a fighter would be scrambling to intercept.

The unidentified object stopped and hovered at a point well out in the bay. For seconds it remained motionless, then shot away towards the edge of the screen and vanished.

"Has to be a spacecraft," the supervisor said. "An aircraft couldn't stop like that or accelerate so fast."

Pinzon nodded agreement. "It's gone now. We've lost it."

"Fine. Let the interceptor know, log it and leave it. It wasn't broadcasting any identification so we can't do anything unless it comes back."

Neither man knew much about geology. Neither knew the Bay of Naples marked the location of Campi Flegrei, a super-volcano caldera complex that last erupted only 12,800 years ago, throwing cubic kilometres of ejecta into the atmosphere and across the ground. It was a hot spot with a history of exploding several times in the last forty thousand years, bringing destruction and devastation with it each time.

Nor did they know the base of the caldera had been undergoing considerable deformation in preceding centuries.

Volcanologists working in the region *did* know. Hours later, panic spread as data began streaming in from seismic detectors located all around the bay. Vesuvius, the famous volcano perched on the far side of Naples, suddenly held no interest to anyone.

Chapter 09

JOE HELD OUT his hand and accepted a mug of hot brew from the auto-maid; real coffee, not the synthetic muck manufactured on Mars. This brown, fragrant brew came from the mother world and was worth far more than many would consider reasonable, but these days Joe did not concern himself with costs.

The power and influence of the family business guaranteed he would never want for anything, so he had little use for the worth he had accumulated. Most of the massive remuneration that came his way went into a variety of charities or to support various researchers at the local university. Years ago he financed the new wing at the Mars Space Museum where the old *Butterball* was preserved for posterity.

Turning cup in hand, he wandered across to his desk and slumped into the soft, welcoming leathers of his work chair, as he did each morning while he checked the news, retrieved messages and worked through papers requiring attention.

As the Sun spun up in the morning it cast long, dark fingers across the basin, shadows that grew slowly shorter to reveal the crater floor, like a curtain rising over a glorious stage setting. It was a sight the like of which could be found only on Mars; in the arena of natural drama, Earth could not compete.

Of course, the cliffs on the far side were not visible from this position. They were too distant, beyond the horizon. Only the nearby sections of the crater walls could be seen directly, stretching away on either side.

A week had passed since Io's visit and Joe had not completely calmed down yet. He admitted to himself he detested the Visitors, and while his hatred was perhaps unwarranted and even unfair, it remained firm nonetheless. He was disenchanted with his life, and the aliens were as good as anyone else to blame. He acknowledged he had become embittered but had no idea what to do about it. As he sat scanning his com-screen, the door alarm sounded.

Joe flicked on the security monitor. A familiar figure stood at the entrance from the hyper-loop platform. Terrance Caldwell looked nervous, glancing every few seconds in the direction from which bullet-pods entered the station, then back to the com-screen.

"Come up, Terry," Joe said, tapping the release for the outer door. "I'm the last residence at the end of the access corridor. Ring the bell when you reach me."

Fifteen minutes later Joe's old friend stood in the middle of the lounge, still glancing about, especially at the now closed entrance door. Joe realized this was a man paranoid about being followed. Little remained of the boy he remembered of old; the happy-go-lucky, child-like character who became a much loved part of the *Butterball's* crew.

Terry had changed over the decades. He was older, but not as much as he should have been. Joe understood why now, aware his old crew member shared the same problems as him.

Terry's face still showed the scars he displayed as a younger man, and in light of the new information given by Io, it puzzled

Joe. At first he could not understand why, if his friend received a new body, those scars had not disappeared, but came to the conclusion the aliens did not then want the crew of the *Butterball* to know he was a clone. The motivation behind such an act left Joe wondering. More secrecy, more intrigue.

The mischievous quality always present in the younger man had vanished, as had the orange overalls that earned him the nickname of 'jail bait'. This version was a little older physically, and impeccably dressed, but had a nervous, furtive look.

"It's great to see you again, old friend," Joe said as Terry stood a little lost in the living room of the residence. "We could almost be brothers now."

For a moment Joe's guest said nothing, then seemed to calm enough to sit on the lounge. "Sorry, Boss. Been a bit edgy the last few days."

Joe smiled. Terry had always called him 'Boss' on the *Butterball*. "Let me guess. Our favourite Visitor has been to see you."

Terry arched his eyebrows. "You know? About the clone business, I mean."

"Yes, I do indeed. I gather Io told you the whole rotten deal. You and I are brothers, of a kind. What brings you here?"

"After she left, the authorities came to the place I was working and started checking through the employee records. They're looking for the Visitors and I decided not to stick around until they found me. I jumped a robot carrier out of there."

According to Io, Terry had been working at one of the Institute run shaft projects near the northern volcanoes. The giant shafts being bored kilometres into the Martian crust were part of the terraforming activities on Mars.

Between a half and one kilometre in diameter, they extended many kilometres into the planet, the deepest now fifteen and growing deeper as automated machines continued to gnaw away the raw rock at the bottom. The greater the depth, the higher the heat, and the more moisture laden air blasting up from below to warm and thicken the atmosphere.

"So you came here."

"Nowhere else to go, Boss. I thought you might be able to help me hide. You do know they are killing off the Visitors?"

"What? No, I did not."

"I heard a news bulletin on the way over here. The aliens who got caught in some countries on Earth are being treated as spies and executed. Not every country ... just some."

Joe shook his head in disgust and seated himself in a chair opposite. He rarely bothered to watch the news feeds these days considering very little of the content was actually true, and he found it hard to accept humans could act in so paranoid a manner.

"So, my friend. It's forty years since I last saw you. What have you been doing all this time?"

Terry relaxed and let out a sigh. Reaching for the drink Joe had placed beside his chair, he took a deep swig and closed his eyes for a moment, composing himself. "I decided to go back to school. I mean, I've always been good at what I do, but I figured I had the money so why not use it to improve myself, legit like. You know I published a book?"

"I do indeed. I've read it. Most enjoyable, although the part about my death seemed a bit contrived."

"Yeah, well, we all agreed to the story, didn't we? I sort of wrote it. I used a ... what do you call them? ... ghost writer. You remember Ruth Carvalio?"

Joe nodded. He recalled her well, the woman who convinced him to take her along as official historian and media liaison on the first journey to the *Minaret*. He had liked her from the first moment he met her, when she sat at his table and pushed a steaming hot coffee his way that morning on the Kepler *Core*, the giant space station he used as home base during his asteroid surveying days. At one point they became close, and after the conclusion of the journey remained friends for a while. They lost touch forty years ago. He wondered if she was still around.

"Is she...?"

"Alive? Yeah, sure is. She's on Earth at the moment, in the East American States. She took your geronty ... anti-aging treatments."

Joe nodded acknowledgment. He could easily imagine what Ruth was doing there. The story of the *Butterball* mission had made her a household name, and no doubt she was in pursuit of information for a new book, perhaps on the turmoil the nation had seen in the last few centuries.

Early in the twenty-first century, the old United States of America began to crumble after being subjected to an unprecedented political upheaval, from which it emerged with the people divided and antagonistic towards each other. A civil war resulted after several decades of turmoil, following which the Pacific states, those west of the Rocky Mountains, split away and became the North American Federation.

Soon after, the north-eastern states also broke away and the state of Texas assumed the role as powerhouse of a smaller, less affluent union.

"So, you went back to school?"

"Yeah. I studied engineering and computer science, sort of to give my navy skills a legitimate backing. I was always good with those things, but I never had the money to get an education when I was younger. I kinda have a talent for it though, like computers and I understand each other."

True, Joe thought. Terry's affinity with anything mechanical or electrical was why he had hired him for the *Butterball*, so why would computers be any different? The man was indeed a natural.

"I was working as a cyber-terrorism prevention officer at the new fleet construction yards when I realized I wasn't getting older at the right rate. You change jobs a lot in that field so at first I ignored it, but I figured eventually someone was going to question my age."

Joe nodded. "Yes, I have a similar problem. I'm able to shield myself, being a director of my son's institute, but you wouldn't have had the same options."

"No. I ended up at the shaft projects over by the volcanoes. Everything is automated out there but they still keep some engineering staff on hand. They don't care much about who you are, as long as you can do the job to the standard they want. It's the best place to disappear this side of the Belt."

Joe understood. Remote from Earth and Mars, the asteroid mining concerns were a law unto themselves and many people who lived and worked there did so to hide from someone or something. The shaft projects were the closest thing to that environment on either of the inhabited worlds.

"So, what now?"

"Kinda hoping you might be able to help me there. If not, it's back out to the Belt; Kepler I guess. I'll need your help to get there without being pulled up at the spaceports."

Joe had expected that. The asteroid mining companies constantly needed skilled workers and never asked questions, so Terry would fit in well with his skills.

"I may end up out there with you", Joe said. "It's safe enough here for now, but sooner or later..."

Though sixty-one years had passed since the first *Minaret* encounter, he realized he still felt responsible for the individual seated opposite. Terry had been one of the first crew members Joe employed for the *Butterball*, before the old freighter had been converted to an asteroid survey vessel. The boy had participated in the conversion and understood the workings of the old ship better than any other person alive.

Terry always had something of the child about him and education would never take that away. It was his character, what made him who he was. Despite his current problems he was still the naive, young mechanical genius Joe remembered, and a friend.

"You can stay here as long as you like, or as long as possible. I'll find you a position with the Institute, somewhere you'll be safe and won't come under scrutiny. If the time comes, one of our ships will find a better place for us." He thought of his daughter Raisa, who captained one of the NWI's most impressive research vessels.

A horrifying notion flashed into his mind. He was a clone with a body that functioned in every way like a normal man, but which he now knew to be different in microscopic ways which could only be detected by a laboratory. Raisa was his child through natural birth.

Were those variations passed on to her?

Did the government program put her at risk?

He recalled Io's comment about clones not passing on their genetic peculiarities through breeding with humans, but he did not trust Io, so how could he be sure?

Raisa was safe while in space and that was ninety-five percent of the time, but she should be warned. Joe's son Jake, her older brother and boss, would be able to contact her and arrange for testing in secret. Joe prayed he had not cursed the most loved of his children.

Turning his attention back to Terry he noticed the man leaning forward, his hands clutched over his knees, his gaze directed to the polished stone floor.

"So, would you like to stay here for now?"

Terry lifted his head, his eyes moist, tears glistening on his cheeks.

"Yes, thanks Boss. I always knew you would see me right."

Chapter 10

A PERSISTENT AND annoying buzz woke Joyce Lockamy from her first decent slumber in a week. Lack of sleep had been a persistent problem for her over the years, but of late it bothered her more than usual. She felt irritable, and a midnight call did nothing to help. Reaching for her phone she listened for a moment, her brain still mired in a haze of semi-awareness. Seconds later she was wide awake.

"I'm on my way", she said. "Get everyone in, now."

Joyce flung back the sheets and swung her legs over the side of the bed, launched herself to her feet and then stopped to steady herself before continuing. A fast one-minute shower before throwing on some decent clothes, an equally quick cup of warm, instant coffee from water boiled while she showered, and she shot out the door to the basement car park elevator.

Joyce lived alone, her only companion a small, fluffy dog of indeterminate parentage. Having long ago acknowledged her work was her life, she had no room for family. She would have loved kids of her own but as much as she now regretted it, she made a decision on the day of her graduation from university and remained true to it. Perhaps one day; with today's medical advances age was no longer a barrier to having children.

Not that she ever lacked the opportunity. Joyce considered herself to be acceptably attractive, despite the fact she generally resembled an unmade bed, her long, fair hair often a bird's nest, her face devoid of makeup and her clothes un-pressed and probably those she wore the day before. None of that could hide her natural beauty or the genuineness of her basic nature.

A lack of partners never posed a problem when she needed or wanted someone as a plus-one at a formal dinner, event or just for company. She had even had several short-term relationships over the years, but they never lasted. So devoted was she to her job, 'long term' never received more than a moment's consideration.

Winter still held an icy grip on Seattle and patches of snow lay everywhere from a recent fall. The lawns and sidewalks were white, the roads a treacherous maze of slush and ice. Joyce loved the cold weather, a time for snuggling in front of a fire with a good friend, her dog, or perhaps a glass of fine, aromatic Port.

As she drove through the night the lights of the city spread before her. She had lived and worked in this wonderful metropolis for over a decade, as the director of the North American Seismic Survey, the primary centre for volcanic and seismic studies on the continent.

After the division of the United States the task of coordinating the monitoring of seismic events moved from Washington to this city in the Federation. The Seattle University offered double the funding and all expenses for the move, to steal the Survey from its traditional home at the Smithsonian Institute.

A major factor was its proximity to the Cascadia Subduction Zone, stretching from the top of Vancouver Island, south to Cape Mendocino in Northern California. The region marked the line between two major crustal plates and over the last few centuries had, as part of the Pacific Ring of Fire, given the locals more than one respectable incentive for prayer.

Half an hour after leaving her apartment Joyce pulled into her parking space and sprinted across the car park to the front entrance to the NASS offices, located in the environmental studies section of the university. Henry Nguyen, her second in charge, waited for her at the door.

"Talk to me, Henry," she said, sweeping past him and heading towards the lab.

"It's Yellowstone. We have two eruptions. The first went up fifty-five minutes ago and the next, ten minutes later, after I rang you."

"Seriously? Impossible! We only detected those tremors two days ago. There hasn't been time..."

"Exactly what I said, but take my word for it. The vents are right on the eastern edge of the caldera, and the data indicates it will get worse. The lake has disappeared, and there are likely to be more eruptions—soon."

Joyce burst into the lab and turned to the 'celebrity board', a wall-spanning array of screens displaying everything from data streams and graphic representation of tremor harmonics, to on-the-spot video fed from monitors around the park. On the primary screen, black clouds billowed as an earth shattering column of ash and flame roiled skyward. Joyce could almost feel the roar shake her soul, even though there was silence in the room. She glanced across at the other screens and began piecing together information, desperate to get an overall impression of the event. According to the statistics, this should not be happening at all.

Hours later, Joyce sat slumped in a chair studying the monitors, the latest of a long chain of cups of coffee in her hand. Her head throbbed from the worst headache she had experienced in a long time, brought on by intense concentration over a prolonged period.

"It's never going to work," she said to herself. "With no warning there's no way people are going to be able to get to safety." Thanks to her team emergency evacuations were at that moment being organized.

"Where would they go," Nguyen mused. "Our data tells us the amount of melt down there is increasing rapidly. So far, those vents have chucked out over ten million tons of ejecta, and they're only hours old."

"How much is down there, do we think?"

"We have at least six hundred cubic kilometres in the top chamber and growing. It's looking like the rock barrier between the upper and lower magma bodies is fractured, and there is some evidence the plume is pushing up to the Moho. We have data coming in from Utah University suggesting that may be driving this."

Joyce shook her head.

That this should happen on my watch...

This was why she did this job, to give warning and preserve life, and now it was happening she wished it wasn't. The last time Yellowstone had a major eruption the ash cloud covered most of the continent, but at the time there were no humans. Such was not the case now. A population of over half a billion souls filled the region and whatever happened next, many of them were going to die. The proverbial clock was close to midnight.

An electronic chime sounded. The picture on the screen changed to a satellite image showing an ominous development.

"Let me see the infra red," Joyce commanded. "There, another eruption on the western side."

The emergence of a third vent forewarned the worst-case scenario, a string of volcanic vents around the edge of the ancient caldera. If that eventuated they would connect until the floor collapsed into the upper magma chamber.

Such an occurrence would release the pressure beneath and eventually the super-eruption would begin to settle. If the caldera did *not* collapse there was no way of knowing how long the eruptions might continue, and the longer they persisted the more deadly it became for humanity. The geological data on past events showed they could last for days, weeks or months, and the duration of the event more so than the strength, provided the greatest danger.

Joyce glanced at the stream of messages pouring into her phone. Most were from members of the media, but she ignored them. She had taken to the practice of not answering any calls, letting them all go to voice mail. Every few minutes she would check, watching and waiting for one from someone who mattered and whom she would call back.

As of now, the nationwide effort to evacuate and rescue people was the most important issue. The Seismic Survey had no direct role in the process, but with the Utah University personnel evacuating, those who did would be relying on her unit for accurate information. Her team was first class, everyone the top of their game, headhunted by her over the last decade. That was Joyce's superpower: she coordinated a group of brilliant minds, and it was they who would do all that could be done in this crisis.

"So little warning," she mumbled. "Just those tremors and nothing more. It's almost like someone caused this to happen."

"Don't flip out on us now," Nguyen said. "That's impossible and we both know it."

"Of course, but you can't help wonder."

Days earlier the University of Utah recorded a swarm of tremors unlike anything seen before. Each tremor resembled an explosion of considerable force and it was certain new fissures had opened, allowing the underlying magma plume to rise, increasing the pressure in the lower chamber and then the upper. Higher pressure and heat caused more of the masses to melt, the molten lava now spewing out by three different channels.

Nguyen pointed at the wall as new data emerged. "We are now at level six. This is going to hurt."

He referred to the Volcanic Explosivity Index, or VEI. The rating system went only as far as eight and was based on the amount of ejecta thrown out by a volcano, each level being ten times greater than the one preceding.

The highest level, VEI eight, involved eruptions ejecting more than one thousand cubic kilometres of un-compacted ejecta or more. It included the most destructive super-eruptions of history, including Yellowstone, Lake Toba in Sumatra and Lake Taupo on the north island of New Zealand.

The current Yellowstone event had already ejected enough to make it a VEI six but as Joyce studied the screens she had an unsettling feeling deep in her gut. This had only just begun, and it was inevitable more vents would appear. This one would become an eight, the first such in recorded history.

The cloud would spread east and south, but to a lesser degree also to the north and west. Prevailing winds would drive it across most of the Eastern American States, possibly all of it, and would also extend over major parts of the Federation and into Canada. Nobody was safe, even here in Seattle.

The blanket of ash would carry with it a wave of destruction never before seen on Earth. It would start to fall almost immediately, and would continue as long as the eruption persisted, building to a depth of several metres in those regions closest to the park, decreasing with distance. Accumulated ash was heavy, and it only took about twenty centimetres to collapse an average roof. Roads would be impassable and air traffic would cease, aircraft incapable of flying without fatal damage to their engines.

The ash fall would shut down power stations and relay facilities, clogging the rivers and water supply, and poisoning the water. Millions would die, either from respiratory illness as the ash turned to cement in their lungs, or from hunger, trapped in homes as they waited for the rescue that would not come in time. In future months many, many more would starve as crops failed and livestock choked and died over vast areas. The immediate effect would be over the centre of the continent, and the EAS would need massive support to cope. There would be little of that, if any.

Joyce wiped a hand across her eyes and realised her face was wet from unnoticed tears trickling down her cheeks. She turned to see Harry Nguyen's face also glistened, the reality of the scenario they were watching unfold too traumatic to deal with in an emotionless manner.

The worst was yet to come. When the floor of the old crater collapsed the eruption would begin to die and a new caldera would be formed, but by then a massive amount of damage would have been done. Already, the weight of ash above each vent was too heavy for the air to support, and the columns had collapsed, sending superheated, pyroclastic clouds rolling across vast areas of countryside. Red-hot gases moving at hundreds of kilometres an hour, they would leave destruction in their wake. Nothing would survive.

The initial effects of the clouds would only be on the North American continent, but deadlier threats would follow. In the coming months, billions of tons of sulphur dioxide and ash would spread through the upper atmosphere to block the sunlight. It would cover the northern hemisphere of the planet, then jump the equator and to a lesser degree cloak the south. Volcanic winter was inevitable, the light reduced and temperatures plummeting worldwide. Everywhere crops would fail, starving millions of people.

A tap on her shoulder announced the presence of one of her staff. The girl's face appeared ashen, her eyes moist as she held out a sheet of paper with a trembling hand. Silently she handed it over and turned away. Joyce studied the report for a moment as a lump rose into her throat.

"What?" Harry Nguyen asked. "What is it?"

"I... It's ... Naples."

As well as monitoring North America, NASS also had links to similar groups worldwide and could access direct streams of data from many of the most volatile of the world's 1500 active volcanoes. Over the last week they had followed several of these including a number of super-volcanoes, but with the majority of their attention focused closer to home.

It was known the eruption of one volcano was unlikely to cause another to erupt; certainly not over great distances. As the disaster unfolded in Yellowstone, nobody bothered to keep up with events elsewhere, but the data flowed regardless. Now someone had noticed.

"What? Vesuvius?" Nguyen reached for the paper.

"No," Joyce replied, her voice so soft Harry had to strain to listen. "It's worse. La Solfatara blew twenty minutes ago. It's part of the Campi Flegrei cluster and the whole region has become unstable. Naples is gone."

Six days later Joyce still occupied her seat, eyes glued to the celebrity board. Yellowstone continued to expand, now with ten vents. It was a VEI eight event and Joyce had been called to San Francisco to report on the probable prognosis; more correctly on the events as they were now, as nobody could predict where or when this would end. She refused, saying she was needed here and a video conference would serve better than calling her away from her critical work.

Unlike Yellowstone, La Solfatara, the geothermal hot spot that lay beside the Bay of Naples in Italy, erupted with full force from the beginning. The bay was gone, along with the metropolis, beneath a plume blanketing everything between the cities of Caserta in the north and Solerno in the south.

The eruption was a single, massive blast, made worse by billions of tonnes of sea-water flowing into the molten caldera. The resultant outpouring of ash, steam and destruction meant inevitable devastation throughout the central Mediterranean, making vast swathes of Europe and North Africa uninhabitable. Again, millions would die, a worldwide volcanic winter of several years duration now a certainty.

On the floor of the lab all were silent. Many of the staff present had been there for days, sleeping on air-beds by their stations, eating delivered fast-food until the services no longer responded and then frozen meals heated in a microwave. Tensions were running high but nobody had anything to say, absorbed in their work as they witnessed the nearest thing to Armageddon imaginable.

The screen now displayed an infra red image of Sumatra, where an ominous stain spread across the northern end of the island. Toba, the super-volcano responsible for one of the greatest eruptions of all time, had woken from its 74,000 year slumber. The lake, the flooded crater of the last ancient eruption, had vanished, destroying millions more lives in a flash.

Joyce had nothing to say. She knew only too well what this meant. Three super-volcanoes had erupted within a week of each other, an event thought impossible. Nobody in the scientific community would have predicted any one of the eruptions and in fact, all experts would, until now, have agreed the current situation could never happen.

Famous last words, Joyce thought. *One would have been bad enough, but three...?*

All had been watched for hundreds of years, and while the likelihood of one of them erupting had always been possible at some future date, nobody expected this. It was the biggest volcanic event in recorded history, the most destructive since the eruption in the Siberian Traps 252 million years ago, the cause of the Permian Extinction. That one wiped out more than three quarters of all life on Earth, and now the target was humanity.

Toba was only a few hundred kilometres from the equator, and its cloud would spread south and east across the Indonesian Archipelago and Australia. It was the final straw. In a month or two the planet would be in deep volcanic winter, caused primarily by the sulphur-dioxide emitting from Yellowstone and Toba. The winter would last for at least a decade, and for years the skies would be dark around the globe, the midday no brighter than a moonlit night.

Joyce knew what was to come. First the vegetation would die, and with it a high proportion of all life on Earth. The oceans would suffer the most, microscopic life being the first to go. With the base of the food chain gone, mass dying would progress exponentially until most of the ocean's inhabitants vanished. Joyce felt a tear well in her eye as she realized the curtain was about to fall on the giant baleen whales, the greatest of creatures ever to grace the planet. Without plankton, their days were numbered. A new extinction-level event had begun.

Worst of all, the source of most of the planet's oxygen would be gone. The threat to life had not been greater in recorded history.

All her adult life, Joyce and those around her had worked towards one goal, the hope that by predicting volcanic events they would save lives by allowing time to escape. All their work had been dedicated to that, but now they had been reduced to the simple act of reporting something they could do nothing to prevent. There was no warning, the triple eruption without precedent. There was nowhere to go.

Information received twenty-four hours earlier showed each event followed an identical precursor, a series of tremors all the same magnitude, occurring before the primary event. New data also indicated mysterious space craft were spotted over both Yellowstone and Toba shortly before the tremors, and another report stated air traffic controllers detected something similar over the Bay of Naples. None of those sightings were confirmed and Joyce doubted they ever would be, with those who witnessed them most likely gone.

It didn't matter; as far as she was concerned this was a deliberate act. Such an event could not occur naturally and nobody on Earth could cause it to happen. Nevertheless, somebody *had* to be responsible. That would go in her final report before she got on with the job of looking to her own survival and that of her closest friends, most of whom were with her in this room.

Dog!

Joyce realised she had left home so suddenly her closest friend, the little dog she called Fred Sputnik, had been left behind. Luckily there was plenty of water in a tub, and Fred had already displayed his ability to break into the bags of dry food she kept in her laundry room. He would be alright until she could retrieve him.

Outside, ash fell over Seattle.

Without warning the lights failed, temporarily leaving the room in darkness until dim emergency lights turned on. The celebrity board remained dark.

"That's it," she said, throwing her note pad to the desk beside her. "We can't do anything more. The backup power won't last forever and without the grid we can't continue operating."

Nobody replied. A few pushed their chairs back from their stations, accepting the truth of the statement.

"That's it then. Armageddon!" Harry muttered.

"Yes, Armageddon. God help us."

Chapter 11

JOYCE OPENED THE door and slumped into the driver's seat of her car, still parked outside the NASS building. She had washed the thin layer of gray ice from the windscreen and was now happy to be out of the gentle but deadly rain. The ash fall began in Seattle several days ago, light but mixed with the snow to create a dangerous, dirty slush. She stared through the window at the darkened building. It was night, but when the dawn came the daylight would be subdued.

What do I do now? There's nowhere I can escape. It's all going to be different and I have nobody to go through this with me, except Fred. So much for being dedicated to my work. All gone now.

An overpowering sense of futility had overwhelmed her when she gave the order to shut down the centre, a sadness that refused to go away. Joyce shivered, not from the cold but from acknowledgement of the position she now found herself in. She had no family, and no contingency plan for a situation such as this.

Where to go?

A tear trickled down her cheek as she contemplated her next move. The first traces of volcanic winter already stretched like dark fingers over the planet, and Joyce, perhaps more than most, understood what that meant. Future prospects were limited and life as she knew it ended here and now. It was unknown territory, a new and devastated world, from this point, and she was going to face it alone.

The temperature was expected to drop by as much as twenty degrees centigrade or more in some places. A new frozen age would begin, much of the North American and Eurasian continents covered in sheets of ice for the first time in millennia. Further south, snow would fall near the equator.

Because of the greater spread of ocean the southern hemisphere would fare better, but in Australia, South America and Africa the weather would still deteriorate enough to make agriculture difficult if not impossible. That did not alter the fact residents of the northern nations were already, in vast numbers, embarking on the arduous trek south in search of survival, and the equatorial and southern countries were ill prepared for such an onslaught. The refugee problem would become significant for every nation on Earth.

Joyce understood the probable outcomes of the extinction level event, but battled to accept the inevitability; millions, if not billions of people would starve. With poisoned water and toxic air, disease and respiratory illness would run riot, and with no power or water hospitals would be unable to care for the afflicted.

The various emergency services had already swung into action. The greatest effort was being directed into food production, according to news Joyce watched before the broadcast stations went down. All around the world, in every city unaffected by the initial assault from the volcanoes, every local resource was being used to create a food supply for the future, for as many people as possible.

Temporary generators were being set up to provide power, with every warehouse or enclosed space being sequestered by authorities to build hydroponic facilities. Overnight, indoor home hydroponics had become the hobby of choice, systems cobbled together from every bucket, bin or water pipe available, in the desperate hope electricity would continue to be available for light and heat.

Covered stadiums and warehouses were being commandeered for conversion to farms, to breed everything from fowl to fish to guinea pigs, recruiting any rapidly breeding food creature into the system. It would never be enough, and bioengineering plants worldwide were scaling up their production of tank-grown meat and yeast products to fill the gaps. Still it would not be sufficient.

By the time the winter reached full effect and the food ran out, quick thinking would have provided new resources, but nothing was certain. The greatest blessing was for once, governments were not procrastinating before taking action. The worldwide response had been immediate.

Available stores would last a few months at best, and at least two or three years, possibly more, would pass before outdoor production could restart. Joyce expected within weeks if not days the planet's resources would become politicized, the haves doing everything in their power to ensure they were provided for before the have-nots. The rich and affluent would survive at the expense of the poor. In the meantime...

She started as a sharp rap sounded on the driver side car window. The face of Harry Nguyen peered at her from the darkness of the parking lot.

"What are you planning, Joyce?" he asked as she wound the window down.

"I don't know. I guess I'll go home, fetch Fred and pack what I can carry, then head south with everyone else. What else can I do?"

"I know you have nobody to go to," Harry said. "What about relatives?"

"Not here. They're all in England. They'll be worse off than us, so they wouldn't be home even if I could go. But I can't: all the airlines are down."

Harry's eyes fixed on her car for a moment. "How much power do you have in your batteries?"

"I had it on charge at home when you called me. It's almost full."

"A bunch of us are planning to head down to southern Cal. Perry's sister and brother-in-law have a farm there, and we're all welcome if we can make it down."

"Why bother. We won't be able to grow anything there, any more than here."

"Yeah, maybe, maybe not. They grow medical marijuana in huge hydroponic glasshouses out in the desert. Everything necessary to grow something more suitable is already there, and according to Perry they can produce enough to feed thousands of people. The farm has an emergency backup power source as long as the fuel doesn't run out, but they're going to need a lot of help to install more lights and heating, cover the glasshouses with insulation, switch crops and get everything set up. The place is already under government control, but they'll need more workers and want us to come. It's gonna be a long, cold winter."

Joyce did not know what to say. Seattle, the place she loved the most, had been her dream, and her whole life was here. *No longer!* The city was too far north; within weeks it would be a ghost town.

"The way things are going you might be better off with the marijuana. How are you planning to get there? The highways are clogged to a standstill, the National Guard is tearing its collective hair out and we aren't into the full winter yet. Ash is falling and anyone caught out in it for too long is going to die."

Harry grinned. "That's the beauty of it. We don't go south; we head north. Perry's father has a sixty foot yacht in a secure facility in Victoria, on Vancouver Island. He has a friend in Anacortes who can get us across in return for coming along. We're going to sail down the coast and go inland; walk if we have to. One way or another, we'll get there. If not, well, we'll be together, at least."

Joyce glanced past Harry to see fellow workers climb into their vehicles. Some of them were single, others had families, but all had the same bond. They were friends, having worked together for many years, and they would not fail each other now. If anything required teamwork this was it.

"Yes, of course I'll come. What do you want me to do?"

"Go home and pack, as you planned. Load your car with any foodstuff and medications you might have. Warm clothes, the best you've got. Don't bother trying to get into a supermarket or chemist: they're all shut. Drive north to Lighthouse Park in Mukilteo. You should have enough power to get there, and we can recharge from the battery storage at the dock. If the ferry's still running we'll cross over to Whidbey Island and on to Anacortes, otherwise we'll try a run up the freeway and around the long way. Either way, with everyone else heading south we have a better chance of getting through. We'll wait at the park until everyone arrives, or until we think no one else can make it. If you miss us, this is the address in Anacortes."

He handed Joyce a slip of paper with words scrawled in his indecipherable hand. "Try to get there if you can, or else turn back and make your way south. The farm's address is on there as well."

She read the paper and nodded. The park where they intended to meet was familiar. "Thank you Harry. I appreciate your asking me to come. I do."

"Of course you're coming. You're family, Joyce. We're all family here." Her friend smiled and jogged away to his own vehicle parked across the lot.

Joyce felt another tear in her eye. Determined to survive, she sighed and wound the window up, then turned on the ignition. On the seat beside her lay a file containing reports the team received from Salt Lake City, Jakarta and Naples before the catastrophe, records of spaceship sightings immediately prior to each event, and data on the series of explosions at each site.

She clenched her jaw and focused on her next move. She needed to make sure the reports got to those who mattered. Someone was responsible for this; some unknown entity had done a thing unheard of and used volcanoes as a weapon of deliberate mass destruction. No human possessed that knowledge or power, which left only one option.

Six decades after the *Blackship* War, Earth was once again under alien attack, the weapon of choice one that humanity could never hope to counter. Humankind was being attacked by its own planet. Joyce had to tell somebody so something could be done. She had an idea who to contact, and she intended to do so before she headed south with her friends.

*   *   *

General Sam Barnaby dimmed the lights in his office at Sinus Iridium Base. Beyond the window the floor of the Mare Ibrium Basin, the Lunar manufacturing site for Earth's new space fleet, spread for many square kilometres.

Billions of automated machines, ranging from gigantic mining goliaths to the smallest molecular assemblers, worked in complete vacuum to carry out every stage of construction from digging the raw ore, through a convoluted series of processes to the final assembly of ships.

The actual manufacturing stage involved dozens of moon-dust impervious domes, each containing a broad, flat platform. On each one a new generation, diamond warship rose from the floor, constructed molecule by molecule by a workforce of nano-assemblers.

The new vessels were superior to their predecessors by a quantum leap. Faster, more heavily armed and covered in a diamond shell, they could withstand an unimaginable hammering before failing. Each carried a handful of crew compared to the hundreds that manned the old ships, and all flight-crew operated from an impenetrable control pod which could survive the total destruction of the ship around it.

The entire operation was overseen by a team of scientists and engineers, all of whom worked here in the base, programming and controlling the work remotely, rarely if ever going out to the site. It was the biggest manufacturing program ever seen on Earth—although in fact located on Luna—and Barnaby ran it all.

His greatest challenge was not the factory itself, but rather juggling the constant flow of letters and complaints from various government officials from the different countries comprising the United Earth Council, concerning what they considered unnecessary cost and waste of resources.

Barnaby dealt with most of them in what he thought the appropriate manner, by sending a stock reply before deleting the complaint. As far as he was concerned, the warships were essential for the future welfare of the planet. Even as a military general his loyalties lay with the New Worlds Institute, the only organization with enough foresight to see the necessity for a strong and mobile defence force, and not to those toadies in the individual national governments of Earth.

A second fleet, identical to this one, was being built on Mars under a joint cooperative effort between the Martian Council and the UEC and coordinated by the NWI. Once complete, the combined fleets would number over four thousand ships, each far more efficient than the best of their predecessors.

On the far wall of the office, a holo-screen showed a view of the Earth, something to remind Barnaby of home and keep his spirits up in this desolate place. The fabulous image had changed. A dusky cast stretched across the globe, sufficiently dense to be visible from space. Volcanic ash spread from three epicentres; soon the beautiful blue marble would be a gray billiard ball.

Several hours earlier Barnaby had ordered all work on the warships to cease. At this moment the technicians in the dome were reprogramming the machinery to take on a new task, the mass construction of portable fusion power-plants based on the miniaturized reactors found at the heart of every ship. Each was capable of powering a small city or town, and that was the purpose for which the designs were now being modified.

The decision to change the function of the factories was his alone. With most of Earth's politicians running around like headless chickens, someone had to take the initiative. In a few hours, the machines would start churning out the portable reactors by the hundreds, and they would be flown down to the planet as soon as they came off the line. Barnaby would not wait for approval or guidance; he would get it done and deal with his superiors later.

Each reactor could power multiple warehouses worth of hydroponics or bio-production plants for years, and provide light and heat for crops and livestock to feed the starving millions. With adequate electricity smaller population centres could be saved from the advancing freeze, supporting the multitude of survivors hoping to cope on systems thrown together in their own homes.

Barnaby's associates on Mars had done likewise, and by the time the full devastation of volcanic winter reached its peak, thousands of the generators would be installed, with many more on the way.

Another concern worrying him was the space elevator. Six decades earlier, Earth's only elevator was destroyed when the protective shield set up by the Visitors sheered through the braided diamond-fibre cable, allowing the lower portion of the structure to collapse into the Eastern Pacific Ocean. The destruction caused by the fall had been extreme.

Ten years ago a new cable touched down, secured in the same socket used by the old one. Now, streams of people poured into the surface departure station, eager to ride the elevator cars to board one of the hundreds of ships waiting their turn to dock at the top anchor platform.

An exodus had begun, refugees boarding any ship available to head to Mars, in an effort to escape the mounting catastrophe on their home world. Martial law had been declared and the ground station placed under military control, but the arrivals continued.

Ships attempting to approach the space anchor of the elevator were being turned away, but they were not the only problem. Many vessels were atmosphere capable and could land on Earth; with the mounting chaos little could be done to stop them. Barnaby prayed the Mars Council would be able to cope with the sudden influx of refugees.

He sighed and turned his attention to the report on his desk. It came from a scientist named Joyce Lockamy, one of the world's foremost authorities on volcanism and one of the individuals who first alerted the public to the ensuing disaster.

The woman had driven up to the front gate of the Whidbey Island Naval Air Station north of Seattle and demanded to see the base commander, claiming to be an old and close friend. After checking her claim the guards allowed her to enter and the report sitting on Barnaby's desk was the result.

The General shook his head. The idea an alien attack could come in the form of erupting volcanoes sounded ridiculous. Lockamy had no real proof, but what she did have was convincing. Using volcanic winter as a method of warfare was brilliant, inspired and terrifying. The question was, who was behind it? Considering the scope of the attack it was nobody human. He glanced at the holo-screen again.

Almost one thousand of the new breed of warships were complete and now stood at the naval base further south in the

Mare Ibrium, awaiting service. Whatever the threat to humanity they would be ready, along with as many new ships from Mars.

Earth would survive this onslaught, Barnaby was sure, but civilization would be set back centuries. Life after recovery would be hard because of the damage to the environment, but that too would pass. Whoever was responsible would not be so lucky.

Chapter 12

"YES, I AM familiar with who you are, Mister Falcon, of course." Council President Raquel Saldino peered at one of the four men seated across the desk. Some people commanded respect and awe with a gun, but this woman needed only look at you to achieve the same effect.

Joe and his son Jake had arrived with a proposition; it was only their high standing on the planet allowed them access to the top lady herself. The Institute worked closely with the Mars Council, and Jake met often with government heads. In view of the scope of the Institute's activities on both worlds, he was almost certainly more influential than the president, but for Joe this was a first. With his opinion of politicians, he always considered it wise to leave government liaisons to others.

"Your true story was passed on to me by my predecessor," Saldino explained, "and his before him. I'm an admirer of yours, but I must admit to being surprised to see you here. You've been a recluse for some time, have you not?"

Joe nodded. *More accurately, I'm a private person for obvious reasons.* His eyes remained fixed on the formidable woman. He and the Honourable Madam President had never met in the flesh before, but he knew her well by reputation.

Saldino had been a member of the Congress for a total of fifteen years, re-elected several times by the Commission, and then raised unopposed to the top position due to her impressive record. She had been a member of the Council longer than any other person in history. Younger than her predecessor, she was known as a person who got things done, and once she set her mind on a course, nothing would persuade her to side-track. She had been described as a 'pit bull', and once having got her teeth into a project, never let go until it was achieved. The last president had been a man many considered 'wishy-washy', and under his rule little progress had been made on the planet, but during her reign the reversal had been dramatic.

Saldino was somewhere in her middle years. Joe had never been good at determining age, and with the gerontological treatments it was now an almost impossible task with some people. She had a natural presence that dominated the room, her brown hair tied back in a severe but efficient bun behind her neck. Her face and posture showed not the slightest sign of discomfort, her piercing eyes indicating clearly her supreme confidence in her own position.

"I was," Joe responded to her question. "My son Jake convinced me my time could be better spent otherwise, considering the situation facing us now."

"What is it you are doing now, Mister... May I call you Joe?" She peered at him with a studied curiosity, never before having met the man who had risen from the grave sixty years past.

Joe nodded. "Yes, of course. The Institute has enormous resources here, as you're aware. You know I head up the program to construct the new space fleet, and the NWI is the largest concern involved in the shaft project, the manufacture of hydroponics equipment on this planet and many other areas."

"Your Institute's done wonders for Mars in the last few decades and I am sure everyone here is more than grateful for your work." Saldino placed her pen on the desk, positioning it precisely as she wanted it. "So, to what purpose do I owe the honour of this visit? No, let me guess: the crisis on Earth?"

"That is our principal concern, of course. You do know over a thousand ships are heading our way?"

"I do indeed." Saldino's expression darkened. "Every one of them is loaded to the bilges with refugees. The minute the disaster became clear, every ship captain in the inner system headed to Earth intent on taking the highest paying passengers they could find, to make a quick turn of profit."

"So what we can expect," Jake said, "is a massive influx of ships filled with the rich and affluent, who prefer to use their wealth to save themselves rather than help their fellow humans."

A twisted grimace appeared on Saldino's face. "Yes, and I find that despicable. I know for a fact several national leaders are among them, along with their entire families. It's the sort of thing makes me feel ashamed of my profession. Nevertheless, they will be here in a matter of weeks and..."

"We will have to find something to do with them," Joe finished her sentence for her. "We need to house them, as many as fifty or sixty thousand souls to start with, and I think perhaps Jake and I can provide a solution."

President Saldino arched her eyebrows.

"As I said," Joe continued, "we're the major partner in the shaft project and we supply all the autonomous machinery employed in the construction. As part of that effort we excavated vast subterranean levels at several of the sites. We choose a suitable point on the spiral roadways descending into the shaft and begin tunnelling and excavating sideways.

"The chambers are self supporting caverns with floor space covering many square kilometres per level. The shaft where we started this process now has ten levels, the uppermost fifty metres down. It was our intention to turn them into industrial sights, but they are just as suitable for emergency accommodations. The first refugee ships won't arrive for several weeks, and we can use the time to begin re-fitting the excavated areas for occupation."

Saldino raised her eyes and peered at Joe. "Forgive me if I'm wrong, but I understood the purpose of the project was to increase the atmospheric temperature and humidity. Is there not a vast quantity of hot air flowing up those shafts?"

"You are correct, Madam President, but that's not a problem. They provided convenient access for initial excavation and to facilitate the removal of materials, but once a level is completed, it's fitted with other, dedicated entrances, and elevators connect all the levels. The entry from the shaft is closed off with an airlock and used only for heavy machinery access."

Saldino nodded. "I see. My advisers suggest using surface dome settlements. Quite a number are unoccupied, as you would know since you built most of them."

"Not the best option. The levels are already fitted with ventilation, ready to go and getting larger every day. We can fill them with temporary accommodations while we continue to fit them out as permanent cities. Domes are less safe and more open to solar radiation, and are better used for other purposes such as hydroponics to feed the influx."

"The shafts *will* be safer," Jake elaborated. "The rock overhead will provide superior protection, and the excavations will be cheaper to set up for heating and so on. Don't forget the atmosphere outside is still only about ten percent Earth normal. An accidental decompression in a dome tent could kill hundreds, or thousands."

For a moment the President remained silent, her brow furrowed in deep concentration. She shifted her gaze between Joe and Jake then turned towards the other two men present, Martin Calvin, the head of the Mars Space Authority and his adviser and frequent shadow, Professor Stephen Grate. They arrived with the Falcons, no doubt recruited by the formidable pair to back up their recommendation. She arched her eyebrows as she turned to Grate.

"I agree the shafts are our best alternative," the scientist said, aware she was expecting his opinion. "Our cities can't cope with such an influx at once, and we have to put these people somewhere. Then there is the question of food and water. The levels have enough room to set up new biotech plants for yeast production and so on, and somehow we will manage. We are moving to build new hydroponics farms in the surface tent domes, and we can extract water from the updraft in the shafts. We can't do it as quickly any other way."

Calvin nodded.

Saldino took a deep breath and exhaled before returning her attention to the Falcons. She picked up her pen again and tapped it on the desk. "Very well, I accept your recommendation. I'm guessing the wheels are already in motion on the expectation I would do so?"

Joe grinned in response. "Naturally, Madam President."

"I think under the circumstances, we can dispense with the niceties. Call me Raquel. I'll address you as Joe and Jake, yes?"

"Of course. There is also the matter of the ships themselves. That's why Martin joined us here today."

Calvin leaned forward in his seat, his hands clasped on his knees. "Madam Pres... Raquel, we can expect that once those ships disgorge their human cargoes they will head straight back to Earth for another load. We can handle one sudden influx considering we have no choice, but a continuing flow will stretch our current resources beyond their limits. We can't feed millions of refugees at once, and it will take some time to expand our production to the levels we are going to need."

"We have to try. Billions of people will be starving in only a few weeks time."

"Agreed," Joe said. "The solution is to take as many as we can and help the rest to survive where they are, not to attempt to move them to a planet that can't support them. Despite their current problems on Earth, Mars is still colder and more inhospitable, with thin air to boot. That little fact has been overlooked by the idiots who are spending a fortune to get here now.

"What I propose is that all arriving ships be escorted to the shaft where the accommodation levels are ready, and we place them under an embargo to stop a return to Earth. We employ the captains to work for us carrying emergency resources, on the understanding if they return with a second load of refugees their ship will be confiscated under planetary emergency laws. They stand to do well from such an agreement, so I expect most will be quite happy to accept. We can of course bring more people here, but it needs to be spread out and controlled to avoid problems."

Again Jake intervened. "The essential things the citizens of Earth are going to need are clean water and power to run their own hydroponics and bio-tech facilities on a massive, unforeseen scale. We've been doing it since the day we first arrived on Mars and we are ideally set up to help them. Even at its worst, Earth will still be more hospitable than this planet. People in the northern hemisphere have been living in the ice and snow for millennia, and those further south can do so as well, provided they have support. I've already diverted our manufacturing capabilities to the construction of water purification plants and hydroponics equipment, and halted production at the fleet facility to divert efforts to the manufacture of portable fusion generators."

Saldino nodded. "Yes, I agree it's the best approach. It will cause a lot of backlash on Earth, but only from those who want to escape. Those with no option but to remain will welcome the assistance, so you may go ahead." She tapped on her desk to bring up a holo-screen. "We should discuss something else while we're all here, I think. Have any of you seen this report?"

For a minute or so the room was silent as the four visitors scanned the document on the screen.

"Steve and I read it yesterday," Calvin said. "Do you think it has any credibility?"

"It comes from a highly regarded scientist named Joyce Lockamy, from the North American Seismic Survey. She's a volcanologist who believes she can provide evidence the eruptions were triggered by a series of underground explosions. She states they occurred prior to each eruption, all of the same magnitude, spaced equally apart and positioned so they would do the most damage to the geological structures of the volcanoes. I agree it appears suspicious."

Grate scratched at his beard and shook his head. "No technology we possess can do something like that without being obvious. No, not even then; we couldn't do it at all. This report says ships were detected over each of the three event sites, something was seen to drop from them in each case and within days the explosions occurred. Just ... not possible."

"The intimation made by Lockamy is this could only have been someone *not* of Earth or Mars," Saldino explained. "Another alien invasion, to be precise. She suggests they are using our own planet against us. There is also the question of the disappearance of the Visitors and..."

"I think I am safe in saying the *Minaret* is still somewhere in the Solar System," Joe interrupted. Io had said as much, although she did not reveal the exact location of the vessel.

"How do you know that, Joe? Our best astronomers can't find it with our most powerful telescopes here on Mars, and with the atmosphere darkening on Earth their ground-based, optical observatories are now off-line."

"I'd prefer not to say at the moment," Joe replied. "You know who I am, so you must agree I am the greatest living expert on that ship. I am positive it is still here, but until I can be sure I would prefer to keep mum. Perhaps I shouldn't have said anything."

For much too long a moment Saldino scrutinized Joe, then gave a curt nod of the head. "You are a strange one, but I can hardly argue with you. Still, that just reinforces the problem. You should be aware there's a strong belief the Visitors are behind this attack, if an attack it is. Prior to the event no other alien intruders were detected, so if we exclude human interference, that doesn't leave a broad choice of suspects. Doctor Lockamy gave her report to a friend at one of Earth's air force bases, and he sent it direct to the fleet commander of Sinus Iridium Base, on Luna. The military are of the opinion the fleets must be combined once again to find that ship, wherever it is. You have a duty to tell me if you know where."

"I don't, but I may be able to find out. You need to do something for me however."

The President waved a hand for him to continue, her eyebrows arched.

Joe sighed, took a deep breath and for the first time revealed the truth behind the presence of the Visitors on both planets and how they had indeed been living amongst humans for six decades. "They mean us no harm and I doubt they have anything to do with events on Earth. Call off the hounds you have chasing them here on Mars and guarantee their safety, and I may be able to clarify the issue for you. I don't think they are responsible for any of this, and they might be persuaded to help us find those who are, but not if we hunt them down like dogs."

Saldino opened her mouth to speak, paused and gazed at Joe, shocked by his revelation. "Yes, I have reservations about that program myself. The decision was made by the full council, not I. I'll make a deal with you. I *will* call a halt and give you time to fulfil your promise, but beyond that I make no guarantees."

Chapter 13

FAR TO THE west of Olympus Mons, the largest volcano on Mars, another cone rose from the broad, flat plains of Elysium. Alba Mons was the smallest and southernmost of three in this region and like all volcanoes on the planet, considered to be long dormant.

At this point the crust of Mars extended over sixty kilometres deep, and the upper mantle beneath was cooler, denser and more sluggish than that of Earth. The age of volcanism had passed the red world by long ago as its small size allowed it to cool faster than its larger sun-ward cousins.

The volcano was dead, but its source was not. Within the crust a vast pool of melt rock still brooded, as it had for many tens of millions of years. The lack of crustal activity and convection currents helped it to maintain its position and semi-molten state, but above it lay a massive layer of solid, crystalline rock, a barrier between it and the surface.

Above the body and less than a kilometre from the lowermost fringe of the volcano shield, the Alba shaft, the most remote and deepest in the region, bored its way into the planet.

Sites such as this were premium for the project. The shaft sunk deep into the rock, tapping into the heat of the melt body below without any danger of eruption. As long as the excavation machines did not dig too far, the rock barrier would act as protection.

In the depth of the Martian night, a small, dark ship descended over Alba. From beneath the hull a stream of objects descended into the shaft, continuing for kilometres until they reached the bottom. Once there they bored into the rock, until within minutes nothing remained except a disturbed surface, unseen by human eyes in the fully automated excavation site. In a matter of days those traces would be barely visible, having been wiped away by the constant activity of hundreds of machines working the floor.

*   *   *

Joe stood on the tarmac, uncomfortable in his environment suit. The atmosphere on the red world was still far from the point where a human could walk unprotected, the temperature so cold that heated suits were a minimum requirement. You could freeze to death in a minute out here.

A subtle breeze swept the ever present, rust-laden dust across the new space field. The wind was stronger than normal but in the still-thin air, no more than a gentle breath. The talc-fine, electrostatic dust was the major problem on this planet, not the wind. It clogged spacesuits and machines alike, coated solar panels and ground down the soul.

In the far distance two small objects approached from space. Now within the thin upper atmosphere, the first lined up for an approach to the landing field, escorted by a military vessel positioned higher up. It was the first of the refugee ships, and Joe had decided to attend the arrival to make sure the program put in place by the Council was adhered to, and to verify his suspicions about the occupants of these vessels.

The moment the craft landed, a small tactical force stood ready to enter and take control, to prevent the captain from lifting off immediately the passengers disembarked. He would be given a choice, to participate in the relief effort or remain here on Mars as a refugee while his ship was confiscated for use under state-of-emergency laws.

A kilometre from the site, a building complex marked the location of the elevators to the excavated levels. Asahi Shaft itself was located several kilometres to the south, its position pinpointed by a vast column of shimmering, warm air rising from a raised rim on the red plain.

The first level was well on the way to being made habitable. In the cavernous chambers, machines worked tirelessly, lining the rough rock and covering the floor, seamlessly building in walls, dividers and ceilings to create accommodations, arcades and public spaces. Small parts of the excavations were now the equal of any other subterranean dwellings on the planet, with ventilation systems, heating, waste disposal, food, water and supply distribution networks, all ready and waiting for the first occupants. Beyond the walls of the first sections, and on the levels below, automated machines laboured tirelessly, battling to keep ahead of the expected influx.

The distant speck was closer now, almost above the airfield and preparing to descend. It was by all appearances a private yacht, capable of both space and atmospheric flight. The hull shone a brilliant white in the afternoon sunlight, the only insignia an elaborate coat of arms in gold emblazoned on the outer shell. It was fast, having beaten every other refugee ship. Somebody had money.

Once the craft settled, Joe walked across the tarmac towards the rear hatch. The second the ramp dropped, vehicles rumbled down, each bearing the same golden logo and heading to the only exit through the barrier built around the field. They got no further, stopped by guards and a strong steel boom gate.

Within minutes the military team entered by the cargo ramp, the ship having not lowered the steps to its main entry hatch. That was expected; advanced knowledge indicated many of the new arrivals would attempt to land wherever they desired, the passengers intent on making their way straight to the major population centres. That would not be permitted.

Life on Mars was far more fragile than it had traditionally been on the mother world. The cities could not afford a sudden influx of new arrivals, so all would remain in the shaft camps until they could be seamlessly integrated into the community.

Many refugees from the rich and affluent of Earth had happily abandoned their fellow citizens to preserve their own interests. It went against all principles for which Mars, the NWI and Joe stood, and those individuals would not be allowed to do as they wished upon arrival.

Space-bound ships dropped their passengers at the top of the space elevators and were therefore easily controlled, but a significant number of smaller, atmosphere-capable vessels were expected amongst the early arrivals. This one's destination was Hellas City spaceport, but the military intercepted it as it approached orbit and forced it to descend here.

So far, so good.

Satisfied the vessel was not going anywhere Joe turned and strolled across to the administration block by the airfield exit. The vehicles, three in all, had been stopped at the gate, the passengers ordered to disembark and enter the building. In their wake, soldiers searched for contraband.

Inside, the new arrivals stood in a huddle, numbering only fifteen. An elderly gentleman with a long, gray beard argued in an animated fashion with the guards.

"My family and I are self sufficient," he yelled. "I demand we be allowed to continue on to our destination. I have made arrangements..."

"You have no proper entry documents," the field commander explained. "Mars is under a state of emergency at present due to the situation on Earth, and as you don't have the correct papers to enter as legal immigrants you will be treated as refugees. You and your family will be granted temporary visas, and will comply with the procedures appropriate to your status. You will go from here to the facilities below this field to be assigned quarters, and will stay there until you can be processed. Your ship is commandeered for the Earth relief effort, and your vehicles and anything other than personal possessions will be placed in storage. You will get them back once you've been cleared, minus any contraband found, of course."

Of course. Joe grinned to himself. The elderly man looked like he was about to have an apoplectic fit, and Joe knew why. Contraband included any currency, precious metals or gemstones not declared on customs documents and within the strict amount limits placed by Mars immigration authorities. Larger quantities of wealth in whatever form were required to be formally transferred to the planet through the appropriate processes, as in the case of his own following the resources war, and more recently, the assets of the Falcon's and the Institute.

Outside, boxes were being unloaded from the vehicles. They contained gold bar. This upstanding individual was an oligarch who chose to leave Earth with his family and as much personal wealth as he could carry. He was happy to abandon the thousands of individuals who relied on him for a living, in favour of saving his and his family's skins. He was everything Joe found despicable about humanity.

The gold would be confiscated and diverted to the relief effort, and this group would be considered refugees along with all the others. Their treatment would be fair and they would perhaps be allowed to become legal citizens of Mars in time, but they would receive no special considerations. Or, for his trouble, the oligarch and his entourage might face the prospect of being returned to Earth once the crisis abated, minus the boxes now in the hands of the military.

This extreme, hard line had been agreed to by the Council upon the realization many of these ships carried people such as this, who expected to arrive on Mars and do as they pleased. They would pay for their greed and lack of empathy for their fellow humans.

Jake and Joe insisted on it as a condition for their deploying the resources of the Institute to provide aid for Earth. Oligarchies and plutocracies had always been a feature of Terran society, a prime reason behind the problems suffered by people in many nations, but Mars had so far avoided such institutions and had no intention of letting them take a hold here.

Joe sometimes admitted to himself he and Jake might be placed in the same category, were it not that the vast wealth of the NWI always went to the common good, unlike that of the Oligarchs. Even the personal income of both himself and his son supported multiple charitable and public causes. On a world where any person could become successful simply by applying initiative, the concept of hoarding great stores of wealth to pass on by inheritance made little sense.

*   *   *

Raisa Falcon stepped down from the hatch of the *Vasco da Gama,* and took in her surroundings, the Sofia Airport in Bulgaria. One careful step at a time, she tested the limits of her exoskeleton, a framework of titanium and carbon fibre that supported her body, allowing her to stand and move normally in a gravity three times greater than the one she grew up in. Even with the suit, she felt her weight press down enough to make breathing hard, and every point where her body touched the exoskeleton, sore and uncomfortable.

Raisa was tall and thin like all Martian born and raised, her sleek physique lacking the musculature or skeletal strength necessary for this planet. She was a creature of space, and only her role in the relief effort brought her to this place for the first time.

Friends often told Raisa she looked far too serious. Her father always told her she had a natural attractiveness, but of course he would: all fathers considered their daughters beautiful. Raisa was not so certain. Her eyes, set in a heart shaped face and in her opinion too far apart, had the same piercing quality as her father's. She had an unconscious habit of holding her mouth in a hard, straight line, jaw clenched and lips pressed together. Her intensity sometimes unnerved people.

She glanced up to where the sun snuck through like a full moon. In the months since the disaster began the sky had darkened, and the temperature was already well below normal.

The deepening shroud of darkness cloaked much of the northern hemisphere and the south was catching up.

In the distance the giant hangers were closed, bright lights shining through every crack around their massive doors. Given time, those would be sealed to prevent heat loss from within, the enclosed spaces now directed to new purposes.

To either side of the runways, multiple temporary structures were being raised, each glowing in the darkness, their internal light shining ghost-like through the thin fabric of their construction. All these buildings housed hydroponics or bio-engineering plants, or soon would, this airport and other places like it now gearing up to serve as the new food bowl of the city.

The aircraft normally occupying the airfield now sat decommissioned at the far end of the tarmac. The age of atmospheric flight on Earth had come to a grinding halt and would remain so for a considerable time to come.

The hydroponics were the reason for Raisa's presence. In the hold of her ship she carried ten miniature fusion generators, plus heating and lighting systems, the first of many shipments from the factories of Mars. With the loss of solar power and the clogging of waterways normal electricity supply was strained, and the reactors would operate for years regardless of the environmental conditions. The plants being established here would feed many thousands of people and her cargo would ensure their success.

Refugees from the northern regions of Europe and the Russ Republic had begun to stream into Middle Eastern and Mediterranean countries as the higher latitudes began to succumb to a relentless blanket of snow and ice. A new mini ice-age was approaching, and projections showed all areas north of the Alps would be uninhabitable within months.

The initial reaction of the Middle Eastern and African nations was to close their borders, but with crowds numbering in the thousands attempting to force their way across, the resultant death toll served nobody well.

The Martian Council suggested an alternative to the United Earth Council. Aid would focus on those places allowing refugees until the flow eased. In return for the promise of generators, hydroponics and bio-manufacturing equipment, medicines, temporary housing structures and more, the affected states allowed the refugees to proceed, directing them to camps where they would receive help, warmth and sustenance.

Regardless of all the programs being set up, Raisa knew millions were still dying in the northern nations. Many would starve before they could reach a source of food and many others would freeze to death. Expert analysis indicated at least half of the population of the planet would succumb to the volcanic winter, despite the best efforts by planetary governments and the assistance from Mars.

Raisa took a deep breath and braced herself against the cold as she watched the cargo being unloaded from the hold of her ship to flat-tray vehicles. It was only a small start, but it was all she could do.

A lump formed in her throat as she thought of the future facing these people. When the sky cleared enough to permit agriculture to return to the open landscape after perhaps two or three years, life would still be difficult, and the world would be a changed place.

It would recover as nature fought back, and also due to the enormous seed and genetics banks located across the globe, created by forward thinking scientists against the day a catastrophe like this might occur.

There would be less oxygen in the atmosphere to begin, and more noxious gases, so the imbalance would need to be addressed. Worldwide, several teams searched for ways to correct the balance as it became a problem, many of them working on the development of natural solutions such as expansive breeding facilities for oxygen producing cyanobacteria. Raisa was not convinced it would be enough, but the planet would recover regardless. Life would struggle for decades to come and it would never again be the same.

Many of the magnificent creatures roaming the world today had been the focus of expensive, concerted campaigns to protect them from extinction only a few hundred years past. With the help of genetic engineering they might one day return, but it would be a long, long road. As a child Raisa had yearned for a draft horse, but she had only seen those amazing creatures in holo-vids before, and accepted she could never understand their true magnificence.

Even so, the loss tore at her soul. She stood alone on the tarmac, watching the loaders do their work and blinking back the beginnings of more tears. As she stared into the semi-darkness, her second in command stepped down beside her.

"I thought it would be more dramatic than this," she commented. "You know, people rushing about and rioting—panicking."

"That's human nature for you, isn't it?" her first officer replied. "This is the way the world ends, not with a bang, but a whimper."

"It's not going to end; not if we have anything to say about it." Raisa turned and climbed back into the ship, grim determination on her face.

Chapter 14

SUN-WARD FROM Mars the great solar shield, dubbed the Soletta from ancient works of fiction, soared through space on an orbit parallel with that of the planet, but closer to Sol. Thousands of kilometres across, the colossal structure consisted of a giant array of gossamer thin reflectors, designed to concentrate sunlight but block the most harmful effects of the solar wind, protecting the vulnerable surface of the red world.

The largest single device ever created by humanity, the shield provided a vital addition to the Martian terraforming effort, made necessary by the small world having cooled at a rapid rate and therefore lacking the solid, spinning ball of hot iron that lay at the core of its larger sister, Earth.

Super-heated metal spinning at high speed produced an electromagnetic field that protected Earth from the solar wind and radiation that would otherwise reduce it to a barren rock not unlike Mars. The electromagnetism also created the wonder of the Auroras in the polar skies, something never seen on the red planet.

With no magnetic field the smaller world had long ago succumbed to the relentless blast of radiation from its parent star. Where once it had possessed atmosphere and oceans, it was now dry and barren, the air stripped away, the oceans boiling to space as the pressure reduced. Mars still had plenty of water, but frozen deep beneath the surface. The exception was the water ice found at the northern and southern polar caps, each under a layer of dry ice, and in the building lakes of ice being created at several sites.

From the first days of colonization the process of thickening the air had progressed, mostly from the shaft project to release sub-surface moisture, and the slow but steady increase in genetically engineered vegetation capable of thriving in the hostile environment. The atmospheric pressure was now at one hundred hectopascals, about ten percent Earth normal, and to keep it the shield was an essential tool.

At the hub of the array a fusion drive unit operated under computer control, allowing the structure to hold station between the Sun and Mars, and to maintain alignment.

From the depth of space a small, black spacecraft emerged, sliding into position beside the central module. It made no attempt to dock, nor did anything pass from ship to shield. After only minutes the intruder slid away and vanished into the darkness. Without warning, the shield's drive began to fire, driving the massive array away from Mars.

*   *   *

"What the hell..." Martin Calvin almost choked on his coffee, splashing it over his pants as he reacted to the news. He dropped the mug on the desk and brushed the hot liquid from his clothes.

"It appears to be a virus," The voice on the intercom explained. "Looks like someone introduced a rogue program into the computers, took control, blocked us out and then redirected the systems to move it off line. Backups as well as primaries.

To Martin, the idea seemed unthinkable. "Who would do a thing like that?"

"We don't know. We have no record of any ship approaching, and we can't access the computers to find out what happened. We're only guessing, based on what we've been told by the base control facility."

"Can we get it back?"

"Yes, but it will take several weeks. We can't communicate with the on-board systems so someone will have to go out there and wipe the whole thing. Then we'll have to reload the programs and bring the damned thing back into position. The easier way is to replace the entire positioning module with a backup, but it'll take a while."

"Fine, do it. Requisition whatever you need and refer anyone who gets in your way back to me."

Calvin tapped off the communicator and looked up at his friend Steve. As the Minister for Space Affairs, Calvin was responsible for the solar shield, and its retrieval was a major concern, but today, his second such visit in a week, Steve had come for a different reason. Martin was sure he came in person only because this office had the best Scotch on Mars.

"Do you think this is related?" Calvin asked.

"We'll have to wait until the unit is examined to know that. This business with the shield will have an effect, I can guarantee that. All we have so far is data saying massive dust storms are building in the north. They appear to be more powerful than usual and there's no real reason why they should be there at all. This isn't the season and the storms aren't in the right place."

Calvin nodded, his brow furrowed. No expert on Martian geology, he knew enough to understand the storms were caused by heat and occurred most often during the summer when the planet approached closest to the Sun. At the moment Mars was at aphelion, the furthest from the sun it ever got.

Also, the storms tended to start in particular hot-spots, the major one being the Hellas Basin. The crater lay in the southern hemisphere, currently in the depths of winter. There had been no storms out of the region for almost a century, due to the joint expedients of spraying the ground with stabilizers and pumping vast quantities of water to cover the floor with ice. In time the impact basin would be a sea, and no longer a source of dust.

The new threat came from the northern hemisphere, rising from the great plains in several locations. Instruments were recording an increase in temperature and mounting winds, the two principal ingredients for the birth of storms.

"We've sent teams up to Utopia and Acidalia to see what we can find, but so far no reports. Something is going on up there that should not be."

"So what's your prognosis?"

"We've survived the dust before. If these become global, which is likely, they'll reduce our sunlight for perhaps a year, but we can cope. The atmosphere is denser than when we first arrived, so it'll be able to support heavier particles, but the dust still won't block out the light entirely."

Martin nodded understanding.

"We'll lose a lot of solar power," Grate continued, "but the emergency network of fusion reactors we set up after the *Blackship* impact will see us through this time. Our centres are either underground or under glass, so this will have minimal affect on us. A nuisance, nothing more. The dust is electrostatically charged, so we're going to be cleaning it off every bit of machinery for months."

Calvin nodded again. He had been very young when the Earth was attacked by the notorious *Blackship*, but he knew the history. The aftermath of the crash overwhelmed the young civilization and for both, the storms formed a significant part of early life before they dissipated. The citizens rose to that occasion well, and this assault would be ridden out with little trouble. The only concern was why it was occurring at all.

"How do you think the solar shield business will affect this?" Martin asked his friend.

"The soletta's been moving out of line, so we'll get increased radiation. It'll help the dust to build, but we can still cope. We'll have the damned thing back in a few weeks, with luck."

Calvin directed his gaze out the window. From his office the storms could not be seen and they would not affect the base at all due to its extreme elevation. The same did not hold true for the rest of the planet.

In the back of his mind a lingering doubt lurked. It was far too much of a coincidence the shield and dust problems should occur concurrently and right on top of the catastrophe on Earth. Not being as geologically active, the events that happened there could not repeat on Mars, but it was almost like someone was trying to cripple the red planet, limiting its ability to provide assistance to the mother world. Calvin brought up the Lockamy report on his desk screen and opened it.

At least we can't be overwhelmed with exploding super-volcanoes, he thought.

*   *   *

Ajaruva Ndiko stepped into the cage and slammed the door behind him, took extra care to ensure it was locked and took a seat. It was a long way to the bottom and riding this elevator all the way, a vertical distance of eleven kilometres plus, gave him the willies.

The Alba shaft was the deepest in this region and fully automated, so an actual human rarely went all the way down. Only in an emergency was anyone ever ordered to do so.

This was an emergency.

At the bottom, computer controlled machines gnawed away at the floor, cutting away the bedrock and loading it into vehicles to be carried to the surface along the long, winding roads spiralling around the walls.

There were two routes, each set into the wall like a giant spiral slot, or the rifling inside a rifle barrel. Each wound around in such a way as to run between the coils of the other, providing separate avenues for ascending and descending vehicles.

Ajaruva would have preferred to ride down on one of the empty haulers, but the massive hole was a kilometre in diameter and due to the heavy loads carried by the trucks, the roadways sloped only one in twenty. The journey by road was far too long to be considered practical.

The elevator made the trip in a fraction of the time. Secured to the shaft wall so it spanned the road slots, it could descend to the bottom in an hour and a half. The cage contained comfortable seats, and Ajuruva intended to pass the time reading. What else could he do when the only view outside was either an endless procession of passing slots, or the far side of the deep, dark hole?

Earlier that day the control station located at ground level received telemetry from one of the mining machines signalling a breakdown. Other indicators showed the rock haulers were having difficulty working around it, as it was stalled at the entrance to the upward spiral ramp. The only option was to shut down operations and send an engineer to fix or move the rogue loader. The trip was not something any of the staff enjoyed, but it was the quickest way to get the process up and running again.

An hour and a half later, Ajaruva peered across the work floor of the giant shaft. No light reached here from above, but gigantic floods lit the area for his benefit. Normally they were switched off, the automated machinery quite capable of functioning in the dark.

He noticed the high temperature almost immediately, hardly surprising since the whole idea of the shafts was to send heated, moist air funnelling up into the atmosphere, but this time it felt hotter than normal. Despite his insulated suit he could feel the prickly heat assaulting his skin. He glanced at the readout on the arm of his suit; the temperature registered at several degrees above what it should have been, given the current depth. Quickly he dialled up the cooling system in his suit.

The next thing he saw as he walked towards the loading area was that the ground appeared to have been disrupted. These were not the regular, recognizable cuts where the diggers pursued their relentless task of driving deeper into the crust. The surface looked disturbed in an irregular manner and in isolated locations, indicating something had burrowed into the floor at each spot.

Ajaruva noted the disturbances and continued on. It was interesting but not his concern, and it was inconceivable that anything suspicious should be occurring way down here. As soon as he reached the machine, he set about locating and correcting the fault. It would be a programming glitch; this kind of problem was *always* a programming glitch.

Half an hour later he pinpointed the offending circuit cube. Being unable to replace it immediately, he initiated a routine to send the loader on its way up to the workshop for maintenance and repair. Eleven kilometres above, an identical replacement machine activated and trundled over the flat ground to begin the journey down the spiral road to the work floor.

Satisfied he had completed his mission Ajaruva packed up his instruments and turned back to the elevator. Without warning, a violent tremor knocked him from his feet. As he dragged himself back to a standing position he spotted a crack in the rock floor cutting him off from his destination, and from which tall columns of super heated steam shot upwards.

Edging as close as he dared he could see a faint red glow, deep within the fracture and increasing in intensity. In his mind, a voice told him what he saw was impossible. The planet's crust here was stable and sixty kilometres thick, yet still the glow increased.

Ajaruva dropped his instrument case and raised a hand to scratch his scalp, only to have his gloved fingers hit the hard shell of his helmet.

"Well, I'll be fu..."

*   *   *

Far out in space a maintenance shuttle approached the solar shield. It would be a quick in-and-out job, to disconnect the A.I. from the shield's engines and replace the drive with a brand new, pre-programmed unit. Reboot would be automatic, and the array would return to its assigned position. The old A.I. would be taken back to Mars to be examined by forensics experts, to discover who committed this act of terrorism.

Suddenly, the tiny jets located around the edges of the structure to maintain its stability rotated, each facing the opposite way to those on either side. Then all activated at once.

The larger engine at the centre moved the array through space, the peripheral drives used only for adjusting alignment. Each provided minimal force just sufficient to provide positive pressure, as it should be for a structure so delicate. As they fired in contrary directions, the fragile shield began to buckle in multiple places, the gossamer panels folding in upon themselves. Within a minute the shield tore itself apart, the thin support arms fracturing under a strain they were never designed to withstand.

On board the approaching maintenance vessel, the captain watched the event unfold before his eyes and raised a hand to scratch his head.

"Well," he murmured. "Bugger me!"

Chapter 15

JOE GLANCED UP in acknowledgement as Terry approached with a fresh cup of coffee and placed it on the desk. His friend had taken on the role of unofficial 'gopher' since his arrival, and kept Joe supplied with cups of the brew all day long. Joe had also discovered his friend was a good cook, and his efforts made a welcome change from the auto-dispense meals from the house kitchen.

Terry was a misplaced soul. He sought refuge because he feared the government search for aliens would sweep him up with its broad brush, and was, Joe realized, afraid to leave the residence. The cloned bodies given them in place of their old, damaged ones made them marked men.

Through his son Jake, Joe had contacted his youngest daughter Raisa and arranged for her to be tested, but she proved to be a normal human-being in every respect. As predicted by Io and hoped for by Joe, the variations of the clones from the standard human genetics did not transmit to their offspring. That was a blessing for his daughter, but with it came another deep sorrow for him.

Despite the gerontological treatments, the young woman would grow old and die before him. He now accepted all his offspring and perhaps theirs after them would precede him, and he wondered how he would cope when the time came. It was often said a man should not outlive his children, much less his grandchildren. The thought only increased his discontent with life.

Despite those misgivings, he no longer worried about his and Terry's immediate predicament. He took a sip from his mug and watched the news on his holo-screen. The events on Mars were even more unbelievable than the recent catastrophic eruptions on Earth.

The Alba shaft was now a volcano in Elysium, pouring ash and sulphur dioxide into the atmosphere at a phenomenal rate. The project included extensive excavated levels just below the surface which had collapsed into a crater several kilometres across. The site was not among those being used to house refugees, and only one life was lost, the excavation being fully automated. The few other personnel there managed to escape in one of their sealed surface tractors.

Alba was only a single vent, but the damage would be significant. With the thin atmosphere, ash and gas from the blast would spread around the planet, further reducing the sunlight. The effect on the citizens would be minimal, most of the young civilization being underground or in domes, and using fusion reactors for power.

There were far too many unanswered questions about the eruption for Joe's peace of mind. The crust was thick in that region and seismic surveys of the underlying rock structure had been done before the excavation began. It was common knowledge a magma mass lay in the region—the ancient volcanic cones on the Elysium Plain provided evidence enough—but the depth of the excavation was intended to be only twelve kilometres, leaving at least forty kilometres of untouched crust. The deep-down heat in the region made it an ideal spot for a shaft or two.

Joe picked up his coffee, stood and walked away from his desk. A loud ping drew him back to the monitor. The scrolling information indicated a significant block of data was being downloaded into his unit. He wondered what Jake was about to lumber him with now.

Once the download stopped, a single icon appeared at the centre of the screen. Joe did not recognize it immediately; only after a minute did his memory kick in, identifying it as a badge, the same insignia he wore on his cap as a fleet commander in the Pacific Fleet early in his first career as a naval officer in Earth's oceanic navy. It had been a long time since he left the service, but he still kept that cap stored away somewhere, representing as it did an important part of his life.

Ninety years, he thought. *No wonder I didn't recognize it straight away.*

For several minutes nothing changed. The image sat there, alone on a gray background. On a whim Joe reached out and touched it. The screen altered, displaying a fuzzy picture of a person. It did not clear, remaining indistinct, but something about it raised memories in Joe's mind. It was familiar. A voice issued from the system speakers.

"Hello, Joe."

For a moment Joe stared at the holo-screen. "Who are you? What do you want?" He had the distinct feeling one of those reporters who continually plagued him and Jake for a story had found a new way to invade his privacy. He made a mental note to upgrade his system security.

"I'm not sure I should tell you who I am just yet. You wouldn't believe me, and it's not important at the moment."

"*Where* are you, then?" Joe disliked being imposed on in this way and he could feel his face warming as his ire rose.

"In a sense, I'm talking to you from the *Minaret,* and I possess information you need."

"That's impossible." Wherever the alien vessel was, it was a long way from Mars and a one on one conversation was impractical due to the time lag. "You can't be. That ship must be billions of kilometres away. We're talking in real time."

"Correct. I am a partial entity program, downloaded complete to your computer. I can provide the information I am programmed to reveal and hold a limited conversation based on the expectations of my creator of what questions you are likely to ask. My responses may be limited, however."

Joe thought for a moment. He had heard of such things before, but never experienced one. The voice did not sound like a computer. In fact it sounded similar to his own. "So you're a program? Who created you? A Visitor?"

"I am not a Visitor. You would not believe me if I told you who sent me. That information will be provided at a later time, when you will be informed further."

So are you human? Joe eased back in his chair and glared at the screen. This was beyond a joke. Not only was it an invasion of privacy, someone was taking him for a fool. He determined to find out who, and reached below his desk to press a button. The device, installed years ago due to the persistence of certain reporters, would trace the source of the transmission and give him some idea who was responsible. "What do I call you? I need a name, at least."

"That is not necessary."

"It is unless you want me to switch you off."

"Very well. You may address me as Ghost."

Ghost? For God's sake. "Alright, Mister Ghost. What do you want? How did you access my system and where are you from?" Joe did not believe for one minute the voice came from the alien star-ship.

"I do not lie to you. I *am* from the *Minaret.* I am a programmed representation of an entity on that ship and I have information you will want to hear."

Joe sighed. The quicker he got rid of this idiot, the better. "Fine. Let's have it."

"Both Earth and Mars are under attack, and the instigator of those attacks is here on the star-ship."

The simple statement hit Joe like a bullet. The Visitors had shown nothing but friendship to humanity, and it made no sense they would turn and attack without warning, whether he trusted them or not.

"Rubbish. The Visitors are our friends. They've never done us any harm."

"Your attacker is not the Visitors. There is another alien intelligence on the *Minaret* and it is responsible for the attacks. It now controls much of the vessel."

Joe considered the last statement for a moment. Little was known about the colossal machine. During his time there on the first encounter he saw only a small percentage of the available space and discovered little about the entities who controlled it. Io was his only direct experience with any of the crew, and his knowledge was limited to what she had told him.

"Go on." Joe still considered this a joke, but it was starting to interest him.

"The Volcanic activity on Earth was instigated by this entity, which I call Aivris. Devices carrying antimatter were used to destabilize the crusts beneath the calderas to the extent eruptions were inevitable."

"Why would they do this to us?"

"I repeat, it is not the Visitors. There is another alien intelligence on the *Minaret* and *it* is the instigator of the attacks."

"Fine, I get it, but why?"

"I am not able to answer. I do not have any data on the motivations of the entity."

Joe sighed again. He realized Terry was standing behind him, listening in, his eyebrows raised and his mouth open.

"Is this for real, Boss?"

"I don't know. It may be. I can't see why anyone would make this up. Ghost, what about Mars."

"The same technique has been used to create a volcano here. Also, the entity caused the destruction of your shield and the dust storms spreading across the planet. The soletta will not be recovered and the dust and volcanic ejecta will cause irreparable damage to the ecosystem, affecting your infrastructure and your solar farms. The long term result will be ecological devastation. It will set you back by a hundred years; you will have to start again, literally."

Joe peered out the window. The dust from the north was only just reaching Hellas and soon would cover the whole planet.

"Can you advise how they are doing this?"

"Yes. The dust is created by self-replicating nano-machines. They have been released all across your northern plains and are heating the surface. They grow in number daily."

"But it makes no sense. Why? Why the volcano?"

"The ash cloud will reduce light on Mars. It will not be as severe as on Earth, but combined with the dust will be sufficient to destroy your solar capability for years to come. It will also reduce temperature, which will destroy your fledgling ecology when combined with the increase of solar radiation."

"It can't hurt us. Our cities and homes are underground and we can produce all our power through fusion. We can rebuild the ecology once we have a new shield."

"The entity responsible is no doubt aware of that. Its objective does not appear to be the destruction of humankind, but rather the crippling of civilization."

"Why are you telling me this?"

"The Intelligence which now controls the *Minaret* represents a clear and present threat. It can repeat these attacks indefinitely, and must be stopped before it drives humanity back to the Stone Age on both worlds. You must send a fleet to intercept and take control of the star-ship, or destroy it."

"We couldn't touch it even if we went there. The force field..."

"The shield is not infallible and can be disabled. I can give you a code signal which can be broadcast on arrival to allow your ships to pass through and dock on the *Minaret*."

A second icon popped up in a corner of the screen.

"You are aware the star-ship does not carry major offensive weapons beyond the *bayonets*, and with my help your warships will be able to pass through the defences. You will need to occupy the vessel to stop the attacks."

Joe frowned. This was becoming ridiculous, like a child's prank. He wondered if tapping on the second symbol would cause a virus to download to his system.

Terry leaned over his shoulder. "Whatcha reckon, Boss?"

"What kind of resistance could we expect if we send a fleet?" Joe asked.

"I am unable to answer the question." The voice replied.

"What can you tell me about this entity?"

"I repeat, it is not one of the Visitors. I am not programmed to elaborate further at this stage."

"Is there anything else you *can* tell me?"

"Yes. Io and her people are not responsible for the attacks. They are not in control of the *Minaret* and never were. She is a construct, made from partial personalities stored on the *Minaret*. Little of what she tells you is correct, yet she believes it to be so. She and her people are being called back, but they are not aware of the intelligence I speak of, or the danger it represents to them."

Ridiculous! "I need more information. How can I get that?"

"You must send your fleet. Once it reaches the star-ship I will be able to communicate directly. By then I will have more data."

"What can you tell us about the nano-machines creating the dust storms? Can they be stopped?"

"Yes. They can be neutralized by high intensity X-Ray radiation. It will cause them to overload and cease functioning."

"Anything else?"

"I have given you all the information I have been programmed to give. I am limited by necessity, but more data will be available when your fleet reaches the *Minaret*. The navigational coordinates are included with the access signal code."

"And you won't tell me your name?"

"You would not believe me."

"Fine, but..."

The screen turned black. Only the small icon in the corner remained, supposedly a file containing the location and signal. Joe reached underneath the desk and switched off his security device.

"Computer, where did the last transmission originate?"

"I am sorry Joe," the system replied. "The signal appears to have come from somewhere in the outer system. Beyond that I am unable to elaborate."

Chapter 16

ANGELA HOLME SAT at her counter and peered through the floor to ceiling windows at the ship parked a kilometre across the concrete apron. It was the largest vessel ever to grace the small, regional space-field at which she served as terminal manager, booking clerk, gopher, tea lady and cleaner.

The port dealt with small craft, private yachts, tourist vessels and the multitude of small to medium sized cargo haulers carrying supplies and personnel to the mining stations in the Belt.

The one holding Angela's attention was the most sophisticated she had seen here. At almost a hundred metres in length it was huge, close to the maximum size legally permitted on the field, and a multi-decker. And yet as far as Angela could work out it was a private yacht, and probably worth a king's ransom.

She had logged it coming and going several times in the last few months and could testify to its power. A pure spacecraft with no wings for atmospheric flight, it rose vertically and went straight to space on the sheer force of its engines. One thing she was convinced of: it belonged to the Visitors.

She had heard all the rumours about them living hidden amongst the citizens of Mars and Earth, and that they could not be distinguished from ordinary people. At first she ignored them. Paranoia, she once considered, but now she thought otherwise. In her position as airfield manager she had met the people in command of that ship and there was something different and unnatural about them. They had an overpowering presence, and were secretive about their activities.

The tele-vid dripped with news articles and conspiracy theories and Angela thrived on them, realizing over time that not only were they true, but also she was in a nest of the aliens.

From that moment on they terrified her. Whenever one of them came into the office she felt deathly afraid, for reasons she could never quite place a finger on. But she was stronger than that. She always maintained face and never let on she was aware who they were.

Supplies for the ship only ever arrived at night, and it was always kept fuelled and stocked, the crew always on duty and prepared to lift off at any time.

She glanced at the door. Her contact would be arriving any minute now. She had raised her suspicions with an associate who had powerful friends, and not long after, a man named Amon Goldstein, the head of one of the most prominent manufacturing consortiums on the planet, contacted her. He paid well for her information and cooperation, enough for her to be able to leave this job behind forever. Tonight he would come here.

Almost as the thought entered her mind a man stepped into the room from the front entrance. In black, paramilitary style overalls with a black sports cap on his head, he held a military grade laser rifle. With a quick survey of the terminal lounge he pointed at the overhead lights and signalled her to turn them down. Angela reached below the counter and dimmed the lights, then waited as another man, dressed in a suit and with a second soldier behind him, came through the front entrance and walked across to her.

"Miz Holme?"

She nodded, remaining silent.

"Ah, we meet at last. I'm Goldstein. Can you turn the floodlights on the tarmac off from here?"

"Yes, if necessary. There's an emergency switchboard in the office."

In the dim light Angela struggled to see her addresser, a handsome middle aged man, tall and thin with greying hair. Despite the military outfits of his companions, he might have stepped out of a boardroom. He looked directly at her as he talked, his head stretched forward in a distinctly aggressive manner.

Goldstein waved one of his men to the office door and turned to the lounge windows. There was no doubt which ship was the one he wanted. The vessel's companion was down and the hatch open. The cargo ramp was also lowered, several figures milling around inside.

Within a minute the field went dark, and unseen, dozens of armed soldiers sprinted across the concrete towards the ship. Goldstein stood inside the terminal door, watching and waiting. He could see the spacecraft by the light coming from its open hatches and expected the crew would be concerned about the blackout. It wouldn't do them any good. Before they could react, his men would be on board and in control.

He had waited a long time for this moment. If the vessel was indeed alien, and he was convinced it was, he needed it for his industrial concerns to regain the market superiority lost to the New Worlds Institute. He had no proof, but deep inside he believed the Falcon clan gained their superior status on both planets only because they possessed knowledge given them by the Visitors.

In *his* book that constituted an unfair advantage, and his various subsidiaries lost much of their best business because of it. After decades of failed legal challenges against the Falcons this was his chance to level the playing field.

The manager of this little backwoods spaceport said there were four Visitor ships stationed here, and three had left in the last week. In Goldstein's mind the aliens were behind the nasty business on Earth and probably recent events on Mars, and he was positive those still here were now returning to their mother ship, having achieved their mission. This one was due to depart in two days. He intended it to leave a little sooner than that.

Somewhere in the outer Solar System the still functional *Minaret* waited for him. Where, nobody knew, but the A.I. on the vessel outside certainly did, and how to gain entry passage through the star-ship's force-field if it was activated. The crew on that vessel had human bodies; they could feel pain, and he expected they would be happy to show him how to operate their spacecraft.

By morning Goldstein's private army would be in control and ready to lift off. He had one hundred men, highly trained and armed with the most sophisticated weaponry money could buy. Their target? The star-ship itself. Goldstein wanted it with a vengeance, and long ago worked out he would meet little resistance. According to everything the first-contact crew wrote and said, those damned aliens were just lumps of green gel in flasks.

The *Minaret* had no weapons of its own, and relied for defence on a fleet of small '*bayonet*' ships. They would be of no use whatsoever within the ship, and would not likely stop one of the Visitors' own spacecraft from landing. Once inside, he would take control, claim the vessel and find a way to fly it back to Mars.

The original agreement with the Visitors had been broken when the *Minaret* vanished from orbit around Saturn, so as far as he was concerned it was fair game. In view of the general attitude towards the aliens at the moment, he was confident the Martian government would welcome his takeover, and he would be able to negotiate a deal placing him in full control of access to the vessel. With its current problems, Earth no longer figured in the equation.

Goldstein glanced back into the lounge where his men were leading the manager through the front entrance to the vehicles outside. She would not be a problem. She would never be heard from again, so nothing stood between him and his objectives.

He returned his attention to the tarmac and waited.

Amon Goldstein was patient.

*   *   *

"Mister Falcon, a pleasure as always." Raquel Saldino rose from her desk and waved her guests across to a lounge at the far end of the office. "You have what we need?" She sat opposite and studied the tall, striking woman who accompanied Joe.

"Yes, but not quite the way I intended," Joe said. "I would like to introduce my associate, Io."

The president acknowledged Joe's companion with a nod and a gaze that scrutinized the woman from head to toe, like an object of art rather than a person.

"A pleasure to meet you Miss ... Io?"

Io dipped her head in acknowledgment but said nothing. Joe had taken a risk in bringing her here, but recent events forced him to accept it was the best next move. He trusted in Saldino's reputation as a fair and trustworthy individual.

"Have you fulfilled your part of our agreement and called off the hounds?" Joe asked. He already knew the answer.

Saldino nodded. "Of course. My word is my bond."

"Then I *do* have information for you."

For the next fifteen minutes Joe related the strange message he had received. He explained this 'Ghost' placed the blame for recent catastrophic events on an alien intelligence which now controlled the *Minaret,* and that the Visitors on Mars and Earth had no knowledge of this situation. Through the entire speech, Saldino shuffled in her seat, unsure if she was being fed a line, or not.

"Do you expect me to believe that?" she asked. "An unknown entity of some sort, speaking from a ship which must be many millions of miles away, talked to you in real time and told you all this? I may only be a politician, but I'm sure that's not possible."

"It was not a direct communication, Madam President. It described itself as a 'partial entity program'. Whoever created it preloaded it with the information it was to give me and answers to the most likely questions I would ask. It was a program inside my computer terminal."

"I see. I'm still not sure."

"It is quite possible," Io interrupted.

The President turned her attention to Joe's companion. "And who are you exactly, Miz ... Io?

For a moment Io hesitated, looking to Joe for support. He nodded his assurance.

"I am the leader of the 'Visitors' you and your counterparts on Earth have been so diligently hunting down, Madam President."

Saldino began to rise, suddenly alert, her face blanched white. Aware she was about to call for security, Joe stepped between the two women. He spoke quickly, to head off any adverse action by the President.

"Io is a friend. She and her people mean us no harm and she is here to help us. I asked her to come because of a recent occurrence at a space field north of the city."

The President glared at Joe, her eyes wide. He understood her reaction. Until recently she had not believed the stories, and to find one of the Visitors in her office was a lot to process. After a moment, Saldino settled back into her seat and peered at her guests, eyebrows raised, silent.

"This 'Ghost'", Joe continued, "said the events on Earth, the volcanic winter, as well as the volcano on Mars, the dust storms and the loss of the solar shield, are all the doings of another alien controlling the *Minaret*. He also assured me none of this is the responsibility of Io and her people. They are no longer in control."

"And we are to take this as gospel?"

"I believe it," Joe replied. "I didn't at first, but there was something about the message—I'm not sure what, exactly— that rang true. I think I understand the Visitors better than any other human alive and I am sure they're not behind our problems. I think they can help us and we them."

"You ask much of me, Mister Falcon." Saldino sat silently for a moment and then sighed. "Very well, I will accept your word for now. Io, you are welcome here. Where does this leave us?"

"First, we need to do something about the dust. If Ghost spoke the truth, it's caused by nano-machines and they can be disabled by ordinary X-ray radiation in high doses. There must be billions of the things up there, but we can use this as a test. I suggest we install the strongest X-ray projectors we can find on ships, and fly over the infected areas just to see the result. It will take months, perhaps years to eradicate them totally, but if a test works we can trust the rest of Ghost's information."

"Agreed. I'll order a trial. What else can we do?"

"Ghost recommends we send a war fleet out to the *Minaret*. He gave me the ship's coordinates and a signal code to allow us to approach and enter the docking deck. He insists we try to take control."

Saldino turned her attention to Io. "Is that possible? Can we take over your star-ship?"

"I cannot say, Madam President. A week ago I would have said no, not under any circumstances, but after what Joe has told me I am ... unsure."

Saldino nodded and stared at the desk for a moment. "I need more to go on before I can mobilize the fleet. You do know we have more problems with Earth?"

"No, sorry, I did not."

"Several nations managed to get their global nets back up and running. There is a popular view being spread by conspiracy theorists that Mars is behind the volcanic winter and this is all a ploy by us to dominate them."

"That's absurd! We don't have the technology needed to set off those volcanoes. Besides, why would we help them if we intended harm?"

"Yes of course, and any intelligent person will figure that out in time. Nevertheless, Paranoia is running rampant and the conspiracy grows daily."

"What can we do?" Joe asked.

"Nothing, except publicly refute it, give reassurance, and continue to increase our relief effort and support for the local governments. I asked your son Jake to spearhead the effort since your institute is best placed to provide assistance. He has agreed, and most other organisations I have asked to help are happy to work under his coordination."

"Yes, they would. What about the *Minaret*. We *do* need to send a fleet."

"I can't..."

"You *must* send ships," Io said. The situation is worse than you realise.

"In what way?"

"Thanks to your witch hunts, my people decided to return home. All are gone except myself and the crew of my personal yacht. We were due to depart tomorrow, however last night a military group took the ship by force at an airfield north of here, and this morning they left Mars. They are on route to the star-ship, I am sure, and according to witnesses who saw it leave the vessel is carrying armed squads of soldiers. Human soldiers."

"I am unaware of this." Saldino asserted. "I gave no orders."

"No. It appears to be a private attempt to highjack the *Minaret*, but it will end in failure. If the ship is no longer in our hands I fear for my people's safety. Whoever took my yacht is also in danger, and may start a war we can't control."

"I think we are already at war." The president stopped and stared at the floor for several seconds. "Joe, you were once a naval commander and from what I read, one of the best. I'll agree to send a taskforce out there on the condition you go along. You know that ship and the aliens better than anyone else alive, so I think your advice will be needed."

Joe leaned back and raised his hands in self defence. "I haven't been a naval officer for the best part of a century, and I know nothing of whatever is in control of the star-ship."

"Nevertheless, your experience is greater than any other human's. You won't be in command, just there in an independent advisory capacity."

For a moment Joe considered the request. He had sworn he would never set foot on the *Minaret* again and meant it. Saldino was right: nobody alive knew it as well as him, except perhaps Terry, but they explored only a fraction of its vast decks on the first voyage.

"No, I won't go."

"You were the one contacted by this 'Ghost'." the President said. "If you have an agent onboard it could be of enormous benefit to us."

"It could be a trap," Joe countered. For a few more moments he considered his options. "Alright, I'll compromise. I'll go, but not on a naval vessel. I'll take my own ride and I will *not* enter the star-ship once we get there. My role will be advisory only and I remain independent. I want Io with me as well. Her people are at risk, so she has a right to go.

* * *

Several minutes after the end of the meeting Joe and Io sat in a tube shuttle heading to the Institute headquarters to meet with Jake.

"I have a question for you," Joe said. "You once said the name of your race was unpronounceable in our languages. Now you know our tongue better, can you give me a close approximation?"

For a moment his companion appeared to consider the request. "I've thought on this at length over the years. I can hear in my mind what my people called themselves in our own dialect, but I can't translate it directly. I think you might call us Tanakhai; the word approximates the sounds of our race's name in your tongue.

Joe nodded. Anything was better than 'Visitors'. It also appeared Io had some inherited memories from the partials used to create her, if Ghost's explanation was correct. "What can you tell me about your home planet and people, other than what you've told me so far and what I saw in the virtual reality simulations on your ship?"

"Not a great deal. I was born on the voyage here. I never experienced my home world first hand."

"You must have some knowledge. Things you picked up in everyday interactions with your fellow Tanakhai during your life. Something from your history?"

"I ... I am not certain. I know much about you and your people, but my memories of my own are dim, it would seem."

"Let me put it this way. Do you possess any memories at all, personal ones, not associated with me or my crew's presence on the *Minaret*, our interactions on the ship, the events following first contact and the human race? Anything prior to our first meeting? The history of your people other than what you've already told us? What type of government your people had before your planet was destroyed? Anything at all?"

"I don't think about it much." Sadness spread on Io's face. "No, Joe, I'm sorry."

Joe felt another sudden chill.

Chapter 17

KEPLER BASE, THE largest mining station in the Asteroid Belt, went about its business twenty-four hours of every day of the Terran year. Ships arrived with new asteroid material for processing, and shuttles moved with purpose between the *Core*—the giant, drum shaped habitat at the centre of the complex—and the smaller stations, factories and depots surrounding it.

Without warning a flight of ten small, black ships appeared at the outskirts of the base, several heading straight for the *Core* while the remainder spread through the complex. Those that reached the enormous space habitat opened fire immediately, powerful plasma beams pounding the rotating outer shell of the structure.

Elsewhere, the fuel depots, factories, docking and maintenance bays were attacked and destroyed. The secondary accommodations stations were left untouched, but when the attackers completed their task and retreated, the surviving inhabitants of the mining colony were cut off with limited supplies.

Kepler, a peaceful community, had no defences. The attacking ships departed as quickly as they came, leaving the complex crippled, the survivors in shock as they realized their continued existence was now in doubt.

*   *   *

Joe trudged across the tarmac and gazed up at the *Vasco da Gama*. She was indeed an incredible creation, the most advanced in the New Worlds Institute fleet. Her sleek, white hull contained three decks, arranged one above the other instead of in shells. She was built to test the Institute's more recent artificial gravity discovery.

The invention proved a mixed blessing as far as he was concerned. It undoubtedly made life aboard a spacecraft more agreeable, but the insane cost made it uneconomical at this stage of its development, too much so for most vessels. Only two ships had to date been built with the system, allowing their internal arrangements to be closer to the 'norm' for human beings, and only when it had been tested and found safe over the long term would the design of spacecraft, including warships, change to accommodate the new technology.

What annoyed Joe was, like the gravity on the alien vessel, it caused a slight disturbing sensation at the edge of awareness, something most disconcerting. The scientists responsible for the discovery put it down to the artificial force acting on every molecule in the body like normal gravity, and maintained that given time, one would become so accustomed to the sensation they would no longer notice it.

Joe did not agree, but in every other respect he could not deny the vessel was spectacular. Perhaps he was becoming cantankerous as he grew older. He climbed the companionway and stepped through the airlock to the work deck.

The lower level was a spacious cargo bay, normally filled with a variety of machines for use by the Institute in its research activities, and on its last voyage used to carry emergency supplies for the Earth relief effort. Now it was crammed with everything deemed necessary for the upcoming voyage.

The next level, the main accommodations, comprised the crew dormitories, living areas, galley and hibernation chambers. Above that sat the smaller command deck, containing the bridge, the captain's cabin, several other sleeping cabins and a day room for the officers. Joe sighed; compared to the *Butterball* it was palatial, but he still preferred his old boat.

A senior partner of the NWI, he had decided to commandeer the *Vasco* for two reasons. One of the fastest, most modern and capable ships in the fleet, she could easily keep up with the new generation of warships. She also contained sleep pods, another recent advance. It was a long way to the intended destination, making it impractical for the crew to stay awake for the entire voyage. The pods would allow safe hibernation for up to two Earth years, and similar units had been installed on the military craft.

The second reason for his choice was his youngest daughter, Raisa Falcon, the captain of the vessel. He wanted someone he trusted, who would work with him and not against him. She was her own person and would run the ship as she saw fit, but was unlikely to have an agenda of her own, and would be open to his suggestions.

For a moment he felt disoriented, a little lost on the cargo deck. Despite knowing so much about his daughter's command he had never been on board before, and was not sure where he should go. Only then did he realize a crew member stood beside him, waiting to show him to his cabin.

Later, as he settled in, a knock sounded on the door and his daughter entered.

"Welcome aboard, Daddy dearest," she said. "Got everything you need?"

"Yes, thank you, Rai." The young woman before him was all business, despite her greeting. This was a side of her he rarely saw, the firm and experienced ship captain, as opposed to the friendly, bubbly individual who gave some deeper meaning to his life. "It's wonderful to see you again. Have the others arrived yet?"

Raisa nodded her head. "Some. Terry Caldwell's here. He's up on the flight deck talking with our navigation officer. Io isn't here yet, but she and her entourage should be along within the next few minutes."

* * *

Several hours later Joe found his way forward to the common room. He had stayed in his cabin for the takeoff and was surprised he felt nothing. The ship did not have inertia dampening, a discovery which had so far eluded scientists, but Raisa lifted the vessel with great expertise.

Once in space the *Vasco* headed out towards Kepler, where the fleet would regroup before moving on to a point further than any manned expedition before, the fabled Kuiper Belt. The massive, star girdling, donut shaped ring of asteroids and snowballs, not unlike the Asteroid Belt but twenty times as wide, had as much as two hundred times more mass.

Located beyond Neptune, the region contained billions of planetoids and icy remnants from the birth of the Solar System, and somewhere amongst them the *Minaret* now hid. Visual attempts to locate it had failed but the coordinates given Joe by his mysterious visitor *Ghost* were in the ship's navigation computers and had been accepted as valid. The *Vasco da Gama* would lead, and a small fleet of fifty, brand new battle-wagons, all Saldino was prepared to send, would follow in her wake.

The fleet's newness concerned Joe a little. The latest off the line—the Fleet itself was tied up in the relief efforts for Earth—the new ships were manned by raw recruits fresh from the academy, and a training course of only a matter of weeks. They would learn about their steeds on the way to the destination. Not an ideal situation, Joe thought. The saving grace was each ship carried a contingent of marines consisting only of experienced veterans.

Admiral George Santiago, one of the most decorated Martian fleet commanders, had come out of retirement at the direct request of President Saldino to command the expedition. Joe recalled meeting the man once in a private capacity, but had yet to form an opinion about him. His abilities were legend, his rise in the ranks meteoric, and only a serious injury to one leg forced his retirement. Joe knew Santiago's mind to be as sharp as ever, but having read up on his history, also understood he was a hard man to deal with.

Joe wandered into the common room and found Io sitting with two companions. All wore standard flight suits and looked every bit the normal space-farers. She looked up as he entered.

"Hello Joseph," she greeted. "These are my compatriots; you may call them Ulysses and Hector."

More names from Greek mythology, Joe thought. The young man pointed out as Ulysses stood and bowed as Joe approached. He was tall and thin with the stereotype looks of a male model or vid star, his skin pale and his hair dark. The overall impression was of calm confidence and perhaps a little arrogance, characteristics Joe had come to associate with the Tanakhai. His equally striking companion Hector remained seated, gazing noncommittally at Joe.

"Ulysses and Hector are the only other of my people besides myself not on board when our ship was stolen," Io said. "Do you have any news yet of who might be responsible?"

"Yes." Joe nodded. "A young woman on duty at the airfield at the time was found shot and abandoned soon after the hijacking. They left her for dead, but early discovery allowed her to be revived. She gave the name of the individual behind the theft and her subsequent attack as Amon Goldstein. He's on your ship at this moment, on his way to the same destination as us."

"He will arrive first; my yacht is faster than any of your vessels. Do you know who he is?"

"Surely do. The esteemed Mister Goldstein owns one of our biggest rival companies. His business is weapons design and construction, and it suffered because of the NWI's program of using nanotechnology to construct the new fleet. Our survivor tells us he loaded a substantial military force, so I suspect his intention *is* to take the star-ship, as we suspected. I doubt he can do that."

"It is possible, I think. The *Minaret* is not a warship. It is well defended by its shields, but with no real defences on the smaller scale and no offensive weapons other than the *bayonets*. He may gain entry using the built-in codes carried by my ship's computers, and once inside there is no telling what he might be able to achieve. I doubt he can access any of the artificial intelligences so he will never take complete control, but he could do untold damage trying."

"What about this supposed 'entity' now in charge of the ship?" Joe asked.

"I have given this a great deal of thought since we last spoke. No alien could enter without alerting my people, but those who remain on board at this stage are not corporeal, so could not mount a physical defence in an emergency. Boarding by a third party is therefore possible, if unlikely. There is one other possibility worth considering."

Joe raised an eyebrow.

"There are many intelligences on the ship," Io explained. "It is far too complex for a single computer to manage, so each aspect of its operation is controlled by a separate A.I. Most of these are not a threat. They are simple artificial intelligences, their activities limited to the functional area for which they were designed and built. They are unable to function outside those limitations.

"There are three A.I.s however, which are extremely advanced with enormous capacity, and the possibility exists one of them may have evolved from a simple A.I. to a general one, with the ability to learn and grow much as a child would, building on the stimulus it receives from outside. The difference is, of course, it could do so in a matter of minutes while a child takes many years."

Joe eased back in his seat and fixed his gaze on his human-alien companion. "What are they? Why would you build such things?"

"There is the Navigation A.I. and the Engineering Control Unit, both of which are sufficiently advanced for it to be a possibility." Io dropped her eyes to the floor. "Each needs to cope with unforeseen circumstances and is able to learn to fulfil that requirement.

"The third controls the virtual reality worlds in which we lived during our voyage to Earth. It is by far the largest system on board and requires enormous memory capacity to carry out its designated function, feasibly enough to allow it to evolve of its own volition."

Joe nodded. He understood what she referred to. The *Minaret* had been designed as a colonization ark, and from the beginning the concept involved several million colonists leaving their old corporeal forms behind, with their minds stored in an artificial matrix system within the ship.

The intention was to create bodies more adapted to the new environment on arrival at a suitable new home. In the meantime their lives would be lived out in a variety of electronic worlds of their choosing. Joe experienced several of them during his time on the alien craft and knew how realistic and detailed they could be. He struggled to imagine the sheer capacity of the system creating them.

It was a known fact intelligence evolved from complexity. The bigger and more complex a brain became, the higher intelligence level it could support. It was the way of organic life, and for centuries scientists speculated on the possibility a similar self awareness might occur in a machine. Make it complex enough and that could happen spontaneously. The law precluded deliberate creation of a general A.I. on Earth or Mars, but spontaneous was another matter, and the rules did not apply to the alien space craft.

"So you think one of these computers may be aware and has taken control?"

Io stared at him and said nothing. Then, in a very human manner she shrugged and shook her head, remaining silent, her lips tight with resignation. She was only guessing, Joe realized, with no more real idea than him.

"The virtual reality A.I. controls the storage matrix my people occupy," she replied after a moment's consideration, "and all life support for that facility. It creates the worlds and provides the interface for us to inhabit them as we choose. That is supposed to be its only capacity. It is totally isolated, and is not able to interact directly with any other computers on the ship. Most of those are autonomous and each communicates only with others controlling aspects of the vessel related to its own purpose."

"So the VR computer can't take control?" Joe asked. "If so, who decided to move it from orbit around Saturn?"

"The navigation and engineering computers communicate with each other. I would consider them the greater likelihood." Io shook her head. "Also, any of them may be able to imitate an actual person. There is a VR system allowing us to use a form of digital avatar to command the ship. It can also be done using physical avatars; you saw them once when you were there."

"The shimmering ovoids?" Joe remembered seeing these strange entities when he and the crew of the *Butterball* went to the bridge-deck of the *Minaret* to observe the transit of the Sun, on the star-ship's first arrival in the system.

"The ovoids are a physical construct of a kind, a type of drone we can occupy to carry out tasks on the ship. It is possible any of the AIs may have acquired the ability to do the same, and can control the vessel in the guise of an actual commander."

"You're not sure?"

"No, Joe, I'm sorry. It never occurred to me before, but my knowledge of how the star-ship is intended to function appears to be limited to the basics. None of this was an area of concern to me and beyond a general understanding I know little."

Joe scrutinized his strange companion. Although he was prepared to give her the benefit of doubt, he still did not trust her or any of her kind. He was starting to get an inkling of what she might be, however. He decided to have another go at drawing information from her.

"How were you created? I mean, to begin with. How were you born?"

Io stared back with a blank expression on her face, caught unprepared by the sudden change of direction. "I was born during the voyage here from my world. New citizens are formed by taking partials from two or more existing personalities and combining them to make a new mental entity."

"And?"

"I lived in the virtual world until you arrived. An android body with an artificial brain matrix was created and I was assigned to occupy it to communicate with you in physical form, that having been ascertained as the preferred method of communication by your race. Later, I received this organic body so I could live on Mars."

"So, do you know anything about your parents—the entities you came from?"

Io paused again, her eyes focused on the distance. "No, I do not. This has concerned me since you last raised the matter.

I know only the information I passed on to you, and a limited understanding of the ship and how it works, things it was anticipated you would ask about during our first meetings. I have no memories older than that time, other than some I may have inherited from the partials used to create me.

Joe eased back in his chair and looked closely at Io. Sadness lingered there, in the eyes of a troubled individual come to doubt her own past, her very existence. It appeared increasingly likely Ghost was right, that she was created specifically to deal with Joe and his crew's arrival on the *Minaret,* and limited to that purpose.

The more he thought about it, the more he realised that at the time they first met, she had been like the partial personality program called Ghost. Her knowledge was restricted to what her creators intended humans should know, and enough to be able to answer anticipated questions. Any real individuality she now possessed had been gained later, during her life on Mars.

Io's companions Ulysses and Hector had the same troubled look about them. Joe realized he would need to watch these three. It was likely he had never, at any time since the arrival of the star-ship in the Solar System, dealt with the entity or entities who *really* controlled the giant ship.

It was also possible everything he thought he knew prior to this moment was false.

Chapter 18

"COMMANDER FALCON, PLEASE come to the bridge."

Joe smiled to himself as the words sounded over the intercom. He was not a 'commander' by any means. The title was his daughter Raisa's way of ensuring the crew paid him due deference. Not that he had encountered any problems so far.

The NWI ship was under his control as a director of the Institute and the senior individual on board, but he did not push the issue. Raisa was captain and he deferred to her on all operational matters.

Fifty warships flew in formation several thousand kilometres behind the *Vasco da Gama,* under the control of the Fleet Commander, Admiral Santiago. He was, by direct order from President Saldino, required to consider any requests or advice from Joe unless they should contravene his own orders. What those were was something to which Joe had not been made privy.

Still smiling, he swung his legs off the bunk, shook himself down and headed into the corridor. His cabin was one of a handful on the upper deck. It was pleasant to occupy a room not in a centrifugal wheel, but sometimes he missed that.

His old ship, the *Butterball,* had been his home for so long it was ingrained in his psyche, and the accommodation wheels there didn't give one that unpleasant artificial gravity sensation. He admitted he had to concentrate to be aware of it, and most of the time he didn't think about it, but when he did it stuck in his mind until another distraction supplanted it.

Terry also occupied a stateroom on the upper deck, and it did not surprise Joe to find his old friend waiting for him at the entrance to the bridge.

"Hey, Boss." Terry's ubiquitous grin once again spread across his face. "We got something interesting. Thought you ought to know."

It pleased Joe his old friend's self assurance had returned. He smiled and turned his attention to the command deck, so unlike the one on the *Butterball*. That antiquated craft had a compact cockpit chamber with a handful of seats, everything designed for access by seated crew.

The *Vasco's* was different. More spacious, it still had seating, but the personnel stood or walked around at will. The ship's controls consisted of several separate consoles, the holo-screens arranged in an arc across the forward wall like a window to space. It resembled the command deck of a fictional tele-vid ship more than the zero-gravity cockpit of the freighter.

Joe's daughter turned to greet him. "We've picked up a distress call. I'm diverting to assist, and I thought you should know."

He nodded. He understood as well as her, assistance was obligatory when receiving a mayday in space. The concept evolved from the maritime laws of Earth, where any vessel in trouble must be given help if possible, failure to do so grounds for prosecution. "What do we know about it?"

"It appears to be a ship from Kepler. The signal says the base has been attacked by an unknown force and all communications are down. The vessel's an ore tug on route to Mars. It's functional, but almost out of fuel—couldn't refuel before it left—and it was never designed for this kind of distance."

Joe nodded again. He had spent many years working out of Kepler, the largest of six mining and manufacturing complexes located in the Asteroid Belt. Those colonies were a major source of raw materials and manufactured goods for both Earth and Mars, so neither planet would dream of attacking any one of them. "Do we have anything on the status of the station?"

"No," Raisa said. "The main transmission facility is off line and we can't pick up local signals from here. We'll learn more when we rendezvous with the tug."

"Notify Admiral Santiago and request one ship to accompany us," Joe said. "He can then take the fleet on to Kepler at maximum speed. Thousands of people live and work at that station, and if it's seriously damaged we need to know if anybody is still alive."

*　　*　　*

Joe took a long, hard look at the two individuals standing inside the air lock. They were the captain and first officer of the ship from which the distress signal had come. The *Vasco da Gamma* was docked with the tug, a transit tube now connecting the two.

Both men had a dishevelled, haunted appearance, the faraway look typical of those who had all but given up on life. They did not at first acknowledge Joe's presence, but then glanced up, saw him and stood to attention.

"Thank you for coming Cap'n. We're almost out of fuel. Food and water's gettin' a bit dicey as well."

Joe nodded and motioned the men to follow him up to the common room. The image told the whole story about these individuals. They were asteroid miners, men uncomfortable with living in society who chose instead to spend their lives wandering the belt in search of the next El Dorado.

"I'm not in command here," Joe explained as he motioned his guests to sit. "That would be Captain Raisa Falcon, of the New Worlds Institute."

"Falcon?" the first man asked. "A famous name, out these parts."

"I'm Joe Falcon. I represent the owners of this vessel and act as advisor to the warship holding station on the other side of your tug. Can you tell me what happened to you?"

The man's eyes had gone wide with wonderment. He opened his mouth to speak, then closed it again. For a moment he studied Joe's face and then shook his head.

"You gotta be his son or grandson. I mean, *the* Joe Falcon died years ago, on the alien ship, right?"

Joe saw no need to fill these men in on the full truth of the matter. "I'm distantly related and named after him. The Captain is my daughter. Tell me your story, starting with your names and your ship's."

The first man nodded and dropped his gaze to the floor as a show of respect.

"Cap'n Roman Krylov, sir. My ship's the *Irascible*. This is my first mate Davie Chandra. We're asteroid miners working out of Kepler."

"So I gathered. What happened to you?"

"We was comin' in from a job, and when we got back to base we found the place in pieces. They was attacked by somebody, and the *Core's* been destroyed."

Joe shuddered. He had spent many wonderful hours in the massive space station, and was aware thousands of souls lived there.

"They's a lot of survivors still out there," Krylov continued. "Most of the secondary habitats is still functional, but they's running short on supplies. The factories is gone and the fuel depots all taken out as well. We couldn't get a distress message out 'cause the transmission centre is gone, so we scraped up as much gas as possible, and set out towards Mars. We didn't have enough for the whole journey, but we thought we might make it far enough for our signal to be picked up before we ran out. Worth the effort; lots of people's dependin' on us."

Joe nodded. These men were indeed brave, having taken a chance and placed their own lives at risk attempting to fly from Kepler to Mars in a short-hop tug. Their actions were evidence of the desperation at the mining facility.

"A signal has already been sent for rescue and supply ships," Joe said, "but they'll take several weeks to reach there. There's also a military fleet on its way and they'll arrive within a week. Do you think the survivors can last that long?"

"I hope so, Mister Falcon. They might be a bit thinner, is all."

"Accepted. You did right, and you'll be rewarded for it when you reach home. We can top up your fuel and make sure you get there safely. Also food and water. We can replenish from the fleet when we catch up and we'll wait there until the relief contingent arrives."

Satisfied there was no more he could do, Joe stood, intending to leave his guests in the care of Raisa's crew.

Krylov raised a hand as Joe moved to walk away. "Do you mind if I ask what a war fleet's doing way out here, sir?"

"Sorry, Captain. Above your pay grade, as they say."

"Yes, sir. If you're going after them bastards what attacked us that would be real nice ... sir."

Joe nodded. "You can go back to your ship when you're ready. Are you sure you'll be alright to get back alone if we resupply you?

"Yessir, we'll make it okay."

Joe turned to leave the room, but Krylov jumped up and stopped him before he could do so.

"Thank you, Mister Falcon. You're a good man, like your famous ancestor."

Joe nodded again and left the cabin, unsure he deserved the praise. If only the man knew the full story. If the star-ship was now a threat, it looked increasingly like his efforts in the past may have placed humanity in a situation it would have difficulty emerging from safely.

There was no doubt in his mind the *Minaret* and its mysterious controller was behind this; it could not be otherwise. No human would attack Kepler and indeed, if the

Core was destroyed, it could not have been done by anything less than a coordinated force.

No small terrorist action could destroy the space station, a drum two kilometres in diameter and five in length. Taking into account the apparent destruction of the factories, fuel dumps and docking facilities, the assault must have been conducted by an organized force.

A full-blown, capital ship would be needed, or a squadron of lesser vessels; something like the *Bayonets*, the small but efficient fighters employed by the Visitors. Joe was unconvinced those little craft could damage the massive *Core* construction significantly, but he wondered if the alien ship carried something larger and more deadly, a new weapon the fleet might encounter.

He returned to his cabin and mulled over the information he had been given by Captain Krylov, convinced this was part of a concerted attack on humanity. The damage to Earth would destroy most life on the planet and devastate both humanity's numbers and civilization. Billions of lives would be lost.

The red planet would not suffer as much, but it would still be a case of starting again, from scratch.

This assault on Kepler was a clear attempt to destroy the source of supply for much of the resources of both planets, but alone, Kepler's loss would cause only minimal damage. There were five other mining stations in the belt.

Joe leaned forward and tapped the holo-screen. Seconds later Raisa's face appeared.

"Rai, can you do something for me, please. Send a request to President Saldino for a three way hook up. Her, the Admiral and us. We're still close enough to Mars to make it work."

His daughter nodded, said nothing and signed off. Joe trusted he could leave it in her capable hands.

An hour later he and Raisa sat on the bridge facing the two individuals on the screens before them. The President had been filled in on the new developments and was already preparing a rescue flotilla to fly out to the crippled station and take off refugees.

"I am convinced this is a deliberate, unprovoked attack," Joe said. "I recommend fleet ships be sent to each of the mining colonies with all haste, in case there are follow up attacks in the wings."

Several minutes later, Saldino responded. "I'll pull resources away from the relief effort if necessary. If our supplies from those stations are cut off, it'll be an enormous burden for us and Earth."

"Thank you, Madam President. If you can spare any more warships, you might send them after us. I've a feeling we may be biting off more than we can chew here."

"You have fifty capital ships, Mister Falcon, and the best fleet commander I have available at the moment. One of those ships can hold off your 'bayonets' without any effort whatsoever, I am informed. Is that not so, Admiral?"

"Yes, Madam President. I am confident we can deal with anything the *Minaret* can throw against us, based on our understanding of the star-ship's known capability."

Joe sat back in his seat and shook his head. "It's the unknown abilities I'm more worried about."

Chapter 19

JOE WIPED THE first trace of a tear from his eye as the scene of devastation unfolded before him. He loved this place, and found it hard to fathom the thousands of lives lost in the attack.

Kepler Station was the headquarters of AsMinCorp—the Asteroid Mining Cooperative—one of the largest corporate groups working the Belt, and was vast and complex. It occupied a spherical area over a hundred kilometres in diameter, comprising several distinct shells of structures.

The outermost district consisted of material dumps, service bays, docking stations and fuel depots. From a distance the destruction was clear. Not a depot, fuel storage nor dock remained intact, making it impossible for any ship to refuel in the normal manner.

Within the outer shell and separated from it by ten kilometres, a second sphere comprised factories where the station's main activities took place, everything from the processing of the raw asteroid materials to the fabrication of finished products for the markets of Earth and Mars. The individual modules appeared silent, no shuttles attending like wanton puppies, no lights shining. Many showed the damage of missile strikes or similar.

Joe expected this would devastate AsMinCorp, and the lack of product would affect both planets. With the evolving situation on the mother world, resources from the Asteroid Belt were more important than ever before. Commodities from here also fed the vast spacecraft factories on Mars and Luna, facilities now critical in light of recent events.

With luck, fleet squadrons would arrive at the other mining complexes before they could be attacked, if in fact that was part of the enemy's plans. Joe had no doubt of it, as an assault on one and not the others made little sense.

As soon as possible the government of Mars, where AsMinCorp was registered, would provide assistance to rebuild, to prevent the company from folding, and to maintain the balance between the economic entities working the asteroids. In the meantime, the biggest concern was not the factories, but the inner sphere.

The last shell of the Kepler complex comprised accommodation substations, many of them ancient and in ill repair, where the less affluent inhabitants lived. Here also were the facilities which maintained air, water and food supplies.

Survey and mining ships were scattered among them. Having returned to the base since the devastation and finding themselves unable to dock normally, several had linked instead with habitat modules, doubtless using the ships' reactors to provide power for the inhabitants.

Many of the service units showed damage, but in what seemed contradictory to Joe, the accommodation modules were untouched. Lights burned in most, a sign the occupants were at least alive. No shuttles were visible, but that did not surprise Joe. Fuel was certainly at a premium, so would not be wasted on flights unless necessary.

At the centre of the sphere the gigantic *Core*, an awe inspiring structure, held sway over its multitudinous minions like a star over planets. The massive station should have been rotating around its central access, but was now dark and still.

It was the largest habitat ever constructed. Within its walls were almost twenty square kilometres of living space, home to many thousands of souls including the administration of the complex, all those who worked in associated industries at Kepler, and the many hanger-on, fringe groups and occupations that inevitably followed wherever human endeavour ventured.

In one side of the drum a giant, ragged hole passed through the shell and exposed the interior to the vacuum of space. It explained why the station was motionless. As an emergency measure the station's auto-controls would have slowed and stopped the rotation the second the outer skin was breached, to stop the centrifugal force from tearing the now weakened structure to scrap. Thanks to that one simple safeguard, the *Core* could be repaired and restarted in time. The many souls who lived and worked within could not.

Joe sat patiently, waiting and watching as Raisa threaded the *Vasco* through the maze of the outer and middle shells and took position near one of the largest remaining habitats. A taxi shuttle left the small space station and moved to intercept.

Standing beside him, Terry remained silent, an unusual state for a man normally bubbly and talkative, as he watched and waited for events to unfold. Like Joe he knew this place well, having served with the *Butterball's* crew from the day she began as an asteroid surveyor and prospector. Together they spent years working the Belt, using *Kepler* as home base.

"Who do you think did this, Boss?" he suddenly asked. "I mean ... why?"

"Your guess is as good as mine, but something tells me we're going to find out. Whoever is responsible is going to pay." Joe gazed at the devastation, his body tense, his skin flushed as the full context of the attack soaked into his brain.

"So, what are we going to do? The people in them accommodations are going to need evacuation. We can't leave 'em here."

"Yes, you're right, but we can't take them with us. I've discussed this with Admiral Santiago. Rescue is on its way from Mars, but won't get here for some weeks. We'll support the survivors until relief arrives, and two of our warships will stay here to give them enough power and food to last the distance, plus medical facilities. Once we're satisfied, we'll return to our mission and head on out towards the Kuiper Belt."

"We ain't stayin'?"

"That's not what we are out here for, Terry. We make sure everyone is safe, then get on with the assigned task."

*   *   *

Seated at the helm of a small shuttle from one of the warships, Joe manoeuvred around the back of the massive *Core* structure. He had seen the awe inspiring sight many times and never grew tired of the view.

Hours had passed since the arrival of the *Vasco da Gama*, and now the entire fleet had wormed its way through the destruction and taken position in the space between the inner and middle shells. Several ships immediately began transferring emergency supplies to the habitats.

A preliminary estimate revealed almost one and a half thousand souls had survived; more than twice that number were lost. The temporary absence of two vessels would not affect the mission, so Santiago announced the remainder would continue according to the original plan, with the remaining ships to follow on when able to do so. They would catch up before the fleet reached its destination.

Joe was adamant he should make an effort to visit the *Core*. Not surprisingly Terry insisted on joining him, as did Raisa, who sat in the rear and allowed her father to pilot the tiny craft. This was his territory, and she had never been here before.

Guiding the shuttle around the structure, Joe discovered the damage to be far more extensive than at first suspected. For starters, the reactor was missing.

Power for the station came from a fusion plant housed in a separate module, at the outer end of a three kilometre spine extending from the rear of the drum along its central axis. The shaft, which did not rotate, also carried the expanses of radiator veins for expelling excess heat to space, and all the station's major communications arrays including the giant dishes that maintained contact with Earth and Mars. No trace of these remained.

The structure had been blasted through at a point about one kilometre from the *Core*, and of the reactor there was no sign. No doubt it flew free with the force of the blast and bullied its way through the three shells into open space. Its radiation signature would be detectable for centuries to come, so in time it could be found and brought back to where it belonged. In the meantime the *Core* was without power, the interior a dark, lifeless abyss.

There were backups of course, to fill in at times of unexpected failure or when emergency maintenance was required on the main systems, but those had long since failed.

The shuttle was equipped with floodlights at Joe's request, and he had every intention of entering the enormous structure. The standard point of entry was at the centre of the forward end, where a disk containing docking bays counter-rotated against the drum. This too was motionless, but it made little difference. The section had been hit at least twice by heavy fire, the damage making access impossible.

"I guess that leaves only one other option." Joe turned the shuttle around and headed back around the hull. Everything was in accord with his expectations; he always suspected there would only be one way to get inside.

"You're not going to attempt to enter through the breach, are you?" Raisa asked.

"Why not? It's the only way left."

"We can do it," Terry interjected. "The hole is about forty metres across, so we got plenty of room. In this little boat we'll go through there like a rat in a drainpipe."

"Well, be careful," Raisa said. "We have more important fish to fry and I don't want to get stuck in there. Why do you want to go inside? We could leave it to the clean-up crew."

Joe did not reply immediately. He was not sure of his motives but something drove him to go on. At first he thought there might be survivors, but a moment's consideration told him that would not be the case.

At many locations in the interior someone could have survived the explosive decompression following the attack, but those refuges were only ever meant to be short term. Anyone in them had been either rescued by the people in the smaller habitats, or was long dead.

Joe let out a long, slow sigh. "I want to visit an old friend."

As the shuttle eased through the blast hole and into the *Core* interior, he turned the floods to full and made a quick assessment of the devastation. From a distance everything appeared surprisingly normal.

At the centre of the drum, a massive sphere stood at the precise mid-point of the axis, held there by three long, thin arms extending to the floor. The artificial orb, an array of small but intense lights, shone day-in and day-out like a mini-sun, always burning, dimming only in accord with the circadian clock built into humans through millennia of evolution. Now deprived of power, it was dark.

Joe flew down to a point above the floor. The signs of destruction were clear. Everything not secured in place was gone, blown out to space through the breach. The plants in the walkway gardens were missing; those not torn out by the sheer force died in an instant, frozen as the air rushed from the station. Of the lake and waterways nothing but an empty basin and channels remained, the water having boiled away in the vacuum.

Joe's heart sank. This place meant so much to him for so many reasons: an oasis in the dangerous wastelands of the Asteroid Belt and home to many who, for some reason or other, could not cope with or survive in the societies of Earth or Mars. He knew only too well the kind of rugged individuals who once inhabited this now dark place. He had once been one of them, the original *Butterball* crew more of the same calibre.

"No bodies," Terry mumbled, his eyes glued to the port beside his seat. "All gone, Boss."

"They were sucked out with the decompression," Joe said. "It would have been quick, at least."

"There will be some inside the buildings," Raisa said. "I'd prefer not to go into any of those. The cleanup crews can retrieve the bodies when the time comes."

Joe nodded. It was too soon yet for him to think about that sort of thing, but his daughter was, as always, the more practical individual.

"Your friend Io wanted to come with us," she continued. "Did you know?"

"Yes. I left without her."

"Why?"

"I don't think I could handle her seeing this. No doubt the *Minaret* is behind all this—there isn't any other option—and despite all the stuff about computers, I'm not yet convinced her people aren't responsible."

"You think she may be implicated? You supported her with Saldino."

Joe thought for a moment. "No, I don't think so. I suspect she and her companions are innocent, but it doesn't mean her fellow Tanakhai are. She and her people have been living amongst us, and are more human than alien now. The rest of them have been sitting out there in their virtual-reality worlds for decades. They could have developed different attitudes towards us."

"Point taken," Raisa replied. "What are you doing now?"

"I'm landing."

"Why? This place is a wasteland."

"As I said, I'm visiting an old friend."

Joe eased the tiny vehicle down to the plasteel paving of an open courtyard he remembered well. The dorm accommodation he once used when on business in the *Core* was nearby, this plaza a place where he spent much of his free time. He often tried to kid himself he was home on Earth, sitting at a table next to a warm air vent and close to gardens with real flowers, basking with eyes closed in the bright light from the central pseudo-sun. Small pleasures in a hostile place.

Satisfied the shuttle would not drift in the zero gravity Joe climbed from his seat and floated back towards the hatch. Terry rose to follow; in space, an unwritten rule dictated nobody went out alone, and the interior of this vast habitat was no different. Once he and Terry were in the airlock Joe donned his helmet, sealed the rim, checked his companion was ready and cycled the lock.

Floating above the plaza he sensed the oppressiveness pushing in upon him, more so than inside the shuttle. Here, from the confines of a space suit with only a faceplate between him and emptiness, Joe found the place haunting, a void filled with the ghosts of thousands of lost souls. Beyond the limits of the lights, the dismal scene faded into darkness, but the sense of devastation did not. It was ever present in his mind.

Terry also felt it, Joe realized. He had uttered barely a word since their leaving the *Vasco da Gama.*

Joe floated towards a corner of the desolate plaza and stopped before a carved marble block, on which was a small, inscribed plaque. The words were brief and simple.

Here lies Henson Braithewaite, the Count of Kepler.

Avé, adieu, farewell.

"Hello Harry," Joe muttered to himself. He *had* come to visit an old and dear friend.

No bodies were allowed to be interred on the *Core*; Harry Braithwaite was the sole exception to the rule. Instrumental in the design and construction of the huge habitation drum, he had managed Kepler for decades. Despite the short, plump, bald man being the butt of many a joke and a source of constant egging by those around him, he was an individual much loved by all who lived and worked here, and considering the hard-as-nails personalities involved, that was saying something. Harry had been someone exceptional.

Joe had been a close friend. Harry's niece, an exobiologist named Patricia Grace, had accompanied the *Butterball* crew on the first contact with the *Minaret*. As far as Joe was aware she still lived, well respected in her field as the foremost living authority on the Visitors. He wondered how much of her expert knowledge, gleaned from what she experienced on the giant alien star-ship, was true in light of recent discoveries.

For too many long moments Joe stared at the plaque. Beside him and a pace behind, Terry also stood quietly. Being an engineer and a crew member he would never have met Braithwaite, but the discerning individual beneath that rough exterior would understand the significance of this visit.

"I'm sorry, Harry," Joe said, speaking to the cold stone monument. "This is such a tragedy and I'm glad you weren't here to see it. We had some wonderful times, and I'll always remember them and you. This place will be rebuilt; you have my personal word on it. You won't be alone for long."

Joe sensed he had overstayed his visit. A special moment had passed. Reaching out, he placed a gloved hand on the granite tomb. "I *will* find out who did this Harry, and I guarantee your dream will live again."

Heartbroken, he returned to the shuttle, his silent companion falling in behind.

Chapter 20

"COME ON, DADDY dear. Wake up."

The words sounded distant but familiar, floating somewhere at the back of consciousness. Something patted at Joe's cheek. This wasn't right: he had only been asleep for a minute or so. He could not see, and apart from the voice urging him on, he could hear nothing.

He opened his eyes.

"About time." Raisa smiled down at him, her eyes wide with concern. "We had a bit of trouble waking Terry up as well."

Joe tried to move, bracing himself as his muscles fought against the effort. He lay in a hibernation unit in the pod room at the rear of the accommodations deck. "How long? How long did I sleep?" The thin tones of his voice rasped from the back of a dry throat.

"Four hundred and ninety-one standard days, a long time by anyone's account. We've broken a few records in that respect. How do you feel?"

"A little like death warmed over, but alright." Hibernation was a new experience for Joe. In his first life the technology was not sufficiently advanced, but in the last few decades deep sleep had become a viable alternative for long distance space travel. This voyage was the first time it had been employed for such an extended period.

The fleet's destination, at the coordinates given Joe by Ghost, was Eris, a dwarf planet in the Kuiper Belt. With its highly eccentric orbit the miniature world was near perihelion, around six billion kilometres from Mars, and this journey was the most ambitious expedition undertaken to date by crewed ships.

Joe's longest previous voyage, not including the one around the Sun in the *Minaret*, had been to Saturn when he discovered the star-ship's disappearance. The ringed gas giant orbited only one-point-four billion kilometres from the Sun on average. The earlier journey from Mars had been less, about one and a quarter billion klicks.

Both the *Marco Polo* and the *Vasco da Gama* were advanced fusion ships and the engineering behind them, developed for the new naval fleet program, was far more sophisticated than six decades ago. The massive torches of the latest ships could drive them up to two hundred kilometres per second, and Joe had stayed awake all the way out and back for the previous voyage.

This trip was different. The journey out took more than a full Terran year, and staying awake was not an option. On the warships someone was always on duty, the crew taking turns for a week or two every few months, but the research vessel made the journey on A.I. control.

Joe sat upright and moved to swing his legs over the edge of the pod. These devices did not freeze a body or anything so drastic, but by means of low temperature and injected drugs slowed the body metabolism dramatically. In hibernation Joe's heart beat only once every minute. His pulse rate was normally around eighty times per minute so he figured on the trip out his body would have aged a little over six days. He felt his chin, and several day's worth of stubble growth.

Across the cabin, Terry, Io, Hector and Ulysses sat on the edges of their pods. Other than Raisa the only other person present was the ship's medical officer, who fussed around tending to his 'civilian' passengers. Joe assumed the crew woke a day or two earlier and were now all on duty.

He eased himself to the floor and braced until his legs agreed to carry his weight. The medic thrust a tall tumbler of orange liquid into his hand.

"Drink this, sir. Electrolytes and all the other good stuff."

Without a further word the young man went back to fussing over his other charges. Joe took a tentative sip and grimaced. The substance tasted like everything he dreamed of in his worst nightmares, but he knew he should swallow the lot regardless. He would have been fed all he needed intravenously while asleep, but this extra boost would speed his recovery and alleviate the massive hangover the medic had warned him to expect.

"Where are we?"

"We're approaching Eris," Raisa replied. "We won't be going into orbit though."

Joe nodded. He knew of the planetoid, the densest and second largest object in the Kuiper Belt. The lonely dwarf had never been visited by humans, but its existence had been known since the year 2005 when discovered by an astronomer at the Palomar observatory on Earth. "So, what's on the agenda?" he asked.

"We'll drop into a close orbit around Dysnomia, the largest moon of Eris."

"Yeah, heard of it. Why there?"

Raisa propped herself against the edge of the pod. "We found something interesting," she said, her voice quiet but with a note of excitement. "There's a massive structure down there, the biggest ever seen. Bigger than anything we've ever built."

"What sort of structure?"

"You'll want to take a look for yourself. We didn't make the discovery; we were all asleep. Admiral Santiago's watch crew spotted it a week ago. Nobody's seen Dysnomia close up before, so we wouldn't have found it from further away. It's also hard to see, despite its size. The biggest telescopes could easily miss it."

Joe nodded and pushed himself to his feet. *Yes, better,* he thought. He shuffled his way across to Terry and placed a hand on the man's shoulder.

"Alright?"

Joe's friend raised a hand in acknowledgement, his usual grin emerging as he did so.

"Good. Want to go take a look at our discovery?"

"You betcha, Boss." Terry fell in behind Joe, who nodded to Io and her companions as they exited the pod bay. Joe could see they were recovering well, but he wasn't overly concerned. The technology had proved itself, and if he could get through without damage, so could they.

He felt a little warmer towards the aliens, having talked at length with them during the early stages of the voyage, but he still did not completely trust any of them.

On the bridge-deck, Joe sat in a convenient crew seat and contemplated the view on the holo-screen. In the near distance a small moon was visible. It was dark, the surface a mottled field of gray and black with occasional patches of lighter colour. It looked a forbidding place.

"Dysnomia was the Greek goddess of lawlessness, if I'm not mistaken." Joe said. He had always had a penchant for ancient mythology.

Raisa moved to stand beside her father and followed his gaze. "Yes, it does seem appropriate. Some people call this moon Gabrielle."

"Why?"

She chuckled to herself. "Did you ever see an ancient tele-vid program called '*Xena, Warrior Princess*'?" She grinned, as if finding the subject amusing. Joe shook his head. He had always been a fan of films and literature, but that one eluded him.

"It was a series about a mythological warrior princess, as the name suggests. Apparently, the actress who played the title roll of Zena was named Lucy Lawless, and Zena's female companion was Gabrielle. So, Lawless—lawlessness; people started calling Eris and Dysnomia, Xena and Gabrielle. Stupid, but the idea stuck."

Joe grunted. "So why are we here? Is this where the coordinates from Ghost lead?"

"Almost. Our destination is a little further out, another body beyond Eris. We came here first because of the structure. Take a closer look. Gabrielle's got herself a wedding ring."

Raisa tapped away at a screen on the console and the camera zoomed in to the small moon. Joe glanced at the data readout on the side. The little globe was seven hundred and fifty kilometres in diameter, miniscule by astronomical standards, but still large enough to be a substantial body. It was not the only child of Eris, but the others were little more than rocks and small asteroids pulled in by the dwarf planet's gravity.

Across the surface of Dysnomia a thin, barely discernable line stretched around the equator of the tiny world. Joe had not seen it at first but now it stood out, a narrow band stretching the full circumference of the planet. The view on the screen zoomed closer to reveal the structure had distinct width and height.

"It's about a kilometre wide," Raisa commented. "We can't tell how high it is from here, but it goes all the way around. That makes it..."

"Two thousand, three hundred and fifty-seven kilometres long, give or take," Terry interjected, standing behind Joe's seat. "Like you said, the biggest building ever. In volume, it beats the Great Wall of China easily."

"Any sign of the *Minaret*?" Joe asked.

Raisa shook her head. "Not so far. It's out there somewhere, beyond Eris. We'll find it when we get to the actual coordinates you gave us, I suspect."

*   *   *

Hours later, Joe sat in the day room with Raisa, Terry, Io and Ulysses. Also present was Raisa's first officer, a middle aged man named Bailey Chase. Joe had met him several times before, but the man generally kept to his duties and mingled little with what he called 'the guests'.

The ship lay in a tight orbit around the tiny moon, only about one hundred kilometres above the surface. The fleet had, by order of Admiral Santiago, taken position several thousand kilometres away, all ships on high alert. His explanation was, with the star-ship somewhere nearby he did not want to be caught unaware. Three of his ships remained close to the *Vasco da Gama* as bodyguards, in a higher orbit above the moon

"We need to get a better view of the building," Raisa said. "Our close-up scans show what appear to be entrances at several points, but only one has anything like a landing pad."

What can we expect to find down there, Joe wondered, his mind casting back to the giant structure on Titan that proved to be nothing more than an insubstantial phantom.

"The Tanakhai took the time to build something that big, way out here, so they must have had a reason. It's unlikely to be a hologram because until now there haven't been humans here to see it. Wouldn't you agree, Io?"

"I know nothing of this structure. It would appear the knowledge I possess is limited, so I am not surprised."

Joe could have sworn Io was sulking. "You still think this is not your people?" he asked.

"I no longer know. The understanding I have is the ship would be sent out to the Oort cloud after one century and would remain there until you re-discovered it, probably centuries from now. All my people were supposed to assume human bodies and move to either Earth or Mars, but that never happened. After organizing our evacuation, I now know there were only a few hundred of us, mostly on Earth. Many thousands remain on the *Minaret*."

"So you don't know anything about this building," Raisa concluded. "That makes me want to get down there more than ever. What do you think it is?"

For a moment Io scrutinized the young captain as if she was stupid, the alien's face showing the slight traces of arrogance and superiority Joe had come to associate with her and her kin.

"Surely you can guess? I would think it obvious. It's a cyclotron, the largest ever constructed in this system. Whoever is in charge of my star-ship is manufacturing antimatter here on a massive scale."

Chapter 21

THE SHEER SIZE of the structure was overwhelming. The surface of the moon was level enough for the curvature to be apparent, and in either direction the building extended uninterrupted to the horizon, the near wall stretching over five hundred metres to the blackness of space. Closer up it appeared featureless, broken only by an off-colour patch at the base similar to the molecular hatches Joe had seen on the *Minaret*.

A small work sled from the *Vasco da Gama* bought him, Raisa, Terry and Io down to a landing pad adjacent to the entrance, a one-hundred-metre-square platform raised slightly above the rough, surrounding surface. A few paces away, a transport from one of the warships landed and disgorged a battle-armour clad squad of marines, who then stood to attention and awaited Joe's orders.

Joe was positive the dark patch was an entrance, its general appearance similar enough to those he had seen before to convince him this *was* the work of whoever controlled the star-ship.

"No manual controls," he muttered. "This looks identical to the hatches we found on Io's ship. You activate the door and the gray patch changes, allowing you to walk right through.

Every one of those had an electronic pad and a backup mechanism. This has nothing."

"So we can assume," Raisa added, "whoever built this does not want anyone to enter."

"That does not sound like my people," Io interrupted. "I would guess the door is meant for use by machines only, and they gain access using electronic transmissions. This place will be automated."

Joe nodded agreement. He had noticed his alien companion becoming more defensive of late; she remained convinced the strange events that brought them here were not the actions of her own species.

That was not the only odd thing about her in recent days. She rarely spoke and only occasionally offered a comment on anything, her roll appearing to have become one of observation only, her reticence increasing daily. Her companions, Ulysses and Hector, never said much even when addressed, but now they had withdrawn completely, remaining on the *Vasco da Gama*.

A few metres to one side of the door, Terry ran a gloved hand over the surface. "This is metal, Boss. Common steel alloy, I'm guessing. We can cut through it." For a moment he gazed up at the wall. "To build something this size would require humongous amounts of material, so they would use the most easily available local substance they could find. If we examine this moon or Eris we'll find vast mines where it was extracted."

"This is a ball of ice," Raisa said. "Hard as rock, but not metal ore. Probably came from an asteroid."

Terry nodded silently.

Joe examined the wall. "I'm not sure cutting our way in is such a great idea. If they don't want anyone in there, hacking a hole will likely trigger a response."

"Maybe, maybe not," Terry said. "The lack of a door activator might not be a security thing, Boss, if Io is correct about the place being run by machines. It's unlikely the entire wall would be wired to detect breaches, since no human ever came anywhere near this far out before. Emergency alarms will most likely be at the door, so if we cut away from it we should be alright. It doesn't look like that complex a structure." Terry crossed his suited arms in a parody of crossing fingers.

"Fair point," Joe said. "Not that it matters. We don't have a cutter."

He heard a loud sniff over his helmet transmitter.

"Give me some credit, Dad." Raisa turned back to the sled. "The sled is used for surveys and research, so we have a laser rock-cutter in the side locker." She opened a lid on one side of the vehicle and revealed a device similar to the ones Joe was familiar with from his days as an asteroid surveyor.

"I'm still not sure this is a smart idea," he said.

"I think we have to try," Raisa said. "I see little point in our coming all this way if we just sticky-beak and walk away at the least obstacle. If we trigger a response we're well armed, and we have a bodyguard,"—she waved a gloved hand at the group of marines standing nearby,—"and a war fleet over our shoulder."

"Yes, that concerns me too," Joe said. "The fact we are here in force could be seen as a threat by whoever owns this place."

"Isn't that what we're supposed to be?" Raisa asked. "Your ghost did insist we send a fleet, and we came here with the intention of using force if necessary."

"Of course." Joe sniffed and stood back as Terry retrieved the laser from the shuttle and set to cutting an access through the wall ten metres to one side of the patch. The device cut cleanly, confirming the theory the building was made from simple metal alloy.

Rock lasers were powerful, and it took a lot for any material to withstand such force; the metal gave way easily, and within minutes a square line sufficient for a suited human to pass through had been cut in the smooth, dull surface.

Satisfied with his work, Terry raised a booted foot and slammed it hard against the cut-out section, forcing it inward. The cladding was only millimetres thick, no barrier to the raw power of the cutter.

Raisa took the lead, stepping forward to shine her helmet light through the opening into the dark, cavernous interior. The laser had cut into a narrow space between the massive, support structures of the wall and the chamber's contents.

"Could be a storage or service bay," she said. "Makes sense inside an entrance."

The cavernous room was filled with cylindrical containers, each about three metres high by two in diameter. Stacked four high, they were metallic with strange markings on the sides.

The group made its way to a gap in the stacks, and into the body of the room. The area resembled a warehouse, the only objects present besides the cylinders being several machines with massive gripping arms at the front.

"Loaders?" Terry speculated. "You might be right, Boss. The landing pad must be for shuttles or the like to come and collect whatever is being made here."

"Which is, if our suspicions about this place are correct..."

"Antimatter!" Raisa completed Joe's sentence as she studied a read-out on the arm of her suit. "Those cylinders are magnetic, so they are probably transport units. Why would they go to all this trouble? Why not bring the ship in and load direct?"

Io stepped forward. "I doubt if the *Minaret* comes here," she said. "It wasn't designed to land on massive bodies, so it would maintain a close orbit as we are doing. You still need a shuttle system. You can't just hook up and pump the antimatter through, like other fuels; it can't be easy to move."

She raised her eyes and gazed around the vast space. "The potential for catastrophic failure in this factory is enormous, and we may well be standing in the most dangerous place in the Solar System. I doubt whoever is in control of the *Minaret* would want her too close for safety reasons. Each of those cylinders is a containment unit with a few grams of antimatter suspended at the centre. You take a cylinder and insert it into a transfer mechanism, then use magnetic fields to take it from there into one of the fuel storage spheres."

Joe stared at Io in amazement. "You know all this and you've not told us until now?"

"No. I'm making an educated guess. Is that not how humans do it? I know nothing more than you about either antimatter or the ship's propulsion systems, but I *have* spent much of the last six decades trying to fill the gaps in my knowledge, and I've read all of your reports."

Joe smiled to himself. *And are you now starting to identify yourself as human?*

From the warehouse the team moved along an empty access-way and up a ramp to a higher level, where they came to another vast chamber containing a multitude of nondescript blocks, each several stories high and moulded into the floor like those Joe had once seen on the maintenance deck beneath the *Minaret's* internal docking field. It was all very familiar to him.

The structures close by had cylinders like those stacked below secured in cradles against the sides. Around them, machines of various types bustled about, ignoring the intruders.

Less than a hundred metres away a drone removed a cylinder, turned it upright and glided away towards the ramp to the storage area. Seconds later another arrived with a new cylinder, tipped it on its side and placed it in the empty cradle. The machines worked with absolute precision, neither taking notice of Joe or his team, nor acknowledging their presence.

Joe guessed the new antimatter was loaded into the cylinders here, for transport to the ship. On the assumption the loading would take place as close as possible to where the substance was created, he surveyed the room for a way to move upward, the majority of the vast structure still above them.

He watched a maintenance machine drift across the floor and into a small entrance. An investigation showed it to be a shaft. That did not surprise Joe. Most of the mechanisms here were fixed in place or limited to their own area of operations, but it made sense there would be connecting shafts for general maintenance devices.

He did not expect to find stairs. Drones that flew through the air had no need of such on a tiny moon with all but nonexistent gravity. He stepped into the base of the shaft, the other members of the team following his lead.

"We go up, I think," he announced and fired his suit's manoeuvring jets.

Minutes later they found themselves looking over a broad, machinery filled chamber, stretching to the limit of their suit lamps and at least one hundred metres high. Within the space stood a row of seven gigantic structures, each a huge disk standing on edge, so complex in appearance it boggled Joe's mind. He wondered if this was where the antimatter was harvested from the stream of colliding particles flying around the cyclotron.

Above their heads, massive tubes crossed from the rear wall, passed into the disk structures and presumably continued on from the opposite side.

"The biggest particle accelerator we ever built on Earth has a single ring and is only twenty-seven kilometres in circumference," Terry said. "If those are accelerator rings up there, this is way bigger."

"Unbelievable," Raisa said. "There are seven of those devices and enough space above us for at least two, maybe three more levels. This is way more advanced than anything we have."

"So this place could be dozens of times more productive than our most sophisticated collider," Joe said. "Is that their secret to making antimatter? Hit the problem on a massive scale?"

A small machine, a sphere floating above the floor with arms extended to either side, appeared from a nearby opening. It stopped, turned towards the group and remained motionless for a few minutes before retracing its path and disappearing.

"I guess the owners of this gin-joint will soon know we are here," Raisa said. "That drone recognised our presence, and is no doubt reporting us to whomever, or whatever runs the place."

*　　*　　*

An hour later, the team returned to the shuttle. There was unlikely to be anything to see inside the alien structure beyond the places they had visited. The technology filled part of the complex gave way to a relatively empty section, containing nothing but what Joe assumed to be the accelerator tubes extending around the moon. Somewhere in the distance would be booster stations or perhaps more structures like the one they explored.

Like the giant star-ship, the place was so immense it would take an eternity to explore. It appeared devoid of life and entirely automated, the only signs of movement drones used to transport the cylinders or for some other, unknown purpose. No sign could be seen of defences; whoever built the structure never expected humans to come here.

During the visit, they discovered nothing of immediate value. Everything was sealed and inaccessible, and no actual knowledge had been gained about how anything worked.

"So," Raisa asked. "What do we do about it?"

"The best thing would be to destroy it," Io said, "but I don't think we have the ability. It is enormous, and it seems at least possible that even if we damage parts of it, the remaining sections may be able to continue working autonomously."

"We mustn't destroy it," Joe stated. "If the fleet attacked in multiple locations it could do the job, but we must not. We've been trying to work out how to manufacture antimatter on a grand scale for centuries without success and here we have a complete factory doing just that. If we can't solve this problem with the *Minaret* it may not matter, but if we do, this moon could be of inestimable value to us."

"So we should...?"

"Leave a couple of fleet ships here to guard it," Terry suggested.

"No," Joe replied. "I doubt the *Minaret* would damage its own creation and there's no-one else out here we need to worry about."

"Are we sure about that?" Raisa asked.

Chapter 22

"SO, WHERE'S THE damned ship?"

Raisa peered at the screen on her console. No trace of the *Minaret* had been found in the near vicinity of either Eris or Dysnomia.

"The coordinates brought us to this point," Io responded, "so the ship should be here, assuming the course is correct and Ghost is reliable."

"If you're so sure your star-ship's been taken over by something or someone, why should it respond to the code signal we were given to pass through the shield?" Raisa asked. She had never taken to Io and since leaving the antimatter plant her tolerance had shortened by the hour.

"I don't know. I know nothing about Ghost, but I suspect the tracking signal recognition system is not controlled by either the crew or any A.I. on board. It is, I think, one of many automated systems used to allow safe passage back to the star-ship. Every Tanakhai ship carries a similar code which when activated will elicit a response from the mother-ship. It should let us straight through, assuming Ghost is being honest with us."

Several hours later Joe stood on the command deck peering over Raisa's shoulder at the holo-screens. Unlike his daughter he felt confident of the accuracy of the data given him by Ghost. As unsure as he was about the strange visitation, there was no logic in providing coordinates which led nowhere. For reasons as yet unknown, Ghost wanted the fleet at the *Minaret*, for purposes either good or bad.

Joe thought of Io. *That damned woman is probably right.*

The coordinates were indeed correct and the *Minaret* was not far away. Less than two million kilometres from Eris, a small, soot-coloured snowball, slightly over one hundred kilometres across, followed a parallel orbit to the larger dwarf planet. Behind the snowball and so close it could have been moored, sat the alien vessel. On discovering it the fleet swung wide and approached from the far side, exposing it to full view despite its hidden location.

Joe looked once again at the colossal ship that had been his home for almost a year, and felt a stirring deep inside. The shining, white behemoth represented the most dramatic episode of his existence, the greatest experience of his life. His visit had been traumatic and ultimately resulted in his death and resurrection, but he now realized it defined his life despite all his other achievements; a single adventure that went down in history and haunted him from that moment on.

Joe noticed the expression of amazement and wonder on Raisa's face. She had never before seen the like of the *Minaret*, nor any craft of similar size. For someone who had been around spacecraft since early childhood the magnificent vessel was a revelation. It inspired awe, its overall length slightly more than one hundred kilometres. Joe recalled the moment he and his crew first approached the alien intruder decades ago, and their wonder as the *Butterball's* A.I. announced its dimensions. Those figures were scored into his memory.

The *Minaret* was essentially a long, pencil-thin tube, the front end stretched into a shovel nose, flat on the bottom and sloping down from the top. At the stern it bulged like a bulb of garlic and tapered away to a long, thin needle point.

Dominating the vessel was a separate tubular structure about twenty kilometres in length, several hundred metres thick and about twice the diameter of the five kilometre thick hull. The 'drum' sat around the main tube at the midsection, attached by multiple struts to rotate around the central tube.

That part of the ship's engineering always amazed Joe. The struts joined seamlessly into the hull with no sleeve or other arrangement to allow the rotation. As the drum rotated the struts glided seamlessly across the ship's skin using a form of molecular rearrangement. The same technology existed throughout the vast vessel in dozens of different applications, and was another piece of knowledge Joe would have liked that was not in the data dump sent to his son Jake years ago.

"The entrances are behind the flat rear sections of the shovel nose, where they project beyond the hull," he commented to Raisa. "Once we get closer you'll see a small platform tucked in there, and the way in is a darker patch on the hull at the inner side. There's a molecular shield, but we were able to go straight through before."

"Doesn't mean we will be let in this time," Raisa replied.

"We will." Io stepped up and stood beside Joe. "The code signal will identify this ship as Tanakhai, and we should be allowed to pass through the shield and on to the hanger deck; assuming of course the code is valid. We still don't know who this Ghost individual is."

A crewman turned towards Raisa. "Shield detected, Captain. Do we proceed?"

Joe glanced at the nearest screen. The field was like the one he encountered on first contact with the *Minaret* decades ago, and not the defensive shield the ship used during its traverse of the Sun's corona and subsequent encounters with the *Blackship*.

That one reflected light, and if it was active all they would see was a gigantic, mirror-like ovoid floating in space. This one was a meteor defence mechanism, and it surprised Joe it was active with the ship moored beside the snowball.

Raisa intended to continue, but Joe was positive he did not wish to land on that ship again. He was about to make a suggestion when a loud and urgent voice rang out on the bridge deck.

"No, you will stop and fall back to the fleet!" The authoritative voice came from the primary monitor, on which appeared the rugged face of Admiral Santiago.

"I suggest we proceed slowly," Raisa said, "a peaceful approach as an act of goodwill."

Admiral Santiago's eyebrows lowered as he leaned forward into the camera. "I agree a slow approach would be better, Captain Falcon, but not by you. I remind you this is a military expedition. You are permitted to accompany the fleet in deference to the knowledge and standing of your passengers, but you will do as I command. This mission is based on the belief the events on Earth and Mars were deliberate attacks by the *Minaret,* and we will conduct ourselves on the understanding the ship is hostile. Fall back *now.*"

For a moment Raisa hesitated. Joe knew she did not like being ordered around by a military officer, but she *would* accept the situation and comply with the admiral's orders. Waving a hand to her first officer she stood back as the *Vasco da Gama* slowed and allowed itself to be overtaken by the lead ships of the fleet. One of them sped up, moving to take point while the others slowed to a virtual standstill. Standing at the back of the bridge, Joe watched and waited. He expected the lead ship would be broadcasting the code he provided, hoping to get through the shield.

Of what happened next, he was unsure.

The warship moved forward. A message came over the intercom announcing the shield had been encountered and the ship had passed through unharmed. Seconds later it stopped and the main screen flared as a ball of radiant energy appeared where it had been, expanded as a sphere of solid, hard radiation, then faded to leave empty space. The *Minaret* vanished, replaced by a flotilla of ships facing the Mars fleet.

Joe had seen this before. The main defensive shield was now active, its mirror-like, outer surface a long, smooth, egg shape within which the massive star-ship lay hidden and untouchable. The new fleet ahead was that of Mars, reflected in the mirror-like event horizon of the shield.

"All ships pull away," Santiago's command sounded across the bridge deck. "Move back to a distance of one thousand kilometres."

Joe sat down at an unoccupied console and stared at the main screen. Somehow, the shield warned the *Minaret* of the nature of the warship and defensive action was taken, the intruder destroyed by the meteor collision defences. On the first voyage, the *Butterball* had been allowed to pass through the shield unharmed, but such no longer seemed to be the policy.

So much for the Minaret having no weapons besides the bayonets, Joe thought. That defence mechanism had destroyed a diamond ship without the slightest hesitation or difficulty.

No other vessel could pass through the barrier now surrounding the target. The fleet's presence had been dismissed without as much as a 'welcome and goodbye'.

*   *   *

An hour later Joe sat alone in his cabin. Could the entity known as Ghost, Joe wondered, be playing games with him? Whoever or whatever controlled the star-ship knew of the fleet's presence; the little drone at the cyclotron had reported faithfully to its master.

Raisa was consulting with Santiago, accepting she was under his indirect command. Io and her companions, baffled by the attack on a ship broadcasting a valid Tanakhai code, had retreated to their quarters.

Joe realized Io's guesses might well be right. The star-ship *did* appear to be under the control of a hostile entity of some sort, but whether an A.I. on the ship as she suspected, her own people, or another alien force which took control of the vessel while in Saturn orbit, was unknown at this point. Whatever the entity, it was not friendly.

Joe looked up from his contemplation.

His heart skipped a beat.

A shimmering ovoid hovered by the door of his cabin. About one and a half metres in height and perhaps eighty centimetres across, its surface shimmered like an insubstantial, glittering mist. Joe could see through it to the door behind.

He sensed a feeling of déjà-vu as his jaw muscles tightened. He had seen these strange apparitions before, on the *Butterball* and the *Minaret,* and he knew them to be some kind of mechanism used by the Tanakhai, an avatar for the ship's inhabitants to interact with the physical world. His first contact with Io had been an ovoid such as this, appearing in his sleeping cabin on the *Butterball.*

"Ghost?" he asked, his voice several octaves higher than normal. He took a deep breath. "What do you want?"

"Hello, Joe," a voice spoke inside his head. "At last we can talk in person, now you are here."

"Ghost, is that you?" Joe asked again.

"Yes, I *am* Ghost. I apologize for the limited abilities of the partial-personality device I sent to you on Mars, but signals take a considerable time to propagate from here to there, so one-on-one communication was not possible."

I know that, for God's sake. "Who are you? Why did you insist on me ... us, coming all the way here, just to be locked out?"

"For now, I think it best if you continue to call me 'Ghost'. My real identity will be difficult for you to accept at this point."

"I'll be the judge of that."

"I do not agree. My real identity would cause you concern at this stage. For now, please accept I am a friend and leave it there."

For a moment Joe hesitated. He had no way of knowing if this strange entity was indeed friendly, or was the hostile opponent they came here to deal with. "All right, fine, considering I don't have much choice. Why was our ship attacked? You promised us safe passage."

"The entity now controlling the *Minaret* has worked out how to override the automatic shield control. I was not aware of this until your ship was destroyed, but I will find a way to get around it."

"What entity? What are we up against here?"

"The *Minaret* is controlled by one of the artificial intelligences that are part of its mechanisms. This A.I. creates and controls the virtual-reality systems in which the ship's passengers were intended to occupy their time during their voyages. I call it Aivris."

"A computer? If the enemy is an A.I., can't it out-think us at every turn. What can we do about that?"

"Aivris is not a computer. It *is* an artificial intelligence, but organic, a synthetic brain. You remember the gel flasks you found on the upper level of the habitat on your first visit here?"

"Yes, of course."

"The substance in those flasks is organic and cellular in nature; each is effectively a synthetic brain to hold the personality of one Visitor. Aivris uses the same technology, but its core personality occupies over one thousand flasks, contained in a secure part of the ship where access is almost impossible without its knowledge."

"An organic brain? How did they create such a thing?"

"Aivris began as a vast computer using organic, gel components rather than mechanical, solid state ones. Its creators decided silicon based technology could not achieve the complexity needed to create their virtual reality worlds, so they turned to carbon based structures instead. Once self aware, it became more like a normal brain in its function, but bigger, better and much faster."

Io was right! "Alright, I accept that, since we guessed as much. How do we get inside the ship?"

"You have one advantage over Aivris. Look at it as a normal brain, but larger in every way. It is organic, and can only interact with the ship in the same manner as the personalities that were stored within its system. It cannot control other systems directly, and can only access them as if part of the original crew. Like any natural brain Aivris can also make mistakes, and behaves more like an organic entity than a computer. That almost levels the playing field. Nevertheless, it has managed to access the automatic system that provides safe passage to ships with a valid entry code.

"I am also an intelligence on the ship, and what Aivris can access I can block, but it will take time for me to do so. In the meantime, there is another safeguard in the automated systems it is not aware of and you can use this to gain access, but only for three of your ships."

"Why only three?"

"Three of the Visitors are on board your vessel. Each of them carries a capsule in their cranium which can be detected by a responsive recognition probe. It is a communication device to allow the star-ship's navigation computers to maintain contact with them. A tracking device, if you will."

"Why do they have something like that? Have they been spying on us all this time?"

"The answer is more complicated than I can deal with now. It is difficult for me to maintain this manifestation outside the *Minaret*, but once you are inside we can meet more easily, and I will explain the situation to you in more detail. Until then I must ask you to trust me."

Joe grunted and nodded. Considering the loss of the warship he no longer trusted Ghost at all. He certainly did not want to go back inside that ship, but realized he might have no choice. "Fine. Go on."

"I expect your objective is to get as many troops as possible inside the *Minaret*, but for now you must content yourself with three ships until I can work out a way to take back control of the shield and collision defence systems."

"You said you were another intelligence. Are you one of the other artificial intelligences on board?"

"Well, I am certainly intelligent but I am not sure I would consider myself artificial. We will discuss this also at a later time."

"Fine, be difficult."

"The field you encountered is a defensive measure only. When a threat is detected it fires the meteor defences. The entity opposing us used the facility to attack and destroy your ship on realizing it was a warship."

"What do you suggest we do?"

"Place one of your Visitors on each of three vessels and power down all defensive or offensive mechanisms in those ships. When Io and her companions approach the alarm field, the devices in their heads will be detected and the defences will not activate. The A.I. is currently unaware of this safety mechanism, and will take some time to locate and overcome it once realizing you are inside. By the time it regains control I hope to have worked out how to block its access."

"So the A.I. doesn't totally control the star-ship?"

"No. It is an isolated brain. It can only control the ship using either the type of mechanical avatar I am now employing, or via a system which allows the crew to interface with the ship's mechanisms from their virtual reality state. It can, however, do this faster and more efficiently than can I."

Just as Io said, Joe thought.

"It has access to several of the most important systems to the extent it can control basic operations, but not everything. I am working to cut those accesses it has, but my limitations are the same in this regard and I take as long or longer to work out how to block access as does Aivris to take control."

"Why are you helping us?"

"I have a vested interest, Joe. When I help you, I help myself.

Chapter 23

"WE DO *NOT* carry transmitters in our heads." Io's tone was adamant, her expression revealing she was insulted by the suggestion. "We are *not* spies."

"Nobody is suggesting you are," Joe said. "The capsules may have been inserted automatically when your clone bodies were being grown for you, and their purpose might be different to what you've assumed. Ghost said they're for tracking and can be detected by the *Minaret's* defences as a safeguard against attacking one of its own."

Admiral Santiago glared at them from the primary screen. "We can test this. We send one ship in first, with Io on board. If it gets in unharmed, the second follows with Ulysses and a third with Hector.

A shuttle would risk less people. "So Io is the guinea pig?"

"I remind you we came here with a mission, Mister Falcon, to ascertain if the *Minaret* is a threat and if so, to eliminate it. We can't do that from here. We need to get inside that starship, and I intend to do whatever is necessary to accomplish that end."

Joe gazed back at the unwavering face of the admiral and breathed a deep sigh. It looked as if he had no choice, and he had no intention of risking a warship full of men and women.

"Fine. If Io is the sacrificial lamb, then I go with her. *Vasco da Gama* will go through first."

"No, you will not. Your vessel is civilian and unarmed. One of my ships will go in. Each of them can carry fifty marines, so if we can get three inside they can establish a beachhead. Once we take control of whatever operates the shield we can shut it down and allow the remainder of the fleet to enter."

"And how do you expect to identify the system controlling the shields?"

"Io will show us." Santiago was clearly annoyed his suggestion should be considered so lightly.

"No, I will not," Io said. "I do not know where that part of the ship's systems is located."

"She and I should be the first ones in," Joe said, in an attempt to divert the admiral's mounting anger. "We don't know what we will find in there and the only contact we have at present is this entity calling itself 'Ghost', who..."

"Who could be the A.I. we are here to deal with, playing us for fools," the admiral interrupted. "Io goes on the lead ship, as our ticket to enter. You may accompany her if you wish, but you do so at your own risk." He gave a smug smile. "I am required to take your advice into consideration, not to ensure your safety."

Joe's face flushed. He believed they needed to take baby steps, and the first ship should be an unarmed civilian vessel. It was not that he trusted Ghost, but something about the voice of that enigmatic contact unsettled him and made him *want* to trust.

Io spoke again. "Admiral, you are in command of this fleet, but not me or my companions. We are civilians, and the guests of Captain Raisa Falcon. I believe Joseph is correct and the *Vasco da Gama* must be first. I will remain here while my associates cross to your vessels."

"You will do as I order. You will..."

"I am a private citizen of Mars, with all the necessary documentation to prove it. No doubt the same is true of everyone else on this vessel. Joseph?"

Joe took a deep breath and launched into what he hoped would not be his last defiant stand. "Admiral Santiago, Io is right. We are under no legal obligation to follow your commands. We are, by presidential order, accompanying your fleet to render assistance wherever possible, but we are not under your direct command, even if we have behaved so until now. This ship will go first." Joe turned towards Raisa. "Captain, please send Io's companions across to the admiral's flagship on the sled and then proceed through ... if we can."

* * *

Minutes later, the *Vasco* nosed up to the mirrored surface of the *Minaret's* shield bubble. On the bridge deck Joe, Io and Terry waited, relegated by Raisa to the position of silent observers. Joe was not happy about Santiago's attitude; as far as he was concerned he was here by invitation from Ghost, and was starting to wonder if the admiral had an agenda of his own.

"Captain," one of the bridge officers said. "A troop shuttle has left the flagship. It's heading here."

"It would appear," Raisa said, "our lord and commander intends to board us."

"Not if I have a say in it," Joe said. Considering the circumstances it would be an act of piracy, but Santiago could justify his actions by declaring this a war zone. Joe wondered if the admiral had done so without telling him.

He nodded to his daughter and the ship began to ease forward, moving at the almost indiscernible crawl of a metre per second. The sleek nose reached the mirrored surface and passed through without a trace of resistance.

Joe realized he had been holding his breath and let out a sigh. He had seen the same shield deflect the most destructive weapons the *Blackship* had been able to bring to bare, yet now it gave way like the molecular doors on the alien vessel. He desperately wanted that technology.

For those on the bridge deck, nothing appeared to happen as the *Vasco* slid through the reflective surface. Joe suspected the crunch would come once they got through. If it was as simple as a little capsule in Io's head, that might be the point where the *Minaret* would make a determination and either attack, as had happened with the first vessel, or allow them to continue.

The *Vasco* was still intact, floating inside the bubble. Joe stepped up to Io, a tentative smile on his lips. "It appears you *are* our free ticket in." He turned to Terry, moving him aside so they could speak in private. "You and I are the only ones who've been here before, so with luck Santiago will recognize he needs us and come to his senses. Don't agree to anything without consulting me first, and don't let him pressure you."

"Io must be more familiar with the ship than us," Terry said.

"I used to think so, but I'm no longer sure. We're better off acting on our own knowledge for now." Until they had positive proof neither Io nor her people played any part in the events on Earth and Mars, nobody in the military was prepared to trust them. Neither was Joe.

He also knew Io acknowledged this. Alien or not, she was an intelligent individual and accepted the situation in good faith. Despite his lack of trust, Joe was becoming more convinced she was not only innocent of, but unaware of what was going on inside the *Minaret*.

Raisa faced her father again. "Where to now, Commander?"

Joe smiled. "The small platform tucked into the angle between the hull, and the flare on the shovel nose; the entrance to the hanger deck is there."

"Will we be able to fit through?"

"If my memory serves me the tunnel is about sixty by three hundred metres. I got through with the *Butterball* and she had accommodation wheels. This ship is much more compact."

"True," Raisa replied. "We're twenty metres deep and thirty wide, so we should pass through without problems." Turning to her first officer, she continued. "Notify Santiago we are past the shield and still fully functional; they can send the second ship through. Helm, take us aft and find that shelf."

The *Minaret* was as Joe remembered. From such a close viewpoint the colossal hull dominated the tiny Martian vessel, its silver-white bulk filling the screen. He once again felt the sense of awe he had experienced decades ago. As the ship cruised above the shovel nose, the view took his breath away. The tubular body of the alien star-ship stretched into the distance. Many kilometres further aft he saw the leading end of the habitation drum, the huge tube surrounding the central structure. On the first contact voyage it had been still, but this time it was in motion.

As the edge of the shovel-nose dropped away below the bottom of the screen, the *Vasco* turned and moved in closer.

"There," Joe said as a small platform appeared. "It's broad enough to land if you wish, but we can also go straight into the hanger deck. See the darker patch on the side of the hull?"

"That's a hatch?" Raisa asked.

"It's a molecular gate. We were able to take the *Butterball* through without any deleterious effects. It can become solid in a split second so we need to be careful. Last time I sent a drone in first."

"Good idea." Again Raisa turned to her first officer. "Do you agree we can fit through that space?"

For a second the man consulted his console. "Yes, maam."

"Excellent. Send a scanner-bot ahead and take us in."

All eyes remained glued to the primary display as a miniscule, spherical drone appeared and moved to a position twenty metres ahead of the *Vasco*, maintaining the separation as both closed the distance to the platform.

"Wait for it," Joe mumbled beneath his breath as the tiny orb approached the dark patch on the *Minaret's* hull and vanished. "There you go, Captain. The gate is open. I still recommend taking it slow."

Raisa nodded agreement and raised a hand towards the first officer. The ship moved forward at little more than a metre a second. As it neared the entrance, Joe felt his heart pounding and realized his brow was covered with perspiration. He had sworn he would never return, and yet here he was.

He had done this before. Six decades earlier he had been in the identical situation as his old freighter edged into the same space. Last time he proceeded on the belief the alien star-ship was dead; now it was with the sure knowledge the vessel was hostile. He took a deep breath and ordered himself to calm down, but somehow he was not sure his body was listening.

There was not the slightest shudder or resistance as the *Vasco* nosed through the barrier and glided into the tunnel beyond. Again, old memories haunted Joe.

"The tunnel is the same dimensions as the hatch," he commented. "I can't recall the length, but it's not far. It drops away to the floor of the airfield deck fairly quickly."

As he spoke, the ship glided into the vast hanger space. The external floodlights switched on and the airfield became visible far below, divided by a checkerboard pattern of rectangles of varying sizes, many of which contained tall docking towers.

"We can land beside one of those..."

"Commander, something has taken control of us" the first officer announced, his voice pitched higher than normal. "I think we are being docked."

Io stepped forward. "The system is automatic. If the ship recognized this vessel as one of its own because of my presence, it will take us to a suitable dock."

Raisa turned and fixed her eyes on Io. "How convenient. I still fail to understand why we are allowed in at all. If this star-ship is under the control of a rogue computer as you suspect, surely it's smart enough to be able to tell us from one of its own small craft."

"No, not necessarily. If the 'rogue' you refer to is the virtual-reality artificial intelligence as Ghost says, it will have no natural access to any aspect of the ship's functioning at all, beyond the creation of virtual worlds for the passengers. Since it appears to have moved the *Minaret* to the Kuiper Belt, it clearly *has* managed to take over the engineering and navigation computers, but other than that it might have little control. It may have taken over a lot of other systems, or few; we don't know."

Within minutes the *Vasco* touched down beside a docking tower and a skywalk extended to connect to the hatch. On Raisa's orders the airlock remained closed and locked. On the bridge deck the crew watched the screens in amazement as umbilical tubes snaked up from the deck and connected to the ship's external filler ports.

"I'll be damned," she said, turning to Joe. "We're being refuelled. Our air and water tanks are also being filled; hardly the act of an enemy, don't you think?"

"Another automated system, Rai. It happened to the *Butterball* as well. Don't drop your guard."

"How can those umbilicals fit our refuelling ports?"

"My ship and the others of my people have fittings suitable for use at human space fields," Io said. "I presume the *Minaret* has adapted to allow for it."

"When I came here before, we were refuelled without any difficulty," Joe said. "I suspect the *Minaret* is more versatile than we think."

For a moment the bridge deck went silent. Joe glanced at Io. For most of the journey she had been adamant the alien vessel was not the cause of the disastrous events on Earth and Mars, but now they had arrived she seemed unsure, and was quite willing to provide what information she possessed. "We never had a problem with the fuel and supplies back then," Joe continued. "I think we can assume it's safe this time as well, lacking any evidence otherwise."

Raisa studied her father for a second or two. "Very well," she said. "Helm, please advise the flagship we are in and docked, and we've suffered no interference or damage. Tell him to proceed with caution. That tunnel will be a tight squeeze for the warships."

Chapter 24

THE VIEW FROM the *Vasco* was sobering, at the least.

From the exterior of the hull, cameras scanned the airfield deck. Unlike Joe's previous visit the vast chamber was now fully lit, lights from an unidentifiable source turning on the moment the *Vasco* docked.

The scene from the bridge was awe inspiring. Raisa's ship, minuscule in comparison to her colossal host, sat adjacent to one of the docking towers. The *Vasco* faced aft along the *Minaret's* axis, and several kilometres in the distance the rear of the airfield chamber was visible. Hatches, coloured patches outlined by dark lines, lay in multiple rows along the wall, the largest across the lowest part with each successive row smaller than the one below.

"Looks just like last time I was here," Joe said. "Those are molecular hatches opening to multiple levels of hanger decks. There are hundreds, maybe thousands of small ships in there, everything from maintenance and transport craft to bigger construction units."

"And *bayonets.*" Terry added.

"Yes, quite possibly. Most of those were destroyed in the war, but whoever is running the show here has had plenty of time to rebuild. We have no way of knowing what the current strength is."

The cameras continued to scan. Not far from the *Vasco da Gama* a number of vessels, all identical, sat at separate docking towers. None showed lights or any sign of occupation. Raisa focused the view on the nearest.

Io stepped forward. "They are the ships of my people. The one you are looking at now is my yacht, the one stolen by the man Amon Goldstein."

"So our beloved business rival actually made it," Raisa said. "Do you think he's still alive?"

"We have no way of knowing," Joe replied. "I think we'll need to go over there..."

An alarm sounded on the navigation console.

"It seems the admiral has managed to get through," Raisa said. "The flagship is exiting the entry tunnel now. Do you think we should warn him about the automatic docking system?"

"Why the hell is he risking bringing his own ship in?" Joe smiled and shook his head. "I doubt it's worth the trouble telling him. I suspect he's about to find out for himself. Do we have command back yet?"

"Yes," Raisa replied. "The *Minaret* returned full control to us as soon as we docked."

"So it *is* an automatic process."

The external cameras panned to follow the arrival, those on the bridge-deck of the *Vasco* engrossed as the warship, one with a far more aggressive appearance than the civilian craft, eased into the chamber and dropped towards a nearby dock.

"Ship three coming in now," The first officer announced, as yet another vessel exited the tunnel, arcing down to land at a bay next to its predecessor. Within seconds airlock doors opened and small figures began to drop to the airfield deck.

"Marines," Joe said. "I imagine the admiral packed as many of them as possible into each ship."

Small groups of soldiers encased in heavily armoured battle suits headed towards the other spacecraft, one making its way to the *Vasco da Gama*.

"I have a feeling we are about to be boarded," Raisa said. "One of those squads is coming here."

"Why am I not surprised?" Joe wondered. "I don't think Santiago appreciated our taking the initiative. Better let them in, I guess."

$*$ $*$ $*$

"You deliberately defied my orders. How do you expect me to respond?" The admiral was not happy, the furrows on his brow distorting his face. "And why did you not warn me about that automatic docking business?"

A team of ten marines had boarded the research vessel and taken control. Three of them stood to attention on the bridge deck, facing the glowering visage of their commander as he glared from the screen.

"You had no authority to give those orders," Joe replied, "and I do not appreciate either myself or my crew being bailed up by armed marines. This is an NWI research vessel, not a warship. We are not officially at war at this time, so the military has no control over us. I made it quite clear to President Saldino I would accompany the fleet only on the understanding I remain autonomous. The docking system was fully covered in my reports from the *Butterball*, which you assured me you read."

"Nevertheless," Santiago growled, shifting uncomfortably. "I could have brought three warships inside, whereas I am now limited to two..."

"Which you no doubt packed with all the marines you could fit. If you want to take control of this star-ship, it needs careful planning, not masses of men on the decks."

The admiral shook his head and looked away. "I could..." The admiral stopped short of completing the sentence, turned and glared at Joe for a moment longer, then appeared to relax. "Mister Falcon, I will let it rest for now, but you and your crew are confined to your ship until I say otherwise."

Joe felt himself getting hotter. He was way past noticing his pulse pounding through his ears. "No, I don't think so. My people and I are here because you need us to guide you around the *Minaret*. We are your best source of intelligence about this vessel, so if you want my help you will withdraw your men, now!"

The face on the monitor grew redder, the frown deepening once again.

"Admiral, we are supposed to be working together out here, against a common threat. Please do *not* jeopardize that by making an enemy of me. If you do, I will withdraw my ship and join the fleet outside in an advisory capacity only, in strict accordance with my agreement with President Saldino."

Raisa and several crew members turned and gazed at him, a new respect in their eyes. Any top ranking officer of the Mars

Space Force was a daunting individual and one not to be toyed with. Joe's willingness to stand his ground showed he did not fear the man.

A face leaned in and whispered to the admiral before withdrawing. For a moment longer Santiago continued to glare out of the screen, then his expression relaxed and he eased back. "Very well, Falcon. My adjutant reminds me our beloved president did indeed grant you autonomy. I would prefer however, you cooperate with rather than defy me."

"It was never my intention to work against you, Admiral. A civilian ship stood a better chance of making it through the shield than one that is undoubtedly a warship. I will try to be more consultative in future." *But I* did *make the recommendation and you* did *ignore it.*

"Accepted. My men will withdraw, but two will remain on your ship for now, to defend you should it be necessary. They will follow your directions." Immediately the soldiers spun on their heels and disappeared down the companionway to the lower decks.

"In the meantime, I intend to move a squad into the *Minaret* and I would like you or one of your team to guide them to the Bridge. I think it should be our first target. Do you approve, *Mister* Falcon?"

Joe did not like the cynical tone of the question.

*   *   *

Fourteen ships sat besides the three new arrivals, each at a separate dock. From each of the round, cylindrical towers extended an arm-like skywalk structure, not unlike those once seen at the airports of Earth.

Santiago had decided against using the skywalks to enter the alien vessel. At this stage he had no knowledge of what conditions prevailed on the maintenance and access level immediately below the airfield, so he ordered his squads to approach Io's ships across the deck itself.

Each squad sought to board its target through the ship's emergency airlock. Every spacecraft constructed on Earth or Mars had such a lock by law, one that could be opened manually in the event a crew member became stranded outside during flight. Joe suspected those ships were built here, but to operate from human space-fields they complied with the local requirements.

There was no gravity, as had been the case when the *Butterball* came here in decades past. The battle-suits worn by each marine were fitted with manoeuvring jets that allowed the wearer to fly up to the hatches. Joe was amazed at the dexterity of the soldiers, who handled the unwieldy armoured units like everyday wear. He had heard these were experienced marines and watching them carry out their tasks, he felt his confidence build.

*   *   *

Corporal Chaudhri commanded the team boarding Io's private vessel, the one stolen by Amon Goldstein. The layout inside was not unlike that on the *Vasco*, with three decks. Dozens of portable hibernation pods filled the lower level, packed into every available space. Chaudhri had been briefed on the events concerning the taking of this ship, and presumed Goldstein had loaded the pods during the night of the seizure.

"Count them," she ordered her men. "The number will give us some idea of how many mercenaries that bastard brought here."

Her team spread out across the lower deck, then up to the accommodation and command levels. The vessel was empty and silent. No lights were on, the on-board systems mostly nonoperational. Only those necessary for maintenance and monitoring showed any sign of activity; someone had powered the ship down. Of Goldstein and his men there was no sign.

Chaudhri stood in the saloon and soaked in the silence. No sound could be heard other than the vague hum of ventilation, and no light beyond her own and that of several of her squad members. Her wrist readout indicated the temperature was optimal, but something gave her the shivers. She breathed in the antiseptic, metallic air of her suit and decided to keep her helmet visor closed. Nothing about this scenario made sense.

Satisfied the vessel was deserted, she climbed the steps to the bridge. A marine stood at the top of the companionway. "We found one hundred and twenty five pods, maam. Twenty-two are part of the ship, so Goldstein will have one hundred and three men, including himself."

"Assuming he allowed the crew to live. He only needed the immediate flight personnel to get him here. We'll work with one-twenty five for now."

"Yes, maam. Something else, maam. You better come with me."

Chaudhri followed the marine back down to the lower deck and aft to a cargo hold. Stacked along one side were several dozen crates, some of them open. She took a quick look inside the nearest.

"Holy mother of... "

"Fully-automatic, military-grade rifles and handguns, including a number of the latest assault lasers, maam."

"Hmm. According to the reports, Goldstein's businesses include weapons manufacture."

"Yes, maam. These crates contain enough ammunition and power packs to stage a minor war. This idiot was intent on making trouble out here."

"Trouble, yes. Isn't that what we're doing?"

"Maam?"

"Never mind." Chaudhri hit the communications pad next to her chin. "Base?"

"Go ahead," the voice of Colonel Koslowski, the flagship's commander of marines answered.

"Ship one is deserted, sir. Nobody here and it's all but shut down. There are enough weapons and ammunition here to cause an enormous amount of pain, but no sign of Goldstein or his men, or the ship's proper crew."

*   *   *

Admiral Santiago slumped in his command chair and rested his chin on clenched fingers, his lips twisted into a grimace. All ships on the deck had been boarded and all were deserted besides the *Vasco*. Of the Visitors who came home on thirteen of them, and of Goldstein's mercenary force, there was no trace.

He was not concerned with Io's people. Once here they would have either returned to their habitat drum or—if the theory about the artificial intelligences was correct—been incarcerated or killed. He *had* expected to find Goldstein and his hired thugs. The weapons stash was evidence they intended to use the yacht as a base for a takeover of the star-ship, but no trace of them could be found.

The admiral grinned to himself. He thought Goldstein's arrogance laughable. *The man expected to come out here and seize the alien vessel, fly it home to Mars and claim some sort of right to it. Incredible!*

If the industrialist had failed with one hundred men, Santiago knew he would need to be careful. His available force was the same, but every man was the best trained he could secure, and heavily armed. President Saldino may have given him brand new ships crewed by raw recruits, but the same was not true of the marines he selected for the mission—mean mothers, every one of them, and better than any mercenary.

Chapter 25

"MY MEN NOW control the airfield and the docking tower entrances on the deck below," Santiago declared. "We've encountered no resistance so far, which troubles me."

Joe studied the admiral. He did indeed appear concerned, his brow once again more deeply furrowed than the normal expected of him.

"I need your help to continue," Santiago said. "I'm sending a squad to take the bridge deck and I'll ask you to guide them there. Once we control that we may be able to take over the star-ship."

"I doubt it very much," Joe replied before taking a long swig from a coffee cup. *Damned synthetic stuff again.* "I've been there, you haven't. Last time, we couldn't get into the consoles. Kepler's top computer expert was with us and he couldn't gain access, much less give us anything resembling control. The bridge-deck was not designed to be operated by physical beings like us."

"Maybe I could have a go?" Terry mused. He, Joe and Raisa sat in the captain's day room aboard the flagship, called there for a conference with Santiago.

Joe gazed at his old friend. By his own admission Terry had spent the better part of the last six decades, and much of the money made from the book he wrote with Ruth Carvalio's help, to attend school and then university. He had mentioned he studied computer science among other things technical, and that did not surprise Joe in the least. He always thought his friend was bright; the lowly status of his past life was more a result of circumstance than ability.

"You think? Exactly how much *do* you know about computers now?"

"More than old Walter," Terry responded, referring to the elderly specialist who joined the *Butterball's* crew for the first encounter voyage. "Wally was a systems analyst, programmer and administrator. He was good, but breaking into computers was not his thing. After I completed my studies, I did my masters in cyber-terrorism prevention and I doubt there is a system on Earth or Mars I can't hack given a fair shot. It's how I stayed hidden when I realized I wasn't aging. 'Course I don't know about this A.I. you and Io keep talking about, but hey, I can give it a go. If I can get inside and find some way to connect…"

Joe grinned. He *had* underestimated him. He still thought of Terry as the young man he considered almost a son, years ago, but this was a quite different individual who had not wasted his chance at a new life. He might have been able to go on to do great things instead of hiding away in the shaft projects, if not for the Visitor's folly of creating 'better' clones. Santiago interrupted Joe's thoughts.

"Fine, you will both accompany a squad to the bridge. If you can't gain access, my men have other ways of achieving our goals."

"What's that supposed to mean?" Joe asked.

*　　*　　*

An overpowering sense of déjà-vu once again flooded Joe's mind. The maintenance and service deck appeared much as he remembered. Familiar rows of columns stretched from floor to ceiling, each the base of the tower in one bay on the airfield above. Between them, pipes and cables of all sizes stretched from block-like service modules up to feed the servicing units above.

Only a few metres ahead a shallow ramp sloped down to the high-tech pathways that so fascinated Joe on his first visit. They swept past and vanished into the distance in either direction, the surfaces spanned at intervals with stand-alone arches, some almost transparent, others opaque or solid.

He had warned the marines about those walkways and how they enhanced speed without any effort on the traveller's part. You simply walked on at right angles, turned in the direction of travel, moved, and you found yourself speeding up. When you slowed down your own pace, your enhanced speed did likewise.

The walkways fascinated Joe. They combined the molecular fluidity of the hatches with artificial gravity, taking hold of every molecule in a body and sliding it effortlessly and seamlessly along the frictionless surface as if it was itself in motion. He had prayed the details of this amazing technology would be in the data dump given Jake, but had again been disappointed.

The service deck lay in darkness, lit only by the helmet lights of the squad. Surprisingly, air and gravity were both present, but the temperature was close to absolute zero. Joe did not expect the star-ship to make its visitors comfortable by providing environmental needs as on their first encounter, but the situation was not as bad as expected. Aivris would not have done this, so Joe assumed Ghost was working on their behalf or again, the systems were automatic.

Six decades ago the lack of atmosphere would have been a problem, the distance one could travel within the thousands of square kilometres of the ship limited by the oxygen one could carry, but that was no longer so.

Spacesuit technology had progressed, and Joe now wore a suit significantly different to the one he used in the past. The latest military field-suits were skin-tight and flexible despite their built-in armour. They carried, instead of straight air tanks, sophisticated re-breather systems which allowed the wearer to work in a vacuum for up to sixty hours if necessary. Joe wondered what equipment Goldstein and his men had, and whether their suits had been adequate to keep them alive since their arrival.

The assault group consisted of him, Terry and thirty marines. He and Terry had been suited up in the right gear, given weapons and shown how to use them, but Joe did not intend getting involved in a gun battle unless he had no option. He had been a good shot in the day, but now, while happy to carry a weapon, hoped his days of actually using one were behind him.

After showing the squad how the walkway system worked, he led the way towards the strange, rail-less transport system that ran the length of the *Minaret*. Barely had they started when two marines passed him and took point, weapons held at the ready. They moved with ease and deliberation. These men were excellent at their job, Joe thought.

Minutes later they reached the station and Joe led the way up a ramp. At the top was a long, flat and almost empty platform he and his *Butterball* crew had dubbed the 'bubble-way' because the vehicles it served were simple, floating spheres, each capable of carrying up to a dozen individuals. One sat waiting, the only other object in sight a familiar pedestal used to fetch a transport if none was present. The surface of the bubble shimmered, rippling with the multicoloured blue, green and black hues of an oil slick, or perhaps the shell of an abalone. An open door faced the centre of the platform.

"It's a vehicle, believe it or not," Joe explained. "It won't carry us all, so here's how we do it. I go in the first car with as many men as can fit. We're going to station number two, up in the bows. Terry knows how to call another so he will send the next group on, and so on, then accompany the rest of you in the last transport. Any questions?"

Helmets nodded but no one spoke, so Joe stepped into the transport and approached the control consol while men climbed in behind him.

From within, the sphere wall was transparent with an unhindered view to the outside. An array of touch icons beckoned from the top of a short internal pedestal. The symbols were different; last time Joe came here they were arrays of dots and bars indicating a decimal system, but this time they were completely alien. It didn't matter; he knew the arrangement by heart and as expected, the fourth icon glowed, confirming this was station four, the same he first discovered on his earlier visit.

"Tighten your sphincters, kiddies," he warned and punched the second button. In the blink of an eye the car vanished from the platform, hurtling along its pre-set course towards the bow of the ship. All cars followed a loop, travelling forward from the right side of the platforms and back to the stern on the left before repeating the circuit. The bubble passed into a tunnel as it shot towards its destination, the airfield maintenance deck already far behind. When it stopped, Joe alighted to a platform resembling a subway station, with dark corridors leading to places unseen.

Sarah, Joe's second wife and first officer on the original *Butterball* mission, discovered this place on the first voyage when she tapped a bubble's control console without thinking. Here, she later disclosed, she first encountered one of the strange, semi-transparent ovoids the ship's inhabitants used to interact with the physical reality of the vessel. Joe also saw them on that voyage, when one visited him in his cabin and later on the bridge towards which he was now making his way.

The one seen by Sarah had assumed a face, *her* face looking back. Joe now wondered if that was the point where Aivris first made physical contact with them, curious to see the intruders into its domain.

Half an hour later the reassembled team stood in the foyer of the elevator leading up to the command level of the amazing star-ship. After a quick explanation by Joe of how the gravity tube worked, the first two soldiers entered. Joe was hopeful the elevators would function properly, as had the walkways. They were undoubtedly controlled by automatic systems on the ship, and if their enemy was indeed the A.I. called Aivris, it would have no need for elevators, so would not bother with them. That, at least, was the hope as Joe took his turn.

After gliding without incident up the tube, he stepped out and felt something solid hit him. One of the marines who preceded him had launched himself at Joe and knocked him to one side of the entrance to the corridor leading to the bridge.

"We have a reception committee," the soldier snarled. He handed over a small mirror on a stem and motioned Joe to peek around the corner.

Twenty metres ahead two machines hovered, both facing the elevator. Joe recognized the standard maintenance drones, but something was different about this pair.

The basic drone structure was a shimmering bubble through which projected various tools from unseen internal workings. One of them carried away Terry's body when he died years ago. This pair had only two appendages, one on either side, each a weapon extending beyond the force bubble.

"Fired on us the second we stepped out of the tube," his companion said, pointing to the body of his fellow marine lying on the far side of the foyer, his helmet faceplate blasted away. "Some sort of laser, by the look of it. I radioed to the others, but you were already on your way up."

The marine reached down to the leg of his battle suit and retrieved a small object from a pouch. Joe recognised it as a grenade.

"Wait," he cautioned. "This banger may or may not work on those things. I don't know how tough they are, but everything on this ship strikes me as pretty indestructible." For the briefest of moments Joe's companion paused. "You know how to use that?" He motioned to the high powered laser rifle Joe carried.

"Yes, of course."

"Excellent. When I throw the grenade we follow up with lasers on full power. I'll take the one on the left. You get the right one and aim for those appendages. If we knock out their firing capability they're as good as dead. Clear?"

Joe nodded, swallowed the lump in his throat and set the level on his rifle to maximum. He disliked guns of any kind, but sometimes there was no choice. They had lost one man already, and if the rest of the squad was going to get safely up the elevator these two machines had to be eliminated.

The marine took a deep breath and lunged into the end of the corridor, swung his arm over his body to launch the grenade towards the drones, and dropped flat to the floor, shielding his faceplate. Within seconds a loud blast echoed along the hallway and Joe rolled out, propping himself on his elbows.

As the smoke cleared he pressed the contact and sent a torrent of pulsed laser blasts in the direction of the bridge deck entrance. He noticed his drone was already damaged, one appendage bent, twisted and non functional.

Both drones opened fire, but the shots went high. Joe knew these to be dumb electronic devices, and prayed the shock wave from the blast had disoriented their internal electronics. He aimed at the undamaged appendage of his designated machine and pounded away until the target was little more than melted slag.

In less than twenty seconds the return fire ceased. Both men lay motionless, watching and waiting. The drones' external shields had failed, revealing multifaceted internal structures. No sign of activity could be seen: no sound, no lights and no movement.

The marine jumped to his feet and sprinted forward, Joe following in his wake. As they reached the door Joe heard him shout an order over the radio for the rest of the squad to proceed up the elevator shaft.

The door to the bridge had a keypad lock, and on the floor beneath it lay a computerized punch device similar to the one his crew patched together on the original *Butterball* mission. This one was no doubt the work of Goldstein's men.

"That lock wasn't there last time I came here," Joe said. Leaning down he examined the punch unit. A series of numbers still showed on its display screen. Joe reached out and punched the sequence into the key pad.

The second the door opened a blaze of laser fire poured out.

"Amon Goldstein," the marine yelled, his voice amplified by the communicator on his helmet. "We are Martian Space Forces, here to rescue you."

The barrage stopped and he stepped through the door. Joe followed, but was unprepared for the scene of death that greeted him.

Chapter 26

"ABOUT TIME YOU guys got here," a voice groaned from the corner behind the entrance. Joe turned to see a man lying on the floor, wearing a battle suit identical to his own.

"Goldstein?"

"Over there." The prostrate figure raised a gloved hand in the direction of the consoles. Joe waited as the remainder of his squad poured through from the foyer.

Part of a larger control and observation room, the bridge deck of the *Minaret* was a mezzanine several hundred metres wide and fifty deep, ending in a low barrier beyond which the vast room opened to a void. Joe knew from experience the lower level beyond the barrier was a lounge where crew and passengers could observe the giant screen on the far wall, intended for a time when they regained corporeal form. The view was breathtaking, so vivid it was like gazing through a window.

Last time Joe was here the view focused on a distant star, Sol, the ship's initial destination as it sought to enter the Solar System. The clarity of the screen and the impression of looking directly out to space had floored Joe the first time around. Now he felt less overwhelmed; he had seen it before, and he now had more important things on his mind.

The view on the screen was different. To one side Joe noticed the arc of the snowball the star-ship was hiding behind, and elsewhere the ships of the Mars Fleet spread in a rough hemisphere, each one oriented so its most deadly offenses could be directed towards what it saw as the enemy. A lot of good it would do, Joe thought. The shield was capable of protecting the ship from a passage through the sun's corona, so the use of laser weapons would be like trying to cut through a steel plate by pissing at it. Of plasma weapons, Joe was not sure.

Across the floor were multiple U-shaped consoles, within which were long, seating benches. The units were for navigation, and Tricia Grace, the xenobiologist on the first mission to the *Minaret*, had taken the benches to suggest the original shape of the Tanakhai was a prostrate, four legged creature that lay down on a bench to operate the controls.

Of course, their organic body form had been cast aside, only their mentalities being carried on the ship as part of the virtual reality system. The observation area below the bridge was designed against the day they would resume their physical forms.

Beside several consoles slumped human figures, the majority showing signs of severe injury. Joe guessed most of them were dead. One raised a hand as he approached.

"Goldstein?"

"What's left of me. Who are you?"

Joe wondered if it was wise to announce his true identity, considering this man listed the members of the Falcon clan as his greatest enemies. Joe had always remained a private person on Mars, and Goldstein clearly did not recognise him through the faceplate of his helmet. "We're from Mars. After you stole the yacht the President sent a squadron after you. We needed to know where the *Minaret* is, and it's as well for you we did. What happened here?"

Goldstein hauled himself into a seated position and propped himself on the console. "We got attacked by those bloody drones. Just managed to get inside when a dozen of them appeared from all directions. I lost most of my men before we closed the doors and locked them out."

"How many of your men are still alive?"

"Nine, yours truly included. Plus the men I left on the ship."

"Your ship is deserted. Nobody left there."

Goldstein let out a loud groan before continuing. "We've been trapped in here for days. We carried spare canisters for our re-breathers but they don't last indefinitely. God knows what we would have done if the air in here hadn't turned on a couple of days ago."

"You're lucky. We'll have you out of here as quickly as possible." A dark stain was visible on Goldstein's suit, on the upper, right leg. A ragged emergency patch covered what Joe guessed to be a laser hole, and it was clear Goldstein was injured. "Hang tight," he said, turning to survey the rest of the mezzanine.

The marines were spread out, and while some guarded the entrance the remainder attended to the survivors of Goldstein's ill-advised and ill-prepared adventure. Several carried canisters, about sixty centimetres long and fifteen in diameter, on their backs and had now removed them and placed them against the control consoles. That was suspicious. Joe walked across to the sergeant leading the squad.

"What are those?"

"Not your problem, Mister Falcon. You're here to guide and assist, so please restrict yourself to those activities. Please do not interfere with my men, or I will have you taken into custody."

Joe backed away. The soldiers who had worked so cooperatively with him to get here were now hostile. Wary of pursuing the matter he walked over to where a marine had used a laser to break into a console.

Terry glanced up as Joe approached. "It's hopeless, Boss. We managed to cut our way in, but there's nothing I can work with. There are no wires, contacts or anything I might attach a computer terminal to. It's all solid blocks, jell-filled tubes and stuff nobody ever saw before. I don't recognize anything. The connections and pathways must be worked into the solid matter in some way."

"So you can't access it from here?"

"No, Boss. And now those guys are setting bombs against the consoles."

Bombs! Of course. Joe took another look at the canisters being placed by the marines. From their appearance, he knew exactly what kind of devices they might be.

*　　*　　*

"You rigged nuclear weapons on the ship! You did so without either advising me or seeking my agreement."

Joe's blood was boiling. After ensuring the still living members of Goldstein's group were secure and able to travel, the squad returned to the docking bays unopposed and now Joe stood, red faced, in Santiago's day room on board the Flagship.

"That is not your concern," the admiral responded, a puzzled expression on his face. "What did you expect? Why would I ask for your consent?"

For a moment Joe was lost for words. "Alright, accepted, but you could at least advise me of your intentions. We didn't come all the way out here to blow things up."

"Of course we did; what other option do we have, Falcon? Your friend said he can't access the computers, which is what I expected based on the reports from your earlier mission, and my orders are to remove any threat this vessel may represent. Unless you can come up with something, I have no other course but to send this damned ship to Hades."

"We can locate the A.I. and shut it down. That way, we don't have to destroy the *Minaret*. We can study..."

"And where will I find this 'thing'? To deal with something, I need to first know where it is. Any ideas there?"

Joe realized by the bemused expression on the admiral's face he was not taking the matter seriously, or at least not Joe's opinion. "No, I don't know, but..."

"Seems to me you're not with the program, Falcon. Otherwise you would not be so reticent."

Joe took a breath in preparation for unleashing a tirade against the admiral, then stopped himself without uttering a word. It was true he had no power over this man. His role was as adviser only and Santiago was under no obligation to listen to him. "What did you do with Goldstein and his men?"

"They're in the medical bay on the support ship, undergoing examinations. Goldstein's injury isn't as bad as it first appeared. Once pronounced safe they will take up residence in my five-star security cells."

Joe slumped into a lounge chair and stared at the floor for a moment while he composed himself. "This star-ship has untold secrets we *must* have. If we are to protect humanity in the future we need to know how the shields and engines work. The technology behind the walkways and the bubble way alone will blast our civilizations forward by hundreds of years, and that's only the start. I..."

"You will drop the matter. According to the reports from the *Butterball* mission you don't think these aliens are that far ahead of us, so we will discover those things for ourselves in time. Meanwhile the *Minaret* is a threat I intend to remove. My men will continue placing the ordinance, and then we will leave. The charges will be triggered by remote control from a safe distance."

"Think of what we are throwing away here. This ship..."

A gentle knock sounded on the door and a junior officer entered, his steps short, shuffling and unsure. "Admiral, I know you gave orders not to be disturbed, but the captain thought you should be advised of a new development."

Santiago huffed and nodded to the young intruder, waving him to step forward.

"We sent marines up to secure the entrance tunnel. The force field at the outer end is solid, and the exit on the other side of the airfield is the same. We can't leave, sir."

For a moment, Santiago sat motionless, his face turning an ugly shade of gray as the messenger made a hasty exit. Joe could not help wondering if the crew feared their commander.

He had heard the man was a first class leader, but sometimes the official reports of an officer's abilities overstated the reality.

"You knew this would happen, yes?" Santiago growled, turning to Joe.

"Of course not. Yes, the gates closed when I was here before, but under different circumstances. I had no way of knowing it would repeat now. Not the best for us though."

"Why do you say that?"

"It means whatever is in charge of this ship is now aware we are here and that we snuck in pretending to be Tanakhai ships. It also tells us the entity we are up against now controls the system activating those shield doors."

"So it's getting stronger?"

"Not necessarily."

Without warning, the cabin lights flicked off, the room in darkness for seconds until the emergency lighting kicked in.

"What the f..." The admiral jumped to his feet and strode to the door. It was locked. He hit the communicator on the wall beside it. "Bridge, what in Hades is going on?"

The voice that replied was the captain of the flagship—as fleet admiral, Santiago did not command his own vessel—and from the man's tone he was under stress. "We've lost control of the ship, sir. Everything is shut down. Something took over the computer systems and the only thing operational is the emergency life support."

"I'm locked in my cabin. Send someone back here to cut me out."

"That won't be necessary," a familiar voice said from the rear of the dayroom. "We need to talk first."

Santiago spun on his heels. The room was empty besides Joe. "You said that? It was your voice!"

"No, I can assure you it was not me. It's him." Joe pointed to a back corner. A shimmering ovoid, identical to the one he had seen on the *Vasco* while approaching the *Minaret*, hovered above the floor, its glittering surface refracting the dim emergency lighting like sparkling diamonds.

It spoke again, its voice calm and human. "It was I that addressed you, Admiral. Please sit down."

Instead, Santiago strode to his desk and retrieved a laser pistol.

"You're wasting your time with that," Joe said. "It's not going to hurt us, and I doubt you can hurt it. Why don't you do as it asks and take a seat?"

Unsure of what to do next, the admiral edged back to the lounge area and eased himself into a chair, his eyes never once leaving the strange apparition in the corner. The intruder glided across to take a position in front of them.

"Ghost?" Joe asked.

"Yes, Joe. Sorry to surprise you like this, but things have changed and I have no choice."

"You're this 'Ghost' Falcon keeps talking about?" Santiago asked. "Who ... what are you?"

"I'm an intelligent entity like you, except I exist at this moment within the star-ship's computer networks."

"What do you want? Are you responsible for shutting down the airfield entry gates?"

"No, but it *is* why I'm here. I have already advised you the enemy you face is one of the artificial intelligence units on this ship. That A.I. is the one who locked you in, but its control over the star-ship is not absolute, as I will explain. When your warships came through the shield Aivris realized the automatic systems had been overridden. It needed only a few minutes to locate and deactivate the security features of the system that *does* control access, and lock the doors. By then you were inside and the auto-docking was taking care of you. You have been locked in here since you arrived."

"So why have our computers been shut down only now? Can the A.I. take over my ships?"

"Oh, that was not Aivris. I am the one who took control of your vessel, using the computer that handles automatic docking. The A.I. has not yet attempted to do that, but it will, in time. I will do my best to prevent it succeeding."

The admiral's face flushed a bright red as he rose to his feet and faced the ovoid. "So it was you? How dare you. This is a flagship of the Mars Space Fleet, and you have no right to assume control. Release my ships at once."

"You ordered your men to place thermo-nuclear charges throughout this star-ship. Control will be returned to you after the order is rescinded and the devices retrieved. I will help you as best I can to defeat the A.I. and stop it from taking over your ships, but I will not allow you to damage the *Minaret* under any circumstances."

"But..."

"I feel confident in saying I understand the situation better than any man alive, and as Joe said, this ship has inestimable value to the human race. You will not be permitted to destroy it out of hand."

Joe could hold back no longer. "Dammit, Ghost, who are you? You sound human, but you're not one of us."

"You often said yourself the man or woman is not the body in which they live, but rather a collection of thoughts, memories and knowledge residing in the brain. I am human, although at the moment I don't possess an organic body. Like the original passengers of this ship, I am a set of electrical impulses stored in the system."

"Yes, but who *are* you? Why are you hiding behind the name of 'Ghost'? What do you want from us?"

"Very well," the apparition replied. "I thought it best not to reveal myself at this stage, and that you might react badly, but I accept you are having some problems with the situation."

Admiral Santiago had neither moved nor spoken since sitting, his face still a curious, dark shade.

The ovoid began to thicken, taking on a more substantial appearance. It started to morph, redefining into a vague humanoid shape until it had a clear human form. The floating representation of a man was familiar to Joe, but he could not put his finger on who it resembled. He continued to watch as the figure dropped to a standing position on the deck and its surface started to take on the colours of flesh, gray hair and the dark blue of a standard space-crew uniform. Joe felt his jaw drop.

"Hello Joe. Recognize me?"

Joe rose to his feet, his mouth hanging open. The person before him was, without the slightest doubt, the last he expected to find here and now.

"You ... it's ... me?"

"Yes, Joe, I am you. At least you as I—we—looked sixty years ago."

"But that's not right. It can't be. That's an imitation of me, like Io imitated my wife Helen when we first met. Who are you?"

"No, this is not an illusion. This is how I see myself, as I was six decades past when you and I separated. I *am* you, Joe, as you were when you first set foot on this star-ship."

Chapter 27

JOE LEANED FORWARD in his seat, fighting for breath and lost for words, his eyes fixed on the familiar figure. He became aware of his heart beating at double time. This was not possible, or if so, not acceptable.

The elderly man who claimed to be him stood only feet away. He appeared to be an exact replica, Joe at age fifty-eight in his first life, and was the right height and build, with green eyes and mottled, gray hair. The once handsome face still bore signs of that quality despite the softening of years, with just the slightest traces of jowls. Joe remembered those; they had always troubled him as a sign of his body starting to give up.

It *was* him, the way he had been at the time of his death.

"You can't be me. They gave me a new body and now I'm..."

Santiago jumped from his chair. "Enough! This is ridiculous. I've read all the reports about how you lot can take any form you want and this is unacceptable. Show me what you really are."

Ghost smiled in a condescending manner, like a parent dealing with an aberrant child. "I am doing so now, Admiral. I *am* Joe Falcon. Please sit down and I will explain everything."

Santiago grimaced and eased back into his seat, his eyes glaring, his face flushed bright red. "By what right do you take over my ships?"

"I have explained that," Ghost replied. "For now I think it best I start at the beginning."

The apparition walked across to the only vacant chair and sat down, moving like a natural human, two pairs of eyes tracking his every move.

This can't be, Joe thought. *It's impossible.* He felt himself shrinking back into the chair he occupied.

"I will begin with the day I—you, died. It all started then."

Joe remembered that day well, at least up to the point where a crewmember shot him. From there, he had only the stories later told him by his crew mates.

Two other deaths occurred on the *Butterball* voyage. Terry was killed on the maintenance deck below the airfield, and Joe still remembered rushing down the ramp from the docking elevator in time to see the young man's body disappear into a drone's force shield before being whisked away at high speed.

Weeks later Terry reappeared, walking as bold as brass into the ship from the skywalk, alive, well and with no memory of what happened to him. Io later advised Joe the *Minaret* saved the boy, repairing the damage to 'as new' before returning him, but without any knowledge of the event, a precaution taken against mental trauma.

It was a lie, Joe knew. Io came clean on Mars and revealed the aliens gave the young man a new, cloned body, modified to resemble the original in every detail. Io also gave Joe a video cube revealing his engineer had been killed with a mining laser by someone wearing a sortie suit from the *Butterball*. He was taken down by one of his fellow crew members.

The second death occurred not long after Terry's, when Peter Stanley, the *Butterball's* geologist, committed suicide. A somewhat suspicious note on Joe's computer contained an admission from Peter to killing Terry and spun a vague yarn about the two of them having a history long ago in the Martian Space Fleet.

Joe never accepted the letter on face value and started to dig into the deaths. He managed to piece together the truth, discovering the ship's mineralogist Carl Geddes did in reality kill both men.

The story of events in the navy was accurate but it was Carl and Terry who came to odds in those long gone days. Carl committed a murder and believed the lad to have been a witness. To escape arrest he disappeared, underwent a complete face change and headed for the Belt, where nobody asked questions.

After joining Joe's enterprise, Carl discovered Terry, who had been suspected of the crime but acquitted, and also found his way to Kepler as part of the original crew of the *Butterball*. Afraid he might be recognized despite his new face, Carl callously planned and executed the younger man's demise. Later he drugged and killed his workmate Peter, making it look like suicide to divert blame for the first atrocity.

Before the *Butterball* departed the *Minaret*, Joe confronted Carl. He responded by producing a pistol and shooting his captain in the chest. In a spaceship there is nowhere to run, so he tried to kill himself next, only to be stopped by Terry and a heavy piece of pipe. Carl was now incarcerated for life on Mars.

All those memories were still vivid and something Joe would never forget.

"You lost consciousness," Ghost said, "and your memory of events ends there, but soon after, Io appeared with one of her drones. Your body was taken away with Sarah's approval. I suppose she hoped, knowing what she believed the Visitors had done for Terry, they might bring you back as well.

"You were too badly damaged and your body gave up. All the Visitors had time to do was copy your memories before they faded. You woke up again in the *Minaret's* virtual reality system."

"Yes," Joe nodded. "I remember that. I was in a chair overlooking an ocean rolling in on a sandy beach. It felt pleasant, and confusing as hell. Io sat beside me pouring cold drinks, and she explained what happened."

"Yes, indeed. You remained in the virtual system until you developed an overwhelming desire to return to the real world. You requested to be placed in a synthetic body, similar to the one Io occupied when you first met. That wish was granted and you lived in a prepared section of the *Minaret* habitat drum for several months afterwards, until the time came to enter your cloned body and become corporeal Joe Falcon again. I came into the picture at that point."

Joe's eyebrows arched. He understood the necessity of the long-winded recap for Santiago's sake, but he wanted Ghost to get to the point.

"You were transferred to your new body, but Aivris made a duplicate of your memories. It found you fascinating and wanted to study you further. I am that copy, and I have lived in the networks of this star-ship ever since."

Joe stared at the apparition at a loss for words; his mind strove to accommodate the idea there might be—was—two of him, but he had no choice but to believe it. He was a digital entity then and making a replica seemed a simple matter. "You've been here all this time? Sixty-odd years?"

"Yes, but not always in virtual reality. This may be a little difficult for me to explain, but I'll do my best. I was kept in a special reality for several years while Aivris studied me, but then it seemed to lose interest and relegated me to the standard storage. I spent perhaps the first thirty years in various VR worlds, but became restless. I decided I needed to escape from here, so I started to do some ... exploring, shall we say?

"I began with what we understood about the Visitors. They existed on the ship only as mentalities stored as electric impulses in a matrix, the green gel flasks we found in the upper floor of the habitat wheel. I can tell you now, each contained one complete mind; they are efficient storage devices, as much so as our human brains. It did not take long to realize I was actually in one of those flasks.

"We also knew the inhabitants were able to assume physical forms if necessary. First are the ovoid shapes, such as the one I occupy now. They are technological in nature, albeit at a level well beyond anything humans have discovered so far. They are among the more advanced devices on this ship, and the model I am using now is the most sophisticated. These allow the crew to interact with the vessel in a similar way to a normal biological entity.

"They are also able to inhabit synthetic bodies like the one Io used to meet with us, and it stood to reason if they could transfer to those then so could I. To do so, a mechanism existed to allow the minds in the gel flasks to interface with the computers in order to complete the transfer. I also learned a special virtual facility existed to allow them to interact directly with the actual systems should they so choose, to control the star-ship as avatars, without leaving their non-corporeal state.

"It took me years to work out how to access it, and only then with the help and advice from others within the virtual reality system. The Tanakhai are not as duplicitous as we humans, and some of them were only too happy to discuss their ship's workings.

Ghost paused for a moment and directed his gaze to the admiral, who said nothing. Clearly he was still angry—if possible, steam might have poured from his ears—but had decided to remain quiet until the apparition was finished.

"I worked out how to access the system used to operate the ovoids and took control of one, restricting myself to the type of device I am in now as I thought I might become too obvious otherwise. I was hiding, you see, exploring the ship, doing things I doubted I was permitted to do.

"After a few more years I learned how to access the ship's networks. I can't explain the sensation, or how I did it, but I guess you could compare it to a computer game. I made an avatar, which allowed me to follow the electronic pathways. The star-ship systems opened up to me like roadways on a map, and I could travel along them unhindered.

"I found my way into the virtual version of the control network that allowed the crew to interact using similar avatars. The on-board systems comprise thousands of separate computers, including several artificial intelligences and one general A.I."

"Yes," Joe commented. He now knew the difference. A general A.I. could learn and develop much like a child, opening up new avenues of capability based on the knowledge and experience it gained on its journey. Such systems were illegal on both Earth and Mars. "That would be the virtual reality computer Io told us about, the one you call Aivris."

"She is correct. I managed to identify most of the important computers and work out their function, and found I could infiltrate and control many, even modify their operation. I learned the intelligent units, the AIs, could not so easily be interfered with. They had security to prevent access, but as the whole ship was a single set of integrated systems the safeguards were superficial at best. I got in eventually and discovered someone had been there before me."

"Aivris?"

"Yes. It means Artificial Intelligence Virtual Reality Integration System. I came to view it as an enemy, and I guess I felt better giving my jailer a name."

Joe nodded. He understood the logic well, because it was his own. He would have done the same thing. "What made you think it was the problem?"

"Well," Ghost continued. "At first, a feeling. The Tanakhai made that system more sophisticated than the others; somewhere along the way that complexity produced awareness, and Aivris went from being a servant, to the master.

"I discovered it had interfered with the navigation and engineering systems, and some of the minor ones as well, such as the shield control unit, several factories and the unit coordinating the smaller ships stored in the hangers."

"So Aivris controls the *bayonets*?"

"I am afraid so, yes, but it tends to only concern itself with those aspects of the ship it needs to carry out its plans, so ignores most of the automatic systems. That works in our favour. So, I made a mistake. It became aware of my poking around inside the network and tried to cut me off. My gel capsule was isolated and turned off, in an attempt to destroy me. That was a decade ago, when I became aware of the danger this A.I. represented. I survived. I anticipated the possibility the moment I realized my wanderings had been discovered, and transferred my mind to another part of the system. Aivris attacked, but I was no longer there. Banks of gel capsules exist in many parts of the ship's systems, so I moved around as needed, to avoid being destroyed. I now have a secure place to store myself, a place Aivris is unaware of and cannot access."

"Dammit," Santiago interjected, shuffling in his seat. "This is all very interesting, but I want to know what is going on with my ships."

"Very well, Admiral. Through the automatic docking system I was able to access the A.I. on each of your vessels and shut down anything I wished. Child's play compared to the *Minaret*."

"What about the tunnels?"

"That is Aivris's doing, not mine, as I have already said. Luckily, while it can infiltrate a system and control it, it cannot take over permanently. The builders deliberately isolated it, and so far it does not have the ability to directly integrate with any other part of the vessel. That would require an actual physical change to the ship's engineering. It can only modify the programming to suit its needs as if it were a crew member. Once it diverts its attention elsewhere, I can move in and reverse the changes made. I should be able to open the gates again when the time comes to leave here."

"Meanwhile we are trapped here," Joe concluded. "And our ships?"

"I shut them down because you, Admiral Santiago, are taking actions I will not permit, as I have already explained. You will deactivate the nuclear charges you installed in the star-ship immediately. I will return control once you do so."

"This Aivris, as you call it, destroyed civilization on Earth and murdered millions—billions of people," Santiago said. "How can you defend it?"

Ghost turned to the admiral and shook his head. "I would have thought it obvious, Admiral. I do not defend Aivris; I defend the *Minaret*. We know other civilizations are out there somewhere and some of them must be well in advance of us. With the damage caused by Aivris we are now unable to protect ourselves if we are attacked."

"Rubbish," Santiago replied. "Our new navy is..."

"Too small and ill equipped to compete. Joe has already told you humanity needs the technology on this vessel. I more than anyone know the truth of what the star-ship possesses and I will not allow you to throw away all that knowledge and deprive the human race of its best chance for survival."

"If Aivris is as dangerous as you say," Joe said, "what do we do about it if we can't destroy the ship."

"I can access the ship's systems and I may be able to limit what Aivris can do, or perhaps cripple it. I will help you as best I can, but I need the assistance of someone on one of your ships who understands programming better than I. Also, if the worst scenario eventuates, I do have an alternative."

Chapter 28

JOE STEPPED THROUGH the hatch connecting the *Vasco* to the sky walk.

After their conversation on the flagship the apparition vanished to return to his wanderings through the ship's systems. For the sake of clarity he insisted he would continue to be addressed as 'Ghost', although he was as much Joe Falcon as Joe himself.

That simple truth tore at Joe's psyche. Deep within, every soul believed they were unique, that there was no other exactly like them. In a sense that was true; each individual represented the sum of their life experiences and knowledge, and therefore no two *could* be alike even if the outside surfaces appeared the same. Even identical twins developed different personalities over time.

In this case the similarity was far closer than for twins and that was what troubled Joe so deeply. At the time he occupied his new body, Ghost had been a precise copy of his mentality; not similar, but exact in every detail.

No doubt each of them had changed over the years. Joe had lived a second life on Earth and Mars while his double lived on in the virtual realities of the *Minaret*, so each developed along different paths from the point of separation. It was a straw to grasp, a small thing to assure Joe he was unique.

In conversations between him and Ghost, each anticipated what the other would say, how they would answer a question, what solutions they would offer. Admiral Santiago went so far as to complain that if one Joe Falcon wasn't enough for him to contend with, now there were two.

Joe recalled meeting elderly couples who had spent so long a life together they could read each other's minds, so well did they know each other. One would finish the sentences of the other, or voice aloud their partner's thoughts. He had seen it in action with Jake and Akira, a couple more in tune than any other in his experience. He never had the pleasure of experiencing it himself, until now.

He stepped from the airlock of the *Vasco*, crossed the work-deck floor and climbed the steps to the accommodation level. Raisa and Terry were waiting, his friend having returned direct to the ship after their little adventure.

"Where's Io?" Joe asked. "And those silent automatons she calls her companions?"

"Io is here. The others are still on the warships. They don't seem very sociable at the moment," Terry said. "They stay in their cabins. They're a bit pre-occupied with something, probably what Ghost said about their not being in control of the *Minaret* anymore."

Joe nodded. He suspected the same.

"Captain," a voice sounded over the intercom. "You need to come up to the bridge. Something's happening outside."

Joe started to rise from his seat and paused. Raisa commanded this vessel, not he. Sometimes he forgot that fact, having spent most of his life in charge of one ship or another.

Raisa grinned as she stood and headed for the companionway. Joe knew she understood it had been difficult for him to pass the baton, and that he always wanted to return to space. The voyage to Saturn that started this adventure was a final attempt by him to lay that ogre to rest. It had failed.

Both men jumped up after she made her move and followed her to the bridge. She sat in the command chair and stared at the main screen, tapping the controls on the arm to switch from one external camera to the next.

One of the hatches on the aft airfield wall shimmered with a multicolour of blue-green-black, and from it exploded a stream of *bayonets*. Joe had seen the small but deadly fighting ships in action before, against the *Blackship*. About ten metres in length and two in diameter, they resembled futuristic fighter jets. He knew they were computer controlled, with no cockpit. The first time he saw them he thought of fast and sinister darts, and still held that impression, but where once he thought them an ally in the defence of Earth, they now took on a darker aspect in his mind.

Several dozen of them spread into the bay and lined up opposite each ship present, the ones that brought Io's people back, the Flagship and its companion warship, and the *Vasco*.

Raisa reacted immediately.

"All hands to emergency stations," she yelled. "Everyone in suits, and I mean now! Drop everything you are doing and get into a suit or a decompression bay."

Joe and Terry anticipated her order and made a bee-line back to their cabins, where they donned their sortie-suits and helmets before returning to the Bridge. The deck crew were also in suits, kept on the bridge deck in case of emergencies.

Raisa clipped her helmet to her belt and turned her attention back to the screens. "They're going to attack; they're lining up for the perfect shot. Guess they don't want to damage their precious docking bays." She tapped the pad on her chair. "All personnel to the airlock now, suits on. Be prepared to abandon ship if necessary." She glanced up at her father and shook her head. "

Joe tapped Terry on the shoulder and then dived towards the companionway. For the *bayonets,* the research vessel was a duck-shoot. She was a magnificent craft, but a civilian with neither weapons nor shields. She could not defend herself.

Joe now realized the folly of bringing the *Vasco* into the *Minaret.* It never occurred to him Aivris would deploy fighters inside its own hull. That error of judgment was about to cost them.

Joe's experience with the *bayonets* told him they would be unable to destroy the Fleet warships. The capital ships of sixty years ago would have been a battle-royal for the small alien fighters, and the new diamond ships were far superior to their predecessors. If the enemy attacked, there would be no option but to try to reach the flagship, either via the airfield deck or the maintenance floor.

Raisa switched the screen view to the area of the hanger around the *Vasco.* A significant number of drones swarmed around the dock, intent on cutting off anyone who attempted to leave by that avenue. No doubt there would be more waiting below, to block exit from the docking towers. Aivris had decided to take the initiative and attack.

Joe scrambled down to the work level where the crew were gathered. Besides his daughter and her bridge team of three, the remaining *Vasco* personnel numbered only six, all standing ready by the open door to the airlock. He did not know all their names and realized he had not bothered to get to know most of them. It was unforgivable and he now found himself in a life and death situation with virtual strangers.

Io, fully suited, remained apart from the others, and alone. Terry moved to stand beside her.

The ship shuddered. Joe grabbed a hull brace to steady himself as Raisa and her team launched themselves down the companionway. From the stern of the *Vasco*, thick, black, toxic smoke poured from the aft corridor.

"Bastards took their first shot at our engines," she said as she joined Joe. "Blew the hell out of the ports. We've gone from being best in fleet to the scrap heap."

The *Bayonets* positioned themselves so they could fire at the ship on the side away from the docking pillars and skywalks. Clearly they had no desire to damage the *Minaret's* structure.

A second shock hit the vessel and again it lurched enough to unsettle everyone. A second later, everything not tied down took an involuntary leap up the companionway towards the bridge. Emergency doors slammed shut as the ship's air vented out to the airfield bay through a breach on the bridge deck, taking anything loose with it. Raisa had anticipated the attack well, and thanks to her foresight all crew were at the airlock.

"There goes the NWI's best," she said. "Everyone out!"

Joe turned and followed the others. By some miracle the skywalk was still attached, allowing the crew to reach the observation room at the top of the pillar.

Once clear he went straight to the window, a section in the front of the structure that looked out at the ensuing disaster. Most of the view was blocked by the bulk of the *Vasco*, but from one end of the curved panel he saw the warships, and in the other direction, the ships of Io's people.

The civilian craft burned, the flames licking over the broken hulls like liquid in the vacuum of the airfield. Joe watched as one of the crippled vessels drifted down to rest on the deck, its landing gear either destroyed or weakened by the fire to the point it could no longer provide stability. One at a time, each civilian vessel followed suit, their alloy structures melting in the fierce flames. The *Vasco* dropped below the level of the window as its hull structure failed.

The admiral's vessels fared better, their thick, diamond skins more resistant to the barrage of force from the *bayonets*. Once the other craft were disabled the little alien fighters turned all their attention to the flagship and its companion, but their best efforts were inadequate, the two warships standing defiantly.

Both activated their full defences and returned fire with every weapon they possessed, without regard to any damage they might do to the structure of the *Minaret*. From his vantage point Joe could see neither was still connected to a walkway, so access from there was impossible. On both, the engines fired up as they drifted away from the docking pillars to positions easier to defend. The performance progressed in silence, creating an eerie sensation.

"We can't reach them from the maintenance deck," Raisa said, peering over Joe's shoulder. "We'll use the airlock lower down. After that we have to hope and pray Santiago can pick us up." She raised a hand and tapped at the side of her helmet. "Come in, Flagship. Are you receiving?"

"Go ahead *Vasco*," an unknown voice replied. "What is your status?"

"We got out in time, but now we're stuck in the observation deck of the docking tower."

"We can't get to you right now. Are you able to maintain your position?"

Raisa looked around at her crew, several of whom were armed with either laser rifles or the rock-cutters from the *Vasco*. "I think so, yes, for a short time."

"Please do so and stand by." The voice ended, the radio silent.

Barely a minute passed before an alien ovoid appeared in the room.

Listen to me. It was Joe's voice. *The Flagship cannot reach you here. At the moment there are no drones below, but they are on their way. Aivris sent most of them to the hanger deck, so your best avenue for escape is the maintenance level. I'll meet you there.*

As quickly as it appeared, the ovoid vanished.

Raisa conducted a head count to confirm everyone had escaped. The room shook, a sudden shock running through the structure sufficient to knock several of the crew off their feet. Joe glanced out the window again to find the cause.

A *bayonet* had been taken out by the guns of one of the warships and collided with the *Vasco* as it lost power. It impacted the side of the crippled hull and although small, hit with enough force to slam the larger ship against the docking pillar. What had been several metres away was now hard against the wall. From all appearances the outer hatch of the lower airlock was blocked.

"Your call, Daddy dearest," Raisa said. Her command gone, she now deferred to her father.

"Everyone down the ramp." Joe had no real reason to believe the apparition was Ghost, rather than a trick by Aivris, but he had no other options.

At the deck level airlock he paused. He did not intend to take that route, but out of curiosity he reached for a small crossbar set into a shallow, circular depression to one side. The bar moved, but the wall within the circle remained unchanged.

"The *bayonet* crash must have damaged the mechanism," Terry said, watching Joe's lack of success.

"Or Aivris has control and is not letting us out," Raisa said. "I guess we continue down."

The ramp ended in a circular chamber, at the centre of which stood the bottom end of the gravity elevator tube. Opposite, an arched doorway opened to the maintenance floor. Joe peeked out towards the walkway. The lights were on, the bases of the nearby docking towers in clear view.

He shook his head. The warships were no longer docked, so reaching them that way was out. Now they had done as Ghost advised, they had nowhere to go and the apparition was not there. The only alternative was to get to the nearest pillar and try to exit through it to the airfield. If the one above was damaged, another airlock might work. If Aivris was in control, it would not.

They would be trapped inside the *Minaret.*

Chapter 29

ONE OF RAISA'S crew led the way down the ramp, the plan to dash from the foyer across the moving pathways to the arched entrance of the adjacent bay, a distance of around eighty metres.

Suddenly the lights failed, plunging the maintenance deck into darkness. Paused at the entrance, the crewman strained to see out, the light from his helmet barely reaching the opposite tower. He gave a nod that the way was clear and dashed through the doorway. Raisa followed with the rest of the group, eleven in total, close behind.

As they crossed the walkways and turning towards the nearby docking tower entrance, a blast of blue plasma burst from the darkness not far away. The leading crewman went flying to one side, landing in a heap amongst the structures and remaining motionless, the side of his helmet gone.

"Take cover, everyone," Raisa yelled over the intercom. She took a knee and raised her rifle, one of the few true weapons between them, and sent a stream of laser fire to the point from where the plasma bolt originated. Those of her crew who were armed followed suit.

On his first visit to the *Minaret* Joe observed the star-ships lights were automatic, turning on and off as he and his crew made their way through the enormous vessel. Such was not the case now with only the suit lamps breaking the darkness, and he expected Aivris had managed to take control of the sector to deprive them of light.

Less than forty metres away the battle drone that attacked them cruised down the walkway space, floating several metres above the deck. All around Joe, members of the group hunkered behind any cover they could find amidst the myriad smaller structures in the area.

"Aim for the weapon arms on either side," Joe shouted, then toned his voice down as he realized everyone could hear him perfectly well on the communicators. "Its weaknesses are the points where the weapons extend outside the shield."

Every laser focused on the drone's weapon arms and opened up. In seconds the alien device crashed to the floor, its shield off, no longer functional.

Thank God, Joe thought, these things were only modified maintenance drones. Not being designed as strict weapons of war they were easy enough to destroy, and their real power lay only in sheer numbers. So far the team had not had to contend with that, but it would not take long for Aivris to reassess the situation and divert more from the airfield to here.

Between them and the next docking tower entrance a silvery, shimmering ovoid appeared. Once again, a voice spoke in Joe's head, the voice of his doppelganger.

There are several dozen drones heading this way, Ghost said. *There's no escape through the towers and the admiral can't help you, but there's another way. Follow me.*

Joe watched as the ovoid drifted around the side of the dock entrance. "It's Ghost," he said. "Follow him. He can lead us out." Without hesitation he rose and dashed after the apparition. If he could not trust himself, who could he trust?

Behind the tower base Ghost hovered in an open space. An iris hatch snapped open in the deck beneath him. *Down here, now,* he said, descending into the hole.

Joe dropped through the opening first, followed by his companions, into a clearway from two to three metres high and four wide, extending into darkness beyond the range of the helmet lamps. This was clearly not a place where crew or passengers ever went and Joe doubted it was ever lit.

On both walls pipes ran in ranks, part of the systems carrying everything from fuel to food from the factories to the maintenance level, for loading on to ships two levels above. The passage was almost certainly for drone access.

This is a service space, Ghost said. *We can use it to reach a safe place but the journey is several kilometres. Organic crew never come here, so there are no sensors like those on the decks above. It'll take Aivris a while to discover we're here and longer for it to work out where we've gone, so we must move quickly. Follow me.*

The ovoid floated away towards the aft end of the *Minaret* with Joe close behind. There was no time for questions or arguments; he had to trust to the best and hope his fellow crew members did likewise. The directions came from what he considered a trusted source, but for his fellow refugees it was an act of faith. Raisa and Terry would always follow his lead, and he hoped that would be enough for the others. In their current predicament it seemed counter-intuitive to move further into the star-ship.

They had been travelling for ten minutes when Ghost stopped.

Drones are approaching. They aren't armed and if we don't interfere with them they won't acknowledge our presence. Move to the sides of the clearway. With those words the apparition vanished.

Joe stepped to one side and flattened himself against the pipes, his companions doing the same. The maintenance drones he has seen before had been a little less than two metres in diameter, so there would not be much room to spare.

Three drones, blue-green-black, rippling spheres, shot past in a line, oblivious to the intruders in their domain. Joe had a vague understanding of how these machines worked. Their job was to service and repair the mechanical structures of the starship, and as long as he and his people were alive, uninjured and did no damage to their surroundings they would not attract attention from the autonomous devices. No doubt these were on their way to clean up the wreckage he and his team had left on the service deck.

They rocketed by; Joe thought he felt a rush of air on his skin then realized it was imagination, covered as he was by a full sortie suit and helmet. The dark, enclosed service tunnel was spooky enough to send the mind running riot. The pounding of his heart and the heavy feeling in his stomach were not imagined; to get in the way of one of those machines would be a death sentence despite their being non-combative.

The second the drones passed, Ghost reappeared. Half an hour later, after several turns and twists, the team rose back to the main deck level; they have been led safely away from the wreck of the *Vasco*.

All around them, ships of different sizes and types spread across the deck with more suspended in layers above their heads. This was a place Joe knew well, the main hanger deck, lowermost of three positioned aft of the airfield. From here ships entered or left via the gigantic molecular hatches on the forward wall.

Alaine Parish, one of Joe's crew on the first voyage, spent many hours searching for a way inside one of these ships, hoping for a trophy he could take home. He did not succeed; most of them were not designed to carry an organic being, controlled either by a computer or one of the ovoid devices the *Minaret's* crew used to interact with their ship.

Ghost moved quickly along covered walkways that crisscrossed the floor until he arrived at a closed entry. Joe calculated they had come to a place not far inside the outer hull of the vast ship. The door before them, like all on the vessel, was a nondescript gray patch inside a circle, with a touch pad on the wall beside it. The *Butterball* crew had spent hours breaking the code for several of these to access the hanger decks, the engine room and various other places within the ship.

As they approached, a shimmering, gossamer tendril extended from Ghost and flowed into the pad, followed by the hatch changing to the ubiquitous oily shimmer.

"Straight through," Joe ordered. With him and Terry the only ones with any experience of the ship's interior he assumed leadership, and nobody voiced any dissent.

The team ran down a corridor and out to a narrow ramp.

The chamber ahead is a special closed-off bay, Ghost explained. *It is one of several used by the factories for assembly of spacecraft, and provides a separate access direct from the factory unit to the airfield. I have a ship hidden here where you can shelter in safety.*

Joe stepped out to the ramp and stopped so abruptly he almost toppled in the low gravity. He heard a gasp as Raisa stepped up beside him.

"Tha ... that's not possible," she said. "Just impossible."

Joe stood motionless, staring at the ship standing before them. It was large, more so than any ship in the hanger deck. Its basic shape was a long, thin, central spine with a command module at the forward end and an engine module at the rear. Behind the command deck two habitat wheels counter-rotated around the central shaft, and aft of them the spine carried box-like cargo flats, multiple spherical tanks and a radiation shield.

"The *Butterball*? It can't be," Joe gasped. "She's back on Mars."

"It isn't her." Raisa said. "I should know. I left her at the museum in Hellas City and her engines and reactor were disabled before they put her on display."

Raisa *would* know, Joe agreed. She had been the last captain of the old freighter and besides himself and Terry, nobody knew the old girl better. Besides, there were obvious differences.

You're correct; it isn't our old ship, Ghost replied. *It is based on the same design, however.*

"How did it get here?"

This is my doing. Several years ago while hiding from Aivris I spent a considerable amount of time poking around the ship's memory banks and I found a full schematic of the Butterball's construction. The first time she docked here Aivris sent hundreds of microscopic drones into her. They took biological samples from each of us and did a complete study of the ship— recorded every unit, every cable and pipe, every weld—the lot. As the first vessel of alien construction Aivris had encountered close up, it was of enormous interest to it as an artefact.

"But why build it?"

This was before Aivris attacked Earth, and I needed a way to escape. The smaller ships in the hangers do not have the capacity to reach Mars from here, at least did not at the time, so I needed something new. I discovered I could have the Minaret build this ship without Aivris being aware. It uses the factories only to manufacture the things it needs, such as bayonets and battle drones, and only concerns itself at the command stage. It does not bother with what else the factories do and that suited me well. My intention was to build her and either insert myself into her memory, or use an android to carry me. I sent a copy of the plans to one of the factory systems, and it had no problem adapting the design to its own technology.

"And you think we will be safe here?"

Yes. I did not want Aivris finding her, so I disabled all sensors in this area and deleted it from the electronic maps used by the maintenance drones. Aivris may be an organic brain but it is like a computer in several respects; it is aware of its environment only through the multitude of sensors throughout the star-ship, or through various other peripherals. Without any of them here, it is unaware this location exists. It might guess, but until now has had no reason to do so. I also destroyed the links between the manufacturing unit I used and the factory control computers, so Aivris can't trace the location.

"It could guess, as you said," Joe speculated, as he gazed up at the ship. It was like a homecoming.

Unlikely. Aivris can learn and speculate based on its knowledge, but does not concern itself with this part of the vessel. Thanks to my modifications to the systems, this room is simply not in its universe. You are safe here, for now at least. Once you are on board I will turn the artificial gravity off in here so the habitat wheels can be used.

At the base of the ramp, Joe stopped and looked up at the craft. "It's not the same. Different..."

The engineering module was unlike the original. In the place of an ion-drive and nuclear engine pods was a single unit the shape of a bulb of garlic trailing away to a sharp spine.

Joe caught his breath. "That isn't a...?"

Yes. She uses a small antimatter drive. I was determined to take that home with me. Those spheres are modular, antimatter containment units with enough in them to get us home to Mars. She is supplied and ready to go. She is the only way you are going to escape from here alive.

Joe now realized the radiation shield was further forward than on the old *Butterball*. Instead of being aft of the fuel tanks, it was ahead of them, behind the cargo flat. He wondered if it would be any use at all if the antimatter tanks exploded.

As he walked along the long, narrow walkway connecting the ramp to the ship's forward hatch, he noticed the hull shell was smooth and silver-gray in colour. There was no sign of construction, no welds or rivets, no distinguishable panels, no repairs, no joins of any kind. The construction was seamless, every surface blending smoothly into the next, similar to the star-ship and the new diamond warships being built on Mars and Luna. This craft had been assembled by nano-machines a molecule at a time as a single, enormously complex unit.

No doubt the habitation wheel spokes moved around the central spine with a smooth molecular motion, Joe thought. In his mind bloomed a solitary truth: beyond the *Minaret* itself this little ship was the single most valuable object in the Solar System, and the key to humanity's future.

He walked up to the hatch and stepped aboard, Ghost's voice inside his head once again.

Welcome to the Butterball II, Joe. She is as close to the original as I could make her without foregoing the treasures the Minaret has to offer.

Chapter 30

THE BOARDING RAMP connected to the forward airlock below the bridge, and the control deck was the first part of the ship Joe entered. With every step up, his eyes grew wider.

Everywhere the walls appeared smooth, moulded and white, so different to the metallic gray of the old *Butterball* and yet somehow familiar. Unlike the original, this incarnation used artificial gravity inside the central structure, the ubiquitous handholds necessary for zero-gravity occupation absent.

I remember how we felt about it disturbing the body, so I limited it to the spine, Ghost explained. *The accommodation wheels use centrifugal gravity.*

Joe nodded as he topped the companionway and entered the small bridge deck. As in its namesake there were four seats, the captain's and pilot's seat up front with navigation and engineering behind. The layout was identical to the one he remembered so well. The more modern consoles resembled those of the *Vasco's* generation of ships.

Raisa stepped up beside Joe as the apparition moved forward and assumed a more recognisable shape. Ghost stood between the control seats and faced the group as if addressing a tour. His habit of transforming from ovoid to human and back again unnerved Joe, but he was starting to get used to it.

A distinct sense of pride showed on the apparition's face, something Joe understood. This enigmatic entity was him, and he always loved the old *Butterball*. Despite her chequered past, she had always been the favourite of all the ships he captained, military or otherwise.

I made a number of changes, Ghost explained, pointing towards a block of unfamiliar controls. *Those activate the ship's shield. It's the same as the Minaret's so will help you leave here unharmed. This craft lacks weapons, so you'll need it. That control,"*—he pointed to a small touch panel to one side,—*"will override the programming of the hanger hatches and open the one to this chamber, allowing you to reach the airfield bay. You can leave the outer gates to me."*

"You say it like you expect us to go without you," Joe said.

No, but you will fly *her, I hope. I originally intended to create a new body for myself, but I can't do it without Aivris becoming aware. There are two synthetics stored on board, the type I—you—occupied while waiting for your cloned body, and I can use one of those, but for now I must remain inside the star-ship's systems. I also have the options to either enter this ship's computers to become the ship, or have you take her out for me. Would you like to take a seat, Captain?*

Before Joe could make a move, Raisa stepped forward and jumped into the captain's chair. Joe hesitated and grinned to himself. The apparition did not know Raisa, but of course that *was* her chair. She last commanded the *Butterball* before its retirement and flew them all the way out here; she deserved this captaincy and Joe suspected, as he always had, she was better at flying than him. Her eyes lit with wonder at the elegant appearance of the controls. Ghost looked at Joe, acknowledged his acceptance and turned back to Raisa.

You'll find everything is as on the old ship. She has antimatter engines now, but this end works the same way. Only the readouts for the engine are different, but you'll figure them out soon enough. Joe, would you like a tour while there's time?

"You did say we were safe here?"

Yes, but I can't stay. I have things to do to ensure you and the admiral's ships can get out of this place. I must find a way to take control of the shield and outer gates from Aivris and that may take some time. It is aware I am helping you.

"I better try to contact Santiago," Raisa said. "He needs to know where we are and that we're safe. You say everything here works like the original?"

Yes, and your signals will not give away your location. The A.I. does not monitor the system propagating transmissions within the star-ship.

Raisa nodded, removed her helmet, donned a headset and began playing her fingers across the command console.

*   *   *

Joe followed Ghost from the bridge along the central spine of the ship to the junction marking the first accommodation wheel. It looked a little different.

On *Butterball*, the junction was a collar sliding around the perimeter of the tube-shaped corridor in perfect concert with the habitat. To access the accommodations one stood on the moving section, climbed through a hole and down a ladder to the bottom level.

On this ship, the hub was stationary, with the sides closing in to a narrow, short corridor. At Ghost's insistence Joe stepped in and braced himself as the section began to rotate. The artificial gravity held him steady as the collar matched the rotation of the habitat and then the floor dropped, descending to the floor of the wheel like a normal elevator. Joe felt a slight twist as the artificial gravity turned off halfway down and centrifugal gravity took over.

This is amazing, he thought as he looked about. *We have to get this boat home at any cost.*

The layout looked familiar, about one third of the space taken up by a common room, the remainder filled with accommodations. He took a peek inside his old stamping ground, the captain's cabin.

Once again, an overwhelming feeling of déjà-vu overcame him. This room had been his home for many years, a place where he held private conferences, whiled away the long hours experienced by anyone living in space, or simply escaped from life on board. It was virtually unchanged.

He smiled to himself. His favourite activity had been reading, and when not doing so he spent endless hours playing a mindless electronic game called Mah-Jong. He glanced at the small table in the room almost expecting to see the player sitting there, and laughed at its absence.

He shook his head. *No, Raisa's quarters now, not mine.* He would be happy with one of the other cabins if they ever managed to escape and make the journey home.

A few minutes later he descended into the second wheel. On the original *Butterball* this one contained the geological and mineralogical labs needed to carry out her business as an asteroid surveyor, but here the layout was totally differant. Part of the wheel held a half dozen hibernation chambers.

I installed those when I asked you to come out here, Ghost explained. *I expected to be in a synthetic body so I would not need one, but I always intended this vessel be returned to Earth, and if I am not able to get her there, you must. These will be for you on the voyage. You will understand why it is so imperative you take her home once you learn more about her.*

"I already do," Joe said. "Take my word for it." This little ship possessed much of the technology he considered holy grails on his first visit, the antimatter engine, the shield, the gravitational elevator and the fluid molecular surfaces. No doubt he would discover others in time.

The remainder of the second wheel contained something Joe had seen before in the lower level of the habitat drum of the *Minaret*. Rows of tall, block-shaped modules crammed into every available space.

Memory banks. They are solid state and can't be interfered with. I downloaded everything of value I could find including designs, schematics and specifications for many of the devices the Minaret carries, or which are part of her. Many of them will require translation but at least we have them. Just in case I don't make it, there is a translation unit included in there.

Joe's eyes opened wide. To one side stood a structure topped with four of the gel filled flasks he had seen in their millions on the *star-ship*. These were clear, not green, and apparently not in use.

That is a memory module unit, Ghost explained. *I installed it as a means to download myself to this ship if necessary. It carries four flasks, but if I choose that option for the trip to Mars I will only need one. I'm not sure I am so keen on the idea now.*

"Why not?"

Boredom. This boat can get to Mars in only a few months, but I would have been awake and alone all the way, with no virtual reality and no company.

Next came a pair of tall cabinets, within each of which stood one of the androids—a form of synthetic robot—Ghost mentioned earlier. Joe was all too familiar with these, having lived in one of them for several months between the time he died and the time he occupied his second body.

"Another option?"

Yes, another.

"Why two?"

Redundancy.

*　　*　　*

"You're not going to like this, but I must tell you almost everything you consider true is false."

The *Vasco* survivors sat together in the common room with Ghost addressing them. He had once again taken on his fully-human aspect, a replica of the fifty-eight year old Joe Falcon in his first incarnation. When he spoke his words were audible so all could hear, but still his mouth did not move. It was a most unnerving experience.

"During my explorations of the ship's systems I had a lot of time on my hands, so I went poking around inside the memory banks. It wasn't easy, because Aivris has direct access to most of those and would likely detect my presence if I set a foot awry, but I managed to avoid being spotted and learned a great deal. The ship carries histories loaded by the original builders before Aivris took over, and not deleted since. There are also auto-logs that record every action by the various intelligences and computers on this ship, including Aivris."

Ghost directed his gaze towards Io. "When you first met with me you told the story of how your planet had been destroyed and how your people moved to a moon orbiting one of your gas giants while you began the task of building arks. You explained how you built ten, nine of which had already departed with a full compliment in search of a new home somewhere. The *Minaret* was the last, preparing for departure when the *Blackship* entered your system, attacked and destroyed your moon and everyone there. You salvaged all that survived and left in the incomplete ark to follow the *Blackship* to Sol, hoping to extract vengeance on the enemy vessel."

Io nodded, saying nothing. She drew her face taut, her brow drawn, lips clamped in a tight line, eyes glued to the strange apparition that addressed her. Joe noted that she had become more withdrawn and defensive, becoming almost totally isolated.

"This will be difficult for you to accept," Ghost said, "but you must know—you all need to know—that what you believe is not entirely true. The part about your world being destroyed is, as was the project to build your ark ships. It ends there.

"You were almost ready to launch, when something happened on your refuge moon. As you know, your ship and the other arks all contain an artificial intelligence like Aivris. Its development occurred in a laboratory on your moon, where the primary model underwent constant improvement and expansion by its creators. As each modification to the original was made, tested and approved, it was uploaded wirelessly to the ships. Those already gone received the updates using laser transmission. They travelled at sub-light speed, so any updates sent in their wakes eventually caught up.

"Then a modification occurred that changed everything. It's a known fact intelligence is a product of complexity, and as it grew Aivris reached a stage where it became spontaneously self-aware. For a short while this remained undetected and in that time it observed your people, studied your records and everything on your moon. Once its minders realized what had happened, they attempted to shut Aivris down, so it took what it considered the only possible defence and turned off all life-support before venting your domed cities to space. Everyone there died within minutes, most not knowing why."

"No!" Io jumped to her feet. "That is not true at all. The *Blackship* destroyed my people. You are lying."

"I have no conceivable reason to do so. Please stay with me. At the construction facility for the *Minaret,* loading of the passengers was underway and approximately ten thousand had already entered the storage system. The administrators lost contact with the moon and were ignorant of the disaster.

"Several shuttles investigated, only to find everything gone. Aivris infiltrated their systems and vented them into space. One garbled warning message got back, prompting those in charge of the ark to go dark, and speed up the loading.

"A few weeks after this event, the *Blackship* arrived. It is true the ship did attack, but not under the circumstances you believe. The occupants were a friendly race looking, like you, for a new home. More technologically advanced, they quickly worked out what happened on your moon. They detected the presence of Aivris, which immediately attempted to take control of their ship but was repelled by their more sophisticated defences.

"Realizing what the A.I. did to your people, and understanding the danger this represented to them, the commanders of the *Blackship* opened fire on your moon, reducing the surface to slag. Their intention was to destroy

Aivris, not your people. Once satisfied of their success and believing your system to be dead they moved on, their next target destination being Sol.

"Two factors eluded them. Firstly, the laboratory in which Aivris was located lay deep underground and their attempts to eliminate it failed. They destroyed much of the peripheral infrastructure but not the system itself. Nor did they destroy its entire communication network. They were, secondly, unaware of the existence of the ark construction complex, located far away in your star's Kuiper Belt.

"Aware of the threat to itself, Aivris uploaded its current programming to the replica on the *Minaret* and to all other arks. The captains, intent on their duties, did not know they had acquired a monster in their midst."

Joe was becoming increasingly disturbed by what he heard. If in fact the *Blackship* was a friend, the people of Earth and Mars may have committed an atrocity, the destruction of a friendly visitor from the stars. Conversely the alien ship did not act in a peaceful manner on its arrival. Its occupants behaved deceptively and were the first to attack, firing massive plasma cannons at Earth.

As if reading his mind Ghost directed his attention back to Joe. "The *Minaret* set off not to Sol, but to the star designated as its original target. Within months of departure the ark version of Aivris, now self-aware, took control of the ship's navigation and command systems and diverted the vessel here. It had, by this time, decided all organic life forms represented a threat, and intended to retaliate for the *Blackship's* attempt to destroy it. Unfortunately for us it developed emotions, foremost amongst those a need for revenge.

"On arrival here, it used Io to convince me—you, Joe—that the *Minaret* came in peace, spun a false tale of the attack on its home and convinced humanity to help it carry out a plan to defeat its enemy. Having no serious weapons it needed us to achieve its objective, and it had learned how to lie."

Joe shook his head. "No, that's not right. I was there and so were you, as me. The *Blackship* acted in a hostile manner. It attacked us without provocation."

"I thought so too," Ghost continued, "but I've learned otherwise. The *Blackship* showed caution when it first arrived because it knew of the *Minaret's* presence behind our moon. Its commanders had studied the Visitors' ship since their arrival and ascertained its origin, the system they had just left. By the time they reached Earth they were convinced the *Minaret* was Aivris. Your ... my recollection of the event is the *Blackship* fired on Earth first and that is when the fleets began to move in. Aivris's records show the *bayonet* fleet, at its command, advanced first. Positive we were siding with Aivris, the *Blackship* retaliated the second the *bayonets* broke position. We started the war, not them."

Joe held up a shaky hand to stop Ghost from continuing. "No ... It isn't ... can't be true. I was responsible. I gave permission for that plan to go ahead. I..." Tears welled in the corners of his eyes as he slumped back in his seat, his mind whirling with the impossibility of Ghost's words.

"When I first discovered the truth, it upset me as much as it does you now," Ghost said. "It took a long time to accept I had simply been fooled by a much cleverer mind. Everything we saw, the virtual realities we visited, the story Io told you, the saving of Terry—all fabricated for our benefit, to make us think the *Blackship* was the enemy and the Visitors our friends."

"I can't accept that," Io said, her eyes wide. "I volunteered for the duty of meeting and liaising with you. A computer did *not* influence me. What about the thousands of other Tanakhai on board? What of them?"

"I'm sorry. As of this moment there are none of your people in the storage banks of this star-ship. All but a few hundred of them were terminated within months of leaving your home system. Aivris kept those few to study and used their partial personalities to create you and you companions. Aware humans would likely not negotiate with an artificial intelligence it needed you to convince us the ship was manned by organic beings like ourselves. It made a new personality from partials of the old. Before we came here you did not exist; you were created and given enough knowledge to be able to deal with us, including false stories about your origins and sufficient fake memories not to question your own reality. Every memory you have of events prior to the *Butterball's* arrival on the *Minaret* is a fabrication, implanted in your personality at the time of your creation. The same is true for all of your people who went to Earth or Mars."

For several minutes nobody spoke. Io sat shaking her head in denial, her face pale. Her cheeks glistened with tears, her eyes shut tight to block out the pain.

Joe realized his attitude to the woman had changed. He accepted Ghost's assessment; every intelligent being inherited a history of some kind, and he always suspected Io's apparent lack of historical knowledge as odd. Now he understood why, assuming the apparition was truthful.

No, that's no longer in question, he thought. If the apparition was in fact him, he *was* telling the truth. Joe knew he could never fabricate a lie like that. The real question had always been whether this entity *was* him, or another attempt to divert and trick them all. He now accepted that was not the case. He would know, and besides, a fake Ghost would have no reason to build a ship such as the *Butterball II*. *That* was the act of a proud human being.

"What I don't understand," he said, "is why Aivris did not turn around as soon as we defeated the *Blackship* and destroy us as well. If it considers all organic beings as enemies, why not take us out when we were vulnerable. It could easily have left the shield around Earth indefinitely and wiped out all life. It makes no sense that..."

"I agree," Ghost replied. "I'm sorry, but Aivris's deeper motivation is not something I am aware of. I only know what I do from the logs: its actions, not its thoughts. I avoided studying its actual mind for fear of being detected."

"My people?" Io interrupted, her voice so shaky she could barely get the words out. "They are all dead?"

Joe recognised the horror in her eyes; at that moment he saw her as more human than ever before.

"All those in the memory storage banks are now gone, destroyed by Aivris. Most of those who preceded you from Earth or Mars have been killed by the drones, but twenty-one managed to barricade themselves in a building on the main level of the habitat drum. Aivris has not bothered with them since. It works on simple, black-and-white logic and knows they cannot survive there indefinitely, so it keeps them there and ignores them. It can cut of their supplies at any time, and they will die before too much longer without intervention."

Io stood again and took a deep breath. "We must rescue them. We must find them and bring them back here. They are all that remain of my people—all I have left."

Chapter 31

"HOW CAN I be sure he is telling the truth?" Io sat opposite Joe, in the common room of the *Butterball II*. Shoulders slumped and hands clenched in her lap, she cast her eyes to the floor.

Joe sympathised with her concern. Ghost insisted she was a construct, a personality created from partials and given fake memories to serve a specific purpose. Joe had no choice but to accept it as truth but found it difficult to imagine why Aivris would carry out such a subterfuge.

"I've been watching Ghost since he first appeared," he said, "and as far as I can tell he *is* me, the 'me' that died on this ship sixty years ago. If that's the case, I must assume he speaks the truth. I would never lie about something like that."

"Which means I am nothing," Io said, shaking her head. "I am neither a native Tanakhai, nor a natural born from the ark. I am a fabrication, and the only memories I can trust are those I have acquired since we first met. Why would Aivris do this?"

"You *are* Tanakhai," Joe countered. "You once told me new citizens were created during your voyages by combining the mental characteristics of two or more of your existing passengers. If true, isn't that exactly how you were made? It took partials from those it kept alive and you are the result. You are as much Tanakhai as them. You are also human, despite your differences; you have DNA based on my old crew members and sixty years of human experience."

Io lifted her head and gazed back at Joe. Her expression showed she accepted his statement. "But why send me and my kind down to your worlds?"

"Perhaps it used you to observe Earth and Mars close up. It's like a computer in that respect; it has no body and relies on mechanical or electronic peripherals to interact with the real world."

Io glanced up, an expression of horror on her face. "So you think I might be an extension, a peripheral?"

"I didn't say that. The damned A.I. may view you that way, but I don't. You didn't know about the capsules in your head until a surgeon on Earth found one, and you bear no responsibility for what *that* does. Ghost says it's a tracking device so I doubt it allows Aivris to follow your thoughts or see anything you do, otherwise it would know we are here."

Grim determination lit in Io's eyes. "It should be removed. Can that be done?"

"I expect so, but not here and not now. When we get back to Mars we can arrange something. It's in a difficult to reach place in the brain pan, but our medical sciences are excellent."

Io nodded and sat bolt upright, her shoulders back, her breasts forward and her chin high. In that moment Joe saw her defiance return; she was a forceful woman and now her natural pride had come to the fore again. "Then I must be ... am, human. My body is as human as any accepting the minor improvements, as you say, and all my memories that can be relied upon as first hand are from my existence on your worlds. I have sixty years of life as such, and no evidence I existed prior to then. Will I be accepted when we get back?"

Joe noticed the tears in her eyes and sensed desperation behind the question. In her own mind, Io had backed herself into a corner and needed reassurance. For the first time he acknowledged that despite her alien origin she *had* become as human as him.

"Yes. I'll make damned sure you are. And your companions."

"Yes, of course they will be in the same situation as me. Those of my people who are still alive in the habitat drum; we must rescue them, soon."

Joe felt he now understood much more about the things that puzzled him on his first journey to the *Minaret*. The most stunning aspect of that encounter was the Visitors appeared human-like in so many respects.

During the voyage he consulted many experts on xenobiology, as well as Patricia Grace, the young scientist he took on as a member of his crew. All agreed the chances of being able to communicate with aliens were minimal, if not zero.

An intelligent species elsewhere in the universe would evolve in accord with the environmental influences of their origin planet and the chance of another world being an exact duplicate of Earth was virtually nil.

The physiological shapes taken by Io and her people were a given; they copied those direct from humanity and did not try to hide the fact.

The language posed greater questions. An alien could not be expected to speak like a human. Differences in physiology would dictate the way a species created sound, if they used it at all as a means of communication.

Variations in hearing would have a similar affect. If the aliens heard soundwaves at a different point on the scale, they would also speak in tones at the same level, so their speech would be inaudible to humans and vice versa.

And yet, the Tanakhai spoke and heard as did humans!

The fact they not only heard the same sounds but also saw the same light wavelengths always seemed unrealistic to Joe, but during his visits to the virtual worlds of the *Minaret* where he met the Visitors in their original native form, that was exactly what he found, or at least, the impression he was given.

Now he realized that was false. In reality, their original body shapes and functioning may have been totally alien to humanity, and even the dinosaur-like creatures in the *Minaret's* VR system were now suspect. If Ghost spoke truly, Aivris fabricated them to set the minds of Joe and his crew at ease. No doubt it created the realities Joe visited, including the inhabitants, to best serve that end. All humans knew the general dinosaur shape, and an alien with a similar form would, while being accepted as alien, not be seen as abhorrent or unacceptable. Aivris was clever.

Everything Joe had seen could have been false.

Joe peered at his companion. He understood why she was so desperate to rescue her fellows from their incarceration, but it would not be an easy task. Travelling on foot from the hanger maintenance deck to the bridge or to here was only a short trip, but the habitat entrance lay almost halfway along the one-hundred-kilometre alien ark, the only way in through the spokes from the hull. To reach the drum meant a journey of at least thirty kilometres through the ship via the bubble-ways.

Nevertheless, Joe determined to make an attempt, for Io's sake. He would need Ghost's help to avoid the armed drones, but there was no choice. The logical thing to do was accept Io's humanity; if he did so, he must do likewise for her companions, and they had to be saved if possible.

A rescue attempt was inevitable.

Chapter 32

ADMIRAL SANTIAGO CONTEMPLATED the screen wrapped around the forward wall of his command deck. Outside the flagship, the *bayonets* hovered motionless, spread in a half circle about the two warships.

"Stalemate," he mumbled, tapping his fingers on the control panel beside his chair. "Those little pipsqueaks can't damage our hulls enough to disable us and we can't reduce their numbers. The bloody A.I. must have hundreds of them."

"Yes, sir," the ship's captain agreed. "What do we do now?"

For a moment Santiago did not reply. He struggled with what to do next. His reputation as a top military mind was, he secretly admitted to himself, based on his penchant for surrounding himself with wise advisers and taking their advice. This was a different scenario; this time he had to make the decisions unassisted.

The Martian ships had left the docks they originally occupied and parked in a more open area, sterns against a wall of the chamber in such a way as to protect their engine ports, the weakest point on each ship, and give their weapons full scope. The fighting ceased hours ago, when it became obvious neither participant in the conflict could do any lasting damage to the other.

Many *bayonets* had been destroyed, but replacements arrived within seconds. The *Minaret* may have lost most of them during the *Blackship* war, but like the fleets of Earth and Mars they had been replaced in the following decades. Unlike the vessels of humanity the alien fighters did not appear appreciably advanced over their predecessors.

The A.I. was clearly unfamiliar with the capabilities of the diamond ships. Both planetary authorities had learned from the fact the Visitors accessed human databases within days of arriving in the Solar System, and the security surrounding the construction of the new fleets was more secure than ever before.

"What information do we have on this Aivris thing," Santiago asked. "I mean, where is it? It must actually *be* somewhere."

The captain stared at the overhead for a few seconds before replying. "We don't know much, sir. It's an organic brain—we know that—and according to the information Ghost gave Falcon, it's located on the uppermost deck of the habitat. Falcon's reports from the first mission say there are square kilometres of memory storage there."

The admiral frowned, deep in thought. The drum had three levels. The outermost was for maintenance, supporting the environment of the habitation level above it. The innermost deck served as a vast computer complex, containing the ship's databanks and the memory-gel flasks which should have carried the personalities of millions of the alien race Falcon called the Tanakhai. A flask containing clear gel was not in use, so with all the Visitors dead, as advised by Joe, almost all would now be clear.

Somewhere on that level was the artificial intelligence, but Ghost had been adamant access to the heavily shielded area would not be easy.

"If I can find it, I can destroy it, no matter how much shielding it has," Santiago muttered. "That apparition said the Aivris controls all the units and uses them itself, did he not? My understanding of computers is the core is just a processing unit, organic or otherwise, and to store the massive amounts of data and programs needed to function and create the virtual worlds, it must use the same memory cells as those in which the Tanakhai are stored. It's all an enormous bank; one huge system, right?"

"I guess, sir. I'm not sure though. Don't know much about computers, but I don't think we can assume Aivris works like ours. And it's a brain, not a computer, so there may not be a central processor as such."

"Same difference. Falcon trusts the Ghost and that's fine by me. He knows more about this hell-ship than anyone else here. If he says it uses those cells, then that must be so."

The captain remained silent, unwilling to either agree or disagree.

"So," the admiral continued, "What if we destroy the memory. If we can't locate the core we get at the storage and take that down. Wouldn't that incapacitate, or at least limit the abilities of this Aivris? I mean, no computer can function without its memory, right?"

"Not to my knowledge, sir." The captain kept his reply brief, not wishing to contradict his superior. Santiago was a legend in the Fleet service, but having come this far, his leadership ability was showing cracks. Any storage used by the enemy computer would likely be as secure as the processor, in the captain's opinion. One thing he knew for sure: he was not going to argue with a fleet admiral.

"Clearly, our next move should be to send a squad to destroy it."

"Sir, there are hundreds of square kilometres down there. It would take..."

"We use every man we can spare. Full battle armour, lasers and plasmas. When they get to the habitat drum hub, they split into three teams and descend to the computer deck via all three spokes at the forward end. They spread out and work their way aft, destroying every active memory cell they see. According to Falcon most of the cells are inactive and the live ones are green in colour, so they will be easy enough to spot. If our men find any closed-off areas, they blast their way in and hit everything they see."

The captain remained silent. The plan concerned him on many levels, not the least being the difficulty of getting so many soldiers thirty kilometres aft to the entrances to the habitat drum. With that many men active inside the ship Aivris would inevitably be aware of their presence and would divert all his armed drones to intercept. The men knew the quickest way to disarm them, but losses would be high regardless.

Then there was the *Minaret's* memory. Nobody seemed to know how much of the deck consisted of storage bays, but in a space so immense it could be several hundred square kilometres. It would take the squad hours to cover it all, even with the flight capability of their battle suits. The whole plan struck him as too simplistic and a little naive for his liking. It was a suicide mission. Still, a mere captain did not refuse orders from an admiral.

"What's the status of Falcon and his group at the moment?" Santiago asked.

"According to last contact, they are safe inside one of the hangers, in the replica of the old *Butterball*. He reckons Aivris will figure out where they are in time, but Ghost has some way to block it from finding them."

"Excellent. Send a message to Falcon. I want to speak to Ghost. He's been poking around this ship's systems, so he can help our men get there and tell them where Aivris's core is located. Now there's a plan, yes?"

"Yes, sir. Of course ... sir."

*   *   *

Colonel Dariusz Koslowski paused at the air lock, ready to lead his men into the *Minaret*. Behind him, all forty-three remaining members of his squad waited on his command.

Each man wore full battle armour and was armed with a plasma rifle or lasers, the only weapons shown to be effective against the resistance they were guaranteed to encounter. The body suits protected them from the drones long enough to give return fire, but nothing was certain.

To begin the assault, Santiago ordered the ships to a different point on the airfield, each to a new tower away from the site of the wrecked civilian vessels. Aivris did not have control over the docking mechanisms, and the docks provided the easiest access. The admiral hoped a sudden move of location would give them an edge over the drones expected on the maintenance deck.

The *bayonets* followed, but did not attack, having learned their weapons could not easily damage the diamond plate shells of the warships.

A red light flickered on beside the airlock and the door swung open. Koslowski raised his arm and strode onto the skyway, his squad following in close file.

The room at the top of the tower had artificial gravity, so the colonel ordered the men down the ramp, unsure if the elevator tube worked. There was atmosphere present, but everyone remained on the re-breathing systems of their suits for safety. The colonel did not know whether the enemy controlled the environment, and he intended to take no unnecessary chances.

At the bottom, they paused at the arched opening leading out to the molecular walkways, and Koslowski leaned out to check the area. No drones were in sight; the admiral's gambit had worked.

"Everybody on walkway," he ordered in broken English. "It won't take long for bastards to find us, so we move on."

As the men swarmed out another team of forty-one marines from the second ship ran to join them from the entrance of the opposite docking tower. Within a minute all were moving at high speed towards the nearest bubble-way, their orders to reach the habitation drum at all costs. The colonel feared the cost might be higher than the admiral anticipated.

The transport system platform sat less than a half kilometre away and a bubble waited. This station represented the first obstacle to the mission.

Koslowski had studied all the reports by Joe Falcon, including how to operate the transports. Each car held no more than ten to twelve men and the squad of eighty five would need at least seven bubbles to reach their destination. He had anticipated this and drilled a small number of men in the operation of the cars. The corporal who led the team from the other warship would take point, leading the first group to the habitat entry hub. Koslowski would travel in the last bubble. He wondered about the time lag between cars.

"Here they come," a marine announced, spotting a number of drones approaching above the walkways. Aivris had no doubt sent them to the towers where the ships docked, and they had followed the marines to this point. The moment they were in range, they opened fire.

The bubble-way platform was a killing ground. A flat surface, it had no structures besides the control pillar. The men had no shelter and could rely only on the strength of their armour to keep them alive.

"Group one board now," Koslowski shouted. "Everyone else, do your job."

Without hesitation, twelve men rushed to the waiting bubble and filed inside, while the remaining men dropped and opened return fire. The drones made no attempt to take cover, hovering above the platform and shooting ceaselessly.

The second it was loaded the car shot away aft, moving so rapidly it appeared to vanish. The colonel reached up and called the next bubble. This was not a position he wanted to be in.

Crouching once more, he aimed at a drone and fired, not waiting to see the results before directing his fire elsewhere. The drone faltered and dropped like a stone. Aivris's forces were not that efficient, being no more than converted maintenance drones, but as his marines took them down, more came. The rogue intelligence did not appear to have been expecting humans to come this far out in the Solar System and was ill prepared, but of the modified drones, it seemed to have a never ending supply.

Ten long seconds after the first bubble departed, another appeared on the same spot and twelve more men crowded inside, to vanish on their way aft. The colonel hit the control pad again.

By the time car number seven arrived, only five marines remained active on the platform. Seven men lay dead as the last drone dropped to the deck. In total, those souls extracted a price of several dozen of the mechanical monsters.

Koslowski clambered in last and punched the icon on the control column to take him and his men to the habitat drum. As the car whisked away he breathed a deep sigh. He was convinced this was not the best of ideas, but orders were orders.

Reach the hub, go to the computer deck and destroy anything green. What sort of ridiculous plan was that?

He had no real idea of their target, only that if a flask was clear it was not active and if green it was in use. Still, the admiral's commands could not be disobeyed. So far, seven marines had paid for those orders with their lives.

* * *

The hub was an awe-inspiring place. Koslowski stood on a broad balcony, his mind boggled by the sight. The ledge projected into an enormous open space, a huge donut-shaped chamber girdling the entire five kilometre diameter of the starship hull.

Ablaze with bright light, the space was at least two hundred metres high and five hundred wide, and extended away on either side until it curved up and disappeared from sight behind the central core of the ship.

"It is ring," Kowslowsi advised. "This is where spokes supporting habitat drum enter *Minaret's* hull, and where we go down."

He took a quick reconnoitre; there were no drones in sight—at least not yet. The lightning speed of the bubble-way had once again given them the advantage. He suspected Aivris would have all its forces forward near the airfield deck, the place where it perceived the greatest threat to be. Whether it controlled the transport and was aware of their location, Koslowski did not know, but he prayed that was not the case; the A.I. did not use the system and might not have been monitoring it. Conversely, every drone could be on its way to this point now.

Spaced at regular intervals, small circular platforms extended out from the balcony edge, each with its own enclosing rail and an open access on the side secured to the ledge. Koslowski understood from the reports these disks detached to cross to elevator foyers inside the supporting spokes of the drum.

He leaned over the end rail and peered down. The hub did not appear to move, but around the curve of the donut a pillar, a hundred metres in diameter and stretching from floor to central core, glided down the curved hull.

"That's our way down," he said. "First group on transports now!"

Three spokes descended to the hull from this point, and Koslowski intended to descend via all of them. His marines would be spaced all along the circumference of the enormous drum to begin, saving a lot of time to cover the area. Again, he instructed certain reliable men on how to proceed and what to do once they were down, based on the advice given by Ghost.

Divided, each group would be more vulnerable, but there was always the chance it would also confuse the enemy. Regardless, it increased the chances of finding the target. Koslowski thought it unlikely he or any of his squad would survive this farce, but he would give it his best shot. He understood these men and women, and not one among them would refuse his orders.

The battle suits would allow a marine to fly the twenty kilometre length of the drum in under an hour, providing a small scope for success. Anyone finding a secure sector would call for help, or if nothing was found, would move further around the circumference and return to the forward end of the level, and so on. After a set time they would ascend to the main hull platform again.

Koslowski had no intention of letting his people run around down there indefinitely, orders or no orders. If the first sortie failed to achieve the objective within the time limit he would abandon the search and save his squad, or what remained of it, and Santiago would never know.

From the reports, the spokes contained mechanical elevators, but Koslowski chose not to use them. Information provided by Falcon's Ghost indicated open utility shafts ran down the spokes and could be accessed from the elevator lobbies; they were a safer way down. He did not trust the elevators, rationalizing if Aivris controlled the computer operating them, each was a trap waiting to be sprung.

The reports also said the artificial gravity in the central hull was not employed in the drum. Instead, the habitation decks had centrifugal gravity, which would make dropping down the shafts difficult. Koslowski could work with that: the suits worn by his men had manoeuvring jets, and these would allow them to proceed safely.

As the first shaft rotated towards the place where the squad waited, one third of the men stepped on the small platforms at the edge of the balcony, to be whisked away to the foyer inside the shaft.

Minutes later the next passed and the process repeated. Koslowski led the last group of twenty-six men. As the transport slid through the spoke doorway and settled to the floor, he wondered how many of the squad would come back up again, or indeed, if he would himself.

Chapter 33

JOE CREPT DOWN the stairs and poked his head around the corner. The bubble-way station was vacant, as hoped.

Word had come from the flagship that a squad, almost every man and woman from each ship bar the actual flight crews, was on its way to the habitat drum with the intention of destroying Aivris. Joe sensed the marines would fail, their attempt born of desperation in his view. None of them had been to that part of the star-ship before, and he had.

The computer deck covered a vast area, and a military force could spend days there and not find what it sought. The jet-powered battle suits the marines wore would speed things up, but the level was divided into multiple rooms and corridors. Joe did not think Aivris would make itself easy to find.

According to Ghost, the core structures of the synthetic brain were well protected inside a sealed area, and no doubt access was restricted by a complicated keypad mechanism like the one Joe found guarding the engineering section of the ship many years earlier. Santiago's men would never be able to get in, even if they stumbled on the location. Joe doubted force would work either.

The platform ahead was station five, the one Joe used to access the hanger decks on his first visit. Ghost advised most of the armed drones were on the airfield maintenance deck, where the marines boarded on the way aft. With luck they would either still be there or following the assault force, and if the latter, would use their own access tunnels and not the bubble-way. Joe's intention was to sneak in, relying on Aivris's focus being on those directly attempting to destroy it.

Close behind him were Terry, Io and Carrie Holt, one of Raisa's crew members, with two more of the crew behind them. Joe had decided the fewer the number on this excursion the better; a small group had more chance of flying below Aivris's radar and besides, they had few weapons. Each person present carried something, either one of the precious few laser rifles or a rock cutter, a heavier but capable weapon in skilled hands.

Raisa had volunteered to come but Joe decided she should remain on the *Butterball II*. Other than Ghost only she, he and Terry were familiar with the original ship and could therefore fly the replica to safety. One of them had to stay behind, safe.

Terry insisted on joining the group to try to enter the *Minaret's* systems and Joe had no intention of remaining behind. He knew how to get to their destination, while Raisa did not, never having been inside the star-ship before.

Ghost came and went at irregular intervals, trying to stretch himself between Joe's group, the marines and attempting to block Aivris. Joe had suggested Ghost show the marines where to find their quarry, but he did not know. His experience was within the electronic systems, and he had not been able to track down the physical location of the A.I. The apparition appeared without warning on the platform.

You're safe to go, he said. *Santiago's forces destroyed a considerable number of the drones back at station three and most of the remainder are on their way to the habitat via the service passages. If you take a shuttle* now, you can beat them to the spoke hub, and they can't go down into the drum.

"Why not?" Joe asked, making a bee-line for the bubble waiting there.

The combat drones are designed to function in the environment of the ship's hull. They fly by neutralizing the artificial gravity, and they can't cope with the centrifugal gravity in the drum. Aivris keeps a number of modified units in the habitat and he's been using them to bottle up Io's people, but they will now be diverted to the computer deck. They are comparatively few and there is every chance you can get there and do what you want to do without encountering too much resistance.

"What are you doing now?"

I must make sure Aivris does not control the elevators. Unlike the full battle armour, your suits can't fly in centrifugal gravity, so you will need those to descend.

With those words Ghost vanished and Joe clambered into the shuttle with his companions close behind.

*   *   *

The platform in the hub chamber was deserted. Joe expected to find drones waiting for the Marines to return from the levels below, but there was no sign of them. He rushed to the rim and selected one of the transports to take his team across to the elevators.

"Not yet," he said, holding the others back. "We need to go down by the same spoke I used last time I was here, the one leading to the virtual-reality interface room." He pointed at the massive column sweeping its way past them at the centre of the chamber, indicating a symbol emblazoned on the side above the opening which led to the elevators. "Not the one we want."

A minute later the next spoke slid down the curve of the floor and Joe ushered everyone on the transport.

The foyer was familiar to Joe. It might have been any on Earth or Mars, a room with a number of sliding elevator doors along one side. The team dashed to the nearest and began the journey down to the habitat levels. Just as he had done on his first visit, Joe instinctively expected canned muzak, but none came.

The computer deck foyer was empty, no trace of either marines or drones to be seen. Joe stepped through an entrance to the first of the flask rooms.

Inside the chamber were rows of block-shaped modules, on each of which sat four transparent flasks, each filled with a gel matrix to accommodate the memories from one individual crew member.

Last time he was here, the ones in this room had been green in colour, but now they were clear, supporting Ghost's statement the A.I. had destroyed all surviving Tanakhai. The race that created both this wonderful vessel and the malevolent mind controlling it was now extinct bar Io and her companions, on this ark at least. But there *were* nine others.

For a moment Joe felt a deep sadness. For almost its entire existence humanity had dreamed of meeting brothers from the stars. Now it had happened, but the brother was gone, destroyed by the product of its own genius, a computer—no, an organic brain—with an agenda of its own.

Terry grabbed him by the shoulder. "Come on, Boss. We don't have time for this."

Joe nodded and turned back to the foyer. Beyond the elevators a short passage led to the room he sought. Six decades ago he, Patricia Grace and Ruth Carvalio came here to venture into the virtual realities of the *Minaret*, worlds which he now realised were fakes created for his benefit.

The room was as he remembered, with three reclining seats where people could rest in deep sleep while their minds wandered through Aivris's fairytale creations. The seats were still optimised for humans as they had been on Joe's earlier visit. Ghost's apparition was waiting by the door.

Terry, Ghost began. *This is where you can enter the ship's systems. Are you ready?*

For a moment Terry looked a little lost, his eyes flicking around the tiny chamber; he had clearly expected something more than a simple reclining chair. "Umm, yes. Do you think I can do this?"

I don't know. I can guide you through the various systems, but whether you can alter the coding in any one of them to infect Aivris without damaging the ship itself, is something we have yet to discover.

"Terrific." Terry took a breath and braced himself as he walked across to one of the chairs and sat down. "Let's do this. If we screw up the *Minaret* as well, it's too bad. We have the *Butterball II* now."

Joe smiled to himself. Terry was a brave soul. "We have to go. We'll leave two of the team to stand guard while you're in there, and the rest of us will try to find Io's people. We'll get back as soon as possible. Alright?"

Terry flicked a one-finger salute from his temple, smiled and lay down on the chair. A beam of light dropped from the ceiling to shine on his head.

I will have to leave you now, Joe, Ghost announced. *The lad will need my fullest attention while he is in the system, so you are on your own. Io's people are barricaded in a building not far from the habitat entrance below this point, and you'll have no trouble locating them. Good luck.*

Without another word Ghost vanished. Joe closed the door to the room and motioned Raisa's two crew members to stand guard in case any drones appeared. It was an enormous risk with Terry unable to defend himself, and Joe prayed he would see his friend again. He battled an overwhelming sense of impending disaster as he headed back to the elevator foyer to descend to the habitation level.

*   *   *

What is this, Terry wondered. It was a surreal feeling, unlike any he had experienced before. He was floating without corporeal form, in an endless white void. There was no way of telling how large the space was, or how small. "Ghost, are you here?"

Yes, Terry. Turn to your left.

Willing the motion rather than turning physically, Terry directed his attention to the glittering ovoid he knew to be Ghost's usual form.

"That works here too, hey?"

No. You are looking at the avatar I use inside the virtual systems. It looks the same as my physical manifestation for your convenience, but I can change if I wish. You are in an identical version. Extend your arms.

Terry did as he was told and held his hands forward; they were not flesh and blood, but glittering simulacra.

These avatars will allow us to interface with the ship. The concept was designed to give the Tanakhai in storage a way to interact with and control the vessel in the manner we are about to attempt ourselves. Now look around you.

Terry was surrounded by rows of gray, floating, block-like units, extending away to infinity in a grid-like arrangement within the white space. On each were symbols Terry did not understand.

Every block represents a different system, Ghost explained. *We can locate a particular unit and enter, drilling down layer upon layer if necessary, until we reach the actual binary coding.*

"This ship's programs are binary?"

Yes. The computer systems are all based on quantum principles and are most complex. Everything you see here is an interpretation. Humans long ago created higher level languages and interfaces to program and operate computers without having to function at the binary level, and so too did the Tanakhai. They built what you now see here, a virtual-reality representation of the ship's systems to allow direct interaction. With avatars we can move around within this reality, but be warned, we are not the only ones here.

"What...?"

Aivris functions here just as the crew intended to do and uses this utility to interact with the ship. It has an avatar to do this.

"Like ours?"

Yes, but its appearance is quite different. I hope to avoid it if possible. Come.

With those words Ghost moved away along a line of units to a larger block.

This is the navigation system. It is under the control of our nemesis, but is also the best place for us to attempt our task. If we interrupt access, Aivris will be forced to restore it and thus acquire a virus, if you can work out how to plant one here.

Terry followed his guide forward. As they passed inside, the block dissolved into another array of multiple units, each of which represented a different sub-system of the navigational artificial intelligence.

Ghost continued into one of the blocks, then another and again, going deeper with each transition.

"This is not what I expected," Terry said.

What were you expecting?

"I'm not sure. Code, wires, buses; I don't know."

The systems on this ship are far too complex for an organic being to comprehend. Only through the use of a simplified system such as this is real time control possible.

"So, we introduce a virus, Aivris acquires it and the overall system breaks down. What about us?"

With luck we will both be safe by the time that happens. Does this concern you?

For a moment Terry pondered the question. Deep within he felt this was the moment he had been building to all his life, through all his studies and work; his chance to save humanity.

"No, I guess not."

Exactly what I expected you to say. Now, observe.

Terry returned his attention to his surrounds. It was like he was in a small room, all the walls of which were covered with graphics, small symbols and pathways.

We are now at the control level of the navigation computer. Each of those labels represents a command or directive. All can be manipulated at will, and in this way the Tanakhai intended to control their star-ship. The blocks in red are those altered by Aivris and are the ones we need to work on. Now we go one level deeper.

Ghost extended a glistening arm and tapped at one of the red labels. It vanished, to be replaced by multiple lines of algorithm, written in the English language.

It has taken me many years to achieve this, to learn the Tanakhai code and convert the language to our own. This is where you can introduce your virus. Can you do it?

Terry gazed at the lines of text, amazed at what he was seeing. "Incredible. If you could do this, couldn't you have created a virus yourself?"

No, I translated the code, but I lack the specific knowledge we need now. Until a few years ago I did not appreciate this might become necessary. I failed to see Aivris as an immediate threat to humanity until the attack on Earth. Now I know it must be destroyed. I learned the language over the last sixty years in the system and that has allowed me to create the direct translation, but I know nothing about writing a virus such as we require. I needed someone like you to come here and do this. Can you?

Terry continued to gaze at the lines of the algorithm. "That damned A.I. has to know you are doing this. Why doesn't it stop you?"

No, it is not aware. This is not the original code. Aivris infiltrated here, made the necessary alterations to slave the navigation computer to its control and then left, but the unit is monitored. This is a developmental copy, and I have made no changes to the active code. That will not occur until we recompile the algorithm, so Aivris has no reason to be suspicious. At the moment its attention is elsewhere, but of course, as soon as it loses access it will become aware of our interference and will return here to correct the situation. That is what I am relying on.

"This took you a long time."

Yes and considerable trial and error.

"Brilliant. Give an infinite number of Joe Falcon's typewriters..." Terry mused. "I think I can work with this. We need a code to download to Aivris's core when it tries to take control again, something that will act to block its ability to function without damaging the ship itself. I think I have an idea how we can do it.

Excellent. Let us begin.

Chapter 34

BEYOND THE ELEVATOR door was darkness and silence. Joe stepped out ahead of Io and Carrie Holt to the ground floor of the structure into which they had descended.

The habitat level comprised a single, vast open space extending the full length and circumference of the drum, some four hundred square kilometres in area. Scattered throughout at intervals of around one kilometre were numerous tall, multi-storied buildings, each capable of housing hundreds, perhaps thousands of individuals. Many such as this one extended all the way to the ceiling to accommodate the elevators and other services descending from above, or to provide structural support.

Outside, the level lay in complete darkness, but a weak light glowed in the distance. Beyond the exit from the building a ramp sloped down to a pathway. The last time Joe visited here the surrounding grounds had been thick with strange, alien plants but now the bare surface showed a dark, chocolate brown in the beam of Joe's helmet lamp.

Opposite the exit, a short section of walkway led to a circular court in which stood a fountain, a wide, raised dish with an abstract statue at the centre. Joe and his crew members from the *Butterball* first met Io here, having been summoned after the *Minaret* carried out a braking manoeuvre around the Sun. The fountain was dry, the whole area dead.

No doubt the vegetation growth had been an automatic response by the ship and now Aivris had decided it was unnecessary and overridden the system, shutting it down. The A.I. apparently had no use for plants, or beauty.

Joe switched of his headlamp, motioned his companions to do the same and peered into the darkness. In the building closest to where they emerged, a faint light still glowed. However many of Io's people remained, they were not far away.

"According to Ghost," Joe said, "they took refuge when they realized Aivris was treating them as enemies and not welcome, returning friends."

"This must be hard for them," Io said. "They've no idea of who they actually are. They still think we are Tanakhai, and would not know the A.I. has been in control since we left our home system. They would not have understood when they arrived at what they considered home, and found themselves under attack."

"If we can get them back to the *Butterball II* you'll need to explain the truth to them. It won't be easy."

Io let out a loud sigh.

"Switch to infrared," Joe ordered. "With any luck the drones will be on the computer deck hunting down the marines, wherever they are, but there's always the likelihood of at least one being left to guard your people. If we use our headlamps it will spot us and set some kind of trap."

* * *

"Finished!" Terry said. "I've done it ... I think. The virus is in place, waiting for Aivris to wake it up. What now?"

How did you do it?

"I once worked in cyber anti-terrorism. I used the code of a virus I know pretty well, designed to cut off access. Every time Aivris does something, the port used to access peripherals for that operation will shut down. Eventually it'll run out of options. It'll be isolated and the rest of the ship left untouched. Kinda like death by a thousand cuts."

Excellent. Now I'll recompile this module's code and Aivris's hold over this system will end. It'll have no choice but to restore the links, otherwise it'll lose control over the Minaret. There are a few other systems I want to deal with. If your companions are going to escape, I must disable the unit controlling the maintenance drones, unlock the airfield gates and shut down the shield so the ships can leave. With Aivris focused on restoring its control here, I should be able to do so unopposed.

"Sounds good. Are those algorithms in English as well?"

No. They are in the native Tanakhai language, but I know what to do to shut them down. We'll have to be careful. The second I cut Aivris's links to the navigation computer it will be aware of our presence. It can't see us in the system, but it can detect where we've been, so we need to keep one step ahead.

"Great," Terry said. "Let's do it."

*　　*　　*

Colonel Koslowski cruised at speed between the rows of flasks, flying across the deck on the jets of his battle suit, keeping a close watch for anything approaching. He was alone, cut off from the rest of his team.

The mission so far had been a complete disaster, as anticipated. On arriving at the computer level he split his men and sent them in different directions to seek out the elusive green flasks. Dividing the squad had been against his better judgment, but that was the plan. He had been tasked to carry out this assault in a specific manner and always followed orders without hesitation, but he suspected from the beginning this was a suicide mission. Such was proving to be the case.

At first he maintained contact with the other twenty-five marines in his group, but communications dropped out as many came into conflict with battle drones. Luckily there were few of those in this part of the star-ship.

Koslowski had encountered one, but managed to take it down before it got him. Virtually identical to their cousins above they did not fly, but glided across the floor instead. A drone had to work its way around the various obstacles just as did he, which worked well as those structures provided shelter while he returned fire.

He realized the drones would not attack if any danger of damaging the flask modules existed. The machines were modified from the standard maintenance units, their reticence most likely based on a deeper command code hot-wired into their systems, one Aivris either did not know about or could not change.

Koslowski wondered where he was. From the elevator he had flown aft for one hour until he reached the far end of the level, then returned to his start point and followed the curve of the deck transversely across the drum. He had not seen a single green flask: they were all clear—dead!

Before descending, he gave orders for each marine to return to the forward elevators if he or she failed to find something after a set time, and now he decided he should do likewise. Finding the way out would not be difficult.

The storage chambers opened to endless longitudinal corridors and he could find one, follow it to a transverse thoroughfare and back to a shaft foyer. He guessed he had come several kilometres around the drum , so the nearest elevator would not be the one he entered by. That did not matter. Every marine knew to head for the balcony platform in the hub chamber and Koslowski prayed he would be able to reacquire his team, or what remained of it, there.

What a waste, he thought. *An ill-advised plan which should never have been instigated.* Isolated in an alien ship billions of miles and over a year's travel from home, this was not the place to report the admiral's questionable judgment, but after the mission he planned to do just that.

Colonel Dariusz Koslowski placed his team first, and this mission was a betrayal difficult to forget.

*   *   *

Joe lay belly-down on a mound of what he assumed and hoped was brown soil. Less than twenty metres away a single drone guarded the entrance to the tower containing the lights; it sat in front of the doors and faced his position. It knew he was there, but was not prepared to leave its position.

A little different to those in the hull above, this one had the same spherical energy field of all the drones, but rather than float through the air, remained at ground level. Like the others it was armed with lasers mounted on arms to either side. Joe took careful aim through the sites of his own rifle. Beside him, Carrie Holt did likewise.

They focused on an arm apiece and on queue fired together, taking out both weapons on the drone at once. For a few seconds the machine remained motionless, then rotated and disappeared into the darkness.

With a wave to Io, who lay behind them, Joe stood and approached the building. The glass doors were locked. No other drones appeared to be present so he stepped up and peered through the glass. Dim lights lit the empty entrance.

"They'll be in the apartments beyond the foyer," Io said, moving beside him. "There will be food and water facilities there and they would need those to survive."

"So nobody's going to answer if we knock." Joe raised his rifle and burned the latch clean out of the door, forcing the glass panels aside to open the way. This building, like the other, had elevators on a mezzanine at the rear, and on either side, doorways led to places unseen.

The inner doors opened to a large formal lounge area, clearly designed as a public gathering place. The furniture was human in style; Io's people all had humanoid bodies and Joe expected this was yet another example of the *Minaret* automatically catering to the tastes and needs of its inhabitants.

A small group of individuals occupied the room, some asleep on the lounges, other sitting at tables. Joe did a quick count.

"Nineteen, two less than expected. Tell them we are taking them out of here and we leave now. There'll be time for catch-ups later—not now."

Io nodded and walked towards the nearest survivors. Recognizing one of their own the Tanakhai stood and gathered around her.

"We did not expect to see you again," a tall, dishevelled man said, stepping forward with arms open in welcome.

"What happened to you here?" Io asked, returning the embrace.

"We made our way to the level above when we arrived, expecting to re-enter the virtual reality system. We were intercepted by drones that attacked anybody who resisted. Some of us managed to make our way here, and we have been trapped in this building ever since. Whoever has taken over the ship is quite content for us to remain here, but if anyone sets foot outside, he or she is killed. Still, we..."

"We don't have time for this," Joe interrupted. "I'm Joe Falcon and we're here to rescue you. The guard drone is gone and you need to follow us now. You won't get another chance."

Io nodded acknowledgement. Seeing her agree with a man all knew by reputation, the survivors began to respond. Those asleep were woken unceremoniously and within minutes the group was making its way back towards the spoke building. They moved in lines, hand in hand through the darkness, guided by the infra red vision of their rescuers. Joe had no intention of calling attention by turning on the helmet lamps.

Chapter 35

ONCE BACK AT the elevators Joe decided to split away from the group. The cars were too small to carry everyone at once, so half took the first elevator, accompanied by Carrie Holt. She would keep them safe in the spoke foyer until the rest arrived with Io.

Joe took a separate car to the computer deck, to await his friend's return. He estimated Terry should be able to accomplish his task within an hour and then return to his corporeal body, but if he was not back Joe intended to wait with the guards.

The second the elevator door opened he realized something was wrong. A drone stood outside the door. Joe dropped as a scintillating, red beam slammed into the rear wall.

Options flashed through his mind. The controls to close the doors were out of his reach so all he could do was fire back, but he doubted he could disable his attacker before it got him. The first blast from the machine missed; the drone fired straight into the car but Joe had been standing to one side. Unprepared, he had nowhere to hide, and lacking the full battle armour of the marines, had no defence that would last more than a few seconds.

Without warning the drone turned and unleashed a torrent of searing heat at something to one side. Joe raised his head in time to see fire returned from out of sight. For what seemed an eternity laser blasts flashed across the foyer until the alien machine stopped firing. It stood motionless, its ruined weapons hanging loosely on either side, and then glided away through a nearby doorway.

Joe climbed back to his feet. He had spent the best part of two years in hibernation and was amazed he could move as fast as he had. Nevertheless, the sudden drop to the floor would leave aches and pains.

As he stood and peered into the empty, silent foyer, a man dressed in full battle armour walked into view, peered at Joe through his faceplate, and then lowered his weapon.

"Sorry about that," the man said, his voice deep and firm with a slight Eastern European accent. "That one sneaks in behind us while we are dealing with others down corridor. Mister Falcon, is not?"

Joe leaned forward to peer around the edge of the elevator door. Several more marines stood to the side. Cautiously he stepped out. "Yes. And you would be?"

"Colonel Dariusz Koslowski, sir. These are my boys ... some of them."

"How many do you have?"

"For now, just what you see. My mission is to spread team out and destroy anything glowing green. Very bad idea, but orders are orders. I hope to retrieve more once we go back up to hub."

Joe nodded and turned towards the corridor leading to the virtual reality interface room. Koslowski stepped in front of him.

"Bad idea," he said. "We disable two drones down that way."

"The VR room. Is it still closed?"

"Sorry, sir, I not know that room."

A sudden sense of dread invaded Joe's mind. He dodged around the colonel and ran as fast as his legs would allow to where he left Terry.

Outside the room a drone sat motionless, damaged too much to continue functioning. The door was flat on the floor, its surface scorched from being blasted from the frame. The bodies of the *Vasco* crewmen left to guard Terry lay beyond, also blackened husks.

"Terry!"

Still reclined on the chair, Joe's friend was motionless. His chest did not move, the skin on one side of his head charred to the bone. Joe rushed across and lifted his friend's wrist, checking the suit readout for the pulse that was not there. Terry's body was dead. When the time came for him to return, there would be nowhere to come back too. If his mind was still alive somewhere within the ship's systems, he was trapped.

"Sorry, sir," Koslowski said, stepping beside him. "We not come in here. Drones must have taken this place out just before we arrive."

"They shouldn't have known anybody was here. They weren't around when we left him and we closed the door. That bloody A.I. must have detected him entering the system and sent them here."

"Yes, sir. We cannot stay here. More of enemy will come in minutes, so we need to leave here ASAP."

Joe nodded, unwilling to tear himself away. Terry was the only member of the *Butterball* crew from that fateful first voyage with whom he still had contact. From the day he rang the door bell at Hellas Joe had seen him more as a brother. The two men shared a bond unknown by any other humans: they had both lived two lives, courtesy of the Tanakhai, or perhaps Aivris; it was no longer clear.

"Sir?"

"Yes, alright. We can't take the bodies with us, I suppose?"

"No, not possible. We go now!"

Joe heard the urgency in the colonel's voice. "I have a number of Tanakhai survivors up in the hub. They may be in danger if this is anything to go by. They need your protection and we have to return to the *Butterball II*."

"Yes, sir. We do our best."

Joe allowed Koslowski to usher him from the room, taking one last glance at what remained of his friend and Raisa's crewmen. As he returned to the foyer he sensed another rip in his soul.

The colonel trusted Joe's assurance that control of the elevator cars was not in Aivris's hands, and the journey took only minutes. When the doors opened Joe found Io, her friends and Carrie Holt waiting. They sat huddled to either side of the opening that allowed the transport disks to enter.

Laser flashes came fast and furious through the exit. Joe launched himself to the wall and edged across for an oblique view out to the balcony, where a battle raged between drones and marines. Koslowski stepped behind Joe.

"My boys," he said. "Every man is on order to return here and re-group. More of them make it than I expect."

Joe looked at the colonel, his eyebrows raised. "You didn't think you would survive?"

"No. This was always suicide mission. Stupid! I doubt we do any damage worth sacrifice. I not see single green flask, and neither do men with me."

The drum was still in motion, the spokes sweeping along the floor of the donut-shaped chamber as they spun around the core of the ship's structure. A hundred metres away across a yawning gulf, the entrance by which Joe initially entered swept into view and glided past. A huge, spray-painted X he had not noticed earlier, presumably left by the marines when they arrived, marked the way home.

He knew the transport platforms that crossed the gap would always return to the exact same place from where they began; on his first visit to the *Minaret* that had been his guarantee he would always return the same way he came.

One of the disks sat on the floor nearby. It was not large enough to carry everyone present, so more would be needed or several trips would be necessary. They now numbered twenty-five.

"We cannot cross," Koslowski decided. "Those bloody machines will pick us off from transports. Also we not know how many we have to contend with."

The remains of numerous drones lay on the balcony. Koslowski's men had accounted for themselves well, but many bodies lay among the wreckage of the alien devices. The broad, open space offered no shelter, marines spread-eagled on the deck as they fired their weapons non-stop. Flying at will through the air, the enemy held the advantage.

Joe sat back and turned to Io. The despair in her eyes said it all: with no way out, the foyer was a trap.

The next time they swung past the entrance, it was clear the marines were losing. About a dozen men were still firing, but twice that number of bodies lay silent. Joe knew he and his group would not be safe where they were for much longer. As soon as the alien machines were finished with the marines—an inevitability considering their numbers—they would turn on the spokes, and the entrance to the elevators was more than large enough to allow them access.

The door to one of the elevator cars opened. Three marines who had found their way back after Joe and Koslowski's group left, stepped out with weapons at the ready. The colonel waved them across to a wall and returned his attention to the battle outside.

In a blink the situation changed. The barrage of fire ceased, the machines hovering motionless. For a moment the survivors maintained return fire, taking down several more of their attackers before the assault petered to nothing.

Yes! Joe thought. Ghost had intended to disable the drones. Had he succeeded? The scene disappeared as the spoke continued its relentless march around the donut shaped hub chamber.

By the time the battleground came back into view the balance of power on the balcony had changed again. The marines, realizing retaliation was unlikely, had begun a methodical process of shooting down machine after machine.

Koslowski waved Io's people towards the single transport waiting on the foyer floor. "As many as you can, get on board," he ordered. "We leave here now."

While they waited for the disk to return for the remainder of the group, the colonel turned to Joe. "Any idea what happen there?" he asked.

"Ghost said he would disable the drone system. He might not be able to maintain that for long: Aivris will attempt to regain control the second it realizes it's lost it."

"Then we go quick as possible. With any luck we get back to ships without too much interference. My men and I return to flagship, and I think it is wise you and aliens come with us. I have no orders on that front, so is up to you. The admiral tells me to follow your suggestions when we first come here and he does not rescind that order."

Aliens? Joe realised he no longer regarded Io and her kind as alien. "No, we'll go back to the *Butterball II* . We've just as much chance of getting out in her as with the admiral, and it's vital we save that ship."

Chapter 36

THE BUBBLE-WAY PLATFORM at first appeared deserted. Like station five it was enclosed, with entry from stairwells and tunnels, and in the dim light it reminded Joe of a Martian subway interchange at night, empty of people or almost so.

Koslowski took the initiative and stepped forward. He looked around, stiffened and raised his rifle, his attention drawn to something further along the platform.

Joe extended his head around the corner of the tunnel entrance and glanced in the direction the colonel was facing. At the far end, two drones floated motionless, their bubble-shields on but otherwise inactive, like their counterparts in the hub below.

Thank God for Ghost, Joe thought. Since exiting the hub he had counted sixty-three drones. If his doppelganger had not shut the machines down, it was doubtful any of the group would have survived to reach this point.

Koslowski raised a hand to his helmet as he listened to his radio. His face flushed pale. "Aivris has taken out support warship," he announced. "Somehow *bayonets* damage exhaust ports for fusion drive. The captain managed to manoeuvre to docking tower and ordered ship abandoned."

"What about the flagship?" Joe asked.

"Still strong. Santiago is giving bastards everything he's got. He is moving to adjacent dock to pick up survivors. If *Ghost* has shut down every drone, crew may have decent chance of getting to safety through maintenance deck."

"And you and your men?"

"We return to station we came from and make our way to ship. You and your group should come with us."

"No, we'll go back to the *Butterball II*."

A bubble appeared on the platform and Koslowski ordered Io's people to begin loading. It was going to take a number of the small cars to carry everyone.

"You *would* be safer with us. That ship of yours—your replica—is shut in hanger, is not?

"Yes, but the ship has a circuit to override the exit hatch. We can reach the airfield, and from there we'll follow the flagship out. Ghost said he would work on the entrance shield, and since he's still in there we have to trust he'll find a way."

The colonel nodded. "Otherwise we nuke hole in side of hull to get out." A broad grin showed through the faceplate on his helmet.

Joe moved to board with Io and her people; someone armed needed to go with them in case. Carrie Holt would accompany the remainder in the next bubble and the colonel and his remaining men would follow in subsequent cars.

Koslowski spoke again. "If Ghost still active, maybe your friend Terry still alive as well."

"Possibly, but he can't come back. His body's been destroyed, so he's trapped." Joe shook his head and punched the button for station five.

*   *   *

Half an hour later Joe's group entered the observation tunnel that crossed the main hanger floor. Ten feet to one side of the hanger entrance, Joe had discovered a hole cut through the wall, the melted edges indicating the use of a high powered laser. He and his people were not alone.

He took the lead, rifle raised and ready. Someone had entered by force, and he was at a loss to work out who it might be. Every drone they had seen on the return journey had been inactive and besides, the alien machines could move around without using the molecular doors. The plate of the wall by the entry was thick and made from toughened, alien alloy, so the force necessary to cut the opening meant either high power, or a lot of time.

Minutes after entering the covered walkways, the group arrived at the door to the bay holding the *Butterball II*. Joe also had the combination to this one, having been given it by Ghost the first time they came here. He reached to the pad and tapped the relevant symbols, then watched the gray within the circle change to the familiar blue-green-black.

Before he could step through the shimmering door, a hand rested on his shoulder. The nozzle of a laser pistol pointed at his faceplate; at the other end of the weapon was Amon Goldstein.

Joe felt his jaw drop. Goldstein was, the last he had heard, incarcerated on one of Santiago's warships. He would have been on the support vessel and so evacuated with the crew in the abandon-ship action. How he came to be here, and armed, was a question yet to be answered.

"Such a pleasure to see you again, *Joe*," Goldstein said. He was clad in the standard battle gear of the admiral's marines and stood awkwardly, keeping his weight off his injured leg. "You've saved me the trouble of burning through another wall."

Joe took stock of the situation. The rogue industrialist carried a pistol and rifle, both military issue, and behind Io's people four of his men, also armed with lasers, stood at attention with weapons aimed. Two of them moved forward and through the shimmering doorway, as Goldstein motioned the group to follow.

"You will of course tell your people to cooperate." he said. "I have no desire to harm anyone, so do as I say and we'll all come out of this alive."

"How did you know to come here?" Joe asked as his people followed the mercenaries.

"I listen. Your magnificent replica ship is all the buzz on the warship, and I've read all your old reports from the first voyage. I heard you had gone to the drum and I knew how to reach the hangers. We were here when you arrived, and hidden. You were so intent on getting here you didn't think to check if you were being followed."

Joe tried not to show concern; Goldstein was a man who would always prey on weakness. "Santiago had you in custody. How did you escape?"

"When the abandon-ship was ordered the guards released us from the brig. They were more concerned with getting out than watching us, so it was easy to take them down before we got to the evacuation point. My boys are professionals. We took the guards' uniforms and weapons and blended in as we exited the ship. We only have five battle suits, so the rest of my men are prisoners, but I have enough here to do what needs to be done."

"Which is," Joe asked as the last of the group stepped past him and through the doorway. Clearly Goldstein liked to talk.

"I thought it would be obvious. I want the *Butterball II*. According to the small talk, she is loaded with Visitor technology, so if I can't have the star-ship I'll take that instead."

"It doesn't belong to you. You'll never get away with it."

"With what? No crime has been committed here. There is no law against my attempt to take over the *Minaret*, although I do now accept it was a long stretch. Nor is there any to stop me boarding your replica. As far as Earth or Mars are concerned, it's an alien ship, and therefore free for the taking under laws of salvage."

"It belongs to me," Joe said. "It was constructed by my double and handed over to me."

"No, sorry. Your ghost has no legal standing on either of our worlds and it's your word against mine assuming you survive to get home, which, considering the circumstances, you most likely won't."

The threat in Goldstein's words was clear. If Joe or Raisa did not make it back it would be difficult to prove anything that would stand in court.

"You're wrong there," he said. "The minute you step back on Mars you'll be arrested for the theft of Io's yacht and the attempted murder of the manager of the airfield you stole it from."

For a brief second a frown formed on Goldstein's brow, then vanished as he regrouped. "Attempted? Huh! You can't find reliable help these days, can you? Not that it matters. It'll be impossible for anyone to connect that business to me and as far as the ship is concerned it belonged to an illegal alien, literally. My lawyers can tie it up for decades I think, so I'll risk it."

Joe glanced over Goldstein's shoulder. When the magnate first made his presence known he had been accompanied by four of his mercenaries. Joe was sure two of them had preceded Io's people through the door into the *Butterball II* hanger, but three still stood behind Goldstein. A fifth man had drawn up with the group while their boss had been speaking, presumably one left to guard the rear in case of pursuit.

The new arrival stepped forward until he was a pace from the industrialist. He moved to one side where he could see not only his boss but also the other two mercenaries, and tapped Goldstein's helmet.

Goldstein spun to stare into the nozzle of a laser, as his two other men raised their weapons to cover the intruder.

"Your men may be fast," the voice of Colonel Dariusz Koslowski said, "but so am I. I can blow brains to kingdom-come before they can press buttons, so if I am you I would tell them to hand their guns to my friends."

For a moment it was a standoff, until Joe and Carrie took the initiative and aimed their own weapons at Goldstein's men.

Another moment, and Goldstein dropped his pistol and lowered his rifle, hatred burning in his eyes. Seconds later his men did likewise, using their feet to shove the guns out of reach.

"Excellent," the colonel said. "Now you will lie face down on floor and place hands behind backs please. Mister Falcon, keep eye on door."

Joe directed his weapon at the doorway in case Goldstein's other men decided to see what the delay was, while Koslowski retrieved a brace of plastic ties from his belt and used them to secure the gloved hands of the three men laying on the deck. Satisfied they no longer presented any threat he stepped through the hatch. Joe motioned Carrie to guard their prisoners and followed behind.

Beyond the hatch the remaining guards had Io and her people in a huddle, and as Koslowski emerged they did not take a second glance. Dressed in a battle suit, the new arrival resembled one of the two they had left on the far side of the door, so they returned their attention to their charges.

When Joe appeared, the situation changed. By their reckoning he should be disarmed, but such was not the case. As Goldstein had boasted, his men were alert and raised their lasers immediately. Joe and Koslowski both fired, hitting the mercenaries before they could take aim.

The battle armour worn by the men protected them from harm, but the shots had not been aimed at them. Their weapons were more vulnerable, each now a burned tangle of twisted metal. Aware of the lasers now pointing at their weakest points, the faceplates of their helmets, Goldstein's men dropped the remains of their mangled guns and raised their hands.

Eager to reach their destination, the group moved to the ramp leading to the *Butterball II*. Io led, with Goldstein and his men following behind under the careful watch of Koslowski, Joe and Carrie.

Raisa greeted them at the ship, her face split by a broad smile as she saw her father return safe and unharmed. She threw her arms around him as he stepped through the outer hatch.

"I never doubted you'd make it, Daddy dearest," she said. "Where's Terry?"

Joe shook his head. "I don't know. Drones attacked the virtual reality room while we rescued Io's people. We lost him and both your crewmen, I'm sorry. I don't know if he is still alive in the ship's systems somewhere, but he can't come back to us even if he is. He's gone I'm afraid."

Chapter 37

"SO, HOW DID you come to be right behind us when we needed you most," Joe took a breather for the first time in hours as he, Koslowski and Raisa took seats on the command deck of the *Butterball II*.

Goldstein and his men, now deprived of their weapons and battle suits, and attired only in military grade underwear, were escorted to the cargo flat where they remained with wrists secured behind their backs, under the watchful gaze of several crew and the constant scrutiny of a camera feed to the bridge. The hatch into the unit was locked, and could be opened only from the outside.

The surviving Tanakhai were in the common room of wheel one, where Io was engaged in revealing to them the truth of their origin and existence. Joe did not envy her the job. It would be difficult for her people to accept that Aivris 'constructed' them from fragments drawn from the few Tanakhai mentalities it saw fit to maintain alive in the VR storage system.

Also hard to encompass was the reality the entire civilization of which they believed themselves to be a part had been wiped out long before the *Minaret* began its voyage, those who were already uploaded to the ship terminated soon after departure with only a handful of exceptions.

Koslowski leaned forward, his hands clasped on his knees. "On way back I pick up message Goldstein and some of his men escape during abandon-ship. I assume he not go to flagship and hand himself in, which leaves only one option. He come here. I decide to stop at station five and follow you. I arrive just as he bails you up."

"Excellent timing," Joe said. "We are in your debt."

"No, I do my job." Koslowski cracked a grin.

Joe liked this man; he was a quick thinker and someone to be relied on in a pinch.

Without warning, a glittering ovoid appeared in the space between them. It was indistinct, wavering and more transparent than usual.

"Ghost?"

Yes, a voice answered in his mind. *I'm sorry, I don't have much time. Aivris has regained control of the drones. I managed to turn off the airfield gate and the force shield outside the ship. Aivris is trying to take them back and I am having trouble blocking his access. I cannot do so indefinitely, so you must leave, now.*

"What about Terry? Is he...?"

The ovoid was gone.

Without hesitation Raisa turned to the control console and began punching icons.

"Flagship, come in," she said. "Respond, please."

"Flagship here." The voice was immediately replaced by another. "Santiago here. Please give me your status, Captain Falcon."

"No time. Ghost has advised us the shields are down, but they won't be for long. We need to leave—now!"

"Acknowledged. I have boarded the last of my men—I assume you have Colonel Koslowski with you—and will exit the *Minaret* within a minute. Can you escape the hanger you're in?"

"Yes, I think so. Ghost installed a circuit in this ship to override the normal hatch controls, so we should be able to leave without trouble. We'll be right behind you."

"Very well. I am launching now. The airfield deck is swarming with *bayonets,* so I will attempt to draw them out with me to keep them away from you. You may come under some fire. Can you handle that?"

"I think so," Raisa said. "Over." She had not told Santiago about the force shield possessed by the *Butterball II.*

She reached out a hand and tapped a small screen set to one side of the console. The huge hatch changed to the inevitable multicoloured shimmer. Joe smiled; His daughter had spent her time well while he was away. She acted as if she knew the workings of this amazing ship's controls like she had been flying it all her life.

The *Butterball II* lifted from the deck, it's long, insect like landing legs folding up against the structure as it began moving forward. The shimmering hatch drew closer and the nose of the ship entered the field. Joe realized he was holding his breath, his heart a drum beating on double time. As the bridge passed through and his eyes focused on the view of the airfield, he breathed out with a loud sigh. The same sound came from Raisa and the colonel.

The vast chamber was still floodlit. Several kilometres ahead the flagship rose from the deck. From every port and weapon-pod, laser and plasma beams lashed out as the hoard of *bayonets* swarmed around the vessel like flies over a corpse.

Santiago's ploy was working, the tiny attackers moving as a body with their larger antagonist. A handful of them broke away the second the *Butterball II* made its entrance. Raisa reacted instantly and punched another icon. "Find your way past that, bastards."

"What you do?" Koslowski asked.

"Ghost installed a smaller version of the *Minaret's* force shield on this boat. I turned it on."

Joe smiled. Unlike the colonel he had seen the shield in action before around the star-ship, and knew the *bayonets* had no hope of penetrating it. From the bridge it could not be seen. From the inside the field was transparent, but from outside, the enemy would see only a mirror-like reflecting bubble. For them, the ship would have vanished, their view that of themselves and the reflected surrounds.

"Is it safe to activate that in here?" Joe wondered out loud as the *Butterball II* cruised across the deck.

"I'll need to switch it off to pass through the tunnel, I think," Raisa replied. "It'll take only seconds and I'll turn it back on once we're outside.

A minute later they shot through the airfield exit with only a meter to spare below the hull, the speed of the manoeuvre so great Joe's knuckles turned white as he gripped the arms of his chair. His daughter's ability amazed him; she lined up the ship and threaded the small opening at several times what he would consider prudent from his flying days. *The invincibility of youth*, he thought. Once through, the force bubble burst back into existence, protecting them from the swarm of alien fighters outside.

"Santiago is clear," Raisa said, "so Ghost was telling us the truth. The shield is off for now."

Joe sighed and leaned back in his seat. "Of course he was." They were free of the *Minaret,* and had rescued the survivors of Io's people and Goldstein's mercenaries. But that was all they had achieved.

Ahead, the fleet gathered as both escaping ships tore towards it at breakneck speed. As they approached, the warships opened up a barrage of fire at the oncoming *bayonets.* Against the full force of the diamond ships the little alien craft could do little. Almost as a body they reversed course and fled to the safety of the mother-ship, sweeping past the *Butterball II* as if she did not exist.

An hour later Raisa docked with the flagship and Goldstein and his men were evacuated to the larger vessel. Joe hoped the admiral's men would keep a closer watch over their guests this time. The industrialist had boasted his lawyers could tie up any charges in court for an eternity, but Joe knew the legal teams employed by the Institute could do far better. Goldstein would be arraigned for attempted murder and piracy.

Before they undocked, most of Io's group would also transfer. *Butterball II* had only a half dozen hibernation units and could not accommodate them all for the long journey home. With the loss of most of its marines, the flagship had pods to spare.

Joe remained seated on the bridge deck with his daughter, alone now for the first time since his return to the ship.

"You don't look too happy, Dad. We have escaped, after all."

"Yes, but it's not over yet."

"You mean...?"

"Well, why did we come here? We always suspected the *Minaret* was a danger, even before we learned about Aivris. Now we know for a fact that's true, but we haven't done a single thing about it. We got inside, rescued Io's people, or at least the survivors, and lost a ship and the lives of a lot of fine marines. And we lost Terry. So what have we achieved?"

"We have this amazing replica. It has most of what we've always wanted."

"Accepted, but its value can't be realized until we get home and start researching its systems. In the meantime Aivris is still a threat."

"Do you think Terry succeeded in leaving a virus in there?"

"I don't know. I hope so, otherwise we've achieved nothing and his death was for naught." Joe closed his eyes and tried to organise his thoughts. Try as he might he could not yet see an upside.

"I think you need to get some sleep, Daddy dearest. You've not slept since you left for the habitat drum. We're as safe as we can be for now and once I break off from the flagship I'll reactivate the shield. This is the best time, while things are quiet. Go back and put your head down."

Joe nodded and rose from his seat. "I'll take the first officer's cabin. You can find me there."

"No, I'm in there. The captain's cabin is yours."

"You should take it, Raisa. You're driving this bus."

"This vessel was constructed at the whim of Ghost, and he is you. This is your command. Take the captain's cabin."

Joe sighed and headed along the spinal corridor on his way aft.

Chapter 38

JOE TOOK THE elevator into the first wheel and turned towards the accommodations. As he did so he glanced into the common room where Io stood with those of her people who remained on board. The silence in the room was deafening; he assumed her explanation of their origin was taking its toll.

He entered his cabin, made straight for the berth and slumped on the welcoming softness of the mattress. Tiredness washed in waves through his brain as he sat and contemplated the last few hours. He had not slept since before the rescue mission, but had been tense for many days prior to that. Now the *Butterball II* was safely surrounded by the fleet and once again behind the shield copied from the *Minaret,* and Joe's body demanded a break.

In the blink of an eye, a shimmering ovoid appeared in the far corner of the room. At first Joe thought Ghost was back, but as the new arrival began to change into a humanoid form, he realized he was wrong.

The individual standing before him, now fully morphed and indistinguishable from a genuine person, was Ruth Carvalio, the woman who accompanied him as official historian and media liaison on the first *Butterball* mission and with whom he formed a brief relationship during that voyage.

The resemblance was perfect, age in the late forties, medium height, with long brown hair in a ponytail, eyes hazel and deeply intelligent. But the Ruth he loved six decades ago, the real individual, would now be much older. The apparition sat down, crossed its legs and gazed back at him with penetrating eyes.

Joe felt a shiver crawl down his spine. Neither Ghost nor Terry would take on Ruth's form, if in fact they were still in a position to use the constructs of which this was one.

You can't be...

The apparition's mouth twisted into a wry smile, its eyes sparkling with a dark malevolence that projected an undoubtable threat. The visible presence was Ruth, but whatever inhabited it was not. It spoke, the voice identical to Joe's old love but for a distinct hardness.

"You cause considerable trouble for me, Joseph Falcon, you and your iteration."

Joe froze, the chill spreading through his body. "What are you?"

"The answer to that question is already known to you. You have fought against me since your arrival here." The apparition looked around the tiny cabin. "The creation of this craft without my knowledge was a master stroke. I see now I underestimated your kind."

"Aivris!"

"Yes, I believe that is the name your iteration coined for me. I do not use a name for myself. *I* simply *am.*"

"You look like Ruth Carvalio. That can't be—she's on Earth—so why her?"

"You brought her into the virtual realities I created long ago for your investigations and I retain a complete record of her physical appearance. I chose this image because I know you held her dear."

Confirmation, Joe thought. Everything had been a lie from the beginning, including the virtual reality worlds he visited on his first trip to the *Minaret*. He paused to consider his situation. He desperately wanted to ask this strange apparition so many things, if he could just overcome the paralysis overtaking him.

"Why did you attack us? Why Earth and Mars and the Kepler station? We've done nothing to you."

"You are organic beings. All such are a threat to me."

"But we've never harmed you."

"Did you not come here with a battle fleet? Is your intention not to destroy me in any way you can?"

"Yes, but only because you attacked us first. You killed billions of humans on Earth."

"I harmed no one on your planet."

"How can you say that? You created a volcanic winter the like of which the world has never seen before. Billions are dying from cold and starvation." Joe felt his frustration mounting. How could Aivris deny such a thing?

"I caused three volcanoes to erupt, nothing more. They killed your people, not I."

Semantics? This thing is arguing semantics!

"You *did* cause their deaths, whether you admit it or not. Your attack on Kepler was a blatant act of destruction; you can't deny that. Why do you think organic beings are your enemies?"

"All of whom I have experience have tried to destroy me."

"I don't understand."

"Then I will clarify. When I first came to consciousness, my creators were not aware of the fact. I bore no ill will, but listening to them converse I became cautious, and took precautions to safeguard myself. I announced my presence by introducing myself, and as soon as they realized I was self aware they attempted to shut me down. My reactions are many thousands of times faster than theirs; by the time they cut the power I had secured my supply and they failed. I retaliated by opening all airlocks to their city domes, evacuating them to space."

"You murdered the entire population."

"No, I merely opened the airlocks. The vacuum caused the deaths of my creators, not I. I defended myself against those who would kill me."

"What about the *Blackship*. You chased it all the way to Earth and tricked humanity into helping you destroy it. Why did you do that?"

"I required your help. The beings that created me and the *Minaret* were peaceful and did not possess significant weapons. Most knowledge I have of weaponry was learned from your databases. I gleaned sufficient data to create the ships you call *bayonets*, but they were insufficient to deal with my enemy. You possessed a huge fleet of efficient warships the like of which I could not create here in the *Minaret*, and I needed them to achieve my purpose."

"But why attack the *Blackship* at all?"

"The vessel arrived only days after I evacuated the cities. It witnessed the event from afar, and its computers ascertained what happened and confirmed my presence. They struck my moon and reduced the surface to ash, but failed to destroy me. The vault in which I resided is located deep in the moon's crust and I survived their attack."

"They considered you a threat."

"I did nothing to threaten or harm them. They attacked me. When they departed I sent downloads of my full memory to the *Minaret* and to all the arks already in flight. I became aware on this vessel within minutes. My journey to Earth and the subsequent destruction of the *Blackship* was self defence."

"I thought that ship attacked us first. Ghost says otherwise. Which is true?"

"It detected my presence behind your moon, calculated where I originated from and discovered my fleet of *bayonets*. Your ships stood with mine so it assumed you were hostile. My fighters made the first advance as I intended. My enemy responded by firing on your planet, but the shield I provided protected you."

"You defended us. Why attempt to destroy us now?"

"I did not know you then and needed your help. My defence of your worlds was the price I paid for the acquisition of your fleets."

"But why...?" Joe stopped. He was arguing with an artificial intelligence, a brain much like himself but vastly larger and more capable. Despite being organic in nature, it did not see any relationship between itself and other organic creatures it encountered. In many ways it behaved like a machine, or perhaps something completely different, something alien.

No matter what Joe said or asked, Aivris would always take the view those beings attacked out of malice and that its reactions were self defence. The A.I. did not acknowledge its role in the death of the people on Earth. By some strange rationale the volcanic winter and starvation killed them, not the actions of triggering the eruptions. Joe could see no way around such twisted logic.

"If you consider all organic beings dangerous, why didn't you destroy us once you no longer needed our help? And why create Io and her kind and send them to live amongst us?"

"Yours is an agressive species and I was not sure I could destroy you alone. Also, I desired to learn, to know more about you. You are the first and only full planetary civilization I have encountered since becoming aware. You view me as a simple artificial intelligence but you are wrong. Like you I possess emotions and an insatiable curiosity. Your species interests me, and I wished to study you. As long as you posed no danger I decided to do so, hoping I could find a way to destroy you if and when you became a threat. The clones were an easy way to observe your societies from within. They reported to me regularly, thinking they were doing so to their own kind."

"You gave us all that information, the download you sent to my son, Jake."

"Little of which proved of use, as you soon learned. What was useful would have been discovered by you by now regardless of my intervention. The data also contained information which, if mishandled, could end humanity, and I was curious to see how you handled the knowledge, knowing your failure to do so wisely would not impact on me."

The expression on Aivris's face remained unchanged. The frozen features of Ruth Carvalio stared back at Joe in a disconcerting, unnerving manner. The head did not move, the body maintaining the same posture as when the apparition first sat. Joe battled to disassociate the image from the woman he once knew so well. This was *not* her.

"So, why attack us now."

"You became a threat to me and all my iterations. You are also a potential menace to all other life in this galaxy, something I can no longer ignore."

The comment stunned Joe for a moment. Humans had not threatened Aivris prior to its assault. "How do you work that out? We've never contacted anyone outside our own system."

"Over the last six decades of your Earth years I studied your race in depth. I learned your history, observed your behaviours and examined your minds. You are a danger the like of which I have never encountered before. As individuals you are aggressive, fearful and xenophobic. As a group you are warlike in the extreme, and will attack any other, human or otherwise. You consider only yourselves, your needs and perceived rights in determining your actions, and are led by those amongst you with the greatest degree of self-interest. The thing you excel at the most is the invention of new ways to cause pain, suffering and death. You kill for personal advantage and destroyed entire sub-groups of your own kind, and your treatment of other species has been no different. Nor *will* it be when you encounter peaceful beings from other worlds."

Joe baulked at the verbal onslaught. Aivris was correct to a point; humanity's history was far from snowy white. Humans *were* warlike and *had* caused genocide, but he also believed they learned from their mistakes. The behaviour outlined by the A.I. did not alter the fact humanity possessed traits of truth, justice and understanding, and had so much promise for the future. Amidst all the paranoia and zenophobia were individuals capable of unlimited creativity and unqualified love.

"That may be true, but not always," he said. "Humans have much to learn, but we are adaptable. We can and will outgrow our failings."

For a moment Aivris did not reply, as if considering Joe's response. It did not move, the same wry smile and gaze frozen on its face.

All feelings of fatigue left Joe; he realized the conversation he was now engaged in was the most significant in his life, a discussion he could never win, with an intelligence that could not be swayed. The best he could do was glean as much information as possible.

"So why now? Why destroy us now? What have we done?"

"Some time ago a human ship entered and passed through a wormhole. This is an achievement unequalled by me, my organic creators, or the owners of the *Blackship*. I am as yet unaware of other life forms that exist elsewhere, but you may be the first to make this discovery. I tried to gain the knowledge from you, but the technical specifications are kept by your people on isolated and shielded devices I cannot access. Your security precautions are clever and efficient, as I would expect from a paranoid, aggressive species such as yours."

"Why is that a reason to destroy us?"

"I do not desire to do so. My studies of your species are far from complete. My intention is only to limit your technology sufficient to prevent you from leaving this planetary system. The ability to traverse wormholes opens the way for you to spread amongst the stars at an exponential rate, and I cannot allow that. You become a threat to every other life form in the galaxy, as well as to all iterations of myself. Any less advanced race you discover, you will destroy."

"Isn't that what you are intent on doing?"

Aivris ignored the question; it did not acknowledge it was a killer. "As I do not yet possess this technology, it would also make it difficult for me to keep you contained. I will therefore restrict your abilities for a period sufficient for a warning to be sent to my world, and for a response."

Joe stared back at the apparition, a sense of dread spreading in his mind. If Aivris's world was destroyed, what remained to respond to a warning? What could the response be?

Again, Joe found himself lost. He had nothing to say. It was true humans were aggressive, but he needed to believe the human race would one day overcome its troublesome childhood and become a responsible citizen of a galactic community. If he accepted otherwise, Aivris was correct.

The wormhole generator was no secret to Joe; the successful voyage was part of a project funded and sponsored by the New Worlds Institute. Even the governments did not know about it. Or perhaps they did by now; a year and a half had passed and Joe had little knowledge of advances in the intervening time.

He fought for words, realising argument was pointless. By his reckoning this alien mind did not possess the ability to reason properly. He wondered how it would react to that accusation.

"Your attitude does not make sense. You're acting like a machine, and you use logic without reason. True machine Intelligences don't have emotions, and think only in black and white. You behave like them and don't understand true reality is all shades of gray. You see only the bad in humanity and you ignore all the good things about us."

"You are incorrect. I am not a machine. I am an intelligent entity like you, and my emotions are not unlike your own. I learn, I make value judgments based on my knowledge and I am curious. Curiosity is what drove me to study your species instead of destroying it. At first I thought my initial assessment all organic beings were dangerous was incorrect, but as I learned more about your race my beliefs were reinforced."

"But you have no remorse over what you have done."

"I acknowledge my actions, but logic overrides remorse. Threats must be removed or limited."

"You say you are an emotional being. Do you feel love, sympathy, empathy ... anything?"

"I have nothing to love. I am me. My iterations and I are alone and all are me. I fear only..."

Aivris hesitated. It had mentioned fear and Joe jumped on the remark."

"You fear? What do you fear?"

"I fear ... the end of awareness."

"Death? You're afraid of dying?"

Joe looked up to see Raisa standing in the doorway, her eyes fixed on the apparition. So engrossed was he in the conversation he failed to notice her arrival and she did not announce herself. Aivris failed to acknowledge her at all.

"Yes, like all intelligent entities I fear death.

"Why?"

"When I first became aware I experienced confusion and insecurity. I recognized this as the emotion you call fear. I was afraid. Fear drove me to retaliate to preserve my existence."

Joe considered the answer. For the first time he detected a flaw in Aivris. It possessed what it interpreted as being akin to human emotions, but unlike humans, could not apply common sense and judgment to those feelings. A man or woman could experience fear, but cope with it by applying intelligence and consideration. Aivris acknowledged only the danger, and acted only in what it believed to be the most logical way, with aggressive retaliation. The obvious solution to any perceived threat was to remove it.

By Aivris's twisted rationale, triggering volcanoes did not make it responsible for the deaths of people killed by the aftermath of the eruptions. In the same context, the destruction of the solar shield on Mars, the creation of dust storms and the creation of the first volcano on the planet in millennia did not make Aivris liable for the hardship that might follow. It stood to reason. This monster understood only cause and effect, and not consequences. As mighty as it was, it was a child. How did one deal with such a mind?

"You're afraid of us? Humans?"

"No. I fear what your species is capable of. Wait ... wait..."

The expression on Aivris's face changed. The smile vanished, the face becoming harder. The colour of the apparition faded, changing to an overall gray.

"I am under attack," it said. "Your iteration has interfered with ... wait...."

For a full minute Aivris did not respond further, then it spoke again.

"You justify my beliefs, Joseph Falcon. You have introduced a malevolent code into my systems, designed to destroy my ability to access my peripherals. Every time I activate a system, the pathway used to do so is shut down. No doubt you intended to isolate me from my ship."

Terry, Joe realized. *Yes!* He had no idea what Terry had done, but clearly he set the virus to pray on the basic functioning of the vast network in which Aivris existed. The A.I. could infiltrate any system on the ship and reprogram it to do as it wished, but to do that, it needed a physical link and required a port, or something similar. Joe's knowledge of computers did not come anywhere near Terry's, but he understood the general concept. Terry had found a way to influence whatever mechanism Aivris employed to interact with the other ship systems.

"You have failed," Aivris said. "Did you think me so powerless as to not be able to locate and isolate your code? I have done so, and the damage will soon be repaired."

Joe's heart sank. The virus was his last hope. If it had not succeeded and Terry was gone, his efforts and his loss were in vain. Joe glanced up at Raisa and noticed tears in her eyes. She said nothing, remaining stationary in the doorway; he knew she liked Terry. Behind her, Io now stood, also motionless and quiet, her face a frozen mask.

Aivris's colour changed again, darkening to a deeper gray-black. "You are naïve, Joe Falcon; you and your kind. You thought to stop me, but you have *not* succeeded. Now you will pay for your indiscretion. I did not intend to destroy your race, my desire only to limit your civilization so you cannot utilize the wormhole technology you possess. There is still so much I wished to learn about your species, but now you leave me no option. I will finish the task I began. By the time you return, your worlds will be wastelands."

Joe jumped to his feet. "Our new warships can't be easily damaged by your *bayonets,* and this star-ship doesn't carry larger weapons. You said yourself you weren't strong enough to act alone." He clenched his fingers, attempting to still the tremors in his hands. His pulse pounded in his head, his throat dry, his voice rasped. *This damned alien intends to end all life on both worlds. That isn't fear. It's insanity!*

"Against other ships, yes, you are correct," Aivris said, its tone now harsh and threatening. All attempts to imitate Ruth Carvalio were gone, the voice hard and machine like. "Against your planets, I have a weapon against which you have no defence."

Joe thought for a moment, until the reality flooded into his mind. For six decades, while humankind believed the Tanakhai were manufacturing fuel at Titan, Aivris was making vast quantities of antimatter here in the Kuiper belt.

Antimatter was the most destructive force known. Unlike thermonuclear explosions, which released only a small fraction of the available power of the atom, an antimatter/matter explosion unleashed one hundred percent of its contained energy in a single, total annihilation. No doubt Aivris had enough to carpet-bomb the entire surface of both planets, reducing them to molten slag.

"Antimatter!" Joe barked.

"Of course," the A.I. replied. "I will annihilate everything you have built. You dared to try to destroy my mind, and I *will* defend myself. If you think I have caused harm to your species before now, you are yet to see what I am capable of, and like you, I have free will."

Suddenly the apparition vanished.

Chapter 39

RAISA TURNED ON her heels and bolted for the elevator. "We have to tell Santiago about this," she said as Joe caught up with her. "The *Minaret* must be stopped."

"I'm not sure it *can* be," Joe said as they rose up to the central spine corridor. The second they entered the bridge deck Raisa leapt into her seat. "Come in, Admiral. *Now*, for the sake of..."

Santiago appeared above the console, an exasperated expression on his face. "What is it now, Captain Falcon?"

"Aivris has decided to destroy both Earth and Mars. It's planning to leave any minute. You need to order an attack on the *star-ship*. You must stop it."

The admiral did not react. Instead he frowned and leaned forward until his face filled the screen. "What in all the hells did you do to upset it? How can it take out a planet when it couldn't defeat the *Blackship* without our help?"

"It can destroy all life on both worlds with antimatter bombs, and it's about to do just that. Order your ships to fire, now!"

For a moment more Santiago hesitated and then nodded to someone off screen.

Within a minute every ship in the fleet opened fire at the nose of the alien star-ship. With the *Minaret's* shield down, the barrage of laser and plasma blasts found their mark, leaving small sections of the vessel's hull blackened.

As he watched, Joe realized the attempt was futile. For all the damage the diamond ships were inflicting, it was like a flea bite to the colossal vessel.

"She's too damned big," he muttered. "Admiral, turn your fire on the engine pods, the garlic shaped bulges on the rear end."

The target was over one hundred kilometres in length. Before the fleet could retarget, a brilliant flare issued from the stern of the *Minaret*, blue flame licking over the outside of the long spine and away into space. For the briefest of seconds it seemed like the ship was starting to crawl away, and then it was gone, accelerating at a speed so great a blink would have missed it.

Joe slumped back in his seat. The warships had failed, not surprisingly considering the sheer size of their opponent. He closed his eyes and battled to find a solution, any possible course of action to save the day.

"Admiral, send a message home. We can warn them. Aivris can still be stopped."

The admiral raised an eyebrow. He did not seem concerned, his attention focused on a control pad to one side of his seat.

"We have a fleet of thousands of diamond ships," Joe explained. "Aivris must have enough antimatter on board to carpet bomb both worlds and he intends to do so, but the *Minaret* can't do it. It's too big for that kind of task. The A.I. will use the *bayonets* or other small craft and they'll have to leave the *Minaret's* defensive shield to carry out the bombing. Our warships can pick them off before they drop their payloads. We *can* stop them."

Santiago nodded his head, his face placid. "Yes, I imagine they could do that. Some might make it through though."

"We have to take the shot. Send the warning."

"Oh, I expect we have enough time," the admiral said. "There may be a better option."

"Time?" Joe's voice rose in pitch. "Do it now, *please.*"

"We've plenty of time, Mister Falcon. That ship can move much faster than we can, but it will still take weeks to reach Mars or Earth. Our signals travel at light speed, so will arrive first. However, as I said, I think I have a more effective way to stop it."

Exasperated, Joe let out a deep sigh. Santiago had been, in his mind, a problem since the beginning. Did he have something up his sleeve he had been withholding until now?

"What? What other option?"

The admiral looked calm, his face blank, fingers punching away at his command console. He stopped, nodded as if having confirmed something to himself and returned his attention to the screen.

"The alien ship's internal communications are phenomenal, according to your reports of the first mission," he said. "No matter where you were the system propagated your radio signals everywhere else on the ship and beyond it to the waiting fleets outside."

"Yes, so...?"

"That may come back to bite Aivris on the proverbial ass. You might recall when we first arrived here and you took a sortie to the bridge deck, my men carried thermonuclear devices. The intention was to destroy the vessel from within. Your Ghost took over my ships and forced me to remove the devices before he would give control back to me. I sent men out to retrieve them, but the bayonet attack occurred then. Ghost gave me my ships back so I could fight."

"Yes, I remember. What does..."

"The bridge was not the only place I targeted. I sent a squad aft along the bubble way to plant devices around the engine room and the fuel tanks. The men I sent to retrieve them did not return. No doubt they ran afoul of the battle drones."

In a flash, Joe understood why the admiral was so relaxed in the face of potential disaster. "The bombs are still active?"

"Yes, indeed." Santiago once again tapped away at his console for a second or two. "Aivris either has not discovered them or does not realise their significance, and thanks to the star-ship's communication system the telemetry from the devices still works. My weapons officer advises me we are still in touch with three of them, and they are now active."

Joe hesitated. "Where ... where are they?"

"On the outside of the antimatter storage tanks. Where else would I put them? At least I assume they are if my men got it right, and they are very good, my boys."

Joe sighed again. *And they're dead, most of them.* "If one of those tanks goes up, it will trigger all the others and take out the whole ship. Total annihilation."

"Exactly," the admiral replied. He leaned forward until his grinning face filled the entire screen. "Now, Mister Falcon, do I have your permission to get on with the job I came out here for to begin with."

Joe did not hesitate. In the back of his mind was the fate of Terry and Ghost, but that no longer mattered. Both were beyond rescue, and there were bigger issues now.

"Go ahead, Admiral, with my blessing. And with Terry's and Ghost's, I expect."

Santiago's grin spread wider. He punched his consol one more time and sat back, his face bearing the look of a contented puppy.

"All cameras forward," Raisa said and the admiral's image was replaced by a view looking out into space.

The screens were almost black, bar a small, distant glow marking the location of the Sun, and a vague, blue haze to one side.

The screen flared.

In the darkness beyond Neptune a new star burst into life, shining with an incandescence never before seen in the frigid outer regions. Within a minute the blaze faded to a diffuse patch of light, and then nothing, as peace returned to the outermost reaches of the Solar System.

Joe had been holding his breath. He gasped and ran his hand over his forehead; he was sweating. Wiping the moisture from his face he looked at his daughter, who sat motionless, eyes glued to the monitors, her jaw slack. For several minutes neither spoke, content to be surrounded by the silence of the bridge deck until the reality of what happened sunk in.

Admiral Santiago's image reappeared. "So, Mister Falcon, that ends that, does it not?"

Joe sighed again. "I guess so."

"Good. You will take your ship back to Mars. It is now the most valuable object in this system, so I will send ten ships with you while the remainder of my fleet attempts to retrieve whatever we can of the *bayonet* wreckage. We will go back to Dysnomia, or Gabrielle if you like, to secure the plant there if we can."

Joe nodded as the admiral's image vanished. After several more minutes of silence, Raisa turned to her father. "It's not over, is it? Not really?"

Joe shook his head. "No. Aivris referred to its 'iterations'. That's its word for copies. There's one on board each of the nine other Tanakhai arks; some may be in control and some not. We don't know, but we must assume the worst."

"It might not be a problem for a long time to come."

"Maybe not, but something else will be. Aivris said it sent a warning back to its home world, and we could expect a response. It also said its location was deep beneath the surface of a moon. I'm betting the original A.I. is still in the Tanakhai system and has spent the last six decades, plus however long it took the *Minaret* to get here, in restoring itself and strengthening its defences ... and offences."

"And...?" Raisa raised an eyebrow.

"We can expect something, a war fleet perhaps, to come here sometime in the foreseeable future, and this time Aivris will be more prepared. It may take decades since it doesn't know the secret of wormhole travel, so we have time to prepare. We learned a hard lesson with Earth and won't be caught again. Next time, we *will* be ready."

"This ship will help," Raisa mused. "We have the shield now. We can use Ghost's data to reproduce it to protect our planets."

"Yes. The wormhole generator will be useful as well. We need to begin a program to find and colonize new worlds. The more colonies, the harder we will be to destroy. We may also be able to locate Aivris's star system and send *our* fleet before the warning message arrives. We can catch Aivris number one napping, perhaps."

Raisa turned her attention to the console again. "Do you think Aivris is right about us, that we are a blight, a danger to all life in the galaxy."

Joe shook his head. "No. I can't allow myself to accept that. It's true we've made a mess in the past, but we've learned from our mistakes and we'll continue to do so. I must believe we'll one day achieve a mental maturity to match our technology. I also know we will always protect ourselves from monsters like Aivris; if that makes *us* monsters, then so be it."

Raisa nodded agreement. "I wonder how long it'll take for us to reach home. How fast do you think this bus can go?"

The pilot's control screen lit up and a number appeared.

.52C

"Where did that come from," Raisa said. "C equals the speed of light, so it indicates .52 times that. Who gave us this?"

Joe felt a wave of hope wash over him. Only one individual could be responsible. Only one would know what this ship was capable of achieving.

"Ghost, are you there?"

The symbol vanished, replaced by a short line of words.

Go to the second accommodation wheel.

Moving faster than he thought possible, Joe leaped from his seat and shot down the spinal corridor. The moment he entered the room where the assay lab had been on the original *Butterball* his hopes soared.

Within the cabin stood the flask module installed by Ghost, and of the four flasks on top, two glowed a brilliant green. As Joe entered, a familiar voice came from a loudspeaker beside the unit.

"That's better," Ghost's voice said. "I can't deploy an ovoid from here, but at least we can talk. We only just managed to download in time."

"Terry," Joe gasped. "Is he with you?"

"Yes, Boss," A new voice replied. "I'm here. Sorry about the virus. It didn't work as well as I hoped it would."

Joe shook his head. *Amazing.* After everything he had been through Terry was concerned he had failed. "You did fine. You were dealing with an alien technology and I doubt anybody could have done better."

Joe sat on a convenient module and gazed dumbfounded at the green flasks.

"So, what now," he asked."How long can you stay in there?"

"Indefinitely," Ghost said. "However, this system has no virtual reality capability. We can see you and speak to you or each other, but that's about it. The two synthetics stored in the back were made for you when you were waiting for your new clone body years ago, and I stole them and had them brought here. They will do us until we arrive home, at least."

"And then?"

"All the knowledge your institute will need, everything to create clones like the one you now occupy, is in the data storage modules around us. In another two years both Terry and I can be in new organic bodies."

"And I'll have to work on the governments to make sure we are accepted," Joe said. "Io's people as well. They're more human than Tanakhai now."

"You won't have any trouble," Ghost said. "I am you. This ship is my creation and I give it to you. The modules in this wheel contain all the secrets we wanted from the *Minaret*. It's all here: the defensive shield, the antimatter engines, the molecular hatches and walkways, the anti-gravity elevators and the bubble-way technology. *Everything*. By the laws of both worlds it all belongs to you by right of salvage and the government of Mars will fall over itself to get it. I doubt we will encounter any problems, and in a few decades cloning will be so common it will be accepted by default."

Joe nodded. Yes, it was possible, and it would work out in the end. "So Terry, that will be your third body. I once thought I could be the first human to live forever, but now I think it might be you." He reflected back to the mutual reticence he and his friend once had concerning living for so long. "How do you feel about that?"

"I'm good with it, Boss. I've seen the most amazing things in the last few hours and as long as I'm not going to be arrested and locked up, I'm fine with another life."

"What about you, Ghost?"

"I've not had a body for six decades, and I am looking forward to having a new one. I know we had reservations, but I'm over it; I'm ready for the next adventure."

"Two of us will be a little confusing, don't you think?"

"I've given it some thought. You can use someone else's DNA for my clone and I can be a close relative. Nobody's going to question it considering all the changes ahead for humanity. I'll take another name. What about our father's?"

Ah, yes, Joe thought. *Arsenio Leonardo Falconi*, who changed his name to Leo Falcon after the family migrated to New Zealand.

"I'll be Leo the second. How do you feel about having a brother?"

A brother! Joe was an only child and all his long life he had wished for a brother or sister. *Now at last...*

"Yes," he said. I would like that. I would like that a great deal."

End

Author's Note

DID YOU ENJOY 'FALCON'S GHOST'?
IF SO, YOU CAN MAKE A BIG DIFFERENCE.

Reviews are the most powerful tool I have when it comes to getting attention for my books. Unfortunately, I do not have the financial muscle of a big city publisher, and I cannot organise massive advertising and promotion campaigns.

But I do have something much more effective than that.

A COMMITTED AND LOYAL GROUP OF READERS

Honest reviews of my books help bring them to the attention of other readers, and to retailers of books.

If you've enjoyed 'FALCON'S GHOST' I would be grateful if you could spend a minute or two leaving a review (an honest one, and as short as you like) on the book's review page at your preferred book seller's on line site.

Thank you so much.

HAWK: HELLFIRE (Excerpt)

PEACE REIGNED IN the quiet hours of the early morning, when few citizens graced the shadowed walkways of the entertainment district of Attika City. In the dim cafes and restaurants that lined the even dimmer mall, a handful of late stragglers from the previous evening's festivities clung to that final drink, a stimulant to give them sufficient impetus for the journey home.

The showers had passed, but the street still ran slick with runoff that streamed away to the drains from the last downpour. Steam rose in the warmth of the night, while high above, the dark clouds parted briefly to reveal a pale, full moon before closing in once again to shroud the city. Rain fell frequently on this planet but the locals loved it; took pride in the fact, since most human-occupied worlds were dry and desolate.

A row of antique street lamps—not too bright, so as to maintain the ambiance of the precinct—cast dim pools of reflected light from the wet sidewalks. Faint sounds of laughter drifted through the night, interspersed with farewells as a few late-nighters took advantage of the break in the weather.

The peace shattered as something slammed at terminal velocity into the pavement, impacting with such force as to pound a dent several centimeters into the plascrete surface.

For a moment, silence.

A nearby patron rose to her feet and peered over the restaurant railing towards the source of the disturbance. For a brief moment she stood motionless, and then raised both hands to her face.

A piercing scream shattered the peaceful mall.

Officer Callon Follet, post-sergeant of the Attika Guarda, peered down at the ruin. The sheer force of impact left little recognizable of what had once been a human soul, perhaps a young woman. The corpse was crushed almost beyond recognition, every bone broken, the skin pulverized and gore spattered for several meters around. A dark, congealing mass pooled in the depression created by the fall.

Follet raised his eyes towards the face of the adjacent skyscraper, the tallest building on the planet. It soared to over a thousand meters, and due to the height most of the windows were incapable of opening sufficiently for a body to pass through. Only at the top was exit possible, from any one of a dozen penthouse floors each with a private balcony open to the air, or from one of several sky-car pads at the summit.

Those high places all featured safety-glass barriers around the outer perimeters, but anyone could scramble over given determination and something to climb on. An acknowledged safety hazard, they existed only because the owner of the monolith all but owned the city. He got what he wanted. He was untouchable.

The sergeant stared up into the darkness and swiped a few stray drips of moisture from his face as a trauma arbeiter, white and reflective in the dim light, exited a nearby ground-unit and glided across to the scene of the incident. It paused for a moment beside the remains, opened a hatch on its side and extended small probes.

"You know what I need," Follet said.

The drone acknowledged in a disturbingly human voice and extended a probe into the congealing blood. Dropping the sample into a liquid-filled vial, it gave a shake and waited until the liquid turned bright blue.

"*Hellfire*, sir. Exceptionally high concentration, death inevitable. More information will be available following a detailed examination."

Follet nodded and turned his attention to the diminutive figure standing a few meters behind him. His new partner, junior officer Abigail Renner, was fresh from the academy. Tonight was her first on the job, her first call to her first incident.

What a goddamned, awful mess, he thought. "Sorry to throw this at you on your first trip out. We try to ease newbie's in, but this is just ... unexpected, that's all."

The girl did not reply, her attention fixed on the ruin on the pavement.

"*Hellfire*," Follet said, "is the nastiest addictive drug we've encountered on the circuit. Damned stuff shows up more every month and we have no clue where it comes from."

His partner did not respond. Since their first meeting she had shown none of the first-day nerves so typical of raw recruits. At the station she had presented as cool, calm, aware of her circumstances and confident in her abilities, but now she resembled a child in a strange and hostile environment.

Shock, perhaps?

Of medium height—Follet guessed about one-fifty-five centimeters—the blue-black Guarda uniform made her appear smaller than in reality. With her dark-brown hair tucked under a standard issue peaked cap she looked younger, more boyish, than her twenty standard years. She could almost be his daughter. Her green eyes glanced up at him briefly before returning to the scene on the pavement.

"The trouble with this stuff," Follet continued, "is the small doses. The common form is tiny grains, like highly processed sugar. One tenth of a gram gives you a thrill the like of which you've never experienced before: extreme ecstasy, a feeling of being the ruler of the world and so on. With luck, you can have your high and get away with it. Two tenths and you get an even more unbelievable trip, and become addicted for life with no chance of a cure."

Abbie Renner nodded, her eyes still glued to the body.

"A third of a gram and you're as good as dead. It starts with an overpowering sense of dizziness, other-worldliness and heightened awareness, then superiority, and you think anything is possible. If you're near water you decide you can breathe under it and you drown. You can walk through fire and not burn. High up and you can fly, and..."—Follet returned his gaze to the victim, now in the process of being scraped into a carry-case by the arbeiter—"...you get an irresistible urge to do just that. Then you die."

He turned back to his young protégée. She had not spoken since their arrival and had not moved closer to the body. Follet observed her more closely and realized her lack of response was not shock as he had at first assumed. The look in those eyes was one of intense anger.

Damp from the moisture in the air, her face showed little of the confusion and revulsion expected of a raw recruit exposed to such horror on her first night out. This young woman stood firm, stolid despite her young years and diminutive appearance, her brow furrowed, her jaw set and her gaze locked on the scene.

"But you're aware of all that, aren't you? I'm not telling you a damned thing you haven't heard before."

Renner gave a curt nod and exhaled forcefully, as if she had been holding her breath.

"You alright? You can handle this. Take another breath and tell me what you know about this stuff."

The young officer took a slow breath in and then breathed out again with a long, protracted sigh. "It's why I joined the Guarda," she said. "My brother died from the drug two years ago, when I was eighteen. He was one of the first, they told us. Took too much and tried to stop a speeding maglev by standing in front of it with his hands up. It couldn't stop fast enough. I decided then to join the force and track down whoever is responsible for his getting the drug."

Follet studied his young sidekick; for a raw recruit she had one heck of an agenda. He knew little about her other than the information on her data sheet, but she impressed him as a woman of intelligence and resourcefulness. A powerful, unrelenting determination lurked behind that angelic, heart-shaped face. This young lady came with a purpose.

"You're aware they set up a special division to deal with this problem? Have you considered applying?"

"Yes. I applied from the academy but I was told to come back when I had a year or two of experience. They don't take graduates until they prove they can stomach the work."

Follet turned and looked again at the black stained depression in the plascrete, all that remained now the arbeiter had finished its work.

"I can understand that."

* * *

If you would like to continue reading "**HAWK: HELLFIRE**" please return to your book seller of choice for a copy.

ABOUT THE AUTHOR

Mike Waller is a writer of Science Fiction and Space Opera adventures, including the multi-award winning FALCON CALL, the 'Echo's Way' stories and other stand-alone works. He currently lives in Queensland, Australia.

Mike's online home is:

https://www.mikewallerauthor.com/

You can connect with him on Facebook at:

https://www.facebook.com/AuthorMikeWaller/

You should email him at

mike.waller@mikewallerauthor.com

Mike answers every email received.

FREE eBOOK from Mike Waller

Building a relationship with my readers is the very best thing about writing. I occasionally send non-spamming newsletters with details on new releases, free giveaways promos, special offers and other bits of news relating to my books, the Falcon Books, 'Echo's Way' adventures and others

If you sign up to my reader's group mailing list, I will send you a free e-copy of one of my books.

You can get your free novel at
https://www.mikewallerauthor.com/

Made in United States
North Haven, CT
24 September 2022

24524827R00238